Critical acclaim for the novels of Vonda N. McIntyre

TRANSITION

"*Transition* is a must for those who enjoy scientific extrapolation and interesting people."

—*Locus*

METAPHASE

"The best Starfarer novel to date."

—*Booklist*

"With this third novel, *Starfarers* clearly becomes the most important series in science fiction . . . the most exciting and satisfying science fiction I have read this year."

—*Ursula K. Le Guin*

DREAMSNAKE

"[*Dreamsnake*] is filled with scenes as suspenseful as anyone could wish . . . but most of all it addresses the humanity of all of us."

—*The Seattle Times*

"[*Dreamsnake*] is an exciting future-dream with real characters, a believable mythos and, what's more important, an excellent, readable story."

—Frank Herbert, author of the *Dune* series

Bantam Books by
Vonda N. McIntyre

The Starfarers Series

STARFARERS
TRANSITION
METAPHASE
NAUTILUS

DREAMSNAKE

And coming in November in hardcover

STAR WARS®: THE CRYSTAL STAR

Transition

VONDA N. MCINTYRE

BANTAM BOOKS
NEW YORK · TORONTO · LONDON · SYDNEY · AUCKLAND

TRANSITION

A Bantam Spectra Book / January 1991
Bantam reissue edition / October 1994

ISBN 0-553-28850-4

Published simultaneously in the United States and Canada

Bantam Books are published by Bantam Books, a division of Bantam Double-
day Dell Publishing Group, Inc. Its trademark, consisting of the words
"Bantam Books" and the portrayal of a rooster, is Registered in U.S. Patent
and Trademark Office and in other countries. Marca Registrada. Bantam
Books, 1540 Broadway, New York, NY 10036.

PRINTED IN THE UNITED STATES OF AMERICA

RAD   0 9 8 7 6 5 4 3 2

Acknowledgments

I'm very grateful to the many people who have given me their time, their knowledge, and their advice (sometimes all three) for *Transition* and for *Starfarers* before it. Both novels benefited from the intelligent readings and the information, on everything from genetic technology to cosmic string, that my friends offered so generously. Thanks to Kristi Austin, geneticist Dr. John H. Chalmers (who also helped me keep my sanity in graduate school, all those years ago), Dr. John Cramer, Jane Hawkins, Marilyn Holt, Orca researcher Jeff Jacobsen, Ursula K. Le Guin, Kate Schaefer, Carol Severance, Jon Singer (yes, folks, I know him too), Sandra M. Smith, classical archaeologist and fellow writer Irene Wanner; and of course the Marmots: Steven Bryan Bieler and Nancy T. Reynolds and Deborah Wessell.

The background of the campus of *Starfarer* depends heavily on the work of Gerard K. O'Neill and the Space Studies Institute.

Any errors and infelicities that remain are my own responsibility.

Transition

1

J.D. Sauvage, the alien contact specialist, drifted in zero g and waited for a message from an unknown civilization.

She floated alone in the observers' circle. The circle's transparent chamber, projecting from one edge of the explorer spacecraft *Chi*, offered a two-hundred-seventy-degree view of the Milky Way, of the star Tau Ceti's second planet, and of Tau Ceti II's satellite. When J.D. oriented herself with the *Chi* at her back, she could imagine herself to be completely surrounded by silent space. The galaxy extended from one edge of her peripheral vision to the other, a great dense spangled disk of light stretching before her, extending behind her.

She had too much to look at. She wanted to laugh and shout with excitement. She was an alien contact specialist: she had spent her life studying for a job that, until today, did not exist. Until today, she had no way of being sure her job ever *would* exist.

A computer-generated image formed in the center of the observers' circle, drawing her attention from the sights outside. She watched, rapt, as a new shiver of shadow and light intensified the image and added to its density.

The alien message hovered, forming slowly between J.D. and the stars. Each bit of information strengthened the image as a whole. Tense with anticipation, J.D. urged it on, as if the force of her will could speed the transmission. As yet, she could not be sure of a pattern within it; she could extract no information.

The *Chi* plunged toward the source of the message. J.D. felt tempted to accelerate, to expend fuel recklessly, to reach the destination a few minutes or a few hours sooner. She restrained the urge. It was unnecessary, unwise.

The on-board computer processed another block of data and added it to the message from alien beings. The image grew denser, but no more detailed.

J.D. kept thinking she could detect a pattern, but the pattern she thought she saw kept changing. Her mind was trying to impose organization on the iridescent gray blur.

Be patient, she told herself. It will have structure, like the first frame. Maybe the meaning of the second frame will be clearer.

She touched the on-board computer via her link, asking it to place the first frame of the alien communication side by side with the second.

A complex symbol formed before her. The first section of the alien message was as complicated as the second, so far, was simple. The maze looked like a curtain, a tapestry, intricately beautiful, beautifully complex. Paths led across its surface, disappeared within and beneath each other, widened and split like the streams of a river delta, narrowed and disappeared. The *Chi*'s computer had traced a single unobstructed path leading from the design's edge to its center. The path lay in gold light, a meander of fractal complexity. It touched every part of the surface. Yet it never crossed itself. It twisted and turned and backtracked, but never knotted or tangled.

The *Chi*'s computer, and all four members of the alien contact department, and all the several hundred people back on board the starship *Starfarer*, had tried and failed to make sense of the pattern. Perhaps its esoteric form required more computer power than *Starfarer*'s crippled systems could offer right now, or more ingenuity than the members of the deep space expedition had been able to apply. Perhaps it was so alien that human minds and human machines could not comprehend it. Or perhaps, as J.D. preferred to believe, it possessed no inherent meaning except what its observer brought to it. J.D. believed it was art, an aesthetic expression so important to the alien beings that they used it as an introduction.

J.D. wished that Arachne, *Starfarer*'s fundamental bio-electronic computer, would complete its healing. She wondered what Arachne would make of the alien message. Besides, she missed Arachne's information web as much as she would have missed her hands or her eyes.

On *Starfarer* and on the *Chi*, many machines were artificial intelligences, and most possessed at least the level of competence referred to as artificial stupidity. J.D. had access to the physical and analytical services of a myriad of auxiliary computers, ASes and AIs alike. Nevertheless, she preferred her connection to Arachne. Without it, she felt detached and lonely. She was impatient for the computer web to finish reconstructing itself. The backups were flavorless, boring, and nearly as involved with Arachne's restoration as Arachne itself.

The second frame of the alien message shivered again, intensifying by another shade. Still J.D. could detect no structure.

She left the second image in the center of the observers' circle, but pushed the labyrinth behind her. When it was in sight it distracted her, constantly pulling at her vision. Now she could look at it, if she liked, by glancing over her shoulder. The translucent pattern hovered, obscuring the entryway between the observers' circle and the *Chi*'s main body.

J.D. let her attention expand beyond the observers' circle, into the alien star system. The most striking feature within her view was the system's second planet. The Earth-like world revolved around Tau Ceti, the G8-type star that lay out of J.D.'s sight, obscured by the flank of the *Chi*. Around the planet revolved a large satellite, airless and dead as Earth's moon.

But Tau Ceti II was alive, clearly and lushly alive. Weather and seas and continents patterned its surface. Already the alien contact team, and their colleagues on the starship, had mapped forests and plains, deserts and tundras and icecaps, river systems and ocean currents, great herds of beasts.

The third planet of Tau Ceti also possessed life, and an environment habitable by human beings. But Tau Ceti III was on the far side of its star, in opposition to Tau Ceti II, so far away that from the *Chi*'s vantage point it was no more than a tiny disk of light.

J.D. considered the implications of finding, in the first star system human beings had ever visited, two worlds possessing life. Her excitement rose toward exultation. Life was *not* unique to Earth. It was not even rare.

She suspected it was ubiquitous.

Strangely enough—for *someone* had arranged to broadcast the alien message—neither living planet showed any obvious marks of civilization.

The alien message, still increasing in density, yet still incomprehensible, emanated from a structure on Tau Ceti II's large satellite.

Directly ahead, the satellite expanded perceptibly as the *Chi* sped toward it.

Like its planet, it was three-quarters full. It was bigger than Earth's moon, younger, rougher, wilder. It spun on its axis, rather than rotating with one face locked toward its world. It was too small to retain any atmosphere. It had craters and plains, maria, like Earth's moon, but it also had active volcanoes and great canyons where faults had cracked and opened. At the top of the satellite's dark limb, a pinpoint of light marked an expanse of glowing molten rock. J.D. recalled a line of poetry, written by Coleridge, disdained by astronomers for describing an impossible astronomic arrangement.

" 'The hornèd Moon, with one bright star / Within—' "

" '—the nether tip.' " Victoria Fraser MacKenzie completed the line of poetry. Entering from the *Chi*'s main body, the director of alien contact for the deep space expedition dived through the holographic image of the maze and joined J.D. in the observers' circle.

J.D. grinned at her colleague. Victoria grabbed the top of her couch and spun around into it, graceful and comfortable in weightlessness. The most intense of J.D.'s teammates, the physicist moved with economy and precision. Her presence was so powerful that people were always surprised, when they met her, to discover that she was quite small. J.D. was a head taller than she.

Planet-light sparkled in her very curly short black hair, and created delicate highlights on her dark skin. She fastened one of the safety straps and smiled across the circle at J.D.

"Coleridge, vindicated," J.D. said.

Victoria chuckled ruefully. "And revenged—he sent his albatross along with us."

J.D. laughed, too. She could laugh, now that the danger was over. Laughter might be the only sane reaction to what had happened.

"I did sort of feel like that missile was an albatross around my neck," she said. "Especially when Kolya said not to let it go." Her arms still ached from wrestling the nuclear warhead out of *Starfarer*'s thick, rocky skin, from holding on to it until she could safely release it.

If it had exploded a few minutes sooner. . . she thought. If I'd slipped, and it crashed into the wild cylinder. . .

She shivered, remembering.

The missile's strike and detonation had left *Starfarer* alive, damaged but repairable. Now, the starship followed the *Chi* at several hundred thousand kilometers' distance, escaping a cloud of nuclear debris.

"I wonder," J.D. said, "how the alien beings feel about albatrosses." It worried her, what they must be thinking. A nuclear bomb was a lousy calling card.

"*I* wonder what they think about our simpleminded signal. Their first one is so complicated, and this one—" Victoria shrugged with perplexity. She turned her attention to the half-formed pattern, gazing at it hungrily, as if she were starving and it was nourishment.

The alien contact team had speculated about the proper first message to send to alien beings. They had tried to create a Rosetta stone, a key to human language and science and culture that could be translated and comprehended by an alien intelligence. But they had to do it without the other half of the stone, the idiom into which the knowledge must be translated. They used universal constants, the table of elements, representations of electron orbitals: all the resources of a technological culture.

Soon they would know if their attempts had succeeded. The *Chi* heralded its approach with a broadcast: a high-speed, compressed, multicopy burst of information in laser light. But compared to the alien labyrinth, their message was simple, graphic, straightforward.

J.D.'s pulse beat through her body, and excitement sparkled in the corners of her vision. She ran her hands through her short straight brown hair and made herself relax, pressing the tension out of her heavyset body, letting it flow away through her fingers and toes. If she closed her eyes, she could pretend she was swimming in Puget Sound with the orcas and the divers. Zero g had a similar, freeing effect.

A breeze brushed her cheek as Satoshi Lono dove through the labyrinth and passed on her left. The team's geographer touched the transparent far wall, pushed off and somersaulted, and came to rest against his zero-g couch. He loosely fastened a safety strap, his athletic body curving forward against the restraint as he scrutinized the alien message.

"God, it's slow," he said impatiently. "You have to wonder if they think we can read."

"Maybe we can't, as far as they're concerned," J.D. said.

"You're so calm about this," he said.

J.D. did not feel calm. She glanced over at Satoshi, wondering if she should have heard irony in his voice. But he smiled at her with genuine regard.

It was too complicated to try to describe the truth of what she felt.

Zev, the young diver, floated into the observers' circle backward, slipping through the labyrinthine hologram as if it were the surface of the sea.

"Come on, Stephen Thomas," he said. "Just swim."

"Swim, huh? Swimming in air is a pain in the ass."

Stephen Thomas Gregory broke through the curtain, paddling awkwardly from the main body of the *Chi*. His awkwardness in zero g was a shock, for under ordinary conditions he moved with assurance, poise, and self-confidence. If Satoshi was the most resolute athlete of the team, Stephen Thomas was the most gifted.

"Are we there yet?" Stephen Thomas asked, putting on a cheerful voice.

"Almost," Victoria said, smiling at her other partner.

The geneticist grabbed the headrest of the couch in the quadrant to J.D.'s right, dragged himself into position, and fastened both restraints. His body language contradicted his tone, his joke. He lay within his couch, looking uncomfortable. He hated zero gravity. The alien contact department balanced on the brink of snatching success from dispute and failure; even that could not erase Stephen Thomas's tension and apprehension.

His long blond hair drifted loose across his face, hiding the cut on his forehead. Both his eyes had blackened remarkably since the accident. The livid bruising of his pale skin almost made it possible for J.D. to forget how strikingly beautiful he was. He tucked his hair behind his ears, absently, impatiently, muttering an offhand curse.

Zev let himself drift near J.D. She reached out and touched his hand. He clasped her fingers. If they had been in the sea, their touching would have been more intimate. Zev had just begun to learn land manners, and sometimes J.D. had to remind herself of hers.

"Please strap in, Zev," Victoria said.

J.D. gave Zev's hand an encouraging squeeze and let go. Obediently, but reluctantly, he took the auxiliary couch to her left and strapped himself in.

Victoria, Satoshi, Stephen Thomas, and J.D. occupied the couches at the cardinal points of the observers' circle. That was as it should be. But Zev's presence was quite contrary to plan.

Zev is so young, J.D. thought. Eighteen makes him too young to be on board the *Chi*, too young even to have joined the expedition. Still, I'm glad he's here, I'm glad he's with me.

Fascinated yet dispassionate, Zev gazed around, as interested in the reactions of the four ordinary human beings as he was in the slowly changing alien image, or in the stars beyond the transparent shell of the observation chamber.

Zev lounged between his couch and the loose safety straps, as easy in zero g as any twenty-year veteran. He let his arms hang relaxed before him, with the palms of his unusually large hands turned toward him and his long, strong fingers gently curved, gently spread. The swimming webs between his fingers looked like delicate sheets of amber. His skin was a deep mahogany color, several shades lighter and redder than Victoria's. His hair was very blond, lighter than Stephen Thomas's.

The message shivered again. It was now almost solid to the eye, yet still it contained no perceptible information. J.D. did not understand why the alien source transmitted with such excruciating slowness. The message arrived at a slow, unchanging rate, without any acknowledgment of the message the team broadcast in response.

Maybe it's just a beacon, J.D. thought. Or—maybe the

alien message *is* acknowledging us, and we just don't understand. Maybe they're slow, deliberate, dignified. Maybe the constancy of the message means, to alien consciousness, that we're noted and anticipated.

"Victoria," J.D. said, "what if we pull out one copy of our message and slow it down? Broadcast it at the same rate this one is arriving?"

"Couldn't hurt to try," Victoria said.

Tentatively, warily, J.D. let her eyelids flicker.

"Be careful!" Victoria said, her voice tense and apprehensive.

J.D. glanced toward her. Victoria grimaced and shook herself all over.

"Sorry," she said.

"That's all right," J.D. said. "Don't worry. I don't want to get caught in another web crash, either." She closed her eyes and reached through her link to check the information and communication computer that formed the nerves and brains of *Starfarer*. She had not been deeply involved with Arachne during the crash; when the web fell apart she had not been emotionally and intellectually bruised, as had Victoria, as had Iphigenie DuPre, the master of *Starfarer's* solar sail. Nevertheless, J.D. approached the web cautiously. Because the crash remained unexplained, its cause undiscovered and unrepaired, it might happen again, at any time, for any reason. Or no reason.

J.D. reached out, but Arachne remained self-involved, intent on the repair of its web.

J.D. opened her eyes. "Arachne's still out," she said.

"Never mind, eh?" Victoria bent over the hard link that extended from the arm of her couch. "I've got the *Chi* working on it, it's almost done."

Touching *Starfarer's* auxiliary computer systems did give J.D. some feel for the status of the starship. The parallel spinning cylinders sailed into the Tau Ceti system. The solar sails reoriented the starship, decelerating it into a course that led to the second planet.

Back in the solar system, *Starfarer* had approached its transition point at dangerously high velocity, fleeing the military carrier sent to stop it. Without Iphigenie DuPre's experience with solar sails, without her preparations and Victoria's backup, the starship would have failed to connect properly with the cosmic string. It would have failed to reach transition energy; it would have lost its path to Tau Ceti. The expedition was lucky to have Iphigenie along. Whether she was lucky to have joined it was another, more difficult, question.

J.D. felt a great relief, observing the course changes.

Iphigenie must be all right, she thought. She must have recovered from the shock if she's in control of the solar sail.

I should start thinking of it as the stellar sail, J.D. thought, now that we've left our own system.

"One copy of our message," Victoria said, touching a key on the hard link. "Now, a control program . . ."

"Be sure you tell them we didn't bring the bomb along on purpose," Stephen Thomas said.

"Any suggestions on just how I should do that?" Victoria said.

"I wish," Stephen Thomas said. He glanced across at the labyrinth. "I wish I could translate that, too."

Their schematic, simple greeting was hardly designed to convey complicated explanations, such as "We didn't mean to explode a nuclear warhead inside your system. Some people back home didn't want us to leave Earth orbit. The missile we dragged through transition was an attempt to stop us."

"Maybe they're waiting for a message from our leader," Satoshi said. His pleasant low voice turned uncharacteristically bitter. "Our silent leader."

"Oh, come on," Stephen Thomas said. "Chancellor Blades is okay."

Satoshi made an inarticulate sound of distaste. J.D. had observed, even on short acquaintance, that Satoshi got along with everybody. He even got along with the assistant chancellor, Gerald Hemminge, though most people found Gerald abrasive. It startled J.D., as it startled Stephen Thomas, for Satoshi to take an instant dislike to anyone. But he did not like *Starfarer*'s new chancellor.

"He *is*," Stephen Thomas said. He glanced around, as if for confirmation.

"I'm sure he is," J.D. said. "But I've never met Chancellor Blades." Though he had put in an appearance at her welcome party, he had left before she arrived.

"He's a little shy," Stephen Thomas said. "Reserved. He

comes off looking aloof. And I'll bet he felt off balance, coming on board and knowing everybody suspects his motives."

"You can hardly blame us," Victoria said, glancing up from the link. The United States had put tremendous pressure on EarthSpace to appoint Blades as chancellor. Everyone assumed his real task had been to oversee the dismantling of the deep space expedition, and of *Starfarer*.

"He stayed with the expedition," Stephen Thomas said stubbornly. "He didn't get on the transport to go home. That says something for him. And it's more than you can say for Gerald. You ought to at least give him a chance."

"I shall," Victoria said. "As soon as *he* gives *me* a chance. As he never troubled to return my call, I have no way of judging him."

Victoria set back to work, every so often glancing at the alien transmission.

J.D. watched it, too. Any pattern it might be forming continued to elude her. Her mind kept trying to make sense of the speckled image, but so far all its structure remained in her imagination.

I think I see something the way people used to think they saw faces and buildings on Mars, J.D. realized. The way Stephen Thomas thinks he sees auras. But I'm making it all up.

"That's it," Victoria said. "One copy of our greeting, transmitted at the same rate as the alien message." She touched the keyboard. "Sent. Sending, anyway."

"It sure is slow," Satoshi said again.

"Maybe its batteries are running down," Stephen Thomas said dryly, "and there's nobody to replace them."

"Oh, don't say that!" J.D. said, distressed.

"Our luck has been ridiculously good," Stephen Thomas said. "It's too much to hope that nothing will go wrong."

J.D. started to laugh. When she heard the high note of hysteria in her voice, she struggled to control herself.

"J.D., what's so funny?"

After a moment, J.D. stopped laughing long enough to wipe the tears from her eyes.

"Nothing's funny! Stephen Thomas, how much bad luck do we have to have, to balance out any good? Half the faculty is back on Earth while their governments sulk, Arachne's operating on the level of an artificial stupid, you and Satoshi nearly got squashed, and we had to steal *Starfarer* to get out here at all—"

"We didn't steal it!" Victoria exclaimed. "We just . . . kept going as if nothing had changed."

"That isn't how they're looking at it back on Earth," Stephen Thomas said. "It isn't how the folks on the transport who are stuck here are looking at it."

Victoria's gaze caught his, then broke away.

"We had no choice," she said.

J.D. wished she had not brought up the subject of stealing the starship, at least not in those terms. She knew perfectly well that Victoria felt sensitive and defensive about their means for continuing the expedition. It had been Victoria's proposal to defy their instructions to drop into a low Earth orbit, where the starship would become a military watching post. At Victoria's instigation, *Starfarer* had continued on course to transition.

J.D. wiped her eyes again, trying to think of something to say to ease the tension.

"There's definitely some structure forming in this thing." Satoshi kept his attention on the transmission; he kept his voice quiet and low and calming.

J.D. forgot her embarrassment; she forgot Victoria's aggravation with her and Stephen Thomas.

J.D. searched for the structure, the evidence of sense, that Satoshi claimed to see.

"I'm not getting anything out of it," Stephen Thomas said.

"Me, either, I'm afraid," J.D. said.

"No, look, there, it's a very fine pattern, a kind of filmy configuration . . ."

"Maybe," Victoria said doubtfully, hopefully.

"Why has it stopped?" Zev said. "It isn't changing anymore."

"What? It—" J.D. protested, then fell silent, fearing that what Zev said was true.

Victoria grabbed for the hard link again.

"He's right," Victoria said. "It's the message. The antenna's okay. So's the receiver, and the hologram imager. The message has stopped."

"Shit," Stephen Thomas said.

"No kidding, Stephen Thomas," Victoria said. "You had to wish for more bad luck."

Feral Korzybski felt like an old-fashioned serial computer trying to solve a parallel problem. The freelance journalist was drawn in so many directions that he could easily spend most of his time moving from one story to the next, instead of with the stories themselves.

Intellectually, he could handle several lines of thought at once. That was not the problem. The problem was that without Arachne's web, the only place he could be was wherever he was physically. One place at a time. The place he most wanted to be, the place that drew his heart and his wishes, he could not reach. He would have given anything to be on board the *Chi* with Stephen Thomas and the rest of the alien contact team. The best story in his lifetime, in the lifetime of human beings, and he had to cover it from a distance.

The limitations were driving him crazy. He could not go with the team. Nor could he participate by way of virtual reality, immersed in a holographic broadcast of the alien contact team's experience, an unseen colleague observing everything from the point of view of a camera. The ship's computer was not yet up to it. Feral could only participate through a hard link, wishing he were in the observers' circle beside Stephen Thomas, in one of the empty auxiliary couches.

Feral tried again, as he did every few minutes, to hook in with Arachne. It rebuffed him, but he could feel the increase in its awareness and complexity. It was healing. But it would not, or could not, give him enough of its capabilities to be of any use. He would be last in line to get Arachne's attention and a place in the web; since he was not a member of the expedition, he had only the limited access of a guest.

He had his suspicions about who had crashed the web. Almost everyone on board *Starfarer* believed it must have been someone on the carrier that had chased *Starfarer* to transition. Feral understood wanting to believe no expedition member could be responsible for the malevolent attack. He wanted to believe it himself. But he thought the desire led to easy answers. Easy, *wrong* answers.

He had some ideas about finding the right answer.

Since he could not be on board the *Chi*, he was in his

favorite spot, so far, in *Starfarer*. The sailhouse was a small, completely transparent cylinder suspended between the starship and the stellar sail, attached to *Starfarer* only by an access tunnel. In the sailhouse, in zero g, Feral had experienced transition.

At the far curve of the sailhouse, Iphigenie DuPre hunched quiet and concentrated over a hard link.

She would have direct access to Arachne if anyone did. In normal space, Iphigenie and the computer navigated the starship. Even if she could not yet connect with Arachne, Iphigenie could link directly with any number of auxiliary computers. Nevertheless, she was using the relatively slow and awkward hard link to control the stellar sail. The ship had come barrelling out of transition, faster than they ever intended, arriving blind in the Tau Ceti system. Iphigenie had to put *Starfarer* on the proper path.

The musical readouts of the sensors whispered and sang. They spoke a language Feral did not know, and without Arachne neither could he translate it. The notes created chords, harmonies, melodies. Every so often he heard a sour note, a minor triad. He knew that was not right. But he could do nothing but watch and remember, and keep trying to talk to Arachne to record his words and insights.

From the sailhouse, Feral could see the enormous sail stretched out across space like a flat silver parachute, slowing the starship's headlong plunge through the system. In the other direction lay the two huge cylinders that made up the body of *Starfarer*: the campus and the wild side. He could see the mirrors that conveyed sunlight or starlight to the interior. Beyond it all hung Tau Ceti II and its satellite: a blue-green three-quarter disk, and a smaller, beaten silver oval.

He could not see Tau Ceti, the star. No nearby star would ever be visible from here. *Starfarer*, in its present orientation, shadowed the sailhouse. Had it not, the transparent wall would have darkened to hide the blazing disk of the sun. In shadow, the cylindrical chamber remained transparent. It responded to radiation, visible or otherwise, by darkening and shielding the inhabitants. Feral was extremely grateful for the shielding properties of the sailhouse, and glad they were much more powerful than they needed to be to protect him from sunlight. If they had not been, he and Iphigenie would both have been fried by the radiation of the nuclear explosion.

Feral pushed off gently and floated toward Iphigenie.

Strange that the sailhouse had remained transparent all during transition. Feral recalled that brief experience.

Disorientation overtook him, unexpectedly, powerfully. Without thinking, he reached for any handhold. He sent himself tumbling. He brushed past Iphigenie, bumping her with enough force to push her away from the hardlink.

"What—?"

Feral bounced off the side of the sailhouse. He managed to damp some of his spin, then had to wait, tumbling foolishly, until the air slowed and stopped him. Iphigenie had already brought herself back to stillness. She watched him, puzzled.

"Are you still here? What *is* the matter?"

"I was trying to think of a way to describe . . . what we experienced during transition."

"Oh," she said. She hesitated. "I think that isn't a good idea."

"You can't do it, either?"

"I was very busy," she said defensively.

"No, you weren't," Feral said. "The sail was furled. Your work was finished. You drifted here right beside me and stared out at—"

"Stop it," she said.

"Sorry."

"You have to understand," Iphigenie said. "When Arachne crashed, I went from complete sensory load to nothing, to emptiness. What we saw, felt, experienced, what *I* felt during transition . . . that was like being hooked in deep to Arachne, but a hundred times over, and with my body as well as my mind. Now that's gone, too. I'm isolated. Disconnected from reality. And I don't know if . . ."

Her voice trailed off.

Feral drifted closer, reached out tentatively, touched Iphigenie's hand. She was shivering. He put his arms around her and held her, hoping he was doing the right thing, hoping that human contact was what she needed to repair her connections to reality. He stroked the smooth tight braids of her hair and rubbed the back of her neck, the sensitive concavities where the skull joins the spine, till she stopped trembling.

"Maybe once through transition was enough?" Feral asked gently.

"May be," Iphegenie said. "It may be." She drew away from him, patting his hand.

"I understand," Feral said. And he did, though he did not agree. He looked forward to experiencing transition again.

But he could not think of words to describe it. This troubled and annoyed him. It was his job to think of words to describe it.

Feral was the only reporter on board *Starfarer*. Other writers with more experience and better connections might have gone out with the expedition, if it had departed on schedule. It had not: it had departed early and in confusion, to keep the military from taking over the ship.

Feral was supposed to have gone back to Earth, but he had never even boarded the transport. He felt embarrassed for his selfishness, but he was glad things had gone wrong. If they had gone right, he would never have been able to stay.

For a journalist three years out of school, he had decent connections. But it took better than decent connections to pull EarthSpace strings. He was free-lance, surviving on royalties from the global communications web. When people read his work, he got paid. The money had increased, this past year, as his stories gained more notice. Enough money to live on and enough money to travel freely off Earth were two very different things. He had no sponsors; "sponsored independence" was, as far as Feral was concerned, an oxymoron. He had bought his own ticket into space, like any tourist, and he had pulled in nearly all the obligations anyone had ever owed him to get on board the starship.

But it was worth it. It was certainly worth it.

Nikolai Petrovich Cherenkov lay on the floor in the main room of his house, stretched out on a small threadbare rug in a patch of alien sunlight. He watched the hardlink, focusing on the image of the alien transmission.

On board the starship, arguments, confusion, and perplexity all hung suspended while the faculty and staff and even the transport passengers watched the communication. Like the members of the alien contact team, they, too, tried to make sense of it.

It disturbed Kolya. Why should it arrive at such a leisurely pace? Perhaps the aliens lived at a rate entirely different from that of human beings. Or perhaps they thought travelers to their system might function very slowly.

The cosmonaut tried to persuade himself that one of those possibilities was true, but he found that he believed neither.

You're just feeling more paranoid than usual, he told himself. Exhaustion and pain will do that to you. You are much too old to wrestle with nuclear warheads.

He wondered how J.D. was, whether she ached, as he did, from their struggle with the nuclear missile.

I should be grateful I'm not a handful of radioactive dust, Kolya thought, rather than bemoaning my aged muscles. Still, I ache.

He found that he badly wanted to talk to J.D. Sauvage about the alien message.

He put his cigarette to his lips and drew hard on it before he remembered he had not lit it. He never lit a cigarette inside; the smoke detector was too sensitive.

He spat out a shred of tobacco. He was trying to quit. He had been trying to quit for decades. He was probably the only human being left alive who still smoked.

And he was, finally, running out of the cigarettes he had begged, borrowed, and bribed people to smuggle into space for him. It was years since he had even found a source, and the few remaining packages had acquired a strange off taste. Freezing in liquid nitrogen was supposed to preserve things indefinitely, but as far as Kolya Petrovich was concerned, liquid nitrogen imparted its own unpleasant flavor.

Kolya was not a scientist. He had been a test pilot, a cosmonaut, a guerrilla fighter. Now he was a man under sentence of death in what had been his homeland. Only off Earth could he be safe.

Safe. His smile was ironic. Not for the first time, he thought: I'm probably the only person in the universe who's safer on board *Starfarer* than I would be back on Earth.

He put the unlit cigarette back in his cigarette case and slipped the case into his pocket.

I *must* quit, he told himself. I am witness to the first message from alien beings, and I am thinking about nicotine.

The hard link's focus changed from the alien message to Victoria Fraser MacKenzie.

"The transmission has stopped," she said.

Kolya forgot about nicotine. Staring into the frozen image on the hard link in his parlor, he rose, fumbling for the audio controls. Tangled voices spilled out as people on *Starfarer* reacted to her announcement.

Kolya listened, but no one suggested a good reason for the termination of the message. His unease increased.

"It must be Arachne." Kolya recognized the voice of Gerald Hemminge, the upper-class British administrator who was assistant chancellor of *Starfarer*. The duties of Gerald's position included acting as liaison between the starship and the *Chi*. He must be feeling ambivalent about the job, for he had been among those who argued for allowing the United States military to recommission *Starfarer*. He had opposed the decision to keep going. He had tried to go home.

Gerald had been on the transport that *Starfarer* dragged along with it to the Tau Ceti system.

"It must be the crash of the web," Gerald said. "The message could still be coming, but..."

Arachne had taken months to create itself and its communications web. It had begun to evolve with the superstructure of the starship, and had taken as long to form as the starship had to build. Perhaps it would require months to re-form, after its inexplicable crash. No doubt the accident would change it. But, then, it grew and evolved and changed all the time.

"Could be, but I don't think we're getting anything at the antenna. What about you, Victoria?"

Kolya did not recognize the second voice. Though he had been living on board the starship since it was barely habitable, he had not gone out of his way to make friends there. He had lived the life of a hermit, letting his fame, or infamy, form a wall between him and the other people on board. He wished he had not isolated himself quite so efficiently.

Victoria MacKenzie's voice reached *Starfarer* after a second or two of transmission delay.

"But our image is the one that's frozen," she said. "It has nothing to do with Arachne. The antenna is working fine. I don't have any more ideas, Avvaiyar. We'll continue to broadcast our own message, and we'll keep on going toward the alien source."

Kolya reached out to Arachne, wanting to send a message to J.D. But Arachne still was not ready to reply to a human being. Though the web had begun to restore its most important function, its control over the starship, it still lacked the attention to spare to handle trivial things like personal messages.

Who crashed the web? Kolya wondered, for the thousandth time since the shocking failure of the starship's control systems. Who would do such a thing?

People remained in the health center, recovering from the effects of being involved with the system when it failed. Other people had gone back to work who probably should still be resting. Deliberately crashing the system was a criminal act. It could have been murder. Only by sheer good luck had no one been killed.

Kolya hoped the deed had been done by someone outside *Starfarer*, someone on board the warship that had chased them to the point of transition.

Crashing the web from outside should not have been possible. Crashing it from inside should not have been possible, either. Yet the system had crashed.

Kolya did not belong to the support group backing the alien contact department; he held no claim to the ship's strained communications resources. If he wanted to talk to J.D. about the transmission, he would have to go to the liaison office and ask to call her directly.

He wanted to talk to her; he wished he were on board the *Chi*, but he was not a member of the alien contact team.

On the other hand, neither was Zev.

Kolya tried to suppress his resentment of the young diver. He failed. The diver had no space experience, no training: he had no right to be on the explorer. Kolya envied him bitterly.

But perhaps he belongs there, Kolya thought. Alone among us, he has lived with a nonhuman sentient species. Perhaps he does deserve to be there, after all.

The image of the alien transmission remained unchanged. Victoria reached out a query to the *Chi*'s computer and tested it again. It responded properly, innocent of locking up. Nor had the antenna drifted.

"The moon's rotating, isn't it?" Stephen Thomas said hopefully. "Maybe the transmitter's gone over the horizon."

"It's got relays," Victoria said. "The signal didn't waver from the time we picked it up to the time we lost it. It didn't drift. It didn't fade. It just stopped." Stephen Thomas could look at the same information and see the abrupt blink from full signal to nothing.

"I still think it's saving battery power," Stephen Thomas said. "Or maybe—"

"What's the point in speculating?" Satoshi said. "If you make up reasons all day, we'll be no closer to knowing the answer than we were when you started."

Stephen Thomas fell silent, his expression hurt.

"Look, I'm sorry," Satoshi said. "I just—"

"Never mind. You're right. You don't have to apologize when you're right."

"Aren't we," J.D. said hesitantly, "transmitting to *Starfarer*?" Her voice was soft, as if the microphones might not pick up her words if she spoke quietly enough.

Stephen Thomas muttered a curse. Victoria hoped the microphones could not pick up what he had said.

"You *are* transmitting, you know."

Gerald Hemminge must have spoken at the same moment as J.D., but his voice had taken a couple of seconds to cross the distance from *Starfarer*.

"I've interrupted the relay to public address," he said. His tone was not nearly so mild as J.D.'s. "You may tell me when you're finished arguing...unless you have some particular purpose in doing it in public."

Satoshi's rueful chuckle earned him a glare from Stephen Thomas.

"Immortalized forever," Satoshi said. "A historic moment. Warts and all."

"Thank you, Gerald," Victoria said. Though Satoshi got along with the assistant chancellor, Victoria did not, and Stephen Thomas disliked him intensely. Gerald had no obligation to protect them from themselves. "We're exhausted, and this new development has thrown us all. But we're finished arguing, I think."

She glanced at Stephen Thomas, who glowered back as if to say, "Who, me? I never argue."

"The day hasn't been easy for me, either, you know," Gerald said. "I have no computer support and several eminent passengers demanding to go home. A demand with which I concur, not that you are likely to listen to me now any more than you did before we left."

Victoria did not rise to the argument. "If you'll put me back on public address," she said, "I'll sign us off and shut down the voice transmission for a while."

Several seconds passed.

"Very well," Gerald said.

"I'm locking channel one onto the image of the alien message," Victoria said for the benefit of the observers on board the starship. "Unless the broadcast starts up again, there's not much we can do till we arrive at the point of origin. At least I can't think of anything else to do. I'm open to suggestions. Channel two is the view in our direction of travel. We'll begin transmitting as we approach orbital insertion. Victoria Fraser MacKenzie out."

"The public audio's off," Gerald said a moment later.

"Thank you, Gerald," Victoria said. "Avvaiyar, don't hesitate to call me if you learn anything new."

"Victoria, my friend," the astronomer said, "I couldn't tell you everything new I was learning in less than three days. But if anything new comes up that relates to the alien message, I'll call immediately."

Avvaiyar's interests focused at the rarefied point where physics and cosmology intersected. When it came to their professional disciplines, only when she and Victoria discussed cosmic string did either have any idea what the other was talking about.

"Good," Victoria said. "I'll talk to you soon."

She shut down all the audio channels and rubbed her eyes. She could not remember when she had felt so tired.

Victoria glanced at her teammates. J.D. was still embarrassed, her fair skin flushed. Satoshi was amused. Stephen Thomas hated to look silly; he was sulking, but his natural good humor would reassert itself soon.

She could probably tease him out of his mood. Victoria tried to summon up enough energy to tease him. She failed.

Dammit, she thought, we ought to be out here fresh and

rested and ready, with everyone behind us. Instead, we're physically and emotionally exhausted, Stephen Thomas looks like the loser in a barroom fight, and the ship is behind us, all right: limping along with a crater in its side, trailing a cloud of nuclear debris. And then there are the transport passengers.

She was glad she had been able to divert Gerald from telling her more about how the passengers felt, because right now she did not want to know.

And even so, it could be much worse. Stephen Thomas could have been killed, not just banged around: the genetics building could have fallen on top of him and Satoshi instead of falling down around them. The missile could have detonated sooner.

I suppose we ought to consider ourselves lucky, she thought. We're renegades. We're fugitives.

But we're alive.

She stared at the frozen transmission, wondering what to do.

She shook off her distress. After all, being a fugitive was a tradition in her family. Her several-times-great-grandparents had escaped from the United States to Canada on the underground railroad. She smiled to herself: She was only following their lead.

The image from channel two faded in beside the alien transmission. Satoshi leaned closer to study Tau Ceti's second planet, a pretty blue-green world with a single airless satellite, a world nearly a twin of Earth. Victoria wondered where its people were, and she knew Satoshi wondered the same thing. Now that the transmission had ceased, the system remained silent all across the useful broadcast frequencies. Where were the system's inhabitants?

Some of Victoria's exhaustion was due to hunger. She released her safety straps.

"I'm going to make a sandwich," she said. "Anyone else want something?"

"That would be great," J.D. said.

"Filet and baby French carrots for me," Stephen Thomas said. He smiled, back to his usual self already.

Victoria returned his smile. "I might be able to fill the order for the carrots." *Starfarer* grew no beef, and the starship had left precipitously and lacking most of its backup supplies. Victoria doubted the starship had any red meat in storage, even for special occasions.

Victoria floated out of the observation room. "Cordon bleu all around," she said.

"I'll help," Satoshi said, and followed her.

Kolya Petrovich limped along the edge of a low, wide, grass-covered hill. At its peak the hill dipped down to form an open amphitheater, where Kolya had spoken in defense of the deep space expedition. That was the first time he had ever gone to one of *Starfarer*'s meetings, the first time he had ever spoken in a public forum on board the starship, the first time since his days as a cosmonaut that he had spoken in front of an audience of living people.

Many years ago, after he escaped from his invaded homeland, he had spoken for the public record, for cameras. He recalled it as if it were another lifetime. Someone else's lifetime. He had believed—he still believed—that his recounting would have made a difference if the world had heard what he saw and experienced under the authority of the Mideast Sweep. But the world had never been allowed to know what he had to say, and now it was too late.

He continued down the trail, favoring his body. He ached all over. He hoped he had only strained his muscles. A muscle strain would heal fairly rapidly, more rapidly at any rate than a torn ligament or tendon. Nothing healed the way it had when he was younger.

There were times in Kolya's life when his body had been badly abused. Some of those injuries he never got over, and some of them were to his soul.

Griffith, who pretended to be from the General Accounting Office of the United States of America, walked fast down a path, his gaze on the ground and his thoughts light-years away.

He needed to walk. He needed the freedom, the motion. During *Starfarer*'s crisis, he had been trapped inside a survival sphere for over an hour. It had seemed like days. He still found it difficult to believe that General Cherenkov had overpowered him, immobilized him. He felt embarrassed, upset, and, above all, confused. He was not used to feeling confused.

He did not like it.

He never would have taken me, Griffith thought, not if I hadn't begun trusting him. That was a mistake. I let my admiration for him get in the way. If I hadn't started trusting him, he never would have taken me.

The landscape looked familiar. He recognized the topography of a small clear stream, a clump of budding white lilacs. He had walked completely around the circumference of *Starfarer*'s campus cylinder. He was, of course, walking in circles.

Griffith swore aloud. When he first came aboard *Starfarer*, he had envied its inhabitants. They lived in a place of beauty, a place that represented limitless freedom. But to Griffith it had come to represent entrapment and isolation and his own failure.

He reached out to the starship's computer web and received a null response. This was the worst system crash he had ever observed. He wondered who could have engineered the collapse of the web and its backups. Whoever did it, however they did it, they had achieved a spectacular success. A few days ago, Griffith would have applauded it. Now he regretted it.

He looked up. A few paces farther on, General Cherenkov rounded a turn in the path. Griffith stopped.

Cherenkov hurried past him.

"General—"

Cherenkov spun around, looming angrily over him.

"I told you not to call me that!"

Griffith stepped back involuntarily, poised for a fight. He did not intend to let Cherenkov make a fool of him again.

Griffith was an unremarkable-looking man; this was one of his strengths. When people described him, they talked in terms of mediums: medium brown hair and eyes, medium complexion, medium build, medium height. Cherenkov was quite tall, especially for an astronaut. A cosmonaut. His height intensified his intimidating presence.

Cherenkov eased back. "I have no wish for a rematch," he said. "We may take it as a given, Marion, that you would win a second round."

"I don't like being called Marion any more than you like being called general. Can we call a truce on this?"

Cherenkov turned and strode down the trail. Feeling like a supplicant, Griffith followed. He caught up after a few paces, but he had to lengthen his stride uncomfortably, or trot, to stay level with Cherenkov.

"You never said you did not like being called Marion," Cherenkov said.

"The hell I didn't."

"You said you did not ordinarily use your given name."

"We're arguing semantics! Will you wait a minute? Where are you going?"

Cherenkov stopped again. "When are you going to keep your promise and leave me alone?"

The tone in the cosmonaut's voice hurt Griffith far more than the physical pain of the fight.

"I risked everything I had," Griffith said. "Everything. And I lost it. To help this expedition continue."

"No one asked you to! No one asked you to help it, and no one asked you to sabotage it in the first place. No one here."

"You have no proof of your accusations."

"Do I need any?"

"To turn me in?"

Cherenkov smiled. Griffith had never noticed before that his front teeth were crooked, one slightly overlapping the other. The flaw troubled him.

"Who would I turn you in to, Marion?"

Griffith hesitated. *Starfarer* possessed no security force, a fact that had leapt out at him when he researched the expedition. As far as he knew, these disorganized anarchists had never even discussed what to do with a criminal, much less set up any mechanism to deal with one. The alternative was mob rule, vigilante justice. When he first came on board the starship, Griffith had felt contempt for the personnel. But in the last few days he had observed their hotheadedness. He could be in serious danger if Cherenkov denounced him in public or in private.

"You think that if I tell my colleagues who you really are, they will deteriorate into a mob."

"I think they already did that," Griffith said.

"Perhaps I *should* tell them what you've done. You hurt any number of people by crashing the web—"

"I did not!"

"They are still in the health center. Many are in shock."

"I *know* people were hurt. But I didn't crash the system."

Cherenkov started walking down the trail again, this time at a more reasonable pace. Griffith followed him.

"Who did, then?"

"I don't know," Griffith said, both surprised and grateful that Cherenkov trusted his word. "I figured it was someone in the carrier."

"I'm not a systems expert. But I would have thought that to be difficult, if possible at all."

Griffith walked beside him in silence for a few minutes.

"I hope it's possible," he said. "Because otherwise I'm the most likely suspect."

"But you are innocent?"

"Of crashing the system, yes, I'm innocent."

"But guilty of other things."

"They don't concern anyone on board *Starfarer*. Only me, if I get back alive. If any of us does."

"Why did you change your mind about the expedition?"

"Because you wanted it—"

Griffith stopped. Not because his words were a lie, but because they were so true. They made him even more vulnerable. First he had begun to trust Cherenkov, and now he was telling him the truth.

"I see," Cherenkov said. "I asked you to think and act for yourself. Instead, you tried to divine my thoughts and you tried to act for me. I don't understand you. If you have to obey someone, what possesses you to choose me?"

"I saw the tapes you made . . ."

Griffith expected Cherenkov to tell him to shut up, but the cosmonaut continued in silence along the rock-foam trail, where banks of pink and white camellia bushes rose on either side. The two men walked parallel to the long axis of the starship's main cylinder, along a cool, green path. The air smelled of damp grass, for a shower had passed a few minutes ago. The cloud lay a quarter of the way farther along the cylinder's circumference, sweeping its course with raindrops.

"You saw the tapes?" Cherenkov said. "I thought they were destroyed. Long ago."

"No. They exist."

Cherenkov shrugged. "Too late, by years, for them to do any good."

"What you said in those interviews moved me," Griffith said. "Deeply. I could see you fighting to control your pain and your outrage, but I could feel it all anyway. Your words, your feelings, were like a sword..."

"I felt nothing."

Marion Griffith looked up at him, uncomprehending. "No. *What*?"

"I felt nothing when I made those recordings. I knew that I should feel something. I knew it was important to tell what I saw, no matter how terrible it was. But I could feel nothing. I turned all that off, months before, just to survive."

"If it wasn't real, you're a damned good actor!" Griffith said.

"Yes," Cherenkov replied, matter of fact.

"You're lying. No. I don't mean that. You're making it up to protect yourself from the truth. I know how to do that—to keep it from hurting anymore."

"Don't rewrite my life for me! I remember how it was. I almost refused the interviews, that's how difficult it was."

"You see!" Griffith heard his own voice, urgent, desperate. "It was too painful—"

"It was difficult," Kolya said softly, "because I no longer wanted to care. I had to force myself..."

Griffith could think of no reply. He felt stunned and numb, as Kolya had claimed to feel.

"Perhaps if they had ever used those tapes as I expected them to be used, if I had seen them again, things might have been different. But I told what I saw, and no one paid attention. No one believed."

"That isn't true either," Griffith said. "I know what happened."

Kolya chuckled. "Marion Griffith, child spy."

"I was a teenager when you escaped. Then, I only knew what was public. The news stories, and the movie—"

Kolya made a piteous sound of agony.

"What's the matter? Are you all right?"

"If you tell me that appalling piece of adventure fiction affected your life, I'll surely throttle you. It had nothing to do with me, and I had nothing to do with it."

Griffith skipped over the subject of his own teenage years

and the things that had affected him when he was a dumb, romantic kid.

"When I was in a position to, I made it my business to find out what really happened. That's how I found your tapes. I talked to people who were involved. It wasn't that no one believed what you said. They did. They knew others would, too. They were afraid of the public reaction. They's why they never released your interviews."

"A political decision," Kolya said.

"Yes. They thought if they didn't do anything, things would ease up with the Sweep. Unfortunately, they were wrong."

"Yes."

Kolya reached the foot of the slope that led up the end of the cylinder. He began to climb.

"At the meeting," Griffith said, "you told me that no one outside the Sweep could do anything that would help anyone inside. Why did you give those interviews? You were trying to affect the Sweep from outside!"

"That was years ago!" Kolya said angrily. "Things change! Different actions are appropriate for different conditions." He glanced over at Griffith. "I think you want everything to be stable, and predictable. But the world isn't like that."

Griffith could think of no reply.

They were halfway up the hill to the axis of *Starfarer*, moving easily along the switchbacks while the gravity decreased with every step. Though the physical angle of the slope increased, the perception was of a progressively easier climb.

"Kolya, where are we going?"

"I'm going to the liaison office. I don't know where you're going."

Griffith stopped. He watched Kolya continue up the path and disappear into the tunnel near the axis of the starship. He hoped Kolya would turn around and laugh, or ask why Griffith had fallen behind. But he glided up the hill and out of sight without another word.

Just follow him, Griffith said to himself. What can he do, if you follow him? It's what you've been doing all along, and he never did anything to keep you from doing whatever you want.

Except, of course, Griffith was no longer following Kolya Cherenkov.

J.D. relaxed, relieved that the audio channels back to *Starfarer* had closed for a while. She never felt comfortable within the view of a camera or the range of a microphone, never grew indifferent to their observation. The public argument had embarrassed her, for herself and for the sake of her teammates. Relieved at the return of her privacy, she pushed herself against her couch, tensing and stretching her muscles.

Until Victoria mentioned it, J.D. had not realized how hungry she was. They would all probably feel better as soon as Victoria and Satoshi returned with sandwiches.

To her right, Stephen Thomas stared at the double image, the pretty planet hovering around and through the solid dark shape of the interrupted transmission.

"Maybe we're supposed to—" he said. He stopped, and glanced over at J.D. sheepishly. "I can't help it," he said. "I keep trying to make up reasons why the transmission stopped. But I can't think of anything that makes sense except by invoking too much coincidence to believe in."

"That could be what's happened," J.D. said. "We wouldn't notice coincidences, we wouldn't even have a word for them, if things didn't happen that were too strange to believe."

"True," he said. He sounded more cheerful. Then he sighed. "But Satoshi's right, too."

"I'm sure he didn't mean to snap at you," J.D. said. "We've been through an awful lot in the last few hours. He looks exhausted. So do you."

"You aren't saying I have dark circles under my eyes, are you?" Stephen Thomas said.

He smiled. J.D. chuckled. He had dark circles, all right. At least the bruises had stopped spreading. The cut on his forehead showed livid under a transparent bandage.

Stephen Thomas gestured toward the holographic display. "I imagined this so often. Before you joined the team, we practiced in here. Just like the Apollo astronauts before the first moon landing. This was supposed to be another giant leap..."

"It still is!" J.D. said.

"I hope so. I hope it's not just a small misstep. But I wish I knew why the message stopped."

As they gazed in silence at the half-completed display, the hard link chimed with a message. It was Kolya Cherenkov.

"Hello, Kolya," J.D. said, surprised that he had called her. Like everyone else on board *Starfarer*, she held him in considerable awe.

"Do you have a moment to speak with me?" he asked.

"Of course."

"This alien transmission," he said, then hesitated. "It makes me suspicious of its creators."

"Why?" J.D. found the behavior of the alien message confusing. She knew she did not understand the motives behind it. But it had not occurred to her to suspect that the motives were sinister.

"I wish I could say for sure. Perhaps I'm only being paranoid, perhaps these are the fears of an old man who has seen too much evil in his lifetime..."

"The message *is* strange," J.D. said. "But... it's alien, after all. Not evil."

"The message feels to me like a trap. Or—bait for a trap."

"If the message were bait, why would it stop?"

"I don't know," he admitted. "It's just..."

J.D. waited. The silence felt very long, much longer than the transmission delay.

"Just what, Kolya?" she asked gently.

"I—" He stopped again, then said, with intensity, "This is a mission of exploration. As I keep reminding myself. I agree with the idea that starfaring civilizations will have given up war. Intellectually, I agree."

"'Intellectually,'" J.D. said. One of the most difficult questions for the starship's planners had been whether *Starfarer* should or should not be armed.

"The truth is, it frightens me that we're unarmed. That you're unarmed." He laughed, but the tone was self-deprecating. "I'm sorry. I've called you to tell you my fears. To worry you, at best. To tell you to be careful."

She was genuinely touched. "Thank you, Kolya," she said. "I will be careful."

After Kolya Cherenkov had signed off, Stephen Thomas whistled softly.

"He's been through experiences none of us will ever come close to. We ought to listen to his perceptions."

J.D. glanced at the labyrinth and at the half-completed

message. Despite Kolya's fears, she could find nothing ominous within the maze. Within the second message, she could find nothing at all.

"Can you see anything there, Zev?" she asked. "Any pattern?"

"Only waves," Zev said.

"Yes." It was like seeing animals and faces in clouds. The mind looked for familiar patterns. What more familiar pattern could Zev see, than waves?

J.D. yawned. She glanced over at Zev. He was wide awake, interested, alert. She envied him his energy and his youth.

"When will we get there?" he said. "Will we be able to swim?"

"We probably aren't going to the planet," J.D. said. "Not yet. Maybe when *Starfarer* catches up. For now we're just going to the planet's moon."

"Oh," Zev said, disappointed.

J.D. glanced back at the transmission. For a moment she thought it had resumed, but like the patterns in the clouds, in the waves, the perception was a trick of her mind. The image remained steady, unchanging.

"Zev..." J.D. said. "If you were swimming with your family, and somebody you didn't know came toward you making a lot of unpleasant noise, what would the divers do? What would the orcas do?"

Zev looked at her curiously. "We would all swim away," he said. "Of course."

2

A few hours later, the *Chi* slipped into orbit around Tau Ceti II's satellite. The intelligence systems guided it, sending it on a course that took the *Chi* over the source of the alien transmission.

As the barren lava plains of the Tau Ceti II's moon passed above the transparent ceiling of the observers' circle, an image formed in the center of the chamber.

J.D. gazed at the first alien construction humans had ever seen. Her pulse raced. She wanted to jump up and cry out: We're here! Answer us, come out and meet us! We're here!

"Not much to look at, is it?" Stephen Thomas said.

J.D. tried to think of a way to express her awe at the sight of the low, nondescript dome, but words failed her. She thought she might be able to write about it.

"Neither are you, Stephen Thomas, just now," Victoria said mildly.

His bruises had faded to a livid purple. He looked like he was wearing lopsided horror-movie makeup.

"What did you expect?" Victoria asked. "Crystal towers? Golden palaces? The plains of Nazca?"

"I would have settled for any of those over a gray pimple," he said. "I'd even settle for a gray pimple, if I thought there was anybody inside it."

"It's very practical," J.D. said. "Looks like it's made of native rock. It could have been there for a long time. Maybe even millennia."

Satoshi glanced at the image of the plain gray teardrop-shaped dome, then returned his attention to the image of Tau Ceti II itself.

"That's probably true," he said. "Especially the last."

"What are you finding?"

31

"Nothing."

"Nothing!" Stephen Thomas exclaimed. "Nothing? Nothing but two living worlds!"

"All I meant was—"

"—that you can't find any roads. Big deal."

"Or any other kind of transportation network, or cities, or lights."

"Or rampant environmental destruction."

Satoshi gestured with his chin toward the dome. "So who built *that?*"

"People who do a better job of cohabiting with their environment than we do with ours."

"I suppose it's possible," Satoshi said.

"We're overlooking two living planets on account of a bunch of radio impulses coming from a sterile satellite."

"We're all anxious to visit the planets," Victoria said to Stephen Thomas. "But the transmission had to take precedence. Don't you agree?"

"Maybe it would have been bad manners to come flying in here and ignore it," he said. "But we didn't. We tried to answer it. We pretty much assumed it would be automated, and we were right. Nobody's home."

"We've got time," Victoria said. "Plenty of time to investigate the dome and plenty of time to visit Tau Ceti II and III."

"I know how Stephen Thomas feels," J.D. said. "What I want to do is explode in a thousand pieces and send each one off exploring."

"Please." Victoria's smile looked rather forced. "We've had enough explosions for one trip already."

J.D. chuckled, relieved that Victoria could make a joke. She hoped they were all finding their equilibrium again. But Stephen Thomas gazed at the low gray dome, kneading his hands together and radiating his disinclination to stop anywhere but on the surface of the planet.

J.D. understood his impatience. While Victoria and Satoshi had plenty to do, neither J.D. nor Stephen Thomas could begin their jobs until the next phase of exploration. A lifeless world was of very little interest to a geneticist. For J.D., an uninhabited alien habitation might be a tremendous discovery, yet it was an incredible anticlimax for an alien contact specialist.

She tried to look at it from a hopeful standpoint. "Stephen Thomas, there may be living beings in the dome."

"There aren't," he said.

"Oh," J.D. said, keeping her voice carefully neutral.

J.D. felt both Victoria and Satoshi stiffen up, their skepticism evident; she saw Zev glance curiously at Stephen Thomas, then at her, then at Victoria and Satoshi. He must be wondering what parts of the conversation he was missing, how ordinary humans expressed what the divers and the orcas expressed in sounds that enfolded the whole body. J.D. wondered what nuances she was missing because Victoria and Satoshi and Stephen Thomas knew each other intimately and she could not enter their triangle.

"Hey, it's too bad if that isn't something you want to hear," Stephen Thomas said. "But nobody's down there."

"You'll forgive us if we double-check your messages from beyond, my dear," Victoria said dryly.

"Sure," Stephen Thomas said. "It isn't as if I'm not used to it."

J.D. realized—startling herself with the realization—that she accepted Stephen Thomas's assertion. She believed the dome would be empty, though she had only his intuition and the ending of the transmission as evidence.

"There's no activity around it," J.D. said. "Nothing that looks like a ship. No broadcast activity on the frequencies you expect people to be using. Maybe it's just set up to signal to us when we arrived. And when we signaled back, its job was over."

"That dome is a hundred meters across," Satoshi said. "You don't need an entire base to transmit a short range signal. You can do that with a beacon, what, this big?" He opened his arms, shaping the antenna with his hands.

"I know, but . . ."

Victoria pushed herself back against the cushions of her lounge. Her long graceful fingers clenched around the open safety straps, tight with tension.

"It's too bad we didn't have our six months in Earth orbit," Victoria said. "We needed that time, for us to learn to work as a team and for *Starfarer* to become a community. We didn't have it. So now we have to do the best we can. I think we should land on the satellite. Satoshi?"

"Yes," he said. "The satellite."

"Stephen Thomas?"

"The planet."

"J.D.?"

She hesitated, irrationally tempted to side with Stephen Thomas.

"The satellite," she said. "The dome."

Victoria glanced back to Stephen Thomas.

"I wish you'd just outvote me, clean and simple," he said. "But I won't break consensus. The moon."

"The satellite it is. On the next orbit."

"But this orientation is making me dizzy," Stephen Thomas said. "I feel like we're flying upside down."

"That I can fix," Victoria said. The *Chi* rotated one hundred eighty degrees. Now, in relation to the couches, the surface of the satellite lay "below," instead of "above."

"Don't I get a vote?" Zev asked.

"No, Zev," Victoria said. "You don't get a vote."

Looking down through the transparent floor of the observers' circle, they passed over craters and flat, unscarred plains.

The *Chi* sped past the terminator and entered night. Tau Ceti's light winked out as the upper curve of the star passed beneath the satellite's horizon. The faint gray luminescence of the holographic image illuminated the observers' circle.

The *Chi* sailed on through darkness.

Infinity Mendez followed Feral Korzybski across the inspection cables that crisscrossed *Starfarer*'s exterior. He kept the young journalist in sight, for this was Feral's maiden space walk.

He's not doing too bad, for a novice, Infinity thought.

Starfarer loomed above them, and its motion spun them over the stars.

"This is fantastic!" Feral exclaimed. "Even better than the sailhouse."

Infinity smiled. He had been on *Starfarer*'s surface at least a thousand times, and he never got tired of the experience. Bone-tired though he was, he enjoyed giving Feral the grand tour. Besides, Infinity wanted to make one more inspection of the damage to the starship. Then he could give himself some rest.

Starfarer's two huge hollow cylinders revolved to produce the effect of about seven-tenths of one gravity on their inner surfaces. All the people lived in one half of the ship, in the pleasant, pastoral campus cylinder. The other half, the wild cylinder, existed as a backup, an ecological storehouse, a safety net.

The spin brought Infinity and Feral between the two cylinders. Below them, the gentle, rocky curve of the wild cylinder rolled past.

"Do you ever go over there?" Feral asked.

"All the time. Nobody lives there, but it's a good place to camp. The terrain's rougher. It's quiet."

"Can anybody visit it?"

"Sure. You can come with me next time, if you want. Once things calm down."

"That'd be great," Feral said.

The bulk of each cylinder consisted of moon rock, flung into space and fused together with rock foam. The thick skin protected the living areas from the extremes of space: radiation, hard vacuum, intolerable temperature fluctuations. The outer surface looked unfinished, rubbly in some places and smooth in others. Inspection cables traced a network all around the outside. Beneath the surface, service corridors and storage compartments and utility tunnels and the water system snaked through, like veins and bones and nerves in an organic body.

Infinity described the invisible workings of the starship to Feral.

"You know this place inside out," Feral said.

"I ought to. I helped build it. Not many of us left on board."

"How'd you decide to switch from construction to gardening?"

Infinity shrugged. "No call for space construction these days." Earth's governments had been looking increasingly inward in recent years. No one had founded an O'Neill colony in a decade. "And I wanted to join the expedition."

Since the missile attack, Infinity had needed his space construction experience. Though he had not used it in years, it came back fast in time of necessity. The damage control committee had come outside as soon as the radiation fell to a safe level. Infinity had been working for hours, sparing a small part of his attention, now and again, to listen in on the reports of the alien contact department.

He moved up beside Feral as the crater appeared over the horizon.

"Here's where the missile hit."

They sat on a cable with their feet dangling above the stars. In awed silence, Feral leaned back to look up at the damage.

To Infinity's satisfaction, a layer of silver covered the jumbled interior. The crater looked as if it were filled with mercury, it's surface set visibly trembling by imperceptible vibrations.

"It's healing pretty well," Infinity said.

Since the starship left transition, he had checked out the damage and double-checked the reports of the ASes and AIs. He missed having access to Arachne. Infinity could have used the powerful intelligence of the computer to help put the repair plan into action.

"We were lucky," Feral said, still gazing into the wound in *Starfarer*'s side. "We were really lucky."

The missile had slammed into the starship, penetrating the skin. Most of the damage occurred deeper, not from the missile itself but from the shock wave of its impact. At the focus of the shock, on the inner surface of the ship, the genetics building lay in ruins.

Had the warhead detonated while it was still stuck in *Starfarer*'s skin, the damage would have been much greater.

Starfarer owed its existence to J.D. Sauvage and Kolya Cherenkov. Infinity wondered if anyone had thought to thank them. He knew where J.D. was. He was not so sure about Kolya.

Feral was right. *Starfarer* was lucky. The isolation doors had worked, sealing themselves around the wound, keeping the loss of air and water to a tolerable level. Now the repair had begun.

Exterior ASes congregated at the damage site, their amorphous silver bodies covering the broken surface. Some of the silver slugs dissolved debris, some reformed it into the proper patterns. Wherever conglomerations of slugs parted to reveal bare rock, the surface looked smoother. The slugs extruded rock foam to ooze between the cracks and seal them. Scar tissue had begun to form.

And there is going to be a scar, Infinity thought. No help for it.

Starfarer should have been safe from impact damage. The

skin of the starship could easily resist hits from space junk. Arachne tracked larger pieces of rock or trash, warned against them, and gave the starship time to avoid the rare asteroid that might approach. Everyone knew about, and accepted, the one point of real, if minuscule, danger: leaving transition blind, reemerging into space with no absolute knowledge of what lay in *Starfarer*'s path.

Starfarer had never been designed to withstand the attack of a nuclear missile.

"Where were you when the missile exploded?" Feral asked.

"Almost over the crater." Infinity pointed. "There, about halfway up in the skin to the interior. I was heading for the point of impact. Looking for what caused the shock wave."

Feral whistled softly.

Infinity shivered, then laughed at himself for his retroactive fear.

Feral glanced at him and grinned uncertainly, his face ghostly behind the gold reflective coating of his face plate.

"Funnier now than then, I guess," he said. "Once you've missed being at ground zero."

"Twice," Infinity said absently. "Ground zero would have been the best place. Quick. Vaporized. Me and J.D. and Kolya. And Griffith. For anybody else ... explosive decompression. Or trauma or asphyxiation or radiation. Not much of a choice."

"Griffith was out here?" Feral sounded surprised. Griffith claimed to be only an accountant, from the General Accounting Office. No one believed him. Everyone believed he had been sent to help stop the expedition.

"Sort of." Infinity considered telling Feral exactly what had happened. The events humiliated the government man. Griffith had threatened Infinity instead of requesting his silence. Infinity no longer feared Griffith's threats. Nor did he need to add to his humiliation. So he kept the story to himself.

"Weird," Feral said. "I've been thinking of him as the most likely cause of all our trouble ..."

"He might be," Infinity said. "His bosses might have decided to sacrifice him once he did his job. Or he might have been trying to get out."

"Infinity ... ?"

"Yeah?"

"What did you mean, 'twice'?"

Feral might have been young; he might even have been inexperienced. But he sure picked up on details.

"My mother was a member of the Southwest Tribes," Infinity said. This was the second time in his life that he had narrowly missed being at ground zero of a nuclear explosion.

"My god," Feral said. "I'm sorry. Did she make it out? Do you remember it?"

"She was in the last deportation. I don't remember it. I was too young."

"Have you ever been back?"

"Are you kidding?" Infinity said, his voice on the edge of anger.

"About that? No."

"Sorry," Infinity said. "You need a security clearance to get in there."

"I know, but—"

"Feral, they don't *give* security clearances to anybody from the Southwest tribes. Not that security clearance, anyway."

"I didn't know," Feral said.

"Forget it. I don't qualify. Ask Griffith what it's like. He probably has the clearance. Maybe he could look at what happened. Why should he care?"

Infinity wished he had not revealed so much of what he felt. When was the last time anyone had drawn him out about his past? Usually people avoided the subject, the questions, the remorse or excuses of those responsible, and the anguish of Infinity's people.

"You care," Feral said. "That's what matters to me."

"I wouldn't want to go back, even if I could," Infinity said. "The Southwest is a myth. For me. For my family. A destruction myth. I think..." He hesitated, then plunged ahead. "I think I came into space looking for a creation myth. For balance. For my soul."

The spin took them out of the valley between the cylinders. The light of the Milky Way washed across them from below, silvering the stony surface, glittering from the skins of the silver slugs. Infinity looked down at the stars spinning past.

The distance between the sun and Tau Ceti, so unimaginably far for human comprehension, meant nothing to the patterns of the stars. The constellations were as recognizable as if he were still in the solar system.

"We should go back inside," Infinity said. "The *Chi* will be landing. I want to watch."

"Me, too," Feral replied, still watching the stars at his feet. "The constellations look just the same."

"The distance between the sun and Tau Ceti isn't enough to distort them," Infinity said. "We've only moved the center of the star chart twelve light-years. From where we sit, Cetus is missing Tau Ceti. And . . ." He pointed out the constellation Boötes, and a small yellow star near brilliant Arcturus. "That's the sun."

Starlight touched the edges of dark craters, and the *Chi* moved through night.

Stephen Thomas scanned Satoshi's data from the surface of Tau Ceti II, pointing out, at J.D.'s request, what a geneticist could learn from the raw chemical makeup of the atmosphere, the seas, the land surface, from the polarization of light and the colors of the vegetation.

Though they needed no complicated mechanisms to detect life on the world—it was obvious to the naked eye from a vast distance—the more detailed information hinted that Tau Ceti II might be astonishingly compatible with Earthly evolution. Attractive as that sounded, it troubled J.D.

"It ought to be more *different*," Stephen Thomas said. His current interest centered around speculative biochemistry. He wanted to look at alien inheritance; he expected, and hoped, to find information-carrying molecules made up of something other than nucleic acids.

"Why haven't they colonized?" Satoshi muttered.

"Hmm?" Victoria said, intent on the dome. It grew slowly; in a minute or two the image would fade, because they would be able to see the structure itself through the observation port.

"Tau Ceti II is temperate," he said. "It has an oxidizing atmosphere, liquid water, dry land, and life forms evolutionarily well in advance of whatever passes here for blue-green algae. But there's no evidence of the kind of technology that's necessary to support building a base. Or a transmitter. So: where are the people who built it? Where did they come from, where did they go, and why didn't they stick around to live on this pretty little world?"

"I read a story once," Zev said. "The people breathed

methane and lived in a sea of liquid nitrogen. Maybe the
beings didn't like this world."

J.D. knew the story he was talking about. He had read it in
a book from her library. It had been written in the early days
of science fiction, when the principles of speculation had
more to do with imagination than scientific plausibility.

"I don't think I believe in methane breathers," Victoria
said. "Or aliens with superconductors for nerve fibers. But
you could be right in essence. For some reason, they didn't
like it. They couldn't find a part of it hot enough, or cold
enough, for their tastes."

"They've got a big range to choose from," Satoshi said.
"They'd have to need it way below freezing or practically at a
simmer, not to find anywhere they'd want to live."

"Or dry or wet or dark or light—they just didn't like it."

"More likely the biological molecules are all the opposite
isomers of what they need," Stephen Thomas said. "Right-
handed instead of left-handed, or vice versa. So whatever
grows here is completely incompatible with their systems,
and they can't grow anything of their own. We could have the
same problem."

"Maybe they left it for us," J.D. said.

Victoria's brow furrowed. "That's an interesting speculation."

"Who knows, it might be the rule in the interstellar
civilization. Tau Ceti is near our sun, and its world is
uninhabited. So maybe they left it alone so we could have it."

"Pretty damned altruistic," Stephen Thomas said.

"Or so many planets are temperate that a few more or less
aren't any big thing."

"And they expect us to colonize the place?"

"It's a possibility," J.D. said. "Though if it's true I'm a little
surprised. I'm uncomfortable with the idea of upsetting the
evolution of an independent ecosystem. And that's what
humans would do."

"Other humans," Satoshi said. "Not us. Human colonists
will have to come on some other ship." Colonization was
against *Starfarer*'s charter, the agreement every expedition
member had signed. This was a research expedition, and it
would do its best not to introduce Earthly contamination—
protozoan, plant, or animal, sentient or not—to new living
worlds.

"Everyone accepted the charter," Victoria said. "That doesn't keep folks from getting into arguments about it. Fairly passionate arguments. People who disagree with the charter consider the expedition the opening of an outer frontier."

"I'm glad I'm not in charge of settling that argument," J.D. said.

Tau Ceti burst above the horizon, and dimmed as the circle wall darkened. The *Chi* emerged into daylight as suddenly as it had plunged into night.

The little ship trembled as the engines fired. The team members waited and watched. The ship took them down.

J.D.'s couch moved beneath her, gradually tilting into gravity mode, turning into a chair. The gravity of Tau Ceti II's satellite took hold of the *Chi* as its engines engaged and decelerated the craft from free-fall. Victoria and Satoshi settled into their new positions as if they barely noticed the change. Stephen Thomas relaxed for the first time since they left *Starfarer*. Zev looked around and under his lounger, slipping out of the safety straps, then slipping back in and stroking the soft arms of the chair. J.D. enjoyed a moment of watching him discover and analyze something new about his new environment.

"So much has changed..." Stephen Thomas said. "I wonder how many of us will decide that the most sensible thing is to settle here? Assuming the place is habitable. Maybe that's preferable to going home—and going to jail."

"What an appalling suggestion," Victoria said.

"Going to jail? I agree."

"Settling here instead of going home with what we've learned. If we disappear, it will be a generation or two before anybody on Earth considers another starship. I'm glad to be here—but I'm not willing to give up Earth in order to stay. I'm not willing to break my word."

"It'd sure make my life easier," Stephen Thomas muttered, as if he were speaking to himself. He might as well have been; neither of his partners replied.

As the *Chi* approached its destination, the image of the dome faded out and left the view through the transparent floor unobstructed.

A cracked and jumbled landscape sped beneath the *Chi*. Volcanic and gravitational activity had created a wasteland of exploded stone, severe lava fields, and great volcanoes.

"If there *is* anybody on Tau Ceti II," Satoshi said, "this satellite must give them quite a show."

"It's not locked with one face to the planet," J.D. said. "There's a theory, that if human beings had been able to see their moon turning on its axis, early cosmology would have been much different. We would have known the moon was a sphere. We might have skipped the Copernican model of the universe altogether and gone straight to Galileo's ideas. We might have had calculus and even quantum mechanics a couple of millennia earlier."

Stephen Thomas slouched forward in his couch. "*Nnnggg*, Grakileo see moon." He imitated a Neanderthal Galileo. "*Eggurrr si muove*. Earth moves! Grakileo deduce $E = mc^2$!"

J.D. giggled.

"Very funny," Victoria said.

"I thought so," Stephen Thomas said.

"But it's such a great idea," J.D. said. "We could have had Renaissance spaceships."

Victoria grinned. "And Regency ones. Can you imagine a spaceship in the style of the Royal Pavilion at Brighton?"

"How about T'ang dynasty?" Satoshi said. "That's when people started printing books, and it got easier to spread information around."

The *Chi* slowed its forward speed and gave up some altitude. It skimmed over the high, uneroded peaks that surrounded the dome. A wide plain stretched out beyond. The dome rose gently from the smooth surface, then blended gently back. The *Chi* decelerated, hovered, descended.

As the *Chi* landed, the dome changed.

J.D. pushed herself forward in her seat, straining against the safety straps, reaching out toward the dome as if she could grasp it and hold it in place.

The radiation shields darkened the observers' circle to opacity. Just before the transparent chamber changed to reflective black, just before the protection cut off the outside light along with the dangerous, higher-energy frequencies, the top of the dome sagged and crumpled.

"No!"

J.D. thought: Kolya was right.

The *Chi* touched down hard. The landing feet scratched and scraped against the surface, and the vibration transmitted itself through the ship.

The faint sound disappeared beneath an interminable shudder that ended with a subsonic rumble. In the darkness, J.D. felt it to her bones.

She slumped against her couch, stunned. She put her hand to her face, afraid she had been blinded by whatever activated the shielding screens.

"Is everyone all right?" Victoria asked.

"Is it dark in here?" J.D. tried to keep her voice as steady as Victoria's, but failed.

"Extremely," Victoria said.

"Then... I guess I'm all right. Physically. Zev?" She fumbled toward his couch. He found her hand, without hesitation, and squeezed it. Divers could see farther into the infrared than ordinary human beings.

"I am all right, J.D." For the first time since arriving on board *Starfarer*, Zev sounded uncertain. The silky webs of his hand warmed J.D.'s palm.

"Stephen Thomas? Satoshi?"

"Yeah." Stephen Thomas sounded as shaken as J.D.

"But what the hell happened?" Satoshi said.

He had been sitting with his back to the dome; he could not have seen what J.D. saw. If she had seen it at all. It was such a brief, shocking sight. She tried to make herself believe she had made it up.

"The dome collapsed," Stephen Thomas said.

"What!"

"You saw it, too," J.D. said.

"Fucking right I saw it. I was looking right at it."

"I saw... something... out of the corner of my eye," Victoria said. "Motion. But I couldn't be sure..." She fell silent.

"I'm sure," Stephen Thomas said. "Hey, is the view coming back? Or are my eyes adjusting?"

Emergency lights glowed on, circling the ceiling and floor of the observers' circle. The alien contact team sat in the center of a room of black mirrors reflecting gold light. The walls and floor and ceiling had not yet begun to clear.

J.D. squeezed Zev's hand. She was worried about him, but he had recovered from his fright. He looked more eager than apprehensive.

"This is very pretty," Satoshi said, "but I'd rather see outside."

"Not right now, you wouldn't," Victoria said. "There's a heavy radiation flux. Fading fast, though."

"Wonderful," Stephen Thomas said sarcastically. "We meet the galactic civilization and they present us with firebombs."

"It isn't that different from what we presented them," J.D. said.

Sensor patterns formed at the center of the circle. They sang quietly to themselves, disharmonious. J.D. could read some of them. A precipitous temperature rise accompanied a seismic spike of considerable magnitude.

"If we're not sitting on the edge of a crater, about to fall in, we're pretty lucky," Satoshi said.

"The *Chi* is solid," Victoria replied. "But I've asked it to respond immediately if we start to shift."

"Come on, Victoria, let's see what's outside."

"Give it another minute, Stephen Thomas. I don't want to burn out any receivers."

Satoshi gazed across the circle at Stephen Thomas. "It collapsed."

Stephen Thomas nodded.

Like a good-luck piece, or a meditation aid, the globe of Tau Ceti II appeared before Satoshi. He stared into the image. Not a good-luck piece. A crystal ball.

"I'm going outside," Stephen Thomas said. He threw off the safety straps, got up, and started for the hatch. Forgetting that he was in a low-gravity environment, he lurched forward with his first step, then caught himself and proceeded in a more dignified fashion.

"Can I come with you?" Zev opened his safety straps with his free hand and stood up, but J.D. pulled him back.

"Zev, you're not going anywhere. Stephen Thomas!"

He did not even hesitate.

"Victoria, you aren't going to let him!"

"I may go with him," Victoria said. "Whatever collapsed the dome, it was very clean. The flux will be down to background by the time he gets into a suit." She frowned at the mass of information, her head cocked in concentration. The songs had evened out nearly into harmony. "In fact..."

As she spoke, the lights went out and the black mirrors vanished. The observers' circle might have been built on a small platform open to the sky and the air and even the ground.

Except that there was no air. The sky was black and filled with stars.

The dome had fallen into a heap of slag.

As soon as the radiation shields cleared, the *Chi* once again began receiving transmissions from *Starfarer*.

"*Starfarer* to explorer, *Starfarer* to explorer. Explorer, please reply." Gerald Hemminge's upper-class British accent rolled into the circle.

"We're here, Gerald," Victoria said.

The distance between the starship and the *Chi* delayed his reply.

"We lost your signal."

"We've . . . got a complication. Are you getting our outside pictures—"

"Good lord!" Gerald exclaimed.

"I guess he got them," Satoshi said.

"You'd better return," Gerald said. "Immediately."

"No!" J.D. whispered.

"I don't think so," Victoria said.

"It's clear we have no idea what we're getting into," Gerald said. "You must return so we can decide how to deal with this, without making the situation any worse."

Victoria's short, sharp laugh was full of irony. "Excuse me, Gerald, but I don't see how it could *be* any worse. I'll call back after we've taken a look. Explorer out." She ended the transmission before he could reply. "Come on," she said. "Let's go."

"Was it such a good idea, to cut him off like that?" J.D. followed Victoria and Satoshi out of the observers' circle. Zev tagged along behind.

Victoria shrugged. "I know what he'll say, he knows what I'll say. We don't even need to say it anymore. Sometimes I think we communicate by telepathy." She sighed. "Isn't telepathy supposed to work between people who *like* each other?"

"That's often the case. In fiction."

"You ought to write a story where the opposite happens. Where you can communicate by telepathy only with somebody you absolutely loath."

J.D. followed Victoria into the changing room beside the air lock. Stephen Thomas was halfway into his suit. The artificial stupid with the holo equipment crouched nearby, inactive, waiting patiently to accompany them. The AS looked like a cross between a spider and a wheeled virus particle, about the size of a house cat.

"Couldn't resist, huh?" Stephen Thomas said to Victoria.

"Resistance doesn't come into it," Victoria said. "Going out there is our job. And I might remind you, you're the one who didn't even want to land."

"True. But now that we're here—"

J.D. took her suit from its hook. She had never worn this one. She had put on a space suit only once before, when, in desperation, she responded to Kolya Cherenkov's plea for help when the missile struck. The other suit was back on the starship, scraped and scratched, heavily used by other people before J.D. came along and abused it in her turn. She had left a layer of her own sweat inside that suit, and perhaps it had also absorbed her fright and exhilaration.

She wondered what kind of emotions this suit would absorb from her. At the moment she felt unhealthily excited, like some nineteenth-century Victorian lady preparing to swoon from nervous exhaustion.

"Which one is mine?" Zev asked.

"You don't have one, Zev."

"But there are enough."

"You have to stay in the *Chi*," Victoria told him.

"But why?"

"For the same reason you didn't have a vote on whether we came here in the first place. You aren't a member of the team. You aren't even a member of the expedition."

"Yes I am," he said. "I'm a member of the art department. I'm Chandra's graduate student."

"You still can't go outside."

Zev turned to J.D. "I want to go with you."

"I'm sorry," she said. "Victoria's right. And we should do what she says, Zev. She's the team leader."

"Like Lykos, you mean."

"Like Lykos."

"But Lykos let me go with you."

Victoria and Satoshi had nearly finished suiting up.

"Are you coming with us?"

"Yes." Though J.D. felt sad to leave Zev behind, she could not abdicate her responsibilities. She did not want to, even for Zev. She stepped into the legs of her suit and pulled the rest of it up around her shoulders. "Zev, Lykos let you come with me because she knew we'd talked about the expedition. She knew you had some idea what you'd be getting into. But here, now—this is something we haven't talked about."

"All right," he said, downcast.

"Go on up to the observers' circle. You'll be able to hear us just like everybody on board *Starfarer*, and see us even better."

"If you can't trust me to go with you, how come you can trust me to stay here alone?"

Victoria glanced toward him, her patience exhausted.

"This isn't a good time for jokes," J.D. said before Victoria could respond. She had seen the mischievous twitch to Zev's lips as he spoke.

"Every time is a good time for jokes," Stephen Thomas said. "Particularly now. Let's go. See you, Zev. Sorry."

"Swim with sharks, Stephen Thomas," Zev said.

The air lock sealed. Through the small window J.D. watched Zev bouncing gently down the hallway toward the observers' circle, light and lithe in the low gravity, his baggy suit pants waving around his slender legs.

The sound around her faded. The threshold interference of her radio receiver shushed in her ears.

"'Swim with *sharks*'?" Stephen Thomas said. "What the hell does that mean? It sounds like a threat."

"It isn't," J.D. said. "It means he hopes you have an exciting excursion."

"It's already that," Satoshi said.

"I'm going to bring the broadcast back to us," Victoria said. "They're probably tired of watching rock slump, back home. Is everybody ready?"

"I hate this," J.D. whispered.

"That isn't an answer."

"I didn't mean to transmit it. I'm ready."

The outer air lock doors opened. Victoria led the way. J.D. followed her down the stairs of the *Chi*.

Victoria's foot silently touched the surface of Tau Ceti II's satellite. The scene reminded J.D. of the foggy film of the first landing on Earth's moon, back in the last century. But Victoria left no footprints on the hard, dustless ground.

When J.D. stepped down, the sound of her booted foot scraping against the rough stone traveled through her suit.

She felt both thrilled and dismayed, to be standing for the first time on an alien world.

"I've never even been to our moon." Then she realized her words had been transmitted, and she blushed violently and in silence. It was, she thought, Victoria's place to speak the first words here. The AS followed them down the ladder. J.D. hoped it could not transmit a picture of her face.

"Neither have I," Victoria said, her tone wry. "None of us has."

She set off across the rock plain toward the slumping, settling dome.

As they approached it, J.D. could feel its radiant heat soaking into her suit. She trusted Victoria's analysis, and believed that the radiation had peaked and vanished. Nevertheless, it scared her to approach a structure that had destroyed itself so recently. For all J.D. knew, it might decide it had not finished its task, and set off another blast of radiation.

The job has risks, she told herself. You knew that when you applied. That's why you're here, that's why you're not essential to the existence and maintenance of the starship. You're here to take the risks.

"What do you think, Satoshi?" Victoria said.

He stopped and settled back, studying the collapsed dome.

"I think it's possible that whoever constructed the dome actually got programmed microbuilders to work. That would be quite an achievement. There's no evidence of heavy machinery." He scuffed his boot hard against the stone. It left a mark. "It's tough to imagine a bunch of people—beings, of whatever kind—living here for very long without leaving more evidence of their presence. Tracks. Lift-off burns. Some general mess."

"That's exactly what's wrong with it," Stephen Thomas said. "The place is too damned clean."

J.D. could imagine alien people who picked up after themselves better than human beings did. But it seemed likely that they would at least have left some scuff marks.

Victoria led her teammates around the edge of the dome. They had to stay some distance away, because heat still radiated from it. It continued to settle in on itself. The rock sagged from the sides inward, making a terraced platform with a hemispherical bulge on top. The bulge, too, drooped slowly, flattening, but held up here and there by some strange infrastructure, or some heat-resistant bit of its contents. J.D. imagined what might be inside, what plans an alien civilization might make to welcome a peaceful, if equally alien, visitor, and she wanted to cry.

How determined would they be to avoid contact with warlike creatures? she wondered.

"I hope it's empty," she whispered. "I hope it was uninhabited."

Victoria swung toward her, unexpectedly clumsy in the spacesuit. After a long silence, she replied.

"I hope so, too."

On the far side of the dome, a single projection, the pointed end of the dome's teardrop-shaped footprint, remained standing. If igloos were made of rock foam, this would be the entrance. There was no door, only an opening that led into darkness.

J.D. stepped toward it, drawn involuntarily by her curiosity, by her despair at the destruction. If she could find *something* intact, something to hint at who had built this place—

Victoria and Stephen Thomas both grabbed her at the same time, one on each arm.

"I just want to—"

"It's too hot." Victoria spoke in a matter-of-fact tone that brought J.D. back to reality faster than condescension or anger.

"Of course," J.D. said. "Of course it is. How long will it take to cool?"

"A few hours of darkness should do it. Say, morning, our time."

"All right."

"Shall I send in the AS?"

J.D. hesitated, surprised at the intensity of her resistance to the sensible suggestion.

"Yes, that's a good idea."

The AS picked its way along, using its spider legs rather than rolling. J.D. watched it till it reached the rock-foam projection, then turned her attention to its transmission. Her spacesuit receivers formed a tiny image for her.

The AS crept forward, casting a shadow unrelieved by any scattered light. J.D. strained her vision, seeking irregularity in the darkness, seeking a pattern, as she had sought it in the original transmission. Again, she could make out nothing. The AS turned on its lamp. The light flashed, then faded.

"Look," Satoshi said softly.

J.D. glanced away from the darkened hologram and into the real world again.

The AS backed away from the entrance of the dome. Or, rather, it swiveled its body on its legs and stumbled in what was now its forward direction.

"What the—!" Victoria took one quick step forward.

J.D. made a connection with the AS through the *Chi*'s computer. Looking at its instructions, she found that it had nothing left in its programming but a single scrambled walk default.

Her hands on her hips, Victoria watched the AS lurch away from the ruined alien structure.

"Something still works, inside that dome," she said. "And it's pretty smart. But it isn't perfect."

Sitting cross-legged on her couch, Victoria rested her elbows on her knees and her chin on her fists.

"I don't like the idea of your going in there," she said.

"I'll be all right," J.D. said. She wished Victoria would stop fussing, stop worrying, because she was making J.D. nervous.

"I'll go with you!"

"Thank you, Zev. One person is enough. It's my job."

"What does that mean?"

"It means . . . I promised to do it."

"It doesn't mean you promised to put yourself in unnecessary danger," Victoria said.

J.D. looked at her askance. "Victoria, don't be silly. Of course it does. That's exactly what I promised."

Beyond the *Chi*'s transparent wall, the dome lay like a beached, dying jellyfish.

"I said 'unnecessary,'" Victoria said. "If we were facing a building full of alien beings and they said, 'We'll talk to you, but only one of you,' that would be something else. This . . ." She tried to smile. "We've had enough buildings collapse on people for one week."

"I'm not going to take any foolish risks," J.D. said. "But I think this is a necessary one."

"Look, J.D.," Stephen Thomas said. "I could go—"

"No!" J.D. said.

She startled them all. They had not expected to see her angry.

"No," she said again, more calmly. "It comes down to me. This is what I'm here for. If we'd had the time we were supposed to, so we could get to be a team, you wouldn't even be arguing the point. But we didn't, so you're just going to have to trust me."

Victoria let her hands fall, and straightened up. "We do trust you. You're right."

J.D. managed to smile. "Besides," she said, "for all we know, the dome might turn me around and send me back like the artificial stupid."

"I don't think that's the least bit funny," Victoria said.

The *Chi*'s living quarters provided a cabin for each person on board. J.D.'s room was on one side of the central corridor; on the other side, the family partnership had three cabins in a row. J.D. assumed that Victoria, Satoshi, and Stephen Thomas folded back the interior walls and shared the space.

J.D. wondered if she would be able to sleep, or even to rest, as she waited for the dome to cool enough to enter.

She led Zev to the unused room next to her own. "This can be yours, I'm sure," she said. "Zev, my dear, you didn't bring anything with you at all, did you?"

"I have my suit," he said solemnly.

Zev had probably never worn clothing before he left his family to join the deep space expedition. The suit was part of the fake identity he had used to get on board the starship. He had already abandoned the identity. But he kept the suit. It was unfashionable, loose and baggy. J.D. kept trying to come up with another metaphor for how he looked, but the only one that fit was that he swam within it.

"You should take it off to sleep," she said. "That way it won't get more wrinkled." She was learning to assume nothing when it came to what Zev did know of the land world and what he did not.

"All right," he said.

"When we're in zero g, you'll want to use the sleeping net. Did you learn how, when you came up on the transport?"

"Yes."

He unfastened the edges of the net and rolled it aside, for it was only necessary in weightlessness.

"Sleeping in zero g is like sleeping in the water," Zev said. "When I was with Chandra, I slept a little on land. Zero g is better."

Stephen Thomas took off the red satin running shorts and the loose white silk shirt he was wearing. He let them fall to the floor.

God, he thought, I'm glad to be out of zero g.

He was too keyed up to sleep. He took advantage of the gravity to take a shower without having to fight with the water. In zero g, it spread and formed a thin clinging layer. He had to scrape it off his skin, then wait for the drain to suck the water back to recycling.

He stayed under the hot water longer than he needed to, longer than he should, holding out his hands and letting the heat soak in. Strange, after everything that had happened, only his hands ached.

Toweling his hair, he glanced at himself in the mirror, and turned immediately away.

Jesus, he thought, I look like shit.

People with black eyes were always being described as looking like raccoons. He looked nothing like a raccoon. There was nothing cute about having two black eyes.

He had planned to change the bandage on his forehead, but decided to leave it one more day. If he changed it, he would have to stare at himself in the mirror. Weird that the cut on his forehead showed almost no bruising.

He went back to his room. Still too troubled to sleep, he called the partnership's house. Arachne continued to ignore personal communications, so he had to do without the holographic display.

Feral's image appeared on the hard link.

"Stephen Thomas!" When Feral smiled, his mobile, expressive lips curved like those of the hero in a Renaissance painting, and his short curly chestnut hair added to the impression.

"Hi, Feral. I'm glad you're still up."

"I just got back from the sailhouse. I stopped at the liaison office, but Gerald is doing a Cerberus imitation over communications."

"He wouldn't let you call us?"

"To put it politely." He grinned, wryly. "He was protecting the channel with all three heads."

"Shit. He's supposed to be facilitating. It isn't his fucking job to decide who we should talk to."

Stephen Thomas scowled, and rubbed the palm of his right hand over the knuckles of his left.

"He might listen to that point if it came from you." Feral hesitated. "Are you okay?"

"He might listen to Satoshi. I'm okay aside from looking like someone beat the crap out of me."

"You look like you hurt your hands."

Stephen Thomas stopped massaging his hands, turned them palm up, turned them palm down, spread his fingers.

"I tried to punch Gerald—"

Feral laughed.

"Something's funny?"

"You guys are supposed to be pacifists."

"Everybody has a breaking point. He went past mine. It was a stupid fight, though. He never touched me, and I didn't think I'd hit him." He looked at his hands again. They both ached. "I must have." But he was certain he had not hit Gerald twice.

"Tell me what it's like out there, Stephen Thomas," Feral said. "Next to the alien base. Tell me what isn't coming over the public broadcast."

They talked for quite a while. When the alien dome destroyed itself, Stephen Thomas had pushed away his reactions of shock and fear, the flashback to being inside the genetics building when it collapsed. He had no time for the memories, no place. Feral asked questions that brought them to the surface.

"Maybe tomorrow J.D. will find something to make sense out of what's happened," Stephen Thomas said. "I hope so. Except... I don't know what she could find that would make things turn out all right. Christ, I sound whiny!"

"You sound like someone who's seen a tragedy," Feral said quietly.

Stephen Thomas took a long breath.

"Yeah," he said, more an exhalation than a word. He collected himself. "Yeah."

"I miss you," Feral said.

"I miss you too. I wish you were with us."

Feral hesitated. "All it takes is an invitation," he said, his tone light. "You'd better get some sleep."

His image faded.

Stephen Thomas stretched, and rubbed his hands up his body, up the back of his neck, through his hair. It had grown past his shoulders. He knew he should cut it, if he was going to spend much time in zero g, but he liked it long.

He felt revitalized. His edginess had passed, and being free of the stress of weightlessness was almost as good as a night's sleep.

The partition between his room and Satoshi's was ajar. Satoshi and Victoria had already gone to bed.

Maybe they'll wake up when I come in, Stephen Thomas thought hopefully. But he knew his partners were exhausted. Perhaps he should let them sleep.

Maybe, he thought, I ought to sleep alone tonight...

But Stephen Thomas did not like to sleep alone, and he did not really want to sleep alone.

Naked, he slid through the gap into Satoshi's room. Satoshi and Victoria lay nestled together on the upholstered sleeping surface, wrapped in a light blanket.

He always woke his partners up when he got into bed in zero g. Last time he had caught his toes in the mesh of the sleeping net and pulled the open edge free of the wall, sending Victoria and Satoshi floating off into the middle of the room. He was glad that tonight he did not have to open the net and try to decide the best way to get in beside them.

On the other hand, he wished they had not gone to sleep so quickly, so soundly. He wanted more than to crawl in beside them and go to sleep. He wanted more than a half-waking murmur of welcome, the unyielding power of Satoshi's long runner's muscles against his body, Victoria's cool cedar scent. He wanted to arouse Satoshi till his skin radiated heat like a blast furnace into his hands, he wanted to make Victoria quiver in his hands, and feel her soft, springy hair against his lips.

He slid under the blanket beside her.

"Stephen Thomas?" Victoria said, half-awake, languorous.

"What?" Satoshi sounded querulous, and more awake than he really was.

"It's only me," Stephen Thomas said. "Go back to sleep."

"Okay." Satoshi stretched and fell asleep again. The cabin's indirect illumination, the light of Tau Ceti II, stroked a blue glow across his gold skin.

"You can have the middle, if you want," Victoria whispered.

Stephen Thomas slipped past her into the center of the bed. His fingers brushed her hip, her breast.

Stephen Thomas snuggled down next to Satoshi. Victoria, behind him, wrapped her arms around his waist. Satoshi woke long enough to gently kiss the outer curve of his eyebrow, where the bruising began.

"I'm sorry you got hurt," Satoshi said.

"It could have been a lot worse," Stephen Thomas said. "It would have been, if you hadn't been there."

"I s'pose." Satoshi turned over and burrowed into the corner.

"You guys looked pretty strange, sitting there with just your heads sticking out of the fog," Victoria said.

Stephen Thomas shivered, turned toward her, and embraced her, drawing her close. "All I remember is, it was cold."

The liquid nitrogen had flowed out of the broken freezers of the genetics department, filling the collapsed rooms and hallways with unbreathable vapor. Satoshi and Victoria had to drag Stephen Thomas out of the building. He had fainted at the sight of his own blood.

Victoria spread her fingers across his back. Her hair tickled his shoulder. Stephen Thomas slid his hand up her side, stroked her arm, and brought her hand to his lips. He kissed her palm. She sighed, sleepily. He guided her hand down his chest and down his belly.

Victoria wrapped her fingers around his, a comforting motion, but one that stopped him.

"I have to get some sleep, my dear," she said. "I'm so tired, I'm trembling."

"Yeah," he said, "okay. Me, too, I guess." He pretended not to care. Probably he just would have disappointed her.

"*Eppur si muove*," he muttered.

"What?" Victoria said, already half-asleep.

"Nothing," Stephen Thomas said.

3

J.D. faced the dark opening of the tunnel. Remembering what had happened to the artificial stupid, she regretted her flippant remark about being turned around and sent back out of the dome. As Victoria had said, it did not sound the least bit funny.

J.D. thought she had done a fairly good job of acting confident. But she was scared, and being watched by a phalanx of recording devices did not help her nerves. Large ones watched from the *Chi*. Smaller recorders of various sorts, little tiny machines, nestled in crannies around her gilded face mask. The LTMs would see what she saw, and both transmit and record it.

She wondered if Chandra, the sensory artist, whose entire body was a recording device, ever experienced attacks of nerves. Did she ever wonder how her clients, watching and feeling what she saw and felt, perceived her reactions? J.D. was glad the recorders attached to her could detect only exterior events.

"J.D." Victoria spoke softly in her ear.

"Yes, Victoria." She glanced back. Her teammate stood beside the *Chi*'s foot, her face unreadable behind the gold face mask.

Victoria raised one hand in a gesture of support. J.D. waved back. Her lifeline swayed in the low gravity.

J.D. sank down on one knee and rubbed her gloved fingertips over the crusted surface. The rasp of the fabric against stone startled her, sharp and loud, transmitting itself to her through her suit.

An alien sound on an alien world, her first alien world.

She stood up and walked forward, cautiously but without any more hesitation.

The entrance to the dome cut off the direct yellow light of Tau Ceti and the reflected blue light of Tau Ceti II. J.D. stood within the entrance like an archaeologist entering a long-lost cave, expecting or hoping to discover fabled paintings. In a moment she would turn on the lights attached to her suit helmet, and find out the reality of what lay within the dome.

She toggled on the headlamp with a touch through its link.

The light pooled on the shiny floor ahead of her. It looked like sunshine on a deep stream, for the floor had a depth to it, and a texture like flowing quiet water.

With no dust to diffuse the beam, the light was invisible except when it touched the floor or ceiling or walls. The tunnel was rather wider than high, the surfaces blending into each other in graceful curves.

J.D. flashed the light around. The circle of illumination darted from spot to spot, finding nothing but polished rock. The light reflected back and forth: everywhere she turned she faced a bright circle. Behind it, washed out by the headlight's beam, moved her own distorted multiple image.

"Your signal's strong." Victoria's voice came softly through the suit radio. "We're receiving fine. What about you?"

"No problems," J.D. said. "I'm going deeper."

"Okay."

Her safety line lengthened from the reel at her waist. She walked forward again. The path curved, and rose, and fell, branching and twisting into the alien station. The safety line snaked after her in eerie silence.

What is it about these people and mazes? J.D. thought.

Walking through the smooth, flowing tunnels in the low gravity made J.D. think about swimming in the sea with the divers. Swimming underwater, with the artificial lung hugging her back and feeding warm, moist oxygen into her face mask. She experienced an abrupt, astonishing rush of homesickness. She managed to push it away.

She wished working in a vacuum were as easy as working underwater. The suit did not weigh much here, but it did not disappear from her perception like the artificial lung. The suit surrounded her with its new smell, and with the faint low rustles and creaks and hums of its workings. Her stomach growled. The organic sound startled her, and reminded her that she had been too nervous to eat breakfast.

A drop of sweat rolled down her temple, making her take notice of the increasing warmth. Only a little distance farther, if the corridor were passable, and she would no longer be able to tolerate the temperature. So far, she had seen nothing but the empty maze.

She paused, watching, waiting, wondering if something would try to stop her, or send her back, or lose her. But she saw nothing to frighten her, nothing she could perceive as a threat.

J.D. thought that perhaps she ought to narrate her exploration for the benefit of her teammates and for the people watching back on *Starfarer*. When she tried to think of something to say, she realized she would only be describing the tunnels. Anyone watching the video feed could see them as well as she. She did not want to describe her feelings about them.

"J.D.—"

She started at Victoria's voice, then relaxed.

"—we're getting some interference. The signal strength is falling."

"How strange . . ." The signal fed through the safety line, a hard connection back to the *Chi*. "But so far, I think it's safe in here. It's warmer. Not too uncomfortable yet. I'm going to go a bit deeper. Don't worry."

"I'll try not to," Victoria said. "But if your position's mapping correctly, you only have twenty meters before you hit the red zone."

"I'll be careful."

She moved forward again. She supposed she should reply to Victoria in EarthSpace jargon, for the record: "Understood." "I copy that." But she had no experience with it; it would be like speaking a foreign language badly to people who expected fluency.

The tunnel twisted again and opened out into a chamber.

The smooth, unmarred surface of the tunnel ended.

J.D. stood in her pool of light, shining the lamp beam here and there, picking out crumpled, twisted forms.

"Victoria?" Her voice caught.

No reply.

She tugged once on the strand to let Victoria know she was all right, but she tugged gently: if the safety line had broken, she wanted it to lie on the floor with the broken ends next to each other. She wanted to be able to follow it out of here.

She was unwilling to backtrack quite yet. She slid one foot forward onto the wavery floor, aware that it might collapse.

The chamber was full of destruction.

At first she feared she might find the burned bodies of alien beings. Her heart pounded, making her pulse throb in her throat. After a few minutes, though, she realized that nothing she would recognize as alive had remained here to be killed by the heat and the radiation.

After she had walked farther into the chamber, and inspected the heaps of debris with her headlamp, and scraped some samples from the melted slag, she decided that nothing alive had been here even if she would *not* immediately recognize it as alive. The chamber did not feel right as a living or working area. The devastation had destroyed everything, but it had left the remnants more or less in place. The placement was careful, and patterned, and devoid of any feeling of life or habitation.

Though it was possible that the alien beings were inorganic creatures, or artificial creations of their own imaginations, or energy beings (possible, even an aesthetically pleasing idea, but not, J.D. thought, particularly likely), J.D. still did not think anything of the sort had been here in a long time. She did not think anything had ever *lived* here. The chamber reminded her of the bare, clean lunar plain surrounding the dome, unmarked by the clutter and debris of builders or inhabitants.

You might just be reacting to what Stephen Thomas said about the dome, she said to herself. Accepting his assumption without any real evidence.

The warmth of the chamber oppressed her. Her suit's cooler labored. J.D. knelt beside one melted heap. It had begun to resolidify into obsidian.

She thought she knew what the dome had been.

The alien beings had prepared for their interstellar visitors. This structure had contained a museum, or a library, or a data base. Perhaps it was all those things: some kind of repository, whether or not its exact form had been familiar to human beings. This reception chamber had been a display of...

J.D. crouched on the floor of the chamber, unable to rise, weak and sick with despair. She would never know what she had been meant to see. It was all gone, all destroyed by the beings who perceived that their interstellar visitors had violent, barbarous intentions.

The alien beings had fled, and they had burned their archives behind them to leave nothing for their enemies.

She felt uncomfortably warm. Sweat trickled down her sides, itchy against her skin.

J.D. pushed herself to her feet and flashed the headlamp around again. The size of the chamber was difficult to estimate with only the lamp, but it was larger than she had first thought. Half of it had collapsed. Its lines were so different from what she was used to that it had taken her a few minutes to understand what she was looking at.

J.D. hoped the archaeology department could excavate the dome and make something of what was left. But she doubted it. The alien beings had prepared their offering well. It had destroyed itself in a manner that would not endanger whoever was nearby, but would get its message across quite clearly:

You are not welcome. Not here, not out among the stars where we were waiting.

J.D. squeezed her eyes shut, trying not to cry.

It's so hard to see through a fogged-up faceplate, she told herself.

Tears ran down her cheeks.

The safety line tugged insistently at her hip. It had been pulling at her for quite a while. She grabbed it, thankful to know it remained intact. She yanked it once to reassure Victoria.

Reluctantly but at the same time gratefully, J.D. turned back toward the tunnel. The safety line rewound itself into its reel.

J.D. passed a cluster of melted pedestals. As she crossed behind them, putting them between her and the direction of the worst of the heat, her toe touched something that caught the light as it spun across the floor. She almost did not notice it, because of course it made no sound. She just barely saw it out of the corner of her eye, a strange little chunk spinning silently, suspended against the translucent depth of the floor.

She waited till it had stopped spinning, reluctant to look at another featureless bit of slag.

But when it stopped, it maintained shape and texture and solidity. She bent down and picked it up.

It looked like granite, not like malleable rock foam. It was sculpted into the shape of a lithe little animal, so sinuous that at first she thought it might be a serpent. Then she saw its legs, back legs holding it upright on dainty feet, the front legs held in close, the front paws precisely crossed over its belly. Its tail curled out behind it. The line from the tip of its tail to the tip of its ears described a small spiral rising into a streak.

The stone creature stood in the palm of her glove, no longer than her thumb, peering at her with two eyes in a pointy, intelligent face.

The safety-line tugged at her, three times quickly. If she did not come out immediately, Victoria was going to come in after her. J.D. tugged once, closed her hand around the stone creature, and hurried toward the tunnel.

The magnified image of the stone creature grew to ten times its real size, then hovered in the center of the observers' circle. The creature itself was in the lab, in a sample case. The *Chi* had begun to test it. J.D. wanted to touch it with her bare hands, to trace the jaunty curve of its back and its tail, but the safety of the team and of *Starfarer* required alien samples to be quarantined and tested.

J.D. believed that the products of two separate evolutions would have no chance at all of biologically interacting with each other to the detriment of either. She did not believe alien microbes would cause disease in humans. She begrudged the time the stone creature would be in the sample case.

For the stone creature, J.D. had overridden all tests that were even minimally, microscopically, destructive. She had picked up plenty of other samples that the *Chi* could pulverize to its code's content. It could examine them for organic matter, alien viruses, toxic materials.

"I hate to say it," Satoshi said, "but it looks like a weasel."

"Nothing wrong with weasels," Victoria said, "unless you happen to be raising chickens."

"It looks like a meerkat," Stephen Thomas said. "Weasel isn't too far off."

"I think it looks like a sea otter," Victoria said. "Don't you, Zev?"

"No," he said. "Not at all."

"It does to me. Why not?"

He regarded the stone creature gravely. "Sea otters don't

stand like that. They're bigger. I mean, more muscular. Different proportions. But mostly, it doesn't look like a sea otter at all, because it's cute. Sea otters aren't cute."

"I always thought they were."

"Maybe you didn't have the chance to watch them closely," he said. His careful courtesy amused J.D., because she recognized it as something she might say herself. "Sea otters are playful, and they're curious. But they're powerful, too. They are predators. They wouldn't look for a fight with a human or a diver, but if they found one . . . they have claws." He flexed his toes, and his own semiretractile claws scraped gently against the deck. "And they have webbed feet. Not little paws like the stone creature."

"It doesn't matter what it looks like," Stephen Thomas said. "It isn't anything we've been talking about. It's obviously something that lives on Tau Ceti II. What else could it be?"

"It could be some other animal from some other world," J.D. said. "It might even *be* a meerkat. It might have been part of a display to let us know the people here had visited Earth. But your supposition is as good as any, until we find out what the creature really is."

"*Unless* we find out," Satoshi said.

"Let's go look," Stephen Thomas said. "Let's get off this rock. We can't do anything here till *Starfarer* arrives with equipment and some trained excavators. In the meantime, we can go down to Tau Ceti II—Shit! We need a name for this place, I'm sick of saying 'Tau Ceti II.' What shall we call it? Something with fewer than four syllables."

"It isn't up to us to name it," Victoria said.

"Don't be such a stickler," Stephen Thomas said. "I don't mean anything formal, just something to call it. Shorthand."

"You should call it Sea," Zev said.

"*C*, as in *A, B, C*? Then it ought to be *B*, if that was the way planets get named, which it isn't."

"Sea as in ocean," Zev said to Stephen Thomas. "Because you call the world we lived on Earth. So you should have a sea. Besides, it is in the constellation Cetus, the whale. A whale needs an ocean to swim in."

"In this case the sea would be swimming in the whale," Satoshi said. "Maybe we ought to call the planet Jonah."

Victoria laughed.

"Whatever we start calling it is probably what it will keep on being called," J.D. said. "No matter what its formal name is. I wonder if we shouldn't be careful about making biblical references?"

"I was just kidding," Satoshi said.

J.D. felt herself blush. Being embarrassed about being embarrassed only made it worse.

"Oh," she said.

"Sea works for me," Stephen Thomas said. "It's even got the right number of syllables."

The hard link signaled. Victoria accepted the communication from *Starfarer*.

"Not much to show for a voyage of twelve light-years," Gerald Hemminge said.

J.D. felt as if her nerves were on top of her skin, and the assistant chancellor had just rubbed a nettle across them. She knew she should have some answer, but she did not.

"Is that what you called to say, Gerald?" Victoria asked, her voice cold.

"No, I have a message," Gerald said. "From Chancellor Blades."

Stephen Thomas glanced at Satoshi with an "I told you so" look. J.D. could not help but feel glad that Stephen Thomas was to be vindicated. She for one would welcome a word of encouragement, sympathy, commiseration from the chancellor, even if he was in most ways a figurehead.

"You're to return immediately to *Starfarer*," Gerald said.

J.D. flinched at the message. The satisfaction in the assistant chancellor's voice distressed her even more. Stephen Thomas glanced up sharply, and Victoria bristled. Satoshi, frowning, kept his silence.

"I'm sure the chancellor knows he's exceeding his authority in issuing such an order," Victoria said.

"He has the authority in extraordinary circumstances," Gerald said. "You must agree this is an extreme situation."

"Don't get in an argument with him," Stephen Thomas muttered. "Gerald thinks arguing is the world's most civilized sport."

J.D. had noticed that Stephen Thomas was all too easy to provoke into arguments. He took them both seriously and personally. On the other hand, she could not recall having seen Satoshi lured into a dispute. Victoria seldom allowed herself to lose her temper, but when she did argue, she argued with passion.

"I don't agree that Chancellor Blades has the authority to recall us," Victoria said.

"His signature validates the order," Gerald said. "You have no choice but to return to *Starfarer*. The expedition has no choice but to turn around and return to Earth."

"Who's trying to make these decisions?" Victoria said. "This isn't the way we work!"

"We should have returned immediately upon receiving the first alien transmission," Gerald said. "That way, we could have had something resembling success. It's pointless to proceed deeper into failure."

"Hey, Gerald," Stephen Thomas said, "when did you decide to grow a beard? It's—"

Gerald jerked one hand to his chin and jerked it away again. His image blinked into gray fuzz.

"—going to look just fine," Stephen Thomas said.

"I shall have to get back to you," Gerald said. "There's . . . er . . . a bit of a crisis."

"What's the matter?" J.D. said. "Is *Starfarer*—? Arachne—?"

"No. No, excuse me, I exaggerated. No need for alarm."

The connection ended.

"Stephen Thomas," Satoshi said, "that was mean."

"I thought I was performing a public service," Stephen Thomas said. "For him and for us."

J.D. glanced around, perplexed. "Would someone explain to me what just happened?"

"Gerald has this problem," Stephen Thomas said. "When he's under stress, he loses all his biocontrol techniques. You can always tell, because he gets five o'clock shadow."

"Oh." J.D. felt herself blushing. She was sorry she had asked such a personal question, even inadvertently.

Victoria tried to keep from laughing. "You didn't have to point it out in public."

"If I'd wanted it to be public, I'd've waited till we were talking on an open channel."

"That wouldn't have been mean," Satoshi said. "That would have been cruel."

"What do you want me to do? Let him walk around with all his controls down till he makes somebody pregnant?"

The discussion made J.D. uncomfortable. Gerald must use

a chemical contraceptive backup, but how terrible not to be able to trust one's own body, and the body of one's lover. For the first time, she felt some sympathy for Gerald Hemminge. No wonder it was so important to him to be in charge and in control, to appear to be perfect.

"He'd have to sleep with somebody who had the same problem at the same time," Satoshi said. "Not very likely."

Stephen Thomas shrugged. "Murphy's Law," he said.

Infinity trudged up the path toward his house. His mind kept repeating the image of the alien dome, collapsing into entropy.

At least he knew that *Starfarer* would be all right. It would be stronger, in the wounded spot, than it had been originally.

He felt slightly disoriented. The light of Tau Ceti was perceptibly different from the light of the sun. Most of the plants covering the inside of *Starfarer* had been chosen for their adaptability, though no one knew for sure how they would react to the light of an alien star. For the garden around and over his house, Infinity had chosen some rarer, more delicate plants. He kept one patch quite dry; there, desert vegetation flourished. Intuition helped him believe that the plants would survive the change, but no one had ever tested anything from the desert. He would have to wait, and watch.

On *Starfarer*, daylight always came from the direction of high noon. Infinity welcomed the cool dusk of his front room, after the brightness of his garden and the peripheral dazzle of his spacewalk. He brushed his fingertips through the cornmeal in the pot on the shelf by the door.

Someone else was in his house.

"Florrie?" he said.

But he knew as soon as he spoke that the stranger was not Floris Brown, the first member of the Grandparents in Space program. Perhaps it was Griffith, the government man, intruding into his home. Griffith despised Infinity. Infinity had feared Griffith, at first. But it was hard for Infinity to be scared of someone he had released from a survival sack. Griffith had spent the duration of the missile attack zipped up and helpless. He was so mad when Infinity found him and let him out that he had appeared ridiculous.

Infinity grinned at the memory, even as he took a step

toward the corner of the room where someone hunched on
his couch. He squinted, wishing his eyes would adjust.

The screen of the hard link in the corner played the dome
collapse. The recording ended, and began again.

"Infinity?"

"Esther. Hi."

The transport pilot straightened up from where she lay,
staring at the hard link. She ran her fingers through her short
curly hair, fluffing it out, scratching her head with both
hands, stretching.

"Is it okay if I stay with you?" she said.

"Permanently?"

"Till we figure out what's going on," she said. She gestured
toward the link. The recording cycled. Infinity froze it before
the destruction began again.

"I guess," he said.

"Thanks for the enthusiasm."

"Sorry. I didn't mean you weren't welcome. It's just that
nobody's ever stayed here longer than overnight. Not even
you."

"I'm never on board more than overnight," she said. "Till
now. I'd a lot rather sleep with you than by myself at the
guest house."

"Once in a while you might have to," he said, without
apology.

She shrugged. "That's okay. I hate to be stuck in one place,
too."

She meant more, Infinity knew, than being stuck in one
single sleeping arrangement. She liked to be flying any
vehicle she rode on; she hated being a passenger. Infinity
managed to smile at the idea that she could be on board
Starfarer and still think of herself as being stuck in one place.

He sat beside her. She put her arm over his shoulders. He
was glad of her presence, her comfort.

"That's better," she said. "You smell good."

"I smell like sweat," he said.

"Right." She cuddled him. "Reminds me of the old days,
building this rock. Before it all got complicated."

They held each other. He liked the way her full body fit
against his, the resilient pressure of her breasts against his
chest, the softness of her arms, and the strength of her
muscles, when he slid his hands from her elbows to her

shoulders. Esther caressed him from shoulder blades to waist, slipped her fingers beneath his shirt, stroked the small of his back.

"I think I'd better take a shower," he said.

"Cold or hot?"

"That depends on whether I'm alone or with company," he said.

A few minutes later, in the shower, Infinity soaped Esther's shoulders and back and buttocks.

Esther began to tremble. Infinity put down the soap and slid his arms around her, holding her close in the warm shower spray. He said nothing, waiting for her to speak if she wanted to talk about what was wrong.

"I was so damned scared," she said. "I couldn't show it. . . . I was mad, too, and that I *could* show. What the hell happened, Infinity? How could they do that to you guys? How could they do it to me?"

He had asked himself the same question, over and over again during his whole life, and he still did not know the answer. Why did people with power so often abuse it?

"They wanted *Starfarer*," he said. "They thought they had a better use for it than letting people live on it and work on it. Just like they thought they had a better use for the Southwest. They didn't care if they hurt us, and they didn't care if they hurt you."

"But I see those guys all the time. The pilot of the carrier—I've slept with her. And the carrier's voice, I know him, we go out drinking together. But I hardly recognized him, he sounded so cold and hard. I didn't think they were like that."

"Maybe they aren't. In real life. But they had their orders. They had to follow their orders."

"Why? You didn't."

She leaned back against him, trying to relax. He stroked her arms and massaged the knots of tension in her neck. He was a head taller than Esther; when he bent down, his long hair streaked over her shoulders in straight dark strands. Water flowed along his hair into streams, over her collarbones, and across her breasts.

The shower was behind Infinity, so he was shielding Esther's face from the spray. But two small rivulets slipped down her cheeks.

"They didn't *have* to follow orders. But they did it anyway. I didn't have to follow *their* orders, but I did it anyway. So now my passengers are stuck here, and you're stuck with them. And me." She started to laugh, her voice strangled, tears still flowing down her cheeks.

Infinity had never seen her cry before; he had never even seen her upset. She was always calm, matter-of-fact, phlegmatic. That was the accepted style for pilots, but she had been that way back when she was a space construction worker. He felt both flattered and discomforted, that she would let him see her in such distress.

"I didn't believe *Starfarer* would go through with transition and I didn't believe the carrier would shoot," Esther said. "So now, if none of my passengers kills me—if nobody on *Starfarer* does—I'll probably be up to my eyebrows in lawsuits for the rest of my life. If I ever get home."

"We'll get home," Infinity said. "But it might be a while. A couple of years, anyway."

"Oh, boy," she said.

"More complications?"

"Sort of. Or maybe not. My personal life will be a lot simpler when I get back."

"They won't wait for you?"

"Why should they? I wouldn't." She shrugged. When she turned to face him, she was herself again. "It's just as well. I want to think about something else for a while. I want to think about you."

They made love in the shower, they made love in his bed.

Esther leaned down and kissed him, playing with him with her whole body.

"Let's go out in the garden," she said.

"It's broad daylight," Infinity said, a little shocked.

"I know it." Her voice challenged him.

"No," he said.

"What's that nice soft patch of grass for, then?" she asked. "You don't even like to plant lawn grass. You said it was boring."

"Maybe tonight."

"Spoilsport," she said. She slid down beside him in the bed and kicked off the sheets.

Lying naked and uncovered on his bed in front of the open full-length windows made Infinity uncomfortable, but the cool air caressed his hot body, and he felt as if he were lying in a small whirlpool of the clean, intense, musky scent of his lover.

He dozed.

Esther fell asleep beside him, her fingers twined in his as she held his hand lightly against her breast.

A knock on Infinity's door brought him fully awake. He reached down and pulled the sheet over himself and Esther.

Outside, Kolya Petrovich stood at his front door, politely not looking through the windows. It was still bright outside, dim inside.

"Come in!" Infinity said.

Kolya opened the unlocked door—as far as Infinity knew, no one ever locked their house doors on *Starfarer*—and came inside.

Before his eyes could have adjusted to the darkness, and before Infinity could speak, Kolya glanced toward him. The cosmonaut used all his senses, not just vision, particularly in the dark.

I guess he'd be dead if he couldn't do that, Infinity thought.

It made Infinity uncomfortable to know so much about Kolya Petrovich's background. He knew things the former guerrilla fighter had not told him personally, things that he had no real right to know. He wondered what it felt like to have one's life so public. No wonder Kolya had spent so much of the past decade being a hermit. He existed at the periphery of the starship's society, seldom participating until the final meeting that set their path, and perhaps their fate.

"Ah," Kolya said, stepping back over the threshold to the outside, "I'll come back some other time."

"No," Esther said. Infinity had not even felt her wake up. "It's all right, please." She pulled the sheet a bit higher.

"Come in," Infinity said again. "Sorry, I've never had time to make any chairs."

Kolya approached. He glanced once, for an instant, at the frozen hard link, the alien dome a moment before its destruction.

"I feared . . . something like this would happen," Kolya said. "We're lucky J.D. was not in it when it fell."

He folded his long legs and sat on the edge of the futon, his back to the display. Infinity joined Kolya and Esther in a tacit agreement not to discuss the dome anymore.

Infinity wished he did have some chairs, a proper place to offer Kolya to sit. The futon lay on the floor. Infinity always rolled it up when he rose in the morning. That was the traditional way. So he had never built a frame for it.

"Would you toss me my shirt?" Esther said to Kolya. Though her voice sounded steady, Infinity could feel her tremble.

Kolya picked up the garment that lay crumpled on the floor. As an informal uniform, the transport pilots had adopted a lurid fluorescent green baseball jacket. Kolya leaned across the bed and handed it to Esther. She slipped it on over her head, then sat up beside Infinity, cross-legged, elbows on her knees. The soft warm skin of her knee slid along Infinity's thigh.

"This is my friend Esther Klein," Infinity said. "Esther, this is Kolya Petrovich."

"I'm honored to meet you," Esther said.

"I'm glad to meet a fellow pilot," Kolya said.

They shook hands gingerly, Kolya obviously embarrassed to have walked in on them in bed, but trying not to show it. What Esther felt, but was trying not to show, Infinity could not figure out at all.

"I'm on my way outside," Kolya said. "Shall I check anything in particular? Besides the crater?"

"I . . . Why are you asking me?"

"Because you have the most experience," Kolya said. "If you aren't in charge of the damage control team, you should be."

"I'm not," Infinity said. "Nobody is. We're a *community*."

"We're a group of inexperienced amateurs," Kolya said gently. "I think it is no longer possible to work as we'd planned, without a leader."

Infinity could see the reasoning behind Kolya's assumptions. That did not make him like it, and it did not make him agree.

"What I was planning to do," he said, "in a little while, was look around beyond the crater's range. The crater's halfway repaired already, and just about every working sensor we have left is pointed straight at the reconstruction. It might be a good thing if somebody who knew the cylinder made sure there isn't any secondary damage."

Kolya lowered his head thoughtfully. "I will do that." He

sounded relieved. "I was not . . . looking forward to returning to the crater."

"It isn't that bad now," Infinity said. "Kolya, are you all right? Did anybody even think to thank you and J.D.?"

"Someone has now," Kolya said. "And I will be all right. I am all right. A bit sore, but that's nothing unusual."

"I give very good back rubs," Esther said. "If you'd like one."

"That's a tempting offer," Kolya said. "May I take you up on it after I come back inside?"

"Sure."

He rose, moving more slowly than usual.

"Thank you," he said, and disappeared into the sunlight. The door closed, leaving Infinity's house in shadows again.

Esther blew out her breath.

"Are *you* okay?" Infinity asked.

"Yes. Sure. Why?"

"I never saw you worry about wearing a shirt before." He turned to face her, propped on one elbow. He laid his hand gently on the bright satin of the ugly fluorescent shirt, just below her breastbone. "And, you were shaking. You still are."

"God!" she said. "You are *so* matter-of-fact about everything! 'Esther, this is Kolya Petrovich,' like it's no big deal to introduce *him* informally!"

"I guess it did look like that," he said. "But once you've talked to him, he can make you feel easy. Besides, you talked to him and you made sense. The first time I met him, I babbled like an idiot."

"Oh yeah?" she said. "Okay, then." She put her hand on his, and slid his fingers beneath her shirt. The satin had a cool smoothness, Esther's skin a warm smoothness. "And as for my shirt, I didn't exactly see *you* jumping up and running around stark naked. Not in front of *him*."

Infinity chuckled.

Gerald Hemminge had not yet called back. The delay made Victoria anxious and impatient. If he persuaded the other expedition members to go home, the *Chi* would have to return to the starship. She had no evidence that Gerald was agitating for the change. But she had known him for a long time; it was something he would do.

To pass the time, Victoria gave her transition algorithm and several sets of variables to the *Chi*'s AI and put it to work on the problems. She was curious to know what transition paths lay open from Tau Ceti.

Even with her improved algorithm, the solution proceeded slowly when Arachne could not work on it. Victoria tried to console herself with the knowledge that the web would soon be healed. But the *Chi*'s AI was still awfully slow. She sighed.

"Problems?"

Victoria glanced across the observers' circle at Satoshi, who sprawled morosely on his couch, the distorted bluish shadow of Tau Ceti II, of Sea, rotating slowly before him.

"Not problems," she said. "Just speed. I want Arachne, dammit! When we go back to Earth, I'm going to find out who crashed the web, and I'm going to..."

"Go on," Satoshi said. "You were just getting interesting."

"I can't think of anything bad enough that I'd still be willing to do with my own hands," Victoria said. "Never mind. I've got plenty of time to think of something suitable."

"I'd like to hear whatever it is you decide to do," Satoshi said. "And the fate you plan for whoever fired the missile at us."

Victoria hesitated, startled. "How strange," she said. "I'd hardly even thought about the missile. I'm much angrier about Arachne. It's as if the missile attack was so alien that I can't even grasp it. Maybe when it sinks in I'll be as mad as I am about the web. About how badly they hurt Iphigenie."

"What if it isn't somebody back on Earth?"

"What?"

"There's no proof that somebody back on Earth, or in the carrier, is responsible for the crash. There isn't even any evidence."

"It had to be somebody from outside."

"I don't think so."

"But none of us—" Victoria realized how naive she sounded, to defend everyone on board *Starfarer* from suspicion of contemptible behavior.

"See what I mean?" Satoshi said.

"There isn't any evidence that it was anybody on campus, either!" Victoria said. "Besides, who would do it, who had the motive?"

Satoshi shrugged. "I'm just saying it's possible. We may not be as independent out here as we thought we were. And if the person who crashed the web once is still on board, they could crash it again."

Victoria shivered: a contraction of memory clutched at her spine. The crash had affected her like amputation without anesthetic. She did not want to experience that perception again.

"It's a complicated system," Satoshi said, "It's unique. Maybe nobody crashed it. Maybe it just... crashed."

"An inherent weakness?" Victoria said. "I'd rather believe the security systems are as infallible as the *Titanic* was unsinkable."

Satoshi chuckled.

"I didn't mean it as a joke."

"I know," Satoshi said. "But sometimes there's nothing left to do but laugh."

"If somebody can open Arachne's security... it could be anybody. Anybody who has the key."

"Anybody whose real reason for being on board was to stop the expedition."

"Florrie's narc?"

"I'm not ready to throw around any accusations," Satoshi said. "But Griffith is a prime candidate as far as I'm concerned."

"He's kind of obvious, isn't he?"

"I don't know. Is he? We hardly even noticed him till Florrie said he was a narc."

"I noticed him," Stephen Thomas said from the doorway. He came in and sat between his partners. "I told you he was weird from the beginning."

"You said he was weird after Florrie said he was spying on us," Victoria said. "What you actually said was that he doesn't have an aura. As far as I'm concerned, *nobody* has an aura, so on that score Griffith is no different from the rest of us."

"He's different, all right," Stephen Thomas said stubbornly.

"Being different doesn't make him the person who crashed the web," Satoshi said. "I think he's the best candidate... but not because he doesn't have something that only you can see."

"You guys are too damned skeptical for your own good."

"We agreed not to argue about auras anymore," Victoria said. "I hope nobody on board crashed the web. But let's face it. It could be anybody. Somebody from the carrier. Or somebody new, sent up here on purpose to do it. Or somebody established."

"Let's not look for trouble," Satoshi said. "If we all start getting suspicious of everybody back on campus..."

"Not *everybody*," Stephen Thomas said. "Just a few prime suspects. Griffith. Gerald—"

"Come on!" Satoshi said. "He disagrees with you. He's a snob. But he's not malevolent. Might as well accuse Feral because he just got here."

"Feral! Just a fucking minute—"

"I didn't accuse him," Satoshi said. "I only—"

"Stop it," Victoria said. "Please, stop it. I knew I should have buried myself in my work."

She let the computer graph a projection of her transition algorithm around her.

"Sorry," Satoshi said.

Victoria did not reply. The complexity of lines and surfaces, the musical tones sketching in unseen dimensions, shielded her from her partners.

"Never mind," Stephen Thomas said. "But, Feral? Christ on a computer node, what a dumb suggestion."

Satoshi whistled softly. "Victoria, that's beautiful."

Victoria grinned despite herself. After a moment, she let the display drift so it no longer completely concealed her.

"It is pretty, isn't it?" she said. "I'm ridiculously pleased with myself. It's about the only thing that's gone right lately." She would have been pleased with her algorithm if only for its aesthetic value, or for the speed and efficiency with which it worked. But it also found better solutions for the approach of *Starfarer* to cosmic string. It had given the starship the option of leaving the solar system six months early: a few hours, or minutes, ahead of the military carrier sent to stop them. It had saved the expedition.

"What's this one for?" Stephen Thomas asked.

"It's an exercise. Where we could get to from here. And the fastest way back to Earth. Which I have no intention of using soon. But it's just as well to have some options. And now, if you guys will excuse me..."

"At least you have something to do," Stephen Thomas said.

Victoria let the display fade to transparency, a few luminous strokes of light above her.

The image of Sea intensified in front of Satoshi. He and Stephen Thomas stared moodily at it.

"No roads, huh?" Victoria said.

"No roads," Satoshi replied. "None at all." He brought the globe in closer. Its colors changed, false colors following some pattern of geology, temperature, air pressure. "I can do some surveys. Topographical maps and ocean charts, currents and weather patterns. That sort of thing. Kind of busy work. It's mostly automated."

"I can't do *anything*," Stephen Thomas said. "Not without some samples. Come on, Victoria, how can you stand it? A living world. And we're sitting on a chunk of rock. Waiting for a bunch of archaeologists to come and dig out a broken library. What the hell *use* are we here?"

Victoria gazed at the image of the globe, and through the wall of the *Chi* into space, toward the planet itself.

"It is tempting," she said.

Stephen Thomas brightened. "We can't stay cooped up till *Starfarer* arrives," he said. "We'll go nuts."

Victoria smiled. "If we go nuts in less than a week, we're all in trouble."

"It's going to take them a *week* to get here? Oh, shit, Victoria—"

"It's not going to take them a week. But, all right. Let's talk to J.D., and if she has no objections, we'll move to the surface of Sea."

The alien contact team sat in the kitchen of the *Chi*, eating lunch. J.D. munched a sandwich. Zev sat across the table. He had taken his sandwich apart and was picking through the destruction of it, eating the meat and the cheese. J.D. suspected he would rather have fresh salmon. So would she.

"I miss Feral," Stephen Thomas said. "We ought to vote to bring along a free-lance journalist as one of the team members."

"I'm sure Feral would appreciate that," Victoria said. "Until he realized you wanted him along as cook."

The young journalist was staying as a guest in their house, in the room that would have belonged to the eldest member of the partnership. Victoria still missed Merry desperately, and it upset her, irrationally, to have someone else staying in the room her partner had never had a chance to use.

"I can think of a *lot* of things to do with Feral besides asking him to cook," Stephen Thomas said. "And he probably wouldn't mind at least making coffee."

"He wouldn't mind anything if you asked him," Satoshi said to Stephen Thomas, teasing him gently.

"That's probably true," Stephen Thomas said, matter-of-fact.

J.D. started to speak, then hesitated, wondering if she should keep out of the matter entirely. But Satoshi had made his comment without jealousy or anger, and Stephen Thomas replied without sounding at all defensive. J.D. knew that Feral found Stephen Thomas attractive; she did, too. It was hard not to. He was the most beautiful man she had ever met.

"Taking a reporter along isn't that bad an idea," J.D. said. "When I first applied to the expedition, I proposed an alien contact team that included a poet."

"I didn't know you wrote poetry, too," Victoria said.

"Not me. That was several years ago. I hadn't even published a novel back then. I thought a poet was a great idea." She smiled ruefully. "I guess the selection committee didn't agree, since they turned down the team and my application as well."

"Never mind," Victoria said. "You're with us now, and you're all the poet we need."

"Maybe. But a reporter still isn't a bad idea." She took another bite of her sandwich, then put it down. "I can cook, too," she said, "but the food we brought along isn't something you can whip up a gourmet picnic with."

"Is there any ice cream?" Zev said.

"There aren't any cows on board *Starfarer*," Satoshi said.

Zev glanced at J.D., curious, questioning.

"Cows give milk," she said. "And milk is what ice cream is made of."

"We have some goats," Stephen Thomas said. "I wonder if you can make ice cream from goats' milk?"

"That sounds awful," Satoshi said.

"Goats' milk isn't so bad once you get used to it," Victoria said. "It's all right in tea. Ice cream, though, I don't know."

"What have you decided, J.D.?" Stephen Thomas said abruptly.

"I told you I wanted to think about it till after lunch."

"I thought you were done."

She picked up her sandwich, stubbornly, about to take another bite. She found she did not want it.

She wanted to land on the world's surface. She wanted it, if that were possible, even more than Stephen Thomas did. But she preferred to make decisions carefully, and she did not like to be rushed.

She put her sandwich back down.

"What I think," she said, "is that I want to go explore Tau Ceti II more than I've ever wanted anything in my life—"

Stephen Thomas yelped with pleasure. He jumped to his feet. "Let's *go*, then."

When he moved, when he exploded with enthusiasm like this, his charm intensified. J.D. wished she could make herself immune to him. As far as she could tell, Victoria and Stephen Thomas and Satoshi lived in a family partnership that was not sexually exclusive. But the last thing the alien contact team needed was more stress of any sort. She was doing her best to keep her feelings about Stephen Thomas concealed. Feral had noticed, though, and teased her, making her wonder if she was completely transparent. She shrugged to herself. Even if Stephen Thomas noticed, she doubted he would be interested.

"—but," J.D. said.

Stephen Thomas sat down again. "But what?"

"But look what happened when we landed here," J.D. said. "Kolya was right. And what if we'd been outside the *Chi* when the dome collapsed?"

"There isn't anything like the dome on the planet's surface," Satoshi said. "I've looked. Believe me, I've looked."

"I just think we should go slow," J.D. said unhappily.

Stephen Thomas grinned. "We can land away from the coast, and we can get Satoshi to figure out where all the crustal plates intersect. That way we won't get hit by a tsunami or an earthquake."

"If you don't start taking this seriously," J.D. said, "I'm going to block the idea of landing on the planet's surface. Look what's already destroyed! Maybe if we'd waited, if we'd orbited for a while and tried to figure out..."

Victoria reached out and gently squeezed J.D.'s hand. "We all feel the same about the dome," she said.

"Maybe it was inevitable that it would collapse," J.D. said, "once we wailed in here trailing a nuclear warhead. But maybe we were meant to take the hint when the transmission ended. Maybe we were meant to stop and wait."

"Maybe we were," Stephen Thomas said. "But we didn't. Look, I was kidding, about the coast and the fault lines. But we *could* land away from them, and check the weather, too."

"What is it you're afraid might happen," Satoshi said, "if we land?"

"I'm afraid . . . the whole planet might collapse."

"J.D., good heavens," Victoria said.

Though Satoshi said nothing, his incredulous expression spoke for him.

"That's fucking ridiculous," Stephen Thomas said.

J.D. looked away.

"It isn't very likely," Satoshi said carefully. "Planets don't just blow up, like in the movies. Even if Sea is in line for a comet impact, we'd have plenty of warning. But the chances of that—"

"Don't patronize me, please, Satoshi," J.D. said. "I don't need a lecture on orbital dynamics or disaster theories. Or old movies. I didn't mean I thought we'd land, and Sea would come apart in pieces. What I'm afraid of is programmed environmental destruction."

The other members of the alien contact team stared at her, appalled.

"That just doesn't make sense," Victoria said. "It wouldn't make sense to destroy a whole world . . ."

"I didn't say it made sense! I said I was afraid of it!"

The *Chi*'s internal communication system formed Victoria's message symbol in the middle of the kitchen.

Victoria waved it toward her. "I'd better see what this is," she said, sounding profoundly grateful for the interruption. Her eyelids flickered for a moment.

"The web's back!" she said.

"About time," Stephen Thomas said. His eyelids flickered, too, and he disappeared into the communications web. Satoshi followed.

J.D. waited forlornly, impatiently, while the others communed with the web. J.D. wished she had thought longer and harder about telling her teammates her fears. As soon as she had spoken, as soon as she heard and saw the reaction, she sounded outrageous, paranoid, ridiculous, even to herself. The beings who collapsed the dome had wanted to conceal the organized information they had assembled. There was no reason to destroy the world.

She had read at least one science fiction story in which the ecosystem of an entire planet self-destructed in response to the landing of a single alien spaceship.

Someday I'll find time to scan my books into the web, she thought. It would be nice to be able to put my finger on the story and the title and the author. But there's so much else to do.

She did remember that the idea was intriguing, and made for an excellent one-punch ending. But like most one-punch stories, it did not bear close examination. An ecosystem that could be destroyed by one mistake, one break in the chain of cause and effect, would never have evolved in the first place.

"Do you think there are people in Sea?" Zev rose and went to one of the ports in the kitchen. He shielded his face from the interior light and gazed into the black sky, toward Tau Ceti II, rising.

"There could be," J.D. said. "Not people like ordinary humans, but maybe people like cetaceans."

"I'd like to swim with them," Zev said. "I think they might be down there."

"Are you sorry you came with me, Zev?"

He remained where he was, as if he had not heard her.

"Zev?"

He let his hands fall to his sides, and turned toward her. His feelings were usually so clear and clean and direct that his expression of confusion startled her.

"I'm not sorry," he said, no longer hesitating. "But . . . I do miss my other family. It's different here, and there isn't enough water."

"*Starfarer* has places to swim," J.D. said. "We can visit them when we get back. You could even have a house near the water, if you wanted."

"You mean . . . not stay with you?"

"You can stay with me as long as you like, Zev," J.D. said. "But I want you to know what the possibilities are."

"I want to swim on Sea," Zev said.

"I don't know if that's a possibility. We have to be careful not to contaminate the planet, and not to let it contaminate us. We shouldn't go out unprotected before we do some tests.

I don't think it would be the same, to swim in Sea's oceans while you were wearing a safe suit."

"I'm getting used to this suit," Zev said. "I think." He plucked at the material of his baggy trousers with his thumb and forefinger.

J.D. chuckled. Zev was barefoot, barechested; and J.D. doubted that Chandra, who had helped him get on board, had bothered to buy him any underwear. The artist struck J.D. as the sort of person who concerned herself with more important matters than the pedestrian details of ordinary life.

"Maybe we could get somebody to make you a pair of shorts like Stephen Thomas wears," J.D. said. "They'd probably be more comfortable than those heavy trousers."

No wonder Zev had dispensed with as much of his clothing as he could. His feet, with their semiretractile claws, must feel terribly confined within shoes. Golden fuzz covered his mahogany body. The hairs were so fine that they barely showed except in just the right light, but Zev's delicate pelt could not make wearing clothes any easier.

"I would like that," Zev said. He plucked again at the trousers. "I think these wouldn't feel very good to swim in." He glanced over his shoulder, toward the planet Sea. "If we visit it, we must swim," he said.

Victoria came out of her communication fugue and resumed her conversation with J.D. as if she had never left.

"J.D., I thought you were eager to visit Sea's surface. How strongly do you feel about your concerns? Do you plan to block the proposal that we move from the satellite to the planet's surface?"

"I . . . No. I won't block, and I am eager." She shrugged apologetically. "I've read a lot of fiction that leans toward the outrageous, and I've trained myself to release my imagination. Sometimes it escapes me completely."

"Then we're going?" Stephen Thomas had come back from the web without J.D.'s noticing.

"Satoshi?" Victoria touched Satoshi's arm.

"Hmm?" He returned to the group. "I heard. You've got my vote."

"We're going," Victoria said.

"Extravagant," said Stephen Thomas, and grinned at J.D., his annoyance completely forgotten.

4

Gerald Hemminge's disbelief erupted into the *Chi* like the blast of radiation from the collapsing dome.

"Land on Tau Ceti II? It's out of the question!" he exclaimed.

He had returned to his post without a word of explanation for his abrupt departure, without even referring to it. His face looked scraped and irritated. A patch of chameleon bandage, nearly imperceptible, covered a spot under his jaw.

J.D.'s perception of him had changed now that she knew his failing. Instead of reacting to him as pompous and aloof, she pitied him. She knew she would find him even harder to deal with from now on.

"Don't you think it's time to cut our losses?" Gerald said.

J.D. pressed back against her couch, distressed by the prospect of another argument. She tried to center herself, seeking all the calm she could draw on. Stephen Thomas sat forward, ready with an angry retort. Victoria silenced him with a glance of warning. She had not yet transferred the transmission to public access, for which J.D. was grateful.

"No," Victoria said. "It's time to have something *besides* losses."

"Chancellor Blades has repeated his request that you return to *Starfarer*," Gerald said. "Several times."

"Why doesn't he tell us that himself?" Satoshi said.

"Because I'm the liaison, Satoshi. It's my responsibility."

"Please tell the chancellor that I appreciate his advice," Victoria said. "But he has no authority over this department. We've discussed the possibilities. We're going to the surface of Sea—to Tau Ceti II."

"It's utterly foolish of you to stand on your team's charter!" Gerald said. "These are extraordinary circumstances."

"Of course they are. Anything that happened once we got

here would be extraordinary circumstances. The charter *exists* for extraordinary circumstances."

"You need all the expertise and advice available to you," Gerald said, his voice curt. "You must come back to *Starfarer* for consultation."

"Next stop, Earth," Stephen Thomas said under his breath.

"We're glad to hear anyone's advice," Victoria said. "That hasn't changed. It won't change."

"I don't know why I bother," Gerald said. "I should have gone on strike the moment you mutinied—"

"Mutinied!" Victoria exclaimed. "This is a civilian—"

"—and stayed out of the aggravation. I should get up and leave right now."

"Why don't you?" Stephen Thomas said.

"Because I take my responsibilities seriously, unlike other people I could name. You've caused the destruction of the most significant discovery—"

"Stop it!" All J.D. wanted was for the argument to end. "The dome collapsed because of the missile. We all know that."

"You can't prove it," Gerald said.

"No. But tell me this. Do you believe the dome would have collapsed if we'd landed—but the missile *hadn't* detonated?"

"No," he said grudgingly.

"Nobody else has challenged that idea, either," J.D. said. "Whoever left a welcome for us decided we weren't worth welcoming. Can you blame them? They destroyed the information they left for us."

"There's no evidence of any concurrent destruction on the planet's surface," Satoshi said. "Not even any evidence for sentient tool-using beings native to this system."

"The dome was a remote beacon, Gerald," Victoria said. "It's gone. Maybe archaeology will be able to resurrect something, but there's nothing left for the team to do here."

"Then don't do anything at all!"

"Doing something is our job." Victoria's smile was sad. "We're going on a brief reconnaissance. A sample-collecting mission. Don't worry about us."

"I'm not—" He stopped. "I didn't mean—"

"We all know what you meant," Stephen Thomas said. "We appreciate your support a whole hell of a lot."

"Stephen Thomas, we must behave in a professional manner. I know we've had our difficulties—"

Stephen Thomas laughed out loud.

"Just a minute, Gerald," Satoshi said. "You can't insist that we junk the expedition plans one minute, and insist on professional behavior the next."

"Satoshi, I'm sorry, but we must admit that the expedition is a failure," Gerald said.

"I'll admit no such thing," Victoria said, "and we're back where we started. It's pointless to go around in circles like this. We're preparing for lift-off."

She ended the transmission.

"I didn't handle that well," she said. "I didn't handle it well at all."

"You didn't have much to work with," J.D. said.

Preparing for lift-off included, among other things, straightening the kitchen. As she wiped off the table, J.D. giggled.

"What?" Satoshi said.

"This ought to be part of our record," J.D. said. "Intrepid explorers on kitchen duty."

"'Wash the dishes, or no superluminal travel for you today'?"

"Exactly. All you ever read about in history books is the heroism, you never hear about the drudgery."

"Right," Stephen Thomas said. "Peary got the credit for getting to the north pole, but Matthew Henson did most of the work, and if they got to the pole at all he got there first."

"When did you develop such an interest in ancient history?" Satoshi said.

"Researching our family."

"Are we related to Peary?"

"Uh-uh. Probably not to Henson, either, though I thought we might be. I figured that Victoria and Grangrana must have heroic predecessors. So I was reading about intrepid black explorers."

"We had heroic predecessors, all right, and they did come north," Victoria said. "But they stopped in Nova Scotia for a couple of generations." She fell silent, polishing a bit of countertop that was already clean. J.D. saw the worry return to her face. Like J.D.'s complex but remote family, and Stephen Thomas's difficult father, and Satoshi's exemplary parents, Victoria's great-grandmother remained back on Earth with no way of knowing whether *Starfarer*, or anyone on board, had survived the military carrier's assault.

Zev's mother, Lykos, and the other divers and orcas could not even be sure he had reached the starship and joined the expedition. The military carrier had jammed *Starfarer*'s normal space communications for several hours before the starship reached transition.

Now the expedition was cut off from home. Communication was theoretically possible but thoroughly impractical, for only an enormous mass could reach transition energy. If it was possible to send electronic communications through transition, no one yet had figured out how.

Victoria clipped the kitchen towel into its place so it would not drift around when they returned to zero g.

"Everybody get on your best behavior," she said. Her voice and her demeanor had returned to normal. "We start transmitting as soon as we get back to the circle. I promise to try not to argue with Gerald anymore."

The collapsed alien dome appeared in the middle of Infinity's living space, then dwindled in the distance to a gray dimple on the silken surface of the satellite's arid and airless plains.

"Look," Esther said. "Arachne's back."

Infinity sat up in bed and watched the scene change as the *Chi* lifted off, transmitting the view behind it. The flat land gradually curved; the sharp horizon came into view, the bright silver gray of the rock stopping abruptly at the edge of the black sky. Within a couple of minutes, the holographic image displayed the entire satellite of Tau Ceti II.

The gray of the satellite intensified, turning blue, bluegreen, brilliant white, as Arachne's attention turned to Tau Ceti II and the planet's image faded in over that of the satellite.

Infinity reached out to his link, checking the web. Arachne's reply felt tenuous, tentative. The computer was testing itself, first diffidently transmitting the *Chi*'s hologram, now allowing a few essential people and services to interconnect while it tried its own strength. Infinity found himself near the top of the web's access list. Being singled out made him uncomfortable.

He detached himself from the web, got up, and collected

his clothes. Esther sat cross-legged in the tangle of sheets, watching him dress. He reached through the hologram to pick his vest up off the floor.

"I better get back to work. Make yourself at home." He slipped into his vest.

"Are you going outside?"

"I've been lounging around about enough."

"What, six hours rest in the last two days?"

"Rest? Oh. Is that what you call it?"

Esther grinned. "I'll come with you. Toss me my pants, will you?"

He did; she grabbed them out of the air and put them on without getting up, sticking her feet through the leg openings and into the air. She sat up and hitched the pants over her hips, then grabbed the fluorescent jacket and put it on again. She had left her shoes by the door.

"I wish you'd signed up for the expedition," Infinity said.

"I think I did," she said, her tone dry.

"I mean formally."

"Not enough flying involved," she said. "The alien contact department didn't request a pilot. And I'm a lousy gardener."

"Have you ever tried it?"

"No."

"Would you want to help with damage control?"

"Sure."

They left his house and walked through the garden, passing through the edge of the desert patch.

Infinity stopped.

"What's wrong?"

"I don't know," he said.

He squatted beside the cactus and slid his fingers in between the thorns. Frowning, he stroked the leathery skin.

"It looks okay to me," Esther said.

Infinity shrugged unhappily.

"Maybe it's got cactus blight," Esther said.

"It shouldn't have anything. It's cloned from a cell stock. Virus free."

"Certifiers can screw up."

"I hope they didn't," Infinity said. "If they made a mistake on this, they could make a mistake on the other stuff. If anything happens to the plants, we're in big trouble. The ecosystem will crash."

"It's just a cactus, Infinity," Esther said. "The ecosystem doesn't depend on one cactus. How can you tell something's wrong with a cactus, anyhow?"

"I don't know," Infinity said again.

"I thought you grew up in cactus country."

"Me? No, I grew up in Brazil. I've never ever seen a cactus in the wild."

"Oh. Then I have more experience with cactuses than you do. And I can tell you, you can never be sure what's going on with a cactus. I had one once, in a window box, and it was dead for six months before I noticed."

Infinity stood up. "Is that supposed to make me feel better?"

"It's just supposed to show you that cacti never reveal whether they're dead or alive. So yours is probably okay."

"Or dead," Infinity said.

He glanced back once as they left his garden. The skin of the cactus had felt spongy, not solid and firm as he had expected. He worried.

"How did you figure out there was something wrong with your cactus?" he asked Esther.

"The cat knocked it over, and it didn't have any roots."

Infinity winced.

The trail led past Florrie Brown's house, a triplex built beneath a hill, with balconies and windows nestled against the slope. Professor Thanthavong lived in the middle house, and Kolya Cherenkov had the top floor. A field separated the house from the trail. Late crocuses, daffodils, and irises glowed in the grass, forming a carpet of Byzantine pattern and complexity. Hyacinths and lilies of the valley had just begun to poke their rolled outer foliage from the ground. The herd of miniature horses stood knee deep in blossoms.

"They're going to eat your flowers!" Esther exclaimed.

"That's okay," Infinity said.

"Wait a minute. You're upset because one cactus might be dead, but you don't mind the minis eating your flowers?"

"They're mostly eating the grass. Besides, they're supposed to eat the plants. The cactus *isn't* supposed to die." It did not upset him that the horses would eat the flowers. It did trouble him that the flowers were blooming simultaneously instead of sequentially.

Half the mares had foaled. Fillies and colts scampered and

squealed, their hooves tapping the ground. They were no bigger than long-legged cats.

The herd's stallion was a five-hand appaloosa with a temper in inverse proportion to his size. But at the moment he was standing on the porch of Florrie's house, nuzzling Florrie's hand, looking for treats. Fox, one of the expedition's graduate students, scratched the little stud behind the ears.

Florrie saw Infinity and waved. Infinity waved back.

"Let's go say hi," he said to Esther. "Be sure she's okay."

"Sure."

He left the trail and entered her yard, Esther beside him. They passed the newly dug area where Infinity had put in rose bushes, protecting them with a spun-glass mesh on bamboo stakes.

"I remember her," Esther said. "She was on one of the last passenger transports. Why's she in mourning? I didn't hear that anybody died."

"Nobody did. She just dresses like that, mostly in black. She likes black eye makeup, too."

At their approach, the appaloosa stud jerked away from Fox and Florrie, stamped his forefoot, snorted, and clattered off the porch. Squealing and nipping, he rounded up the patient, indulgent mares and their excitable foals. The herd moved ten or fifteen meters before the mares stopped to graze again.

Fox laughed. "You embarrassed him, you guys. He wasn't enjoying himself, nope, not him."

"We'll have to plant him some carrots," Florrie said.

On Fox's arm, Florrie started toward Infinity and Esther. Moving carefully, she planted one foot on the porch and stepped sideways to the ground. Tiny bells, braided into one of the three long locks of her hair, jingled in a high register.

A hologram of Tau Ceti II followed her.

"Hi, Florrie," Infinity said. "Hi, Fox."

"Infinity." Florrie's voice, always soft, sounded feathery.

"This is my friend Esther Klein. Is everything all right?"

"Yes. Yes. I never thought—Esther, is it? Hello, do you know Fox?—I never believed I'd see this. A new star system, a new world."

Infinity smiled. People reacted strongly, for or against, to the Grandparents in Space program. Infinity had always thought it was a good idea. It had taken Florrie a while to get her bearings here, and she was a little eccentric. Everybody on board *Starfarer* was eccentric. The quality had nothing to do with age.

Florrie was doing fine. Fox had practically adopted her. Or maybe it was the other way around.

"Thank you for the roses," Florrie said.

"You're welcome." Roses took a lot of hand labor, a lot of care, but he did not begrudge it to her. "It might be a while before they bloom."

"No," she said. "Look."

She moved to the bushes, where they could get a better look past the fence.

The white bud of a rose had just begun to open.

In the *Chi*, Victoria waited while Gerald Hemminge, brusque and disapproving, signed off after lift-off. She signed off in her turn, and transferred the public channel to an exterior view.

She let her breath out in a short, sharp sigh.

"No arguments, anyway," she said. "This time."

"That was masterful," Stephen Thomas said.

If she had been in a gravity field, Victoria would have let herself flop back in her couch. As it was, in zero g, she grabbed the headrest, pulled herself against the cushions, and shook herself all over.

"Masterful! I sounded like a zombie!"

"You did keep your voice flat. Restrained. Our friend Gerald, on the other hand, showed some evidence of tension."

"I could barely understand him," Zev said.

"He was doing his upper-class Brit number on us," Stephen Thomas said. "It doesn't even work on Victoria. It took me weeks to figure him out. He has this weird accent he can use. From a distance it sounds like perfect English. But when you try to listen to it, none of the words make any sense." Stephen Thomas raised his chin and made an exaggerated *O* with his mouth. "Too many rounded tones," he said, extending all the vowels. He did sound just like Gerald, nearly as incomprehensible. "You're supposed to be intimidated."

"I was confused," Zev said. "I thought perhaps he was ill."

Stephen Thomas laughed out loud.

"The accent used to intimidate me," Victoria admitted. "Until I spent some time in England. It's all a game. I quit playing it."

Stephen Thomas let the image of Sea coalesce in front of him as he unbuckled his safety straps and floated out of his couch.

"I'm going to take a nap before we orbit."

"It's awfully early," Victoria said.

"So?" he said impatiently. "What's the big deal? I want to be rested when we land. Maybe having a black eye makes you tired." He paddled through zero g and disappeared into the body of the *Chi*.

Frowning, Victoria watched him leave.

"I've never known him to take a nap during the day," she said to J.D.

Satoshi chuckled. "Go to bed, yes, but sleep?"

"Maybe things just caught up with him," J.D. said. "I know my physical energy feels low."

Victoria felt physically and emotionally stressed, but intellectually aroused and on edge. She let go of the headrest of her couch and stretched her arms forward, rounding her spine. Her vertebrae cracked, one after the other, an inaudible *pitter-patter* from the base of her neck to the small of her back. She wished Stephen Thomas had stayed a few more minutes. He gave the world's best back rubs, and she could use a back rub just now. She wondered how hard it was to give a back rub in zero g.

"I'm anxious to reach Sea." Victoria raised her head and glanced across at J.D. "I keep hoping that something, somewhere along the line, will work out the way we planned for the expedition."

J.D. managed to smile.

The holographic globe of Sea hovered in the center of the observers' circle. Beyond the hologram, beyond the transparent wall, Sea itself grew perceptibly larger.

Alone in the circle, Victoria slid into Arachne's web. It was like walking through a new house, all the rooms clean and uncluttered, a house as yet unfurnished.

How much did we lose? she wondered uneasily. If she had been walking, she might have stumbled at the sudden shock of apprehension. If the web crash had wiped out all the data bases...

She had stored her new transition algorithm outside the web. In fact the only place it *was* stored was outside the web.

In a moment of sheer paranoia that had embarrassed her at the time, she had taken all her research on transition approach vectors, archived it in hard form, and erased it from Arachne's memory. Only in retrospect were her actions eminently sensible.

Under ordinary circumstances, the web kept everything for everyone: research data, operating instructions, health profiles, meeting announcements, interdepartmental sports standings, love letters, recipes, entertainment schedules... everything.

Victoria tried to reassure herself. It could not all have been lost, or the ship would not now be functioning as well as it was. The web must want to increase its strength before it replaced all the multifarious sets of information from its continuous backups. The web had recreated its linkages, the paths along which information could travel and in which information could be placed.

And then, as she watched, and listened, and perceived, the web began to fill itself with information.

A sharp signal attracted Victoria's attention. Avvaiyar, a member of the astronomy department, wanted to talk to her by direct connection. Victoria hesitated. Like most people, she found it unnerving to communicate with another person directly through the web links. Victoria could never quite escape her feeling that it was too intrusive, too close a communication.

But it was private, and under normal conditions it was very fast. Its speed was a major reason for Victoria's trepidation: the speed made it too easy to say something without thinking about it first.

Stephen Thomas is the only person I know who can get away with talking before he thinks, she said to herself, and smiled.

Victoria connected herself to the web. With Arachne back on *Starfarer* and Victoria on board the *Chi*, the inevitable time lag of distance both interfered with the communications speed and intensified Victoria's discomfort. Now she could reply too quickly, and have to suffer through the lag while a message crossed space to its recipient, as yet unheard, but irretrievable.

"It's the system survey," Avvaiyar said, her voice as clear and as distinctive as if she were standing, invisible, nearby.

"That was quick!" Victoria replied.

"I'm not nearly done. Only five percent. But what I've found in the five percent—!"

"Tell me."

"Look."

Victoria took a bit of her attention and glanced at Avvaiyar's representation of the Tau Ceti system. The web poured the information directly into her vision centers.

She jerked back, startled by the brilliance of the conical volume Avvaiyar had surveyed. Tangled brush strokes of lambent blue filled space above and below the plane of the system, and faint fine strands passed through the plane, between the paths of the orbits.

"What!" Victoria exclaimed, more an expression of surprise than of confusion.

"It's cosmic string," Avvaiyar said.

"I know, but . . ."

"A whole skein of interstellar string. Even if the other ninety-five percent of the system is completely bare of the stuff, even if I just managed to luck onto an unusual concentration—'Unusual'!" Her strained, disembodied laugh made the image of the star system pale. "Victoria, it's as if we drove out of the back woods on a gravel road, and ended up on the world's biggest freeway interchange!"

It was wonderful. The false color of the strings twined above, below, and through the system. In the small mapped segment, fully ten separate strands twisted through space. The more kinks, the more possibilities for changing direction and distance. Her eyes closed, Victoria gazed with rapture at the map.

"Victoria?"

"I'm here. It's amazing." She looked closer, with a quick laugh when she realized she had physically leaned forward, as if to bring herself closer to the internal screen. She would have thought she had far too much experience with the web to fall into that novice's reaction.

The web interpreted her body language, and brought the image closer and larger in her mind.

"Does anything about it strike you as odd?" she asked Avvaiyar.

Avvaiyar laughed again, a low, hoarse chuckle. "Such as its being here at all?"

Victoria's smile spun over the web to the astronomer.

"That, too," she said. "But I mean, a pattern."

Avvaiyar remained silent for several long seconds.

"I see what you're saying," she said. "But, Victoria... this is a very small part of the system. Let's look at ten percent, at least, before..."

Avvaiyar's voice trailed off; the link between them weakened. Victoria caught it and strengthened it with her own energy.

"... before we start speculating," Avvaiyar said.

"All right." Victoria did her best to keep her message calm, but excitement trembled along the edges of the link to Avvaiyar. "I'll wait for at least ten percent before I start speculating that the alien beings put the string here... left it here, on purpose, for us to find."

Avvaiyar's presence gave the impression that she was drawing a deep breath, none too steady.

"Just in case, I'll give the distribution to a statistician or several," she said. "Can you apply your algorithm to some of the strands?"

"I need one more magnification of structural detail," Victoria said. "Then, sure, if Arachne's strong enough. I could put a couple of copies to work at once."

"Do you want to pick the strands, or shall I grab some at random?"

Victoria brought the image even closer, and extended a probe into it.

"That one," she said, choosing a straight streak of false color. "For simplicity's sake. And this one over here." She touched two strings that intersected, tangling in a Gordian knot. "For the challenge. Then if Arachne can handle it, pick a couple more that look interesting to you. And the closest one."

"I'll send you the magnification in an hour or so."

"Thanks."

After Avvaiyar's presence faded from the link, Victoria sat silent and thoughtful, her subjective gaze directed at the radiant blue filaments.

Victoria sailed into the kitchen, grabbed a handhold, and swung herself to a stop.

"There you are!" she said to J.D.

"Here I am," J.D. said. "I thought I'd make some dinner. Are you hungry?"

"No," Victoria said. "Wait, yes, I am. I'm ravenous!" She giggled.

"Victoria, what happened?"

Victoria could not help acting silly. She felt immensely joyful.

What she wanted to tell J.D. burst from her like bubbles from champagne.

"J.D., we can go anywhere!"

J.D. listened in silence to Victoria's description of Avvaiyar's discovery. She worked methodically, steadily, finishing the preparations for dinner.

"This system is right in the middle of a concentration of cosmic string," Victoria said. "As if someone were weaving a three-dimensional tapestry with it, using the orbits of the planets as the warp!"

The alien contact specialist appeared remarkably calm, almost indifferent, as she put sandwich filling inside pocket bread and squeezed the opening closed. Instead of spinning with excitement, she remained braced against the counter, her feet tucked into the steady straps.

She looked up.

"It's deliberate." She began to smile.

Victoria moved: had she been standing, she would have drawn away. As it was, she started to rotate around her center of gravity. She reached out and stopped herself.

"I just meant we have a lot more possibilities. I'm not quite ready—" She stopped, surprised by her own reaction. "Yes, I am," she said. "That's just what I think. Avvaiyar doesn't want to agree yet, but that's what she thinks, too."

J.D. gripped the edge of the counter. One of the pita sandwiches floated away. She grabbed for it, slipping her feet free of the steady straps and diving into the air. When she turned toward Victoria, spiraling as if she were swimming underwater, she started to laugh. She skimmed past Victoria, caught herself easily against the wall, and stopped. She hugged Victoria, wrapping her strong heavy arms around Victoria's shoulders.

"I was so afraid," she said. "So afraid we only had one chance, and we ruined it..."

Victoria patted J.D.'s arm.

"We're lucky," she said.

J.D. snagged the sandwich out of the air without losing any

of its filling. She handed it to Victoria with a zero-g mock bow: when she bent at the waist, her head moved toward her feet and her feet moved toward her head, as if she had dived again, in the pike position. She straightened, giggling.

"Have you told the others?" J.D. asked.

"Not yet. I don't want to wake Stephen Thomas, but let's go find Satoshi and Zev."

"Okay." J.D. wrapped the extra pita sandwiches into a packet and put them under a strap on the counter. "Those are ready whenever anyone wants them."

"Stephen Thomas will probably be hungry when he wakes up. If Satoshi's in the exercise room, he won't want anything to eat for a few hours."

"Zev's always hungry," J.D. said. "He used to visit me at my cabin and eat all the ice cream."

Victoria bit into her sandwich, savoring the crisp vegetables. The hydroponics that cleaned and freshened the air and water of the *Chi* created a pleasant by-product: fresh vegetables. Carrying her dinner, she headed out of the kitchen.

J.D., floating nearby, plucked an escaped leaf of spinach from the air, popped it into her mouth, and followed Victoria.

"I hope Stephen Thomas isn't coming down with something," Victoria said.

"That would be a shame."

"Yes. But everybody always gets colds, every time a transport comes to *Starfarer* with some new bug. Once in a while a nasty strain of flu comes along as well." She ate a bite of her sandwich. "J.D., how do divers interact immunologically with ordinary humans? What I mean is... is Zev in any danger from us? Could he catch a minor illness and get seriously ill from it?"

"I doubt it," J.D. said. "The divers have evolved several of their organic systems. Their lungs. Their immune systems. Zev is less likely to catch anything from us than you are to catch it from any new group of people."

"Good," Victoria said, relieved. "I didn't know. When it isn't your own field, and you don't know for sure, you worry."

"Do you and Satoshi and Stephen Thomas have trouble talking about your specialties with each other?"

"Yes, it's awful. Physics and geography and genetics are so far removed from each other. Once in a while our projects have weird little points of intersection. Some of the algorithmic work I do, for instance, and the work Stephen Thomas used to do with superconducting bioelectronics. He needed some multidimensional networking analogues—" She stopped, and grinned. "But you see what I mean, eh? I'm talking Old High Martian."

"I don't suppose it was intuitively obvious that the quickest-paths results and the electronics work would dovetail so gracefully."

"No, it wasn't . . . until after we did it."

Victoria bounced off a wall, using the bounce to turn a corner and head toward the exercise room. Music filled the hallway, getting louder as she moved forward.

Trees sped past. Following the topography of a hilly road, they leapt upward, dropped downward, their leaves fluttering as if from the wind of their motion.

Satoshi, within the hologram, pedaled hard on the stationary bike. He wore nothing but shoes and a tight pair of riding shorts. Toe clips secured his feet so he could expend energy on the extending stroke and the contracting stroke alike. Sweat covered his body with a fine sheen. A droplet reached the limit of its surface tension, formed a sphere, detached itself, and floated, quivering, toward the ventilator intake.

A fast drum rhythm filled the room: several drums, steel and leather, very loud.

Zev sat on the other bike, outside the hologram. He watched Satoshi for a moment, pedaled furiously, then stopped and let himself float off the seat. He had rolled his trouser legs up to his knees, exposing his bare, clawed feet and his brown, gold-furred calves. When he saw J.D., he let himself slip free of the bike and glided past her, brushing her shoulder with his fingertips.

"Satoshi!" Victoria had to raise her voice to be heard over the noise. "Stop! It's making me dizzy!"

Satoshi glanced around and saw her. His eyelids fluttered once. The music softened. The hologram faded away.

"Hi," he said. He stretched. "That's better. I was beginning to feel the calcium jump right out of my bones." He grabbed a towel and wiped his face and his chest. "And I needed to think."

"I'll never understand how you can think through all that racket." Victoria smiled. "And when your brain is deprived of oxygen, too."

Satoshi always claimed that he got some of his best ideas while running plus-spin—the hard, "uphill" way—around the inside of the campus cylinder.

"I thought it was loud at first, too," Zev said. "But Satoshi said, feel it through your skin. He's right. It's almost like being back in the water. Now I understand about loud music."

J.D. handed Zev half her sandwich. He bit into it, floating beside her in reverse orientation.

"I have something to show you." Victoria let Avvaiyar's map form in the middle of the exercise room, then watched in pleasure as Satoshi realized the implications of the information.

Quite late, Feral returned to the partnership's house. It was lonely and silent, with the family gone. The distillation apparatus that Stephen Thomas had liberated remained in the middle of the main room, waiting for Stephen Thomas to keep his promise to Victoria to put it away. In time he planned to use it in making brandy from the wine he planned to ferment from the grapes of the vines he intended to plant.

Feral requested the broadcast from the *Chi*. As it came on, Victoria locked the visuals onto the planet, bid *Starfarer* good night on behalf of the whole team, and shut down the audio feed.

Disappointed not to see Stephen Thomas, Feral requested a repeat of a broadcast the *Chi* had sent earlier in the day. Arachne complied.

On the audio, Stephen Thomas discussed the possibilities of what they might find when they landed. Life: that was certain. Life teemed, abundant and obvious, on the surface of Tau Ceti II.

The image formed, overlapping the mechanical jumble of the still. Tau Ceti II appeared, ghostlike, with the still's condensing tube sticking out of its north pole.

Feral laughed, moved the image to a clear space, and shrank it a bit. While he watched, he set to work dismantling the still.

Now and again the image switched to the observers' circle, to Stephen Thomas. Feral noticed his friend's increasing comfort in zero g; he noticed that the bruises around his eyes had begun the multicolored process of fading, and he noticed that his hands still hurt. Every so often, as he spoke, Stephen

Thomas rubbed the skin between the first knuckles of one hand with the thumb and forefinger of the other.

Feral liked to watch Stephen Thomas; he liked to listen to him.

The scene cut away. While it played in the background, Feral made contact with Arachne and did some snooping. He had a good deal of experience at gleaning information from public records. First he browsed through biographies. Gerald Hemminge: a straightforward, academic-administrator résumé. Good degrees from upper-class British schools. An idiosyncratic tinge here and there: a three-month Antarctica International Park fellowship.

"Lucky bastard," muttered Feral, who had applied for the same fellowship, and been turned down.

If Gerald Hemminge's bio was faked, it was what Feral thought of as an official fake: composed by experts and backed by fraudulent information in primary sources.

He looked up Griffith: nothing. Griffith, a visitor, had no reason to file his curriculum vitae. Arachne knew his date of arrival, his guest house room number, the reason for his visit, his job. GAO accountant. Feral snorted. He did not believe Griffith was a GAO accountant. Nobody believed Griffith was a GAO accountant. Unfortunately, that did not prove he had crashed the web.

Feral skimmed the bios of everyone on board, flashing through them, hoping some anomaly would leap out at him. Part of the problem was that most of the members of the deep space expedition had achieved recognition before they ever arrived on *Starfarer*. Their bios were long, complicated, and littered with hypertext links to papers, commentaries, articles, exhibits, competitions. Avvaiyar, Iphigenie DuPre, Chancellor Blades, Crimson Ng, Chandra.

"They really *did* all this stuff," he muttered. "If I didn't know it, I'd think they were snowing me with information overload."

Even Fox had published several papers as an undergraduate.

Feral had a talent for turning the defensive tactic of information overload back on itself, pulling out details people never meant to reveal. Tonight, though, his talent failed him.

Before he ever came into space, Feral had read the biographies of the members of the alien contact team. Nothing then, or now, struck him as suspicious. But he could hardly pretend to be objective about the alien contact team.

He picked out the other people who were, in his mind, the *least* likely to be spies, and he spent extra time looking at their bios. Kolya Cherenkov, cosmonaut and hero of the Soviet Union. Miensaem Thanthavong, Nobel laureate. Florrie Brown. Infinity Mendez. And Iphigenie DuPre, solar-sail designer, millionaire, and the person hurt most deeply by the web crash.

He found nothing.

Tired and dispirited, Feral disconnected from Arachne. He sat cross-legged on the floor and watched Stephen Thomas talk about Sea.

"I *like* too many people here," Feral said out loud. "I don't want anybody to be guilty. Not even Gerald, the arrogant sod. Stephen Thomas, what am I going to do?"

The image of Stephen Thomas, of course, did not answer. Feral let the repeat cycle a second time.

An hour later, as the broadcast ended, Feral finished storing away the still.

It was the middle of the night, and Feral was tired. He was hungry, too, but cooking for just himself was too much trouble. He went to the fourth bedroom, the room he had begun to think of as his. It looked just the same as when the family offered it to him. Back on Earth, he never made much change in his physical surroundings. He traveled too much; he seldom stayed at home. Nevertheless, this room felt like his.

He took off his clothes. The air was cold, and so were the sheets. Tonight was the coldest the weather had been since his arrival. It was the middle of spring on board the starship. Feral supposed the temperature would bounce down the thermometer once in a while before summer came along.

Pulling the blankets around him, he closed his eyes and waited for sleep. But once he got in his cold bed, he felt wide awake. The air was more a draft than a breeze. Feral made himself lie still for a quarter of an hour.

Just relax, he told himself. Any second you'll fall asleep. You'll wake up with sunlight, starlight, Tau Ceti's light, reflecting into your room.

He remained awake. Though he was used to sleeping

alone, and had been too busy getting his career started to do anything but sleep alone for a couple of years, he felt lonely.

He threw off the covers, got up, and pulled the window shut. Outside, on the bank surrounding the yard and the garden, early white carnations glowed in starlight.

Turning away from the window, he found he did not want to lie down again on the cold futon. Instead, he went to Stephen Thomas's room.

The windows were open, and the room was just as cold and just as silent as the rest of the house. But incense lingered on the air, and the clutter of projects and clothing, the earring tree, the rumpled bed, made the room comfortable and friendly.

Feral straightened the sheets and slid between them. The bed smelled like Stephen Thomas, like the faint musky incense of his hair.

Feral had never fallen for anyone, man or woman, as fast and as hard as he had fallen for Stephen Thomas Gregory. It was more than his extraordinary physical beauty. There was much more to him than that, charm and strength and intelligence, and self-centered vulnerability. Feral wondered if Victoria and Satoshi took their youngest partner too much for granted.

No point to feeling jealous: the connection between the members of the partnership was strong and solid. But Feral thought Stephen Thomas needed something he was not getting. Something had hurt him, and the wound had never quite healed. It was Feral's intention to heal it, if he could.

Victoria slid her fingers between the door frame and the folding fabric that closed off Stephen Thomas's room. The door opened a crack. The room was dark except for filtered blue light from Tau Ceti II.

The net of the sleeping surface hung loose, and Stephen Thomas drifted free outside it, his whole body relaxed, arms and legs extended, uncoordinated, as if he were floating underwater.

He probably would not hurt himself, but it was not safe to sleep while floating around unrestrained. Victoria pushed off, came to a stop at his side, and put her arm around him.

"Stephen Thomas—" The heat of his body scared her. "Stephen Thomas!" she said again, urgent.

"Huh? What?" He came awake slowly, sluggishly, his body hot, his skin dry. "What's wrong?"

She held him; he struggled against her, as if fighting in a dream.

He relaxed suddenly: she was afraid he had fainted.

"Are you all right? Stephen Thomas!"

"*Yes*, what? What's the matter? Lights, low."

He sounded awake. In response to his voice command, the lights faded on and stopped at dusk. Stephen Thomas's blue eyes had dilated to black.

"Are you all right?"

"Yes, sure. Why do you keep saying that?"

He always woke up quickly, smoothly, with a languorous stretch. This awakening was different, discomforting.

"Because I was worried, eh?" she said. "You were in here floating around loose in the dark—"

"Was I?" He glanced toward the open sleeping net. "I guess I was. I had a dream, I was floating, and I got trapped . . ."

"Of course you did. You're supposed to be trapped, and stay trapped, when you're sleeping." She put her hand to his forehead. Now he felt cold and clammy.

He flinched when she inadvertently touched the half-healed cut. He pushed her hand away.

"It's still kind of sore, you know?"

"Let's get you in some covers."

"Okay."

Stephen Thomas had a mild tendency toward hypochondria, and he enjoyed being fussed over. As long as he had nothing better to do, he never minded taking advantage of being ill. Satoshi had the opposite habit: on the rare occasions that he became ill, he invariably denied being sick.

"We don't have time for you to catch cold," Victoria said.

"I know it. But I haven't finished my perfect cure yet."

It annoyed Stephen Thomas, as it annoyed most geneticists, that they still could not cure common minor viral diseases. Thanthavong's viral depolymerase had defeated most of the formerly fatal viruses, but the cure was unwieldy and unpleasant, involving as it did a deliberate infection with an artificial virus, and a couple of weeks of being very sick. For life-threatening diseases, the cure was worth it. But for the minor scourges of humankind, a depolymerase cure was worse than the illness.

Stephen Thomas shivered. Once he started, he could not stop.

Victoria towed him to his sleeping net and positioned him within it.

His patchwork quilt, a wedding present from Merry's family, had floated free. Victoria retrieved it, fastened the quilt to the inner surface of the net, and tucked her partner in.

"Somebody must have brought a new strain of cold germ up on the last transport," Victoria said. "Damn! I hope we don't all get it."

"My germs are thine," Stephen Thomas said. "Thanks for the sympathy." He really did look miserable, but that was partly because of the bruises. They had gone from black to livid purple and green, fading to sickly yellow at the edges.

"I'll get you some flu-away," Victoria said. "And some tea. You rest. Maybe you can fight it off, or maybe it's a twelve-hour variety."

Stephen Thomas pulled the quilt closer under his chin. "I hope so," he said. "I'm not staying inside the *Chi*, that's for sure."

"Of course not," she said.

But Stephen Thomas never responded very well to symptom-treating drugs like flu-away.

Victoria thought: Stephen Thomas will be awfully uncomfortable in his safe suit, where you can't even blow your nose.

She left his room and went to get the medical kit.

"I'll bet it's Zev who's got the flu," she muttered irritably, uncharitably. "Probably some weird whale germ, and we'll all catch it."

She took a couple of medical patches back to Stephen Thomas: thermometer and flu-away.

He was already half-asleep. Victoria stuck the thermometer to his skin, trying not to wake him, and watched with concern as the central numerals changed and the patch's color intensified. Nearly 40° C: much too high. She peeled the backing off the drug patch, pushed Stephen Thomas's hair aside, and applied the patch behind his ear.

He winced, the bruised skin around his eyes tightening.

"I can taste it," he said, sounding groggy. "Awful."

"Let it work," she said. "You'll feel better in a while."
She kissed him.

As she left him alone to sleep, she realized she had not told
him about the string. She glanced back, but decided that the
news would have to wait.

5

J.D. lounged in the kitchen area, drinking cocoa. She drifted with her hips and her knees flexed, as if she were floating down a wide quiet river in an inner tube. The room was comfortably warm and the lights remained dim. The brightest source of illumination was the system map hovering nearby.

Everyone in the alien contact department was supposed to be getting a few hours' rest before the *Chi* entered its orbit around Sea. Though the idea made good sense, J.D. was not yet ready to sleep.

Every so often, J.D. glanced at the map. Avvaiyar's survey was progressing rapidly, updating itself with a quiver of light every quarter hour. Each interval brought new strands of cosmic string to the map.

The implications were incredible. J.D. had to restrain her excitement, hold it in and tame it.

Back home, a single strand of cosmic string had vibrated over the solar system, tantalizingly near, near enough to reach from Earth. *Starfarer* had used the unlimited power and the strange space-time properties of the string to make the transition from Earth's sun to Tau Ceti.

Some people believe that the string was a lifeline, thrown to humans by an advanced technology. Some people believed it was an invitation to join an interstellar civilization.

Sometimes, late at night, when her critical facilities and her skepticism were at their lowest ebbs, J.D. found the idea powerfully attractive.

And it's late at night again, J.D. thought. Maybe my critical facilities haven fallen all the way into negative numbers. There are so many possible explanations for that pattern, explanations that don't require the intervention of consciousness. But it's tempting to imagine a deliberate, knowing force, the way people used to see the mosaic courtyards of Atlantis in columnar basalt, or control by gods in the path and existence of life. I *want* to believe in a conscious force guiding that string.

She reached out to Arachne to find out what her colleagues back on the starship were thinking.

No one—no human being—knew enough to do a proper statistical analysis of Avvaiyar's discovery. Or, rather, no one knew enough to do anything but guess at the values of the variables. Several people had made the guesses and done the analyses and posted the answers within Arachne's web. The results varied by several orders of magnitude. One hypothesis proposed that alien control was the simplest, rather than the most complicated, explanation for the concentration of cosmic string.

Victoria grabbed the edges of the entryway and pulled herself into the kitchen. The blue glow of the system map glistened on her shiny dark hair.

"Hi, Victoria," J.D. said.

"Oh—hi. I didn't know anybody else was up."

J.D. smiled. "Just me, disobeying orders."

"Hm?" Victoria said, sounding distracted.

"You did say, Let's all get some rest."

Victoria extended the straw from a packet of fruit juice and sipped from it.

"Issuing orders isn't my best ability. Can't even follow them myself, eh?" She scowled at the fruit juice. "What I really want is tea, never mind whether it's got vitamin C in it or not. Would you like some?"

"I've still got some cocoa, thanks."

Victoria began the moderately complicated routine of making tea in zero gravity. Tea bag and covered mug bobbed in the air before her, gently moved by random air currents. She heated some water.

"How's Stephen Thomas?" J.D. asked.

"He's got a bad case of the flu. This is terrible timing."

"How about you and Satoshi?"

"We're okay so far. You?"

"So far."

"And Zev? Is he asleep?"

"He's resting. Divers don't sleep the way ordinary humans do, they sleep like cetaceans."

"How? Underwater?" She grinned. "In the shower?"

"He'll nap for a while, wake up and breathe for a while, then go back to sleep."

"I thought divers could breathe underwater, like fish."

"They can. But it isn't very efficient. Just for emergencies."

Victoria sipped her tea gingerly. She made it, as she said, right, with the water at the boil instead of tepid.

"That'll do," Victoria said. "Not too bad for a tea bag."

Neither J.D. nor Victoria spoke for a few minutes. J.D. felt suddenly awkward and shy. She wondered whether Victoria was keeping a companionable silence, or whether she was wondering when—if—J.D. would bring up a question that lay between them. It had troubled J.D. for several days.

She drew a deep breath. In the silence of the spacecraft, in the silence of the dim light, Victoria heard the sigh, and glanced over at her.

"Why did you kiss me?" J.D. said.

Victoria turned away; or perhaps one of those random air currents had touched her.

"In the waiting room," J.D. said. "When I was about to get on the transport and leave."

"I remember," Victoria said. "I'm just trying to figure out how to answer you. I'm not sure I know all the answers myself."

"If you don't want to talk about it . . ." J.D. said, then stopped. It was too late to pretend she had never mentioned what had happened, too late to pretend she assumed it all meant nothing.

Victoria sipped from her tea mug, then let it drift at her side.

"When you said you had to leave, to find Zev and help him, I realized how much I'd miss you. We haven't known each other very long, but it's wonderful to have you with us. I love Satoshi and Stephen Thomas. And we work well together. But until you joined the department, I hadn't realized how much I wished it included another woman."

"It was an awfully personal response to a professional connection."

"That response didn't have much to do with our professional connection."

J.D. sipped her cocoa, watching Victoria curiously.

"I didn't know how you'd feel about that," Victoria said.

J.D. finally replied. "I don't know how I feel about it, either. You kissed me when I was about to go back to Earth to find Zev. When you thought I was leaving, and probably not coming back. Since I didn't go after all..." She shrugged. "Confusing. Difficult."

"I kissed you on impulse, J.D. I didn't want you to go. Maybe I hoped you'd change your mind and stay. I wouldn't blame you if you thought that was unfair. You did make it clear to me why you thought you had to leave."

"What if I had stayed?"

"You did stay!"

"I came back. There's a big difference. I left, but when I realized Zev had arrived with the transport I was just about to take off on, I came back."

"My opinion of you didn't change when you got on the transport."

"I still don't know what your opinion of me *is*!" J.D. said. "Is it just that you're glad to have another woman, any woman, in the alien contact department? Did I just happen to be in the right place at the right time?"

"I'm glad to have you as a colleague. *You*. Not just anybody."

J.D. could not gaze into her mug, seeking dregs of cocoa to read, like tea leaves. The mug was closed. Even Victoria's tea leaves were folded up in a package. Instead, J.D. stared into the system map. The framework of cosmic string nearly enclosed the Tau Ceti system; Avvaiyar had nearly finished her survey.

"I hope—"

"I'm not ready to hear more right now," J.D. said softly.

"I'm sorry," Victoria said.

"Don't apologize," J.D. said. "I did ask you. I thought I had to. I guess I thought you'd say, Oh, it didn't mean anything, I kiss everybody."

"I don't kiss everybody," Victoria said with a smile. "That answer would have made things simpler, eh?"

J.D. chuckled, though she did not feel very happy. "I was risking the probability that things would become simpler, against the possibility that they'd become more complicated." She glanced around the kitchen. "This is complicated," she said.

"I know," Victoria said.

"The department is complicated. So is your family. And then there's Zev."

"Is he your lover? Would he be jealous if—"

"Jealous?" J.D. giggled; she could not help it.

"Some people are."

"Divers are about the least jealous and most—I guess the only word we have is promiscuous, but it isn't quite right— most sexually active human beings, ordinary or changed, that you can find. Divers are very sexual. A lot of their play is sex. A lot of their sex is play. Victoria, I don't know how to answer the question, 'Is Zev your lover?' It doesn't mean anything in the sea, and Zev hasn't been with *Starfarer* long enough for me to know the answer to it here."

"He must be feeling some culture shock."

"Yes. And worry." J.D. tried to relax the tight muscles of her neck and shoulders. "I haven't even had the time to talk to him about leaving home, leaving his family..." She took a deep breath. "What about Satoshi and Stephen Thomas?"

"What about them?"

"You asked me if Zev would be jealous. I'm asking you if your partners would be."

"No."

"But—" J.D. stopped. The details of Victoria's partnership were none of her business, and she felt awkward about asking.

Victoria's eyes crinkled at the corners when she smiled.

"We are a confusing bunch, aren't we? Everybody wonders the same thing. Especially since Stephen Thomas falls in love with someone new about every other week."

J.D. felt a quick pang, not of jealousy but of envy, followed quickly by embarrassment. She felt herself starting to blush as she tried not to remember her first reaction, of stupefied speechlessness, to Stephen Thomas.

"You noticed him and Feral eyeing each other, eh?" Victoria said, mistaking the blush.

"Feral... mentioned an interest," J.D. said. She was surprised that her own feeling of attraction had continued so strongly. Stephen Thomas could be very aggravating.

"We'd none of us be in the partnership if we were particularly monogamous," Victoria said. "Stephen Thomas isn't the only one who gets involved with other people. He just does it more often, the way Merry did." She giggled. "When Merry brought Stephen Thomas home the first time, Satoshi and I thought he was one of Merry's passing fancies."

She fell silent. Her expression was serene, wistful, thoughtful.

"Victoria?" J.D. asked after several moments.

"That's the first time I've been able to think of Merry . . . without feeling sad. Without only feeling sad, I mean. The first time I've been able to think about the fun we had, too."

J.D. wanted to hug Victoria, to offer comfort for the loss of her eldest partner. But she hesitated too long, and then felt too self-conscious.

"I'm glad you can remember the good times," she said.

"When Merry died, people kept saying, After a while, you'll forget. I could never understand how they thought it would help to try to forget someone you loved. Then all you'd have left would be the grief."

"People get clumsy when they want to help but don't know what to say. They mean well."

They gazed at each other in silence.

"What do you want to do?" Victoria asked.

J.D. suddenly felt wilted, as if she'd been picked from her roots and left out in the sun.

"I want to try to get some sleep."

"All right." Victoria had drifted closer. She reached out slowly, as if she were afraid J.D. would flinch away. J.D. did not move. Victoria clasped J.D.'s hand and pressed it.

The system map hung before them. As J.D. watched, the survey's last connections formed, and the star and its planets spun within and among a tenuous pattern of luminous blue lines. J.D. tried to imagine the system within the larger framework of the galaxy, of the universe, moving swiftly away from the center, the point of genesis of everything now existing, the primordial big bang; and the cosmic string moving along with it in perfect synchrony.

A tiny silver point indicated the position of *Starfarer;* a tiny gold point placed the *Chi* almost halfway to Tau Ceti II, in transit from its satellite.

Beyond the kitchen viewport, the system showed no visible evidence of the tangles and patterns of cosmic string. It looked perfectly empty. But it was not.

"It's incredible," Victoria said.

"It is." J.D. slipped her fingers free. She put her hand to

Victoria's cheek and looked into her face, into her dark brown eyes.

"Good night," J.D. said.

J.D. returned to her cabin with too much to think about. The fabric door between her cabin and Zev's stood ajar the width of a finger. Afraid her lights would wake Zev, J.D. stopped at the door to close it. She paused to listen to her young friend, wondering if he was awake or asleep. When she could not hear him breathing she felt frightened for a moment, then laughed at herself. Habits were hard to break. Back in the wilderness, when she swam with the divers and the orcas, it never bothered her when the divers stopped breathing to nap. Here, on land—or at any rate out of the water—she listened for the soft regular breathing of a sleeping youth.

You just finished explaining to Victoria what normal behavior it was, J.D. said to herself.

She undressed, pushed her clothing into a storage bag, and wrapped herself in a thin quilt—another habit hard to break; she could easily turn up the heat in her cabin and sleep completely bare if she wanted, but the blanket was necessary, somehow comforting. Besides, on the transport she had once tried sleeping with only the net against her skin, and she ended up with a diamond pattern impressed temporarily into her back and her butt.

She fastened the net across the quilt and tried to relax, expecting to have trouble sleeping. She had not sorted out any of the things that had concerned her when she went to the kitchen for cocoa, and she had walked straight into having even more complicated subjects to consider.

J.D. took a deep breath that turned into a sigh.

Before she took another breath, she was soundly, deeply asleep.

She dreamed she was swimming with the orcas. The cold water streamed past her body. Her powerful legs kicked hard, pressing her through the sea. Even so, she could not keep up with the orcas or the divers, and she fell far behind.

J.D. woke. She felt hot and sweaty.

Oh, no, she thought, I've caught the flu from Stephen Thomas.

Her heart was pounding. The strange warmth of her metabolic enhancer created a physical pressure within her body. The artificial gland, implanted in her abdomen, pumped out extra adrenaline, endorphins, adenosine triphosphate. It raised her blood pressure, her heart rate. She could call on it to increase her endurance beyond her usual limits when she was swimming. When she first joined the alien contact department she had meant to let the gland atrophy, but had decided to keep it for the time being. The extra endurance had perhaps made the difference between her being able to hold onto the nuclear missile, and having the weapon slip out of her grasp too soon and crash into the wild cylinder.

Not that she expected to have any more wrestling matches with bombs.

The enhancer had kicked in during her dream, in response to her memories of swimming. Strange: it had never done that back on Earth.

I'm not getting enough exercise, J.D. thought.

The exercise bicycle interested her not at all. She wanted to swim, and swimming would have to wait. *Starfarer* contained a couple of large lakes, wide shallow salt marshes, a pseudo-ocean. She wondered if any of those would provide a satisfying place to swim.

The light from Sea moved across a free-floating shape. At first J.D. thought she must have failed to secure her clothes, or some other possession, then recognized a human form.

"Zev?"

He woke with a great, explosive exhalation and a gasping breath, shocking here, normal in the sea, where all the orcas and the divers would come to the surface together, blow, inhale, and sink beneath the surface again.

He touched one toe to the wall and drifted toward her. He looked sad, confused, frightened.

"Zev, what's the matter?" She could not remember ever having seen him frightened. She thought of him as completely fearless. "What are you doing in here?"

"Did I do wrong to come into your room?"

"No, of course not. Do you need something?"

"I don't know enough about the land world. You told me we shouldn't touch each other the ways we touched each other in the sea. And on land, when ordinary humans sleep, they sleep each in a separate place. In my room, I woke up to breathe, and I listened for my brothers and sisters and cousins, I listened for Lykos and I listened for you. But none of you were there. I just wanted to be near you. I came in to sleep where I could hear you. J.D., I felt so . . . so . . ."

"Lonely?"

"I don't know what that word means."

"It means . . . all by yourself, but wanting to be with other people."

"Yes. That's how I feel. How do I make it stop?" He was crying, the tears forming small bright spheres that popped out into the air and spun away, quivering.

J.D. fumbled at her sleeping net. "I should have thought, I should have realized—" This was the first time she had ever seen a diver cry.

He had probably never spent as much time all by himself as he had spent in the few days since he had come on board *Starfarer.* J.D. was responsible for his loneliness.

She pushed herself from the sleeping surface and moved the short distance to him. She put her arms around him and stroked his hair. He cuddled gratefully against her. Victoria's questions came back to her: Is Zev your lover?

"A lot of things are different on land than in the sea," she said to him. "Most ordinary humans don't sleep in groups." She wondered how to explain her teammates to him. She started to tell him that ordinary humans only slept with people they loved, but that would not help him understand, either. Love was exactly the relationship between and among the divers and the orcas.

"Do they all sleep by themselves?"

"No. Ordinary people sleep with each other when they want to make love."

His tears forgotten, even his loneliness forgotten for a moment, Zev laughed. He was amused, and perhaps a bit shocked. The one time divers and orcas did not think of having sex with each other was when they slept.

"That is very silly, J.D."

"I know it sounds silly, but . . ."

"Why do they do that?"

"It's kind of more convenient." This late at night, that was the simplest and truest explanation she could think of.

"I understand," Zev said. "It's because of wearing clothes. It takes too long to get in and out of them. So ordinary humans just make love when they aren't wearing anything anyway. Is that right?"

"Not exactly," J.D. said. "But it's part of it."

His preternaturally warm body melded close to hers. He let his head rest between her heavy breasts. She liked the way his smooth cheek felt against her. The fine gold hair on his mahogany skin slid across her body like delicate, soft fur.

"Would you like to sleep with me?" she said.

"I want to make love with you," Zev said. His dark eyes glistened in the faint light. She felt his penis extruding from his body, slick and resilient, very hot against her leg.

She kissed him. She had never seen divers kiss each other on the lips. He did not know what to do.

"Open your mouth a little," she whispered. She moved his hand to her breast. The swimming webs caressed her nipple like silk. Zev opened his mouth. J.D. touched her tongue to his lips, to his teeth, to his tongue. His prominent canines pressed against the sides of her tongue. She moved her hands down his back and his sides and his legs, smoothing the soft gilt hair.

He kissed her with his eyes open. J.D. took his tongue between her lips, between her teeth. He tasted salty, and sweet.

In zero g, their bodies drifted apart as they kissed. J.D. drew Zev closer. His penis was fully extended, now, but not yet fully erect. She stroked him gently, then more firmly. He opened himself completely to her as he never had in the sea, releasing the muscles of his scrotum and letting it descend from the protection of his body, leaving himself entirely vulnerable in her hands.

"Don't worry," he whispered. "I haven't chosen to be fertile. I only want you to touch me everywhere."

"Don't worry," J.D. said, replying to his politeness with courtesy of her own. "I haven't chosen to be fertile either."

She was ready, as was he, but in zero g their eagerness created a complication. Zev started to enter her. Their motion pushed them apart. J.D. giggled, and Zev laughed against her chest, his warm breath tickling her breasts.

"We are too slippery," he said. "Like eels."

She burst out laughing, kissed his forehead, kissed his lips when he raised his head. She touched the tip of her tongue to the tip of one canine tooth, savoring the sharpness of it. To the eye his teeth were little different from anyone's, but to her sensitive tongue they were sharp and dangerous.

Zev slid his hands down her back, trying to hold her hips against his. In weightlessness, the angle was too awkward. J.D. did not want to stop long enough to get inside the sleeping net; she wanted the freedom of the whole room. It was as if they were in a quiet cove, lit by a bluegreen moon.

"Wait," J.D. said. "Wait—"

He groaned softly. She wrapped her legs around him, riding him, and held him to her. She sighed as he moved inside her. In the sea, the sexual play of divers and orcas was a long intermittent series of touches and caresses. People came together and parted, swam and played and enjoyed themselves and their companions. In zero g, Zev and J.D. teased each other, led each other farther and farther, and had only each other to concentrate on.

Stephen Thomas lay wide awake within his sleeping net. He wished he could see his own aura, but he had never been able to do that. He could see the auras of other people. Once he had looked for, and found, the aura of the starship.

He knew he was just sick with the flu, but this did not feel like any illness he had ever contracted. His muscles ached and his body alternated between shivering and fever that never broke into sweat.

He drew his consciousness away from his body for a moment, letting it drift at a distance, acute, observant, and indifferent to his physical discomfort. Though he did not wish illness on any of his teammates, he was curious to know what he would see if he looked at the aura of someone who caught this particular bug.

Though it hurt to move, he unfastened the sleeping net and let himself free. Instead of dressing as he usually did, in running shorts and bright silk shirt, he dug out a pair of long pants and a sweatshirt. He put them on. He was glad of their warmth, though he wished he had something warm to wear other than regulation clothing.

As soon as he got a chance, he would slash fluorescent orange paint across the EarthSpace half of the *Starfarer* insignia on the front of the sweatshirt and the thigh of the pants, and rip the clothes in strategic places. Roughing up the clothing was his reaction to having been ordered to dress according to "regulation," when it looked like the ship would be taken over by the U.S. military. He wished he still had the sweatshirt he had already edited, but he had thrown that one away after bleeding all over it.

Starfarer should not even have regulation clothing, as far as he was concerned. If the members of the deep-space expedition had wanted to wear uniforms, they would have joined the Space Command.

Not that anyone was still trying to enforce the order. It was the principle of the thing.

He felt dizzy, weak, distracted. He always felt uncomfortable in zero g, irritated and embarrassed at being the only member of the alien contact team, probably the only person on board *Starfarer*, who had never gotten the hang of weightlessness. Zev had picked it up instantaneously.

For the moment, though, Stephen Thomas felt almost competent.

Must be the fever, he thought. I'm probably hallucinating it all.

He pushed off toward the door and moved into the corridor and drifted toward the observers' circle with barely a hesitation.

Everyone else slept on. The *Chi* projected itself toward Tau Ceti II. Stephen Thomas settled into his couch and created a link to *Starfarer*. Arachne responded smoothly, normally, with only the brief delay caused by *Starfarer*'s distance.

The *Chi* remained on the same schedule as the starship: it was night back there, too. While the interior of the cylinder lay in darkness, the communications channels were nearly silent. Stephen Thomas sidestepped the link to the team's liaison. No point to waking anyone up, not even Gerald.

All the links to the genetic department were completely blown. Though that did not surprise him, it disappointed him. He had hoped the devastation was not as bad as he feared. He barely remembered Victoria and Satoshi dragging him out of the wrecked building, and after that he had only seen it from a distance.

He put in a call for Professor Thanthavong. He did not expect a reply, so he made sure not to attach any intensifiers to the transmission. If she were asleep, like everyone else, her AI would not wake her.

"Yes, Stephen Thomas?" Her image formed before him in the observers' circle. "I'm glad to see you looking better."

"I'm glad I look better than I feel."

"Are you ill?" She leaned forward.

"I just picked up the usual transport flu," he said.

She relaxed. "I was . . . afraid you might have encountered a serious pathogen."

"No! Jesus christ, is one loose?"

Her safety standards had kept the collapse of the genetics building from turning into a complete disaster. She ran her department with a gentle hand, but made it exceedingly clear that she would put up with no safety risks. No one ever created a pathogen from DNA transcription without her permission and counsel. When the building fell, Thanthavong could say for certain that its labs held no illnesses that might contaminate the starship.

"No. I think not. But when you said you felt unwell—" She stopped. "No. Nothing virulent is loose. But I got the results of your test, and you have been exposed to sensitizing virus. Everyone else is clear of it."

Stephen Thomas shrugged. "It's no big deal, then. It isn't what's making me sick, and it'll die out in a couple of days at the same time I fight off this other bug."

"Nevertheless, be careful when you reach the surface of the planet. If it supports a biology compatible with ours— don't object, I know your feeling on that—you could find yourself in serious trouble."

Some people believed DNA was the most likely carrier of genetic information all over the universe; some people believed no ecosystem that evolved on one world could have any points of compatibility with that of another. Until now, human beings had only one example to test. In a few hours, Stephen Thomas would be able to answer the question one way or the other.

Stephen Thomas's most recent project dealt with alternate chemical carriers of genetic information. He wanted Sea's life to be based on something besides DNA. He wanted something new to study.

"I'll be careful," he said. "I would anyway, but thanks for letting me know the test results. Professor, how much did we lose?"

He still felt guilty about leaving her and his colleagues to face the destruction themselves, while he went off on the *Chi*. But this was his job; he could not have chosen to stay behind.

"We lost... a great deal. Most of the equipment, almost every experiment in progress. Stephen Thomas, your lab was completely crushed."

"Shit," he said. "Oh, *sh*—" He stopped. He seldom cursed in front of Professor Thanthavong, even though cursing never bothered her as far as he could see.

"I'm sorry to have to tell you," Thanthavong said.

"Back home," he muttered, "they have a lot to answer for."

"Yes," she said bitterly. "They do. But we may be sure they are inventing reasons why we should first have to answer for our actions."

"Yeah. At least we don't have to worry about that for a while. The longer the better, as far as I'm concerned."

"And, Stephen Thomas..."

He waited with trepidation, reacting to her ominous tone.

"It isn't only the experiments we lost. When the web crashed, we lost a great deal of basic information."

"That's impossible!"

"Yes. But it happened."

He pressed himself into his couch, appalled, stunned.

"But we hit transition dead on! And *Starfarer's* still running. What about the backups?"

"Iphigenie was navigating with new information. A new course, impressed on hard copy."

"Victoria's algorithm."

"Yes. Whoever crashed the web didn't want to cripple the ship permanently. They wanted to keep us from transition. They wanted to demoralize us."

"We're here," Stephen Thomas said. "We're going on."

"I hope so."

"Is everything okay back there? People aren't talking about turning back?"

"Of course some are. A few always were, but most were anxious to go ahead. The message, and the dome, though— that is causing distress."

"Here, too," Stephen Thomas said. "Believe me. Can we keep going? Exactly what did we lose?"

"The web crash acted like damage to the higher neural facilities. As if it attacked the cerebrum, but left the brain stem. Some restoration will be possible, but some of the backups are garbaged. Medical records. Environmental balances."

"Oh, christ," Stephen Thomas said. "What an ungodly mess." He stared into space, thinking of his own six months' work lost.

"The students want you to bring back some samples for them," Thanthavong said.

"How are they holding up?"

"Better today than yesterday." She smiled affectionately. "They are young. Adaptable. Have you spoken to them?"

"Uh, no," he said, wishing he did not have to admit it. "We've been—"

"You needn't apologize to me, Stephen Thomas, I have no need of your attention." Thanthavong left the rest unsaid.

Stephen Thomas changed the subject. "Nobody's figured out *how* the web crashed, or you'd've said so."

"True. No one knows how, no one knows who."

"Somebody on the carrier that was chasing us."

"I think not. Not directly. After all, they cut off most of our communications. There was hardly a channel they could hide in to send such a command."

"You can do a lot of damage with something that looks pretty simple," Stephen Thomas said stubbornly.

"Ah," Thanthavong said. "I've upset you, too."

"I'm not upset! Why—" He stopped. He had raised his voice in pitch and volume, and his pulse rate increased. "What do you mean, me, *too*?"

"You aren't the only one to resist the idea that someone within *Starfarer* did this deed. I'd like to prove someone outside our community did it, too. But I think the alternative is more plausible."

Stephen Thomas knew almost everyone on board. He hated the idea that one of his friends might be a government spy, sent out to ruin the deep-space expedition and turn *Starfarer* into an orbiting military base.

"It must have been Gerald," he said. "That—"

"Don't throw around accusations for which you have no evidence," Thanthavong said. "I know you don't like him. That isn't evidence."

"Who else could it have been?" Stephen Thomas said. "Except maybe that guy Griffith . . ." He paused. Griffith was an even better possibility than Gerald Hemminge. Stephen Thomas suddenly shivered.

"What's the matter, Stephen Thomas? Perhaps you should go back to bed."

"Yeah, that's true. But listen, Griffith—"

"Do you have any *evidence*?"

"How about Florrie's reaction to him? How about mine?"

"What reactions, exactly, are you talking about?"

"Florrie took one look at him and said he was a narc."

Thanthavong laughed. Unlike Stephen Thomas and Victoria and Satoshi, she did not have to be told what a narc was.

"My dear," she said, "a certain segment of my generation will regard *any* member of the government as a narc. I believe Floris belongs to that segment. What reaction did you have?"

He hesitated. He had never tried to persuade Thanthavong of his ability to see auras. Indifferent to the opinions of most people, he cared deeply what she thought of him.

"Go ahead," she said.

"I . . . looked for his aura, and I couldn't find it."

"His aura."

"Yeah."

"I see," she said, her voice neutral.

"You aren't laughing," he said.

"Why should I?"

"Practically everybody else does."

"It's true that I don't believe in auras. But you are very perceptive, when you care to be. Your instincts about people can generally be relied on. An 'aura' may be your way of perceiving character."

"People keep saying that to me." Stephen Thomas sounded grumpy even to himself. "I don't see what the hell's so weird about seeing auras, if you *don't* think it's weird for somebody to take one look at another person and be able to make accurate statements about their personality."

Thanthavong chuckled. "Perhaps you're right. What makes you think Griffith may be our culprit, just because he has no aura?"

"I don't know," Stephen Thomas said. "I never had that reaction to anybody before. It . . . shook me."

Thanthavong's mouth quirked in half a smile. "I'm afraid,"

she said, "that your evidence would be of little use in a court of law. Or in a meeting."

"Everything was going fine until Griffith turned up," Stephen Thomas said. "Who else could it be?"

"That's what you said about Gerald! If you accuse Griffith because of when he arrived, you must also accuse Floris Brown—"

"Florrie Brown!" Stephen Thomas started to laugh, until he realized how serious Thanthavong was.

"—or J.D.—"

"But that's ridiculous."

"—or Feral."

"Now wait a minute," Stephen Thomas said. "Feral—"

"I didn't say *I* suspected him. I said you could apply the same evidence to him as to Griffith."

"He's on our side," Stephen Thomas said. "I'd stake my life on it."

"My friend, the most likely person to be a spy is the most unlikely person to be a spy. It could be anyone on board the starship. It could be any of the transport passengers. They would have been most likely to survive, if the missile had breached *Starfarer's* hull. One assumes the government would not throw away a capable agent unnecessarily."

"If the warhead had gone off when it hit, nobody would have survived."

"But it didn't go off when it hit. We'll never know what was intended—a scare shot, or a crippling strike, or a killing shot with a defective trigger. The missile didn't leave us any clues to who crashed the web."

"Christ on a carousel," Stephen Thomas said. "If whoever it was is still on board, they could do it again. *Shit.*"

"You do have a way with words," Thanthavong replied.

"We've got to *do* something."

"I'm open to suggestions."

"I still think it's Griffith. Maybe I could make him tell us what's going on."

"Assuming you're right about him, just how would you propose to do that?"

Stephen Thomas shrugged. "I don't know. But he doesn't have the whole government behind him anymore, and I'm bigger than he is."

As soon as he said it, he wished he had kept his mouth shut.

"You're talking about physical force? When is the last time you were in a fight?"

"I never get in fights—I mean..." He glanced away sheepishly.

"When?"

"Gerald and I kind of went at each other."

"Your black eyes—"

"He never hit me!" Stephen Thomas brushed his fingers across the bandaged cut on his forehead. "This is all from the accident."

"That is what I believed, but when you said you had fought..."

"It was more like we sort of whacked at each other for a while and bounced into the wall. It was in zero g."

"Did you win?"

"Nobody won."

"Threatening violence is a dreadful precedent. Besides— let us be pragmatic—if Griffith is a government agent, an undercover agent, and you fought him, someone would win. Probably not you."

"Maybe you're right."

"'Maybe'?"

"Do you have a better idea?"

"Lots of them. I intend to ask him. Maybe I'll ask Gerald, too. And Feral, just to be impartial."

"Wait—"

"For what?"

"For me to come back, so I can come with you. At least don't talk to Griffith alone. Please."

"That's a sensible precaution," Thanthavong said. "Very well. What about Florrie? Do you think I can hold my own against her?"

"I don't know," Stephen Thomas said, deadpan. "If she's a government agent, she might be pretty dangerous. Maybe you'd better take Feral along with you as a bodyguard."

Thanthavong chuckled.

Stephen Thomas let himself relax in the loose straps of his couch. He had forgotten, during the whole time of his conversation with Thanthavong, that he was in zero g.

Maybe Satoshi was right, he thought. I just needed some extended experience.

"Would you do me a favor?" he said.

"If I can."

"I don't want to wake the kids up in the middle of the night. They're probably exhausted. In the morning, we'll be landing. I won't be able to leave the circle to make private calls. Would you tell my students . . . that I'll bring back some new work?"

"Certainly," she said. "But you could tell them that yourself. It wouldn't destroy your reputation entirely to appear sentimental on the public link. Good night, Stephen Thomas. Get some sleep."

Her image faded from the center of the circle.

Stephen Thomas spent another quarter of an hour looking through the transparent wall at the approaching planet. Its beauty and promise soothed him and allowed the tension and apprehension to flow from him, as if they were diffusing into space. Finally, yawning, he unfastened the safety straps and let himself free. He swam easily to his room.

He got into bed, deciding against joining Victoria and Satoshi. They had enough to worry about without getting sick, too.

He fell into a deep and quiet sleep.

Early in the morning, Victoria laid her hand on Stephen Thomas's forehead. The fever still burned.

He woke up. In the dim light, his beautiful sapphire eyes looked gray.

"You sleep so pretty," she said.

He snorted. "I don't feel pretty this morning."

"You are, though." She kissed him; he turned his head so her lips brushed his cheek.

"You don't want to pick up this bug," he said. "It's a real pain. Literally."

She gave him more flu-away, and the package of fruit juice she had brought him.

"That'll help the ache."

"I hope. It didn't last night."

"Do you feel well enough to join the circle?"

"No, but I'm going to anyway." He opened the sleeping net. "Are we in orbit? Damn, I didn't want to miss it."

"Not yet. But look." She gestured with her chin toward the port.

He looked out the window.

"Holy shit."

Sea filled the circle, the shapes of its continents perceptible beneath white clouds. Zev had suggested naming the continents after the islands of his home, in the Puget Sound wilderness. Stephen Thomas liked the idea, but Victoria resisted any more gratuitous naming.

Stephen Thomas pushed himself out of bed and dove toward the window. Victoria grabbed for him, afraid he would crash headfirst into the glass. To her surprise, he stopped gracefully and easily in just the right place.

"You're getting better," she said.

"I still don't feel too great," Stephen Thomas said offhand, mistaking her comment. "Will you look at that."

Victoria joined him by the port.

She wondered if she perceived Tau Ceti II as beautiful because it looked so much like Earth, green and blue, streaked and swirled with white clouds, three-quarters in sunlight and a quarter in shadow.

"Can you see the lightning?"

"No, where?" Victoria said.

"Northern hemisphere, middle latitudes—"

Victoria looked for lightning in the night crescent, but saw only darkness.

Her message signal formed. Victoria ignored it for the moment, wanting to get Stephen Thomas back to bed.

"Why don't you try to get a little more sleep?" she said. "You might feel okay by the time we land."

Stephen Thomas's message signal formed beside Victoria's.

"That's a good idea," he said. "Would you do me a favor?" He gestured toward the message signal. "Would you check my messages? My brain feels like it's full of fur. God only knows what I'd answer anybody."

"You'd probably answer with your usual restraint," Victoria said, her tone dry. "Sure, I'll check yours when I answer mine. Traffic's busy for so early in the morning. Do you need help getting back to bed?"

"I can make it." He moved away from the window, turned with grace, and pushed off to cross the short distance to his sleeping surface. "I'm getting better—oh, is that what you meant?"

Satoshi's voice reached them through the intercom.

"Victoria, where are you? Avvaiyar wants to talk to you. Sounds serious. It's something about the strings."

Victoria touched Stephen Thomas on the arm. "Will you be okay?"

"You can keep an eye on me," he said. "I'm coming."

He followed her to the observers' circle. Victoria was amazed and amused at how well he was navigating in zero g. He had avoided it for so long, complained about it for so long, that he had convinced himself he could not cope with it. Now he could be the first one chosen for the team in zero-g sports, as well as in the traditional variety.

J.D. and Zev and Satoshi had already reached the circle, where Avvaiyar's image occupied the center.

Victoria's couch enfolded her. Stephen Thomas took his place.

"I thought this could wait," Avvaiyar said, skipping all the preliminaries. "But it can't. Victoria, the strings are moving."

Strings always moved; it was their nature. The string by which *Starfarer* had entered transition had vibrated into the vicinity of the solar system. Someday it would vibrate out of range. That "someday" was several thousand years in the future, however, so it was not an imminent threat.

Victoria brought up the system map beside Avvaiyar's image.

"Moving how?"

"Moving away. All at once. Accelerating. Untangling. It's like they're opening up..." She put her hands together, palm to palm, laced her fingers, then drew her hands apart again.

"All of them?" Victoria said, stunned.

"All."

Nothing in cosmic string theory accounted for this behavior.

"What are we going to do?" Avvaiyar said.

She sounded even more shocked than Victoria felt. Her voice held a note of hopelessness, of despondency, as if the heart had gone out of her.

"Avvaiyar, I don't understand what you're telling me. If they move, they move. There's nothing we can do to stop them. We'll have to add the motion to the algorithms; they'll take more time to solve. Other than that..."

"Victoria, you don't understand! They're moving *fast*. Unless they stop and start moving back the other way, they're going to be moving faster than *Starfarer* can accelerate within a very few weeks. And I don't believe they're going to be moving back the other way!"

"Christ on a broomstick," Stephen Thomas said. "Is this stuff going to strand us here?"

"It could."

"Oh, damn," J.D. whispered. "Damn . . ." She was looking not at Avvaiyar's image, but through the clear wall of the observer, toward Tau Ceti II. "We're not going to get to land after all, are we?"

"I don't see how," Avvaiyar said. "If Iphigenie doesn't realign the sail soon—very soon—*Starfarer* will never catch up to the transition point for Earth. You're going to have to sling yourselves around the planet and come back. ASAP."

"But—" Stephen Thomas exclaimed.

"But what, Stephen Thomas? I don't—"

"Never mind," he said.

"—see that there's any choice!"

"Never mind! I understand! My whole career just got snatched out from under me! Let me have a *little* disappointment!"

"I'm sorry," Avvaiyar said. "But . . . I'm frightened. I don't understand why or how this could happen, and I'm afraid that if it could happen this way, it could start happening even faster." She tried to smile; she failed. "I didn't sign onto this expedition for my life's work, you know?"

"None of us did," Victoria said.

J.D. made a quick, suppressed motion of objection. She stopped almost before she started, but not before Victoria noticed.

J.D. *did* sign on for life, Victoria thought. Or she'd be willing to.

"All right," Victoria said. "We're coming back. We won't land. Is Iphigenie prepared to change course?"

"Yes."

"Go ahead. We'll catch up."

Avvaiyar's image vanished.

The members of the alien contact team stared at each other for a long slow painful minute.

"Excuse me," Stephen Thomas said. "I'm going to go find a

quiet, private place for a little while. Don't pay any attention to the noise. It's just the neighborhood geneticist beating his head against the wall."

He left the observers' circle and vanished into the main ship.

"I can't bear this," J.D. said softly.

Zev reached out and took her hand.

"Don't give up hope yet." Victoria tried to keep up her own spirits, but the encouragement sounded hollow even to her. "We don't know that much about cosmic string. It might be indulging in a momentary local variation. A hiccup. There's so much of it in this system, I can't imagine how it could all vibrate out of range at once."

"But you've changed the course of the *Chi* already. Haven't you?"

"Yes," Victoria admitted. "It's a safety precaution. I think it would be better to delay our landing on Tau Ceti II, rather than risk being stranded in this system forever. Don't you?"

J.D. did not answer.

"I would not like it, never to go home again," Zev said.

"We'll go home, don't worry." Victoria glared through the *Chi*'s transparent wall, out into the system, as if she could see the cosmic string, as if her anger alone could force it to retrace its path. "Maybe a lot sooner than we thought."

Satoshi flung off the safety straps and shoved himself out of his couch.

"You know what I'd like to know? I'd like to know what general is pushing the buttons *this* time."

He propelled himself through the entryway, out of the observers' circle.

Victoria and J.D. and Zev remained. J.D. looked enervated. If she had been in a gravity field, she would have been slumping with dejection.

"I'm so sorry, J.D. . . ." Victoria stopped. Anything she said would be inadequate.

"Yeah. So am I."

"You weren't serious . . ."

"About what?"

"About staying here. Forever."

J.D. did not even bother to point out that she had not actually said she wanted to stay here forever.

"There's a lifetime's work here. Work I spent my life preparing for."

"You're an alien contact specialist. There aren't any aliens to contact."

"Victoria, there's a lifetime's work back in the dome, even crushed as it is. How can we leave it behind, unexcavated?" She thrust out one hand to stave off Victoria's objection. "No, I'm not suggesting that everyone on board *Starfarer* should stay here while our route home disappears. But I am admitting that if it were only up to me, if I were the only person involved, I'd stay."

Victoria hesitated, wanting to say something but afraid of offending her teammate.

"There's nothing . . ." she said carefully. "There's no way to leave behind an artificial environment that would sustain a person for more than a couple of years."

"I know it." J.D. smiled sadly. "I'm angry, I'm disappointed, I'm frustrated, and I'm going to be very depressed for quite a while. But I'm not suicidal."

"I'm glad to hear it," Victoria said.

J.D. glanced through the wall of the observers' circle, not, this time, at Tau Ceti II, but at its satellite. The orientation of the *Chi*, the arc of its path, put the satellite to one side of the spacecraft, rather than behind it.

"I wish, now, that we'd stayed. I wish we'd tried to excavate. Salvage archaeology." She sighed. "Too late now, I suppose."

The *Chi*'s computer took only a couple of seconds to answer J.D.'s question: They could not land again, much less spend any time excavating, and still catch up to *Starfarer*.

"I'm sorry, J.D.," Victoria said. "We have to go straight back to the starship. We have to go home."

6

All its recording instruments set on high detail, all its cameras focused, the *Chi* sped around Tau Ceti II, from light to shadow to light again, and headed toward the starship.

The planet passed, beyond J.D.'s reach. She yearned to stop and explore it, at least visit it. The telemetry would tell them a great deal about the world, but it was not the same. She had spent her life learning things about other places by means of telemetry, speculation, words and equations and pictures. She wanted something real.

J.D. felt the whisper of the steering rockets, not slowing the *Chi* but speeding it up. It would never be captured by the gravity of Tau Ceti II. It would arc around the planet and sling itself back toward *Starfarer*.

No one on the alien contact team spoke during the passage. Tau Ceti II lay behind them.

In despair, J.D. let herself out of her couch and drifted to the transparent wall of the observers' circle, as if she could look back and reach through it and touch the surface of the planet.

Zev joined her. She was afraid if he touched her, if she had to speak, she would break down and cry.

"I would have liked to swim in an alien sea," he said.

J.D. grabbed at hope, clutching it blindly.

"Maybe you can."

"J.D.—" Victoria said.

"Hear me out," J.D. said. "We can't stay here, because the string is receding. But we still have access to transition points that will take us other places."

She paused, waiting for reactions from her teammates.

"It could work," Stephen Thomas said.

127

"Your algorithm tells you whether the destination is empty or full, as far as string goes, right?" J.D. asked Victoria.

"It wouldn't be much use if it didn't," Victoria said dryly. "It tells me if the stuff exists there, so we could go someplace else, or if it's absent, so we'd be stuck. It doesn't say how much—"

"But how much doesn't matter!" J.D. said. "As long as you pick a 'full' destination, as long as we keep going to a place where there's more string, we can go wherever we like. True?"

"Within limits." Victoria sounded intrigued. "Instead of one stop, we could make a grand tour."

"Just like a bunch of debutantes," J.D. said.

"What?"

"Nothing," J.D. said. "Dumb joke. Before your time, and out of my class."

"Nothing's out of your class, J.D.," Victoria said. "God, what a great idea. Why didn't I think of it? Too preoccupied with the string. It's not supposed to behave this way."

J.D.'s despair had turned to excitement; from the verge of tears she had traveled to the verge of giggles.

"We could try Epsilon Indi or 40 Eridani—or maybe it would be better to try a star that isn't very much like our own. Sirius? Maybe we should look for the alien people in a much different environment—" J.D. stopped, for her voice was rising with excitement. "I'll have to think about this for a while."

"It's got my recommendation," Satoshi said.

Within a few minutes, they had put together a meeting proposal and posted it, with all their recommendations.

"We could do it," Victoria said. "There's no reason why we *couldn't* do it!"

In the sailhouse, Avvaiyar said, again, "I'm sorry. The expedition is a failure. We have no choice. We must turn back." Her image faded.

Iphigenie stared at the place her friend had occupied, then shook herself and turned, without a word, to the hard link.

"Iphigenie—" Feral stopped. Shocked and angry and distressed and confused, he was for once at a loss for a question or an observation.

"Be quiet," she said, without glancing at him. "This is a

dangerous maneuver. Too much stress. I have to think about it."

Feral remembered his first sight of her, at the first deployment of *Starfarer*'s solar sail. Iphigenie's sail was as magnificent, beautiful, elegant, as Iphigenie. She controlled it, she controlled the starship, with the touch of her intellect and her will. The harmonies of the sensors, reporting in musical tones, sounded like a new symphony. Iphigenie's presence had filled the sailhouse; she had, by right, been the center of her colleagues' celebration. She quieted the group with a single word, and released them with a single gesture. Feral remembered her floating in the middle of the cylinder, drinking a shimmering, fizzing globule of champagne with a kiss.

She had belonged here, within walls so perfectly transparent that they gave the impression of allowing her unprotected access to the stars.

Now, though, she huddled—as much as one could huddle in zero gravity—over the hardlink. The pale glow of the screen lit her dark, drawn face. She was still beautiful, and elegant, but anguish replaced the magnificent, fierce joy.

He knew how she felt. He had always expected to have to face the consequences of his actions eventually. But not quite so soon. Not with quite so little to show for the rebellion.

Feral tried to call Stephen Thomas, but received no reply.

The harmonious melody of the sensors broke up into discord. Feral felt useless. He wanted to help. He wanted to be a part of the expedition, not just an observer, and now he would never get a chance. The expedition was at an end.

He drifted in the center of the sailhouse, where Iphigenie by rights should be, directing the spacecraft with her mind, her body moving in small, involuntary ways in response to her commands. Body English, Feral thought, or maybe, for Iphigenie, body French. She spoke English with a barely perceptible accent. Feral wondered what language she thought in, dreamed in. Sometimes he himself dreamed in fluent French, much better French than he spoke when he was awake. It was only after he woke up that he realized he was making most of it up in his sleep.

The sail harmonies followed a long slow slide into key. The melody changed. Feral glanced out toward the sail.

The sail moved, altering its angle to Tau Ceti's light. Feral's first reaction was to look around for one of the transparent glass handholds in the sailhouse wall. But he felt nothing. The ship was so large, the acceleration of the sail so delicate and gradual, that the change was imperceptible. It was the cumulative effect that redirected the starship. One could not go hot-rodding around in a ship the size of *Starfarer*. The physical stresses would rip it apart.

And when *Starfarer* returned to Earth, the political stresses would as surely rip it apart. This time the expedition would not escape. Feral had no official place here, but he was ethically allied with it. He would not pretend he had been dragged along unwillingly.

Home. The word carried few resonances for him. He had rented the same room for the past two years, and it still held boxes he had never unpacked. *Starfarer* was the first place he had ever been where he thought he might feel at home.

Iphigenie straightened up, leaning back from the hard link. But she left her feet secured in the steady straps. The iridescent beads on the ends of her thin, smooth braids drifted till the motion of her head pulled them together in a staccato of faint clicks. Feral stroked over and joined her.

"You'll get your wish soon," Iphigenie said.

"My wish?"

"To pass through transition again."

The memory of transition was one of the most vivid of Feral's life. Yet, so far, he had been unable to describe the experience in words that conveyed its impact on him. He felt changed, but he could not describe exactly what about him had changed, either.

"I didn't want it to happen like this," he said. "Isn't there some other possibility? Don't you cheerful anarchists have to have a meeting before you can make a change like this?"

"We seldom make drastic changes without several meetings," Iphigenie said. "We hold meetings so everyone can contribute. We thrash out differences when we aren't under great stress. This time, when there's only one possibility, it's my job to keep it within our reach."

Feral's message symbol faded in nearby. He accepted the communication. The image of Stephen Thomas appeared

before him. Seeing him gave Feral a quick sharp thrill of
pleasure, of desire, of loneliness.

"Hi," Feral said. "Stephen Thomas, I'm so sorry—"

"J.D. has a suggestion." He must have started speaking as
soon as Arachne made contact. The rush of explanation cut off
Feral's attempt at sympathy, comfort, commiseration.

"What a great idea!" Feral said. "Can we do it?"

"It's possible," Iphigenie said, listening in. "It would be
possible."

"Then what are you waiting for?"

"We could *decide* to do it," Stephen Thomas said in reply
to Feral's first question, but it reminded him of the answer to
his second as well. "I called to ask, will you help? Will you
talk to people, help us pass the idea around, get them to
support the meeting?"

"Sure! I—"

"Great. I have to make some other calls. I'll talk to you
soon." He vanished, leaving Feral's enthusiasm hanging.

The air currents took the tendrils of Iphigenie's narrow
braids and pushed them together, apart, together. The beads
on their ends clinked, like tiny castanets seeking the measure
of the whispered harmonies.

"I'd better get started," he said. "Will you be all right?"

"You are very committed for a journalist, Feral," she said,
not answering his question. "Aren't you supposed to be
objective?"

"No," he said. "I'm a participatory journalist. Involvement
is my intention. Objectivity is the furthest thing from my
mind."

The *Chi* sped toward *Starfarer*.

Stephen Thomas lounged within his couch, alone in the
observers' circle. He had turned the couch so it faced the
Chi's direction of motion, resolutely leaving Tau Ceti II
behind. He looked out with nothing between him and space
except the invisible glass wall. The on-board computer flew
the *Chi*; no one on the alien contact team had to be concerned with its course.

Starfarer grew. It was a distant dot, silhouetted against the
expanse of its sail. It was a moving clockwork toy. It was an
enormous, complex, spinning world.

Stephen Thomas had nothing to do but watch the docking,

regret the lost opportunities of Tau Ceti II, and worry and wonder about the reaction the team would get when they disembarked. J.D.'s suggestion was intriguing, tempting, but would their colleagues have the resilience to attempt another change in plans? If they did continue, could they hope for another star system as perfect as this one?

He drifted easily between the couch and the loose safety straps. *Starfarer* came closer, its paired cylinders spinning silently against the silver backdrop of its sail.

The *Chi* moved so smoothly that from Stephen Thomas's perspective the starship approached him, rather than the opposite. The crater moved past, concentric circles of jumbled rock around a bull's-eye of silver. Stephen Thomas was surprised that the slugs had not yet completed the repairs.

I wonder if we'll always carry the scar of the attack? he thought.

He stretched, arching his back, curling his toes. *Starfarer* drifted closer, appearing to turn as the *Chi* approached the dock on the stationary end of the cylinder.

Stephen Thomas felt remarkably well, considering how terrible he had felt a few hours ago. The fever had not yet died away, but the muscle aches had faded. He rubbed his palms together and pinched the skin between his fingers. His hands itched.

He had no samples to pack, no experiments to transfer. What little useful information he had about Tau Ceti II resided in the memory of the on-board computer. He could transfer it to Arachne any time, anywhere, as soon as he was certain the web had finished its reconstruction.

Not that I can do much with spectroscopic data and photographs, he thought. Dammit! I wanted to look at living organisms from another world. I'd've settled for exotic algae. To have to leave the whole evolved ecosphere behind...

He tried to relax, tried to resign himself to whatever happened, tried to interest himself in the docking. He had never watched it up close before.

A shadow passed across him. He glanced toward it. Zev gazed at him, silently.

"Hello, Zev," Stephen Thomas said.

Zev hesitated, "Hello." He sounded uncertain, shy. "What are you doing?"

"Just watching. I never did before. I usually hide in the bathroom and puke when we do these maneuvers."

"Do you get seasick?"

"Space sick. I must have adapted. Finally. I haven't lost my lunch once this trip."

Without replying, Zev continued to hover nearby. Stephen Thomas went back to watching the approach. After a few minutes, Zev's unwavering observation began to make him nervous.

"Zev, what's going on?"

"J.D. said you were ill. I wondered how you were feeling. But you say you're well."

"I didn't get space sick. I got the flu instead." He grinned. "The trade-off's worth it, I think. Besides, I'm almost over it."

The walls of the starship enclosed the *Chi,* nesting and securing it. A faint vibration rose to perceptibility, then vanished.

They were home.

J.D. joined Victoria and Satoshi at the access hatch. J.D. carried the alien sculpture, the meerkat, in a transparent sample box.

J.D. almost went to her teammates and hugged them. She felt the need of some comfort and encouragement. But she did not know how Victoria would feel about being hugged, after last night's conversation. Now, with Zev, J.D.'s feelings were even more complicated. The possibilities surrounded her, more synergistic than exclusive.

"Ready?" Satoshi said.

"I wish I were."

Zev floated in. "I'm here," he said. "I didn't forget."

He stopped next to J.D., his shoulder rubbing hers.

"I knew you wouldn't forget," J.D. said, "but I didn't know if you'd keep track of the time."

"I wish Stephen Thomas would keep track of time," Victoria said.

Satoshi glanced back into the *Chi,* puzzled. "He's usually the first person through the hatch and into gravity."

"Zev, have you seen him?"

"Yes."

"Where is he?"

"Floating."

"We're all floating, Zev," Victoria said. "Oh, hell, I'll get him in a minute. He probably doesn't feel up to facing a crowd."

Responding to her command, the hatch unsealed.

Stephen Thomas arrowed into the vestibule, turned and touched the wall with one foot, and came to a halt among his teammates. He was carrying his patchwork quilt.

"Feeling better, eh?" Victoria said.

"Quite a lot."

"Glad you could join us."

"Hey, I almost forgot my blanket."

The hatch opened.

The waiting room was full of people. Professor Thanthavong hovered near the front, accompanied by Fox and a dozen other graduate students from the astronomy and physics and genetics and geography departments.

Feral greeted the team with a grin; he was intense and involved, in the midst of everything, surrounded by Crimson Ng and Florrie Brown and Infinity Mendez and Esther Klein. Even Kolya Cherenkov had joined the crowd. J.D. looked, uneasily, for Griffith, who could usually be found tagging around after Kolya. For a change, he was nowhere in sight.

Chandra, the sensory artist, drifted outside the group, taking everything in with her strange body and her weird, all-seeing, opaque eyes, recording what surrounded her, collecting raw material to sculpt into virtual reality.

Stephen Thomas crossed to Feral and kissed him.

Gerald Hemminge eeled between his colleagues, heading for J.D.

"I've heard of foolish suggestions," he said to her, "but haring off into nowhere is—"

Professor Thanthavong interrupted. "What Gerald is trying to say is that we have more than a quorum for a meeting, if you're up to it."

"I am," J.D. said.

"We all are," Victoria said. "Eager for it."

"You don't understand the problems," Gerald said. "You don't even *begin* to understand—"

"You can have your say with everyone else," Thanthavong told him. "Things have happened to disappoint all of us. Nevertheless, our friends have visited a world outside our solar system, for the first time in human history, and I believe we should congratulate them."

The Nobel laureate hugged J.D., who returned the embrace gratefully.

"Thank you," J.D. whispered.

Thanthavong patted her shoulder and hugged Stephen Thomas, Satoshi, and Victoria.

"And here's our young stowaway." She hugged Zev, too.

Crimson Ng moved closer. "Can I look at the sculpture, J.D.?"

J.D. let the sample box free. It floated, turning slowly, before Crimson. It became the center of a sphere of people.

"It isn't very *alien*," Chandra said with disdain.

"May I touch it?" Crimson was a sculptor, most recently of fossil alien bones. She buried them in artificial strata, leaving only tantalizing bits exposed. She touched the plastic shielding, moving her fingers along the lines of the stone creature.

J.D. longed to take the meerkat out of the sample case. She still had never touched its graceful curves with her bare hands, only through gloves. But it would be a mistake to open the box, a mistake to indulge herself and pass the sculpture around. It was too precious.

"The protocol calls for quarantine and testing," she said, yearning to stroke its stone surface.

"I know," Crimson said. "But it's been out in hard vacuum, and heat sterilized, for god's sake, it's not going to emit some alien germ to eat my face—"

Interested, Chandra moved closer. "I wonder what an alien illness would feel like?" she said, out loud, but to herself.

"We'll observe the quarantine," Professor Thanthavong said. "But we are likely to be as unpalatable to alien germs as alien people would be to our diseases."

"Then why can't I touch it?" Crimson asked.

"Because of precautions," J.D. said.

"It looks like something from back on Earth," Chandra said scornfully. "A weasel or something."

"A meerkat. That's what Stephen Thomas thought it resembled. I looked it up, and he's right."

"Parallel evolution," Thanthavong said. "Quite common back on Earth, for unrelated species to evolve to a similar pattern, in similar environments."

"Or it could mean the people who made it have visited Earth," Kolya Cherenkov said. "In secret."

"It could," Thanthavong said, unwillingly.

J.D., too, resisted the idea that alien beings had visited Earth without making their presence known to humans, or at any rate to humans in public. She had been teased about little green men and UFO landings and the unconvincing reports of flying saucer abductions. She had been teased by people who knew she wrote science fiction novels, and she had been teased by people who knew she wanted to join the alien contact department. She supposed every member of the expedition had faced the same derision.

"Where will it go?" Crimson gazed at the sculpture as if mesmerized. "You don't have to damage it to study it, do you?"

"No, of course not," J.D. said. "I thought it could sit out the quarantine period in the art museum."

"I'd like that," Crimson said.

"It's an excellent suggestion," Thanthavong said. "But one to be carried out later. It's time to convene the meeting."

J.D. found herself between Victoria and Professor Thanthavong as they left the dock. They passed the waiting room for the transport ship. Apprehensive, J.D. glanced inside. The waiting room was empty.

"What a relief," she said.

"Hmm?" Victoria asked.

"I kind of expected the other transport passengers to be blockaded in there. On a hunger strike or something. Gerald made it sound like they were carrying out mass protests. . . . Where *are* they?"

"Almost everyone returned to their homes and their jobs," Thanthavong said. "They didn't *want* to leave us, you know. They were recalled. When the transport remained with *Starfarer*, they had the opportunity to stay with the expedition without disobeying their orders."

"That's an anticlimax," Victoria said. "I was a bit worried about them, too. It beats a civil war."

"Except," J.D. said to Thanthavong, "you said, 'almost everybody.'"

"Everyone except the observers, and—"

"EarthSpace observers?"

"U.S. Congress observers. Senators. Two of them."

What J.D. felt, she would not have dared use as description in one of her novels. She hated cliché, and "shock of recognition" was practically prehistoric. Nevertheless, she did feel as if she were in shock. The blood drained from her face; her stomach clenched.

"Oh, god," J.D. said. That tears it, she thought. How could I forget? Because I *wanted* to forget. We'll *have* to go home, now. "I saw them on the transport. Orazio and Derjaguin."

"Yes. One for us, one against."

"Maybe two against, after what's happened," J.D. said sadly. "I guess they're pretty upset."

"Gerald did mention something of the sort. . . . He said, I quote, more or less, 'I cannot imagine anything worse than shepherding two American senators. Except, perhaps, shepherding one British MP'" Thanthavong sighed. "The U.S. government frowns upon people who kidnap members of its government."

"It wasn't our fault, dammit!" Victoria said. "*Their* carrier ordered the transport pilot to stay docked."

"Orazio and Derjaguin are politicians," Thanthavong said. "They're pragmatic. They dislike their situation, but they're in no danger—no more than any of the rest of us. They won't behave foolishly. But . . . I *am* worried about Alzena."

"Alzena!" Victoria exclaimed. "Was she hurt? Was she in the web?"

"She has . . . withdrawn."

"Why?"

"Her family will be angry with her."

"Seems to me her family is always angry with her," Victoria said, sounding angry herself. "Seems to me her family would be angry with her no matter what she did, unless she hid away in a closed room."

"Perhaps," Thanthavong said.

They made their way through the transition zone between the stationary axis of *Starfarer,* and the main cylinder. Zero g gave way to microgravity, and they moved onto the slope that formed the end of *Starfarer*'s cylindrical body. Switchback trails led from the axis and down the end slope to the floor of the cylinder, the living area.

As J.D. descended, the microgravity increased. It became

a definite force, seven-tenths of Earth's gravity, imparted by *Starfarer*'s spin.

Below her, Stephen Thomas and Feral and Zev bounded down the hillside, sure-footed as mountain goats.

"Alzena ought to dump her whole crew of relatives!" Victoria exclaimed.

"Could you abandon your family because they had opinions other people don't agree with?" Thanthavong asked.

"My family *does* have opinions other people don't agree with," Victoria said. "Lots. But their opinions don't require me to give up my autonomy. It's hardly the same."

"Not to you. Not to me. But it is the same to Alzena. Try to understand."

"I have tried. Believe me. I've done my best. And she's done her best to explain. It doesn't work. It's as if I'd gone back a couple hundred years, and my ancestors were trying to tell me that they'd changed their minds about risking the underground railway. That they'd decided to stay slaves."

"Alzena does not think of herself as a slave. And through no fault of her own, she's disobeyed a command she believed she must follow. I'm concerned about her, Victoria."

Victoria shrugged uncomfortably. "She's depressed. She'll get over it."

"I hope so," Thanthavong said. "*Starfarer* will be in difficult straits without our director of ecology."

"She can speak at the meeting," Victoria said. Bitterness tinged her voice. "Maybe she doesn't care about *Starfarer*'s ecosystem anymore. Maybe she'll convince everyone we should go home. Maybe her family will win after all."

Victoria and Professor Thanthavong continued on ahead. J.D. paused on the slope leading into the starship, struck by the beauty of her new home. At the bottom of the hill, the cylinder curved up to either side, circling the sun tube that carried light to the interior. Overhead, the opposite floor of the cylinder formed a green, growing sky, its contours traced by footpaths, all overlaid by a delicate pattern of puffy white clouds. Small streams led in erratic spirals from their sources at this end, occasionally pausing at a lake, spreading through the mud flats and wetlands at the far end, spilling finally into the sea. Bushes and grass covered the gentle hills, and young evergreens with spring-pale needles sprouted in the meadows. J.D. found the hill that covered her own underground house, and then, inevitably, her gaze traveled to the circle of jumbled ground where the genetics building had collapsed. Genetics Hill looked as if an inexorable force of erosion had begun to dissolve it back to earth and basic elements.

The ASes had cleared away some rubble, but J.D. could see no signs that they had begun to rebuild. The site lay silent and deserted.

J.D. looked away from the destruction.

It was evening. The light from the sun tubes began to dim. J.D. set off down the hill again, lengthening her strides to catch up with Victoria and Thanthavong. They chose the path that would lead most quickly to *Starfarer*'s amphitheater.

On the paths below, other people, the rest of *Starfarer*'s faculty and staff, headed for that same central meeting point.

7

As the faculty and staff of *Starfarer* gathered in the amphitheater, the sun tubes lowered the daytime illumination. The starship's luminous evening began.

J.D. took a seat halfway down the hillside. Zev hopped onto the terrace beside her and sat with his knees drawn up and his arms wrapped around them, his bare toes curled over the corner of the seat. His claws extended, scraping the riser.

The amphitheater was nearly half full. People congregated in the seats near the center as if they were in a funnel; a few scattered in the higher terraces. J.D. recognized quite a number of her colleagues, considering how short a time she had been on board, and how immersed she had been in work and plans—or conspiracy.

Her teammates entered the amphitheater with her, but split up to sit apart as was their custom: Victoria toward the center, Satoshi in the middle of the slope, Stephen Thomas on the other side and near the top, with Feral and the genetics graduate students. J.D. also found Kolya Petrovich and Iphigenie DuPre and Dr. Thanthavong. Griffith stood at the very top of the amphitheater, on the ramp surrounding the top row of seats. J.D. wished he would either join the meeting or leave; his lurking made her nervous.

Avvaiyar entered, looked around, and moved easily down the ramp. She was striking, a human version of an omnipotent goddesses from ancient India. J.D. could easily imagine Avvaiyar dancing and exchanging flirtatious glances with a demigod of life or death, four-armed, eight-armed, naked except for gold bangles on her ankles and a silken scarf around her narrow waist, to set off the flare of her hips.

140

She sat beside Victoria; the two spoke quietly together, bent over a tiny display that glowed in Avvaiyar's hands.

Crimson Ng and Chandra sat just below J.D., where Crimson could see the meerkat that J.D. still carried. Florrie Brown sat across the way, resolute, gripping the top of a short walking stick, pressing its end into the ground between her feet.

A flash of chartreuse caught the corner of J.D.'s vision: Esther Klein, wearing her ugly, lurid pilot's jacket. Infinity Mendez accompanied her.

Passing Griffith, Infinity paused. To J.D.'s surprise, Infinity grinned at the man who probably was not an accountant from the General Accounting Office. At any rate Infinity did not believe he was, and neither did Florrie Brown. J.D. was inclined to agree with them.

"Hiya, Griffith," Infinity said cheerfully.

Griffith glared at him, as if the greeting were somehow insolent. Infinity continued on; he and the transport pilot greeted Florrie and sat on either side of her.

One person conspicuously absent was Gerald Hemminge. J.D. had begun to think of him as the loyal opposition, for he was the loudest voice among those who thought the expedition should have returned, at least temporarily, to low Earth orbit. He was also the mouthpiece for *Starfarer*'s chancellor. Chancellor Blades was also absent, but that did not surprise J.D. He was always absent. She had never met him. She had thought perhaps he might come to this meeting, but apparently he had decided to maintain his reserve.

The light from the sun tubes faded completely, sinking the amphitheater into intense darkness. The only spot of illumination was the display between Victoria and Avvaiyar, shining like fox fire.

The last time the personnel of *Starfarer* had met to discuss the starship's fate, someone had flooded the theater with brilliant light, as if to frighten them from their rebellion. The tactic had not worked.

"Hey!" someone called out in protest. At the same time, half the people in the theater ordered Arachne to turn up the lights. Reflexively, hardly thinking about it, J.D. did the same. At the same time, she glanced up.

The light brightened to glaring intensity, brighter and hotter than any midday. J.D. flung up her hands and turned her head away, but too late. The brilliance of the sun tubes dazzled her.

"Damn!" Temporarily blinded, she blinked, squeezed her eyes shut, put her hands to her eyes, and pressed her palms against her eyelids. Afterimages flashed from black to bright to black again. She opened her eyes. The afterimages flashed more vividly, tangling with her view of the theater. Zev grabbed her arm and steadied her.

She gripped his hand. Her eyes filled with tears that spilled down her cheeks.

"Oh, what a dumb thing to do. Zev, did you look? Can you see?"

"I didn't look," he said. "I'm not going to."

"Good." J.D. could not see far, but she could tell, from the sounds of cursing and questions, that she was not the only person to make the mistake. Along with everyone else, she wondered whether Arachne's feedback mechanisms had healed incompletely.

The alternative was that the overwhelming intensity of light was meant, again, to frighten them.

If that were true, whoever crashed the web was still on board.

J.D. hoped it was a malfunction. She did not remember it as being this bad before, this bright, this hot. Sweat beaded on her forehead and trickled down her face, onto her eyelashes, mixing with the tears. She wiped her eyes on her sleeve. A drop of perspiration ran down her spine.

J.D. tried to reach Arachne, demanding the reason for the change, objecting to it. But the queue was jammed. Surprised, J.D. backed off. Arachne had plenty of channels to accommodate multiple demands. For the computer not to answer... J.D. reached out again, gently this time, fearing the shock of a second web crash.

The web reached back, sturdy and undamaged, except for the blocked strands leading to information about the sun tubes.

Maybe it is just a malfunction, J.D. thought. Maybe Arachne hasn't healed quite enough to handle all those queries at once.

"Or maybe it's Gerald..." J.D. said softly.

"What?" Zev asked.

"At the last meeting—before you got here—we got spotlighted. It was meant to scare us, because we weren't supposed to be having the meeting. If Arachne's all right, Gerald's the most likely person to want to disrupt the meeting."

Maybe that was why he had not come. But his absence only served to draw attention to him. Besides, though he disagreed with almost everyone left on board, though he was one of the people who had been trapped on the transport, he disagreed vocally and unequivocally. Sneakiness was not Gerald Hemminge's style.

Though the changes in the sun tubes could be effected from anywhere on board, surely they could not be changed by just anyone. J.D. tried one more query, for information about who was permitted to alter the lighting; again Arachne rebuffed her.

The amphitheater fell silent.

"They're all looking at you, J.D.," Zev whispered.

J.D. took a deep breath, wiped her dazzled eyes on her sleeve, and stood up. The amphitheater remained a blur.

"J.D. Sauvage," she said, and paused, as was customary for someone wishing to speak. It was a tradition observed for its own sake, a ritual. Everybody knew everyone else; everyone had the right to speak without interruption, and everyone else had the right to disagree.

"We can't stay here," J.D. said. "My proposal is that we keep going. Not home, but to another star system. That we continue the expedition." She blinked again, trying to make out people's faces, trying to see who was on her side, who disagreed. Everyone already knew her proposal for the meeting. Stating it aloud was another ritual.

"That's all," she said simply, and sat down again.

Arachne routinely broadcast meetings throughout the starship. Though one had to be present to have a say in the decisions, one could observe from a distance. J.D. was about to hook into the transmission and watch the meeting from within her mind. She was reluctant to make such a close connection with Arachne, since the possibility remained that the computer would crash again. The aberrant light was very bright, and heat pooled in the amphitheater.

She wiped the sweat and tears out of her eyes and looked around again. To her relief, her vision began to clear.

Victoria rose and turned once around, as if picking out each of her colleagues individually.

"Victoria Fraser MacKenzie," she said, and waited.

No one spoke.

She raised one hand; in it she held a hard-copy module from the computer. "These are the solutions to the transition approach. We can return to Earth, a failure, or we can choose J.D.'s path, and—"

"There is no choice." Gerald Hemminge appeared at the mouth of an entrance tunnel at the top of the terrace.

"You're interrupting," Victoria said.

Gerald started down the ramp. Two other people followed. Their tailored clothes marked them as visitors. Most of the starship personnel chose attire of uncompromising informality.

Derjaguin, senior senator from New Mexico, who was unalterably opposed to the deep space expedition, and Orazio, junior senator of Washington state, who was one of the expedition's strongest supporters, followed Gerald into the amphitheater.

"You've used up the possibilities," Gerald said. "We have to return to Earth—unless you think being stranded light-years from home is an option."

"Sit down and listen, Gerald," Stephen Thomas said from his place high in the theater. "Take your turn like everybody else."

"You shut up, or I'll blacken your eye again!"

Stephen Thomas jumped to his feet.

"What the fuck do you mean, 'again,' you bureaucratic brownnose?"

Feral grabbed his arm. Gerald threw his hands in the air, backing up a pace, though he was twenty meters away. Stephen Thomas shrugged off Feral's restraining hold.

J.D. was midway between the two. She prepared herself to try to keep them apart.

"Stephen Thomas!" Victoria exclaimed. "Gerald! For heaven's sake!"

"I'm sorry!" Gerald said. "That was a foolish thing for me to say. I didn't mean to imply I'd blackened your eye the first time." He lowered his hands, slowly, gradually, as if he were holding Stephen Thomas off with an invisible force field.

"Damn right you didn't," Stephen Thomas said. Scowling, he allowed Feral to pull him back to his seat.

"We're all under a great deal of strain," Gerald said. He turned toward J.D. "You can't seriously be proposing *not* to go home."

"Yes," J.D. said. "I can. I am."

"If you and your guests sit down and join the meeting," Victoria said, "there's plenty of time for everybody to have their say."

"Very well," Gerald muttered.

"And now you're here," Satoshi said, "you can turn down the lights. You made your point."

"I didn't turn them up," Gerald said. "It isn't my responsibility to turn them down."

"Dr. Fraser MacKenzie—" Senator Derjaguin said.

"You have the advantage of me, sir."

J.D. repressed a smile. Victoria knew who she was talking to. But Victoria had a habit of stressing her Canadian heritage, and of playing down her knowledge of U.S. politics, when confronted with the assumptions of U.S. citizens.

"I'm Senator William Derjaguin, of course, and this is—"

"I can introduce myself, Jag, thanks," Senator Orazio said. "Ruth Orazio, Dr. MacKenzie."

"An honor to meet you, Senator." Victoria's Canadian accent was more noticeable than usual. "You and Senator Derjaguin are welcome to observe the meeting. As guests."

"Mr. Hemminge's right, there's no point to—" Derjaguin said.

"This is neither the Senate chamber nor the United States," Victoria said, her voice low and tight. "Now please *sit down.*"

"I'm afraid we must insist, Senator." Professor Thanthavong rose to back Victoria up. "We have rules of procedure to maintain."

Derjaguin, accustomed to being treated as an elder statesman, had considerable justification for his expectation. But even a senior senator could meet his match in a Nobel laureate.

"Very well, ma'am, if you wish it."

Gerald and the two senators sat down a few rows in front of J.D.

"Avvaiyar and I have a proposal for where we should go," Victoria said.

An image of a star system formed in the center of the

theater. The bright light washed out its clarity, but it remained comprehensible: the solar system, a small yellow star, Earth in its accustomed place, third from the sun. A bit of cosmic string, made visible by false color, hovered above the plane of the system. After the profusion of string in Tau Ceti's system, Earth's meager strand looked terribly inadequate.

"This is a re-creation of what observers from Earth saw when *Starfarer* entered transition," Victoria said.

A minuscule silver dot approached the string, and suddenly vanished in a flash of lambent light. The release of transition potential had a distinct spectral signature.

Victoria glanced toward Avvaiyar, who rose and spoke her name and waited a bare moment. The holographic display changed abruptly, fading from the solar system to the system of Tau Ceti. Avvaiyar gestured toward it. She was not quite as perfect as a goddess; her fingernails, instead of being long and buffed above rouged fingertips, were bitten short.

"This is what *Starfarer*'s instruments observed a few minutes after our arrival," Avvaiyar said.

The same lambent light burst from a node on the tangle of Tau Ceti's cosmic string.

J.D. gasped. All around her, people reacted to the implications of the pattern.

"They were here," J.D. said, her voice barely a whisper. "Alien beings were here, waiting for us—how could they know to wait for us?—and when we got here . . . they ran."

"Who, J.D.?" Zev asked. "I don't know what this means."

"The alien people, Zev. The ones who built the museum."

A spectrogram streaked its colored bands down one side of the holographic display.

"The theoretical spectral signature," Avvaiyar said. A second spectrogram, not quite identical, but nearly so, scrolled down next to it. "The signature of the emission we just observed. The signature of a spacecraft attached to a cosmic string, reaching transition energy."

"The spacecraft of alien beings," J.D. said aloud, forgetting not to interrupt.

"Oh, *now*!" Gerald Hemminge exclaimed. "Alien beings waiting for us?" He snorted.

"Quite likely it was an observation post," Avvaiyar said. "It must have been here—who knows how long? Automated. An

AI. Like the dome. It detects us, it went to report on us."

J.D. grimaced. She could imagine what the report might say: "These folks are dangerous. Go back and slag them the way we slagged the dome."

"And it did go *somewhere*," Victoria said. "Whatever or whoever it was, it went somewhere. We could follow. If we just had a chance to explain..."

Avvaiyar's system map expanded. The tangle of cosmic string had unraveled and dispersed.

Victoria glanced up the terrace toward J.D.

"J.D., what do you think?"

"She has no more experience than the rest of us!" Gerald said. "All this is new."

Victoria smiled. "New to us. J.D. has thought about it."

A ripple passed through the system map. The relative positions of cosmic string and planetary orbits changed, as the scan recorded the string's motion. When the image settled, the strands had pulled even farther apart. Some dangled into the system from below, some from above.

They were flying off toward the poles of the galaxy, and there was no way to stop them.

"We should follow the alien ship," J.D. said. "Where did it go?"

"To Sirius," Victoria said.

"Sirius!" Sirius was a binary system, not expected to host Earth-type planets. Sirius A was large and young and hot, Sirius B tiny and dim. Beings who called it home would be very different from humans.

"Arachne's solved the transition algorithm," Victoria said. "Sirius is a 'full' system. That is, cosmic string exists. If we go there, no matter what we find, we'll still have the freedom to enter transition and move elsewhere when we choose. All we have to do is continue the expedition."

She and Avvaiyar waited for questions.

Chandra rose.

"Am I understanding you right? You want to go off chasing aliens that you don't know still exist, who might be flying a ship that you can't even prove was there?"

Her blank, translucent gray gaze rested on Victoria, and the hypertrophied nerve clusters on her face darkened.

"I thought Chandra wanted to be in space," Zev whispered.

"I think she's just stirring things up to make a good sensory recording!" J.D. said, outraged. "Look, she's taking this all in!"

"She takes in everything, J.D.," Zev said.

"Maybe." J.D. was unwilling to be placated.

"We know the alien beings were here, Chandra!" Victoria said. "We know a ship left this system right after we arrived . . . with our bomb."

"We know the aliens were here sometime within the last million years," Chandra said, "and Avvaiyar photographed a light flash that maybe was a ship. Those two spectrograms didn't look all that identical to me."

"There's always a bit of noise," Avvaiyar said. "This is the real world—not a sensory recording."

"It's risky," Victoria said. "Of course it's risky. I'll admit that as many times as you want. We all knew it when we signed on."

"Not this kind of risk."

"Exactly this kind of risk. Look at the alternative! Do you want to go home and go to jail?"

Chandra started to reply, then frowned thoughtfully, off in her own imagination. Maybe she was wondering what a prison recording would be like, and whether it would sell.

"Chandra," Victoria said, "let's take a chance on a successful expedition. After we get back—you can go to jail and the rest of us will rent your experiences."

Everybody laughed. Almost everybody. Chandra was not among them, nor Gerald. J.D. glanced at the senators. Orazio did not even smile.

Victoria stood for an hour, answering questions, referring the cosmology to Avvaiyar. J.D.'s sense of the meeting was that most people wanted to continue, but she was afraid to feel secure in her perception. She wanted the result too badly.

She remained mindful of Gerald and the two senators, aware of their potential. When Derjaguin rose to question Victoria, J.D. felt, not precisely relief, but a break in tension that had been building in her. Zev patted her hand. She took his long webbed fingers and held them tightly.

"There's no question of continuing the expedition," Derjaguin said, his voice flat. "The threat of the Mideast Sweep is too great—this spaceship can help us combat it. You people talk as if it belonged to you. It doesn't. It belongs to the members of EarthSpace, your own countries that you left behind without a second thought." He leaned forward, radiating his intense charisma. "If you go back now, I assure you that Senator Orazio and I will intercede on your behalf in the matter of kidnaping."

"We all know your opinion of *Starfarer*," Victoria said. "But—"

"Ah, and here I thought you'd never heard of me," Derjaguin said.

Some people laughed despite themselves, but J.D. found herself blushing in embarrassment for Victoria's sake.

Victoria tightened the muscles of her jaw.

The laugh died away.

"I'm sorry to have to tell you this, Senator, but you aren't a member of the expedition. You have no say on the question."

"That's absurd."

Senator Orazio rose. The considerable presence of Washington's junior senator silenced the hum of discussion.

"You know I disagree with my honored colleague on a number of subjects, most vehemently, *Starfarer*. I've always supported basic research in general and the deep space expedition in particular. It seems to me that returning is your best option. You *have* found that life exists outside the solar system. You *have* found that alien beings exist. If we go home, a second expedition is possible. It's even possible that the news you bring will encourage world peace."

"Or increase suspicion," Thanthavong said. "Against us, against EarthSpace. Even against you."

"Suspicion? Why?"

"Senator, imagine the reaction if we return with nothing we can prove."

Orazio started to object, then hesitated.

"You have proof!" Senator Derjaguin exclaimed. "You have the alien message. The telemetry from the planet. Samples from the dome. And the sculpture!"

"Not even very imaginative," Thanthavong said.

"I don't follow you."

"They could have made it all up," Orazio said.

"Everything we have, we could have created ourselves," Thanthavong said. Her voice held no satisfaction. "Unless the samples J.D. gathered in the dome prove to be something unimaginably beyond our ability to duplicate, we have nothing that cannot be challenged as fabrication."

"And they would be challenged," Orazio said, also without satisfaction.

"Yes. We're all very talented," Thanthavong said. "J.D. with her novels and the rest of us with our laboratories. . . . We could easily create a persuasive record of everything we've found."

"Nonexistent aliens," J.D. said. "To fool the world's governments into forming an alliance."

"It has been done, I believe, in fiction," Thanthavong said.

"An old plot." J.D. refrained from adding that the usual result, even in fiction, was more weapons of war. "And the aliens are customarily much stranger than a meerkat."

"The expedition cannot be considered a success without persuasive proof of extraterrestrial life or extraterrestrial civilization."

"In that case," Orazio said, "I'm afraid I have to agree with Jag. *Starfarer* has to return to Earth. I came into space to try to help the expedition continue. But I never had any intentions of joining it for the long term."

"I know," Victoria said. "And I'm sorry."

"Is that all you've got to say?" Gerald exclaimed. "You're *sorry?*"

"Victoria shrugged. "That's about it."

"But—"

"Look at yourself, Gerald. You accepted the argument that the military needed *Starfarer* to use against the Mideast Sweep. But that's a debatable point. You heard what Kolya Petrovich said about it! If you were as distressed as you pretend, you never would have continued to act as liaison between *Starfarer* and the *Chi*."

"It was my responsibility," he said angrily. "And in retrospect, perhaps it was a responsibility I should have eschewed."

"Too bad you didn't," Stephen Thomas said, just loud enough to be heard.

"Victoria, *Starfarer* is carrying an entire transport full of passengers who have been kidnaped—"

"I don't feel kidnaped," Avvaiyar said. "I feel glad to be back on board. Most of the other people were returning under duress, too."

"*I* feel kidnaped!" Senator Derjaguin said.

"Agreeing with the senator from New Mexico twice in one day troubles me," Orazio said, "but given my choice I'd've had the transport undock."

"*Starfarer* had no responsibility for your predicament," Victoria said, her voice flat and hard. "We gave you notice. We gave you time. It was the military carrier that ordered the transport pilot not to undock."

Beyond Victoria, the transport pilot shifted uncomfortably. She stood up and waited for silence.

"My name is Esther Klein." Esther's shrug shimmered the loose lime-green satin of her jacket. "What Victoria said is true. I'm the transport pilot. We should have been gone. I had plenty of time to take us out of there."

"Why didn't you?" Derjaguin asked angrily.

"Because the carrier *Hector* ordered me not to. Because..." She was not meeting his eyes, or anyone's. Then she raised her head and looked the senator in the face. "Because I fucked up big," she said. "I wish I hadn't. But I did." She turned toward Victoria. "And that's what I'll testify to. Whenever we get back."

J.D. wanted to cross the amphitheater and hug the young pilot for admitting what she clearly considered an inexcusable lapse in judgment. Victoria gave her a short glance of acknowledgment and faced the senators again.

"You're here by mistake," Victoria said. "But it's the mistake of your own country's military, not a mistake we made. I'm sorry that you may have to pay the consequences of their illegal action."

"*Their* illegal action!" Gerald exclaimed. "Good lord, Victoria, you have nerve. You're the one who stole the starship."

"So I stole the starship!" Victoria cried. "So shoot me! Keep saying I stole it, that doesn't make it true. That doesn't change why most of us stayed on board—out of choice. We upheld *Starfarer*'s charter, instead of creating a war machine!"

"I must warn you, you're at risk of seeing *Starfarer* put under martial law."

Victoria stared at him, speechless.

"Martial law!" Professor Thanthavong looked close to laughter. "You can't threaten martial law! We've got no militia!"

"Perhaps you aren't aware, Professor, that the administration has certain measures we can take, under extraordinary circumstances."

Thanthavong sat back, startled, and J.D. became uncomfortably aware of the hot sun beating on her shoulders. She brushed her hand across the top of her head. Her hair was hot, her scalp damp and itchy with sweat.

"Such as what?" Satoshi said. His voice was very low, stripped of its usual humor, and scary. "Such as crashing the web?"

"No!" Gerald exclaimed. "Good god, Satoshi, no, not at all! I meant only that we can take control of the mobile AIs and the ASes—"

J.D. imagined a squad of squat little machines advancing on the amphitheater with dusters and vacuums, instructed to disrupt the meeting.

She started to laugh. She could not help it. Her colleagues imagined similar scenes. The whole meeting burst into laughter. Gerald glared at Victoria, as if it were all her fault. He waited in silence for the hilarity to die down, his forehead furrowed with anger and embarrassment.

"There are resources," he muttered.

Victoria had not laughed at the assistant chancellor. She had not even been close to laughing.

"You're welcome to have your say," she said coldly. "The senators are welcome to have their say. Even Mr. Griffith is welcome to have his say. You can all persuade us. Or threaten us. You can *try*."

She sat down.

The amphitheater filled with hot silence.

"Tell them what to do, J.D.," Zev whispered.

"I already told them what I want," she said softly. He expected her to behave like Lykos, leading and directing her colleagues. She almost wished she had that power.

"Alzena Dadkhah."

The director of ecology, dressed in black robes that covered her completely, rose and waited for a few seconds after speaking her name. No one interrupted her. She stood with her head down, her shoulders slumped, everything about her revealing deep distress. She had been on the transport, heading home, believing that her honor and that of her family depended on her leaving. Nothing about the circumstances that kept her on the starship had changed that debt of honor, except to make it heavier.

"I would like to remain here."

"I'm so glad, Alzena—" Victoria said.

"Here," Alzena said again. "Whether you of the expedition decide to go on, or return home, I wish to remain in the Tau Ceti system. On Tau Ceti II."

"Alzena, it's impossible," Thanthavong said.

"I must not go on," the ecologist said. "And I cannot go home. I have no choice but to stay here."

Her voice was quiet, and intense, held tautly under control.

"You can't stay here all alone. You'd be in a wilderness," Satoshi said. "Did you listen to my reports? There's no evidence that any sentient being has ever visited Tau Ceti II."

"I don't care. I've lived in deserts. I've lived in mountains. I can live on a new world."

"We can't prove you'd be able to eat anything down there," Stephen Thomas said. "We can't even prove you'd be able to *grow* anything."

"I don't care."

"This discussion—" Thanthavong said.

"Wait a minute!" Chandra exclaimed. "That's not a half-bad idea. If she stays, I'll stay too."

J.D. was not the only person shocked when Chandra interrupted Professor Thanthavong. Thanthavong regarded the sensory artist with an expression part amused and part outraged.

"It would be great," Chandra said. "God, there would be material there to work with that nobody else has ever imagined, let alone experienced!"

"You've only just come on board!" Victoria said. "Why did you join in the first place, if you want to abandon the expedition when we've barely gotten started?"

Chandra shrugged. "Space is boring," she said. "I didn't know it would be boring."

"Boring!" Kolya Petrovich, breaking his silence for the first time, reacted with horrified incomprehension.

"Yeah. Boring. There's nothing at all out there, and there's nothing much in here. It's like living in the suburbs. I could have moved to a second-rate college town if I wanted this atmosphere." She gestured with both arms, taking in the amphitheater, the faculty and staff, the whole ship.

"Thank you for your opinion," Thanthavong said dryly. "We like to think we're at least a first-rate college town."

Chandra shrugged, oblivious to the sarcasm. "Whatever. Look, we've got to quit pretending that nothing's changed from our original plans."

"I agree with Chandra and Alzena." Floris Brown spoke without standing up, then remembered the conventions and rose to her feet, slowly, solidly. Like Alzena, she dressed in black, but where Alzena's clothing was intended to make her invisible, Florrie's was designed to draw attention. She also wore black eye makeup, applied today in a style reminiscent of Cleopatra. The three long locks of her hair, one natural white, one pink, one green, draped over her shoulders, heavy with bright beads.

"Florrie Brown," she said, waited, and continued. "I want to stay, too. I'd go along to the new world, if they'll have an old woman."

"But you joined the expedition!" Victoria said.

"No. I came to a new home. Tau Ceti II looks more permanent to me than this starship." She sat down.

Griffith stood up. "My name is Marion Griffith," he said. "I'm not a member of your expedition. Can I say something anyway?"

"You, Mister Narc!"

J.D. jumped at Florrie's shout. She had never heard the elderly woman speak so forcefully, even at her welcoming party when she grew cross with Victoria and snapped at her.

Griffith turned toward Florrie, equally startled.

"You, Mister Narc," Florrie said again. "Where do you get off, coming up to *Starfarer* and trying to ruin everything? We're not talking about what you want right now, we're not talking about packing up and going home!"

"Let him talk, Ms. Brown," Victoria said. "Everybody has a right to speak their piece."

"You're sillier than I thought, young lady, if you want to let him talk."

Victoria stiffened, angry and insulted.

"He'll just try to make us go home," Florrie said, "like he tried to make us stay." She glared at Griffith. "You narc."

"I'm trying to agree with you," he said.

"You . . . what?"

"I want to go with you. I have skills you'd find useful."

"I—I don't care! We don't want you! We don't trust you!"

"You nearly killed me," Iphigenie said. "Go into space, and good riddance to you. Go without a spacesuit!"

"I didn't crash the web!" Griffith said. "I did a lot of things to stop this expedition. I was wrong, and I knew it before the web crashed. There's no way to convince you of that. But I didn't do it." He turned toward Kolya Petrovich, silently asking for support, trying and failing to hide how much he hoped to get it.

Kolya leaned against the terrace behind him and regarded Griffith with grave concern, his arms folded on his chest.

"I believe him," he said.

"Why, Kolya?" Florrie said. "They pay him to lie."

"And so they paid me, when I was his age, and had a job and a mission like he had," Kolya said. "But I changed. He has changed. I believe him."

"*Someone* did it," Iphigenie said. "Someone infested Arachne with hibernating moles, and planted a trigger to tell them when it was spring, or sent Arachne a Trojan horse and opened it. He's the most likely person."

"Maybe I am, but I didn't do it," Griffith said. "And I'll tell you this—if anybody had asked my advice when this starship was being planned, I'd have told them to take whatever they used to crash the web, and make it redundant. That stuff would still be in it. I'd watch it, if I were you."

Iphigenie stared at him as if he had directly threatened her life. Griffith faced her, and the whole meeting, with his fists clenched at his sides and his shoulders hunched, defensive and angry.

"Never *mind* the narc," Florrie said. "Who else will go? If there are enough of us they'll have to let us. It doesn't matter about him. If he dares to come along . . ." She left unsaid whatever fate she might imagine for Marion Griffith.

Florrie rose. She turned toward Esther. "You could fly us down in your transport, couldn't you, my dear?"

"I could but—"

Infinity turned sharply toward her, shocked, but Florrie interrupted Esther and looked for more allies.

"Good. Kolya, won't you come, too?"

"It's very tempting," Kolya said. "It's *very* tempting to

think of touching a planet's surface again. To live on a world where I don't have to worry if each person I meet might be the one sent to kill me. But...I want to stay with the expedition, Florrie. I want the expedition to continue."

Next to J.D., Zev shifted in his place. She felt him gather himself. She glanced at him, quickly, shocked.

"Zev, you wouldn't leave!"

For a moment he remained motionless, not meeting her eyes. Then he reached out and took her hand and enfolded it between both his own, covering her fingers with the warm amber silk of his swimming webs.

"No," he said. "I'd like to swim there. But I won't leave. I won't leave you."

Chandra stood up. She nudged Crimson Ng, who shrugged a denial. Alzena wearily pushed herself to her feet. Griffith remained standing. Satoshi's underage graduate student, trapped on *Starfarer* by her own plan rather than by accident, slid off the edge of her seat and stood in a sort of crouch.

"Fox, what are you doing?" Florrie asked.

"I want to stay with the expedition," Fox said. "But I want to stay here with you, Aunt Florrie, if *Starfarer* goes back to Earth."

Satoshi lowered his head and covered his eyes with one hand.

"Good lord!" Derjaguin said, when he saw Fox. "You're—"

"No, I'm not!" Fox exclaimed.

"Not only have you people kidnaped two U.S. senators, you've kidnaped President Distler's—"

"I'm not, I'm not, I just look like her, everybody says so!"

"—niece."

"Thanks a *lot*," Fox said, with feeling. She looked around the amphitheater. "I'd divorce my whole family, if I could," she said to her colleagues. "They wouldn't have let me stay with the expedition even if I had been twenty-one. You didn't kidnap me, I stayed on purpose."

J.D. could see how that would go over in court; she could hear the prosecuting attorney making reference to the Stockholm syndrome and claiming that Fox had identified with her kidnapers to protect herself.

Fox sat down. A few others stood up.

Only a dozen people chose secession; a dozen too many.

"We don't care about the risks," Florrie said. "We want to stay."

"That's quite enough," Professor Thanthavong said. Contrary to custom, she remained seated, unwilling to take any action that resembled support for the new movement. "The risks are immaterial. You're wasting our time. *Starfarer* is a scientific expedition, not a colony ship. This is not a wagon train. Whatever we decide, no one is staying behind."

"I *must* stay here." Alzena's voice quavered; she was near tears.

"I'm sorry," Thanthavong said. She crossed the center stage and sat down next to the ecologist. She took her hand. "I do know what you're facing, and I'm sorry. But no one can stay behind."

Without replying, Alzena drew her hand from Thanthavong's. She rose, climbed to the exit tunnel, and disappeared into its mouth. Her dark shape vanished in the shadows.

J.D. wanted to go after her, but she had no idea what she could say to Alzena, no way to ease her despair. And J.D. could not, would not, leave the meeting.

"Who appointed you the leader all of a sudden?" Florrie said to Thanthavong.

"No one," the professor replied. "Nor am I taking on that responsibility. I'm only pointing out what we all know. You should know it, too. You signed the same agreement as the rest of us."

"What if I did? Everything's changed."

"Things have changed. But they will not change as much as you propose."

Iphigenie rose to her feet. "Iphigenie DuPre."

Reluctant and grudging, the members of the secession resumed their seats.

"We have to decide now," Iphigenie said. "I have to make the course changes soon, I have to pick the proper transition point. What's it to be? Back to Earth, the expedition ended? Or farther into space, to try to catch the alien ship?"

"Farther into space," J.D. said immediately, and rose to her feet.

"Farther," Zev said. He stood beside J.D.

"Yes!" Fox jumped up a fraction ahead of Satoshi and Victoria, Stephen Thomas and Feral. Almost everyone else rose with them.

Even Florrie and Chandra and Griffith supported continuing, over going home. In the end, fewer people supported a return to Earth than had supported the secession.

"This is illegal and an outrage!" Derjaguin shouted.

"I block the decision," Gerald said.

"Please, Gerald," Victoria said. "Don't."

"You aren't going to let me, are you?"

"Let you send the ship into suicide?"

"We can't let you block us from making a choice," Iphigenie said. "We have to pick one or the other. If we don't choose, we keep moving through the Tau Ceti system at subliminal speed. We go nowhere, we lose our chance of going *anywhere*, when the cosmic string vibrates out of our reach."

"At least stand aside," Victoria said.

"No," Gerald said. "I want it on the record that the first time your ideals came to the test, they failed."

"Then you have your wish," Thanthavong said.

"I'll set the sail," Iphigenie said, and hurried from the theater.

"You can't *do* this," Derjaguin said. "At least—at least give us the transport and let us go home!"

"They can't, Jag." Orazio's voice was flat with dismay.

"You can't reach transition potential without a lot of mass. The transport is far too small. *Starfarer* itself is near the lower limit of what you need." Victoria spoke much more sympathetically than she had before. "I'm sorry, Senator. It's impossible."

No one spoke to Griffith after the meeting. He was prepared for abuse, for threats. He was not prepared simply to be shunned. Even Floris Brown, on the arm of the transport pilot, walked past without a look. The only acknowledgment of his presence was silence: conversations faded away as people passed, and started up again when he was out of earshot.

No matter how the personnel of the expedition felt about him, he found himself admiring them. He had spent the greater part of the past two years devising ways to undermine their morale. Even though a number of his suggestions had been put into practice, even though some of his suggestions had worked, the faculty and staff was somehow managing to hold things together.

I guess I'd feel pretty good, too, Griffith thought, if I'd taken an unarmed ship against a missile carrier . . . and won.

He wiped his forehead on his sleeve, blotting up the sweat; he rested his elbows on his knees and slumped forward, staring at the ground between his feet. The heat in the amphitheater had climbed beyond body temperature; it must be at least 45°C.

What am I going to do now? he wondered. A new world. A new start, and the expedition would have been rid of me. It would have been perfect for all of us.

Someone sat down beside him.

"I didn't have anything to do with the sun tubes, either," he said without looking up. "I wish whoever turned them up would turn them down, too."

"I believe you," Kolya Petrovich said.

Griffith jerked upright.

The cosmonaut rested his chin on his fist and gazed at Griffith curiously.

"I believe you," Kolya said, "but you confuse me."

"Nobody else believes me. They don't believe you, either. Not when it comes to me. Why do I confuse you?"

"I can understand why you might wish to continue with the expedition. After all, you took great risks to help us escape."

"For all the good *that* did," Griffith said.

"And I can understand why you might wish to return to Earth. Until you spoke, no one else knew you had changed your loyalties."

"No one but you."

"I have long practice at keeping my mouth shut," Kolya Petrovich said.

"And you think I'd let you all go home and go to jail, while I pretended to be a returning hero or a prisoner of war?"

"Nothing quite so melodramatic. I felt it was your decision to make, not mine."

"I'm not a hypocrite. I may be a . . ." He stopped. This was the first time he had had to say, out loud, or even voice to himself, the word they would use for him back on Earth. He thought of himself as an honorable person, resolute and constant. He had never behaved this way before in his life. "Oh, god," he said, and buried his face in his hands.

Kolya Petrovich patted him on the shoulder. "You said you

were to be married next month. You are thinking of your fiancée."

"She won't be my fiancée when she finds out what's happened," Griffith said. "If you thought *I* was gung ho.... She won't understand why you're right and we were wrong. There's no way I'll be able to explain it to her. She'll think... I'm a traitor." His voice broke on the last word.

"It's difficult," Kolya Petrovich said, with sympathy.

"I wish we could send the transport back," Griffith said.

"You would go? Turn yourself in?"

"I'd send word that she shouldn't wait for me. That she's free."

8

J.D. could hardly believe it.

"We won," she said to Zev.

Victoria sprinted up the terrace and joined her.

"We won," J.D. said again.

"We sure did."

Satoshi joined them, and they walked around the curve toward Stephen Thomas.

"It's almost morning," Satoshi said. "By the clock, anyway. Why don't we all have breakfast together? Maybe we can even get Feral to cook."

Victoria hurried toward the group of graduate students standing around Stephen Thomas. Concerned, Satoshi jogged after her.

Stephen Thomas sat leaning forward, his forearms on his knees, his head drooping, his hair falling loose around his face. Feral had his arm around his shoulders.

"Take it easy," Feral said.

"Stephen Thomas—" Victoria said. She sat on his other side.

"It hit me all of a sudden," Stephen Thomas said. "Maybe it's just the heat."

He straightened up, taking a deep breath; he wrapped his arms across his chest and squeezed his eyes closed.

"Turn off the damned lights, okay?"

Whoever was controlling the sun tubes paid him no attention.

J.D. stood nearby, feeling helpless. Zev passed her and moved toward Stephen Thomas, watching him closely.

Stephen Thomas opened his eyes again and looked straight at Zev.

"Zev," he said, "why do you keep looking at me like that? *What* do you *want*?"

The diver drew back, scared.

"Take it easy, Stephen Thomas," Victoria said. "Come on, let's get you home."

Infinity sprinted across the field, ignoring the path, feeling the grass and the ground yield beneath his feet. Exultation overcame apprehension: the expedition would continue. No matter what, the expedition would continue.

Sweat poured down his face and his sides. It was years since he had spent time in a tropical zone; he was accustomed to the temperate climate of *Starfarer*. At the moment it was not temperate. Light blazed down and the temperature continued to increase.

The windows of Alzena's house were shut and curtained, the door closed.

Infinity crossed the porch and knocked on the door. He received no answer.

"Alzena!"

He was worried. He was worried about *Starfarer* and he was worried about Alzena, too. He tried the doorknob.

It opened. He hesitated on the threshold, squinting into the stuffy darkness. The brightness outside could not penetrate the shelter of the wide porch roof.

"Lights."

Nothing happened. The house was not set to his voice. He fumbled for the manual control.

One light glowed in the corner, as if all the others had been taken out or broken. Infinity could barely see.

"Alzena, are you here?" Finally he made out that she was hunched in the window seat, huddled up against the dark curtain.

"Did you change the sun tubes? You've got to put them back to normal. I can't get through."

She remained motionless, never looking at him, never answering. He sat on his heels beside her.

"The whole place is going to be cooked if you don't do something," he said.

"I did nothing before," she said. "I'll do nothing now."

Infinity stood. Alzena flinched away, as if she expected him to hit her, then straightened again as if acceding to any violence he might do her. He backed up, too appalled by her reaction to be insulted.

Alzena had been the last ecologist on board, when she entered the transport to return to Earth. The ecology department should never have been allowed to become so depopulated.

We thought we had time, Infinity thought. We thought we had six months.

He closed his eyes to concentrate, trying once more to reach Arachne, trying to find a way to bring *Starfarer* back to night. The web gave him a strange response, not quite a rebuff, but a request for him to restate his question. He did so, and Arachne refused to understand him.

Infinity was staff, not faculty; he lacked the technical credentials that would allow him to alter the environment.

Infinity left Alzena alone, concerned about her, but more concerned about the starship. He opened the door, bracing himself for heat like the Santa Ana, the unpredictable hot desert wind of California.

Darkness welcomed him.

Beyond the shelter of Alzena's porch, Infinity stood with his head thrown back, staring into the sky. The glow of house windows speckled the far-side hills, but the sun tubes were completely dark. Before, the light had been too much. Now it was too little. The sun tubes reflected nothing, not even specks of starlight.

At least the temperature was dropping, and a shutdown of the tubes was less dangerous, temporarily, than their blasting the cylinder with heat.

But whatever was wrong, with Arachne or with the mechanism itself, had better be tracked down and fixed, fast. Or *Starfarer* would be a tin can full of dying and dead vegetation. The animals, humans included, would not be far behind.

Victoria slipped quietly into the cool, dark bedroom. Stephen Thomas lay in his rumpled bed, the patchwork quilt pulled over his head. Now that the light outside had dimmed, returning night to its proper place, Victoria opened the curtains. Fresh air poured past her face.

She sat down on the edge of the futon. Stephen Thomas did not move; there was no motion except his breathing and the gentle drift of the curtains in the breeze, *Starfarer's* breath.

She was worried about him. Her distress, over Stephen Thomas and over the persistent flaws in Arachne's control of *Starfarer*, warred with her elation at the decision to continue the expedition. She wanted to leap up and cheer.

But she did not want to wake Stephen Thomas.

Professor Thanthavong promised that no pathogens had been growing in the lab. Her attention to safety was legendary; still, suppose she was wrong? Suppose one of the geneticists had been doing research the head of the department did not know about?

Victoria touched Arachne and asked for a health AI. A few tests could not hurt, and Thanthavong had no reason ever to hear of them. They would ease Victoria's mind.

As she rose to rejoin the others, Stephen Thomas turned over and pulled the blanket down just far enough to look out at her. The purple and green bruising around his eyes had faded to sickly yellow. Under the transparent bandage, the gash in his forehead was nearly healed.

"Hi," Victoria said.

He made a hoarse, inarticulate sound; maybe it was "hi."

"Love," Victoria said, "you sound almost as awful as you look. I hope you don't feel that bad."

"No, I feel that bad too." His voice was a croak. "My throat hurts. My hands itch."

She sat down beside him and pushed his hair off his forehead. He was feverish and sweaty. She had never heard of any flu that made your hands itch.

"Can I get you anything?"

He moved around so he could put his head in her lap. The sheet slid away from his bare shoulder. Victoria tucked it around him.

"I asked the housekeeper, but that seems like a long time ago."

"Maybe it's recharging." Victoria queried, but got no reply from their household AS. She frowned. Unusual for it to be *this* stupid, but perhaps it had run its batteries down to zero. It did that once in a while. Victoria kept trying to remember to track down that glitch, but had never gotten around to it.

"I just want something to drink," Stephen Thomas said.

"I'll get you something. What would you like?"

He looked up at her. "Isn't champagne supposed to be good for treating the flu?"

"Grow up," Victoria said fondly.

"Champagne's a grown-up drink." His voice cracked, as if he really were an adolescent.

"I have no idea if it's good for treating the flu, but I do know alcohol dehydrates you. So I doubt it."

"Oh." He was so hoarse now that she could barely hear him.

"Don't talk any more, Stephen Thomas," she said. "It hurts to *hear* you, so I can imagine how you must feel. Let me up, so I can straighten the sheets."

He started to move, then collapsed back into her lap.

"Shit!" he whispered. "God, Victoria, it hurts just to move."

She felt helpless, and she was beginning to feel scared.

Stephen Thomas saw her eyelids flicker. "What are you doing?"

"Asking Arachne about a health AI. I got a busy signal."

"I don't need..." His voice failed him.

"Just a little personal attention, hmm?"

He grinned sheepishly. With Victoria's help, he moved to the edge of the bed. She pulled the sheets straight, then shook out his quilt and smoothed it over him.

"You can't be sick for long," Victoria said. "This is way too domestic for me."

He reached out and squeezed her shoulder. His grip was strong. She patted his fingers gently. The bones felt sharp beneath his skin, and the skin looked red and irritated.

"I'll be right back," she said. She wondered when he had last had anything to eat.

He stroked her arm all the way to her fingertips as she rose to leave, but he did not try to hold her.

Feral had started to make breakfast; it smelled like French toast. Satoshi lounged near, kibitzing while Feral cooked.

Victoria hurried into the main room.

"How is he?" Satoshi asked.

"He's awake. He sounds terrible." She opened the refrigerator. Feral had ordered some food to put in it. No one in the partnership was much of a cook. That had been Merry's province. And now, maybe, Feral's.

"He asked for champagne," Victoria said.

Satoshi chuckled. "He's got the right idea. A celebration." He yawned. "He can't be too sick."

"I don't know. This isn't his usual hypochondria."

She got out some fruit juice, found a glass, and poured the juice into it.

"I'll put his breakfast on a tray," Feral said.

"Don't give Stephen Thomas too much chance to send you fetching and carrying," Satoshi said. "He's the world's worst patient. The housekeeper could take stuff to him, but he likes the attention." Satoshi glanced toward the electrical plug where the household AS recharged its batteries when it was idle. The machine was not there. Satoshi had not seen it puttering around the house, and he knew the bedrooms were tidy. Except Stephen Thomas's, of course, but Stephen Thomas had programmed the housekeeper to leave his things alone.

"Where's the housekeeper?" he said.

"Haven't seen it," Feral said. "But I haven't been looking."

"I haven't seen it either," Victoria said. "And I can't get any answer from the health AIs."

Satoshi put out a query. To his surprise, he received no reply.

"You don't suppose Gerald really did take emergency authority? He wouldn't pull in all the artificials?"

"After the way everybody laughed at him when he suggested it? I doubt it."

Outside, J.D. crossed their yard and stopped at the open window. Zev stood in the darkness behind her.

"I just stopped to see how Stephen Thomas is feeling," J.D. said.

"He's been better," Victoria said.

"Breakfast's almost ready," Feral said. "Would you like some?"

"Come on in," Satoshi said. "Visit the house of pain."

J.D. entered through one of the open floor-to-ceiling windows that formed most of the front of the partnership's underground cottage. Stephen Thomas was the only one who regularly used the door with the fan-shaped top. Zev hovered on the threshold.

"The house of pain?" J.D. said curiously. "Do you read Wells?"

"Satoshi, are you sure you feel okay?" Victoria asked.

"Sure, why shouldn't I?"

"Because I don't know what kind of bug Stephen Thomas has. I don't know where he got it."

"Professor Thanthavong said—" Feral said.

"I know that!" Victoria said. "Everybody screws up once in a while, though. Maybe even Nobel laureates. Maybe somebody was working on something she didn't know about."

"That's hard to believe," Satoshi said.

"You might have broken some culture dish without noticing—"

"Victoria, we were up to our knees in spilled stuff," Satoshi said. "It was melting all over the floor. I noticed it, I just didn't worry about it after Professor Thanthavong said not to. And, look, I'm okay. If there was something there to get, I'd've gotten it, right?"

"I guess so. I probably would have, too. And Zev. Zev, are you feeling okay?"

"I am well," he said. "I am always well."

He spoke in a defensive tone, which Victoria thought strange.

"I must sound completely paranoid," Victoria said. "It's not as if I think we're in some horror movie being stalked by the Creature from the Genetics Lab." She took a deep breath. "I'll be back in a minute." She started for the hallway, carrying the fruit juice. "But I sure never heard of any kind of flu that makes your fingers itch."

J.D. came in and sat down, but Zev remained in the doorway.

"Come on in, Zev," Satoshi said.

Zev hesitated before he replied.

"I'd rather go swimming," he said finally.

"Are you afraid of getting whatever Stephen Thomas has?" Satoshi asked. "If he caught something in the genetics department, and you and I were exposed, we ought to have it by now. If he caught the usual transport flu, that goes around *Starfarer* more or less at random."

"I am not afraid of getting ill," Zev said. "But..." He backed onto the terrace. "I need to swim." He walked away fast, his baggy pants legs flapping around his bare ankles.

"What's the matter with him?" Feral asked.

"He's just a kid, Satoshi," J.D. said. "He's in an environment that's alien to him and he's not used to having anything to worry about. It's the older divers, and mostly the women, who make the decisions where he's from."

"Do you want to go after him?" Satoshi asked.

"I guess I'd better." She glanced wistfully at the kitchen nook, and smiled at Feral. "But I'm famished, and that smells awfully good. I don't suppose it will last long—"

"It'll last long enough." Feral grinned at her. "I'll make sure of it. Come back when you find him."

J.D. set off across campus. It was still dark, but the sun tubes had begun reflecting starlight again. J.D. hoped that the malfunction was minor, a remnant of Arachne's crash or a control sent out of true by the impact of the missile.

J.D. missed the Earth's moon, and all its different phases and shadows. She wondered if any of the plants or animals on board reacted to the rhythm of the moon; she wondered if people would react to its absence. The salt marsh had artificial tides . . .

She touched Arachne and sent Zev a message, asking where he was. She received no answer.

J.D. climbed a small rise. Her eyes grew accustomed to the dim light. *Starfarer*'s herd of miniature horses dozed in the meadow, fifty meters away. J.D. was beginning to get used to them, but she still did not feel entirely comfortable about miniature horses. People liked to have animals around, and Alzena, who had designed the interior, had forbidden mammalian predators. She had only recently allowed an eagle, a few falcons. The starship contained no ferrets, no rats, particularly no dogs or cats. But people like to have pets.

J.D. found it difficult to think of horses as pets.

She received no answer from Zev through Arachne. She asked the computer about the nearest body of water that was deep enough to swim in. Her eyelids flickered as she concentrated on the map she got in return. It appeared as a three-D image in the visual center of her mind, a curving plane that she could follow all the way around to her starting point. She remembered the difficulty she had had in drawing a map for one of her novels. Her characters had lived in an O'Neill colony, a larger version of *Starfarer*'s rotating cylinder. Mapping it presented none of the problems of distortion that occurred in representing a sphere on a flat surface. The problem, instead, was where to slice the cylinder and still preserve spatial relationships. She had never found a perfect solution.

A lake lay half a kilometer away. The wetlands were at the far end of the cylinder, at least an hour's walk. She had not yet had time to visit them. Hoping Zev had chosen the freshwater lake, she set off in its direction.

Sand slid softly beneath her feet. Wavelets lapped at the shore. Frogs groaned and crickets chirped, and far off across the water, something splashed on the surface.

"Zev!"

She called his name in a hoarse whisper. She had no idea how far sound carried on *Starfarer*. It was five o'clock in the morning. If anyone lived on the shore of the lake, and had managed to go back to sleep after the meeting, J.D. did not want to wake them.

Again, she received no answer. She kicked off her shoes and unfastened her pants, then glanced around, a bit nervous, a bit embarrassed. She saw no lights nearby, no sign of habitation. She might have been back in the Puget Sound wilderness. She took off her pants and her shirt and her underwear and left them on a distinctive rock.

She waded into the cold water.

It felt wonderful. She waded deeper. She paused when the water was chest deep. It always amused her that men hesitated when the water reached crotch high, and women hesitated as the water touched their breasts. She pushed forward and stroked down into the dark water. It flowed through her hair, over her skin. The metabolic enhancer had already kicked in, fortifying her body against the chill.

She broke the surface and took a breath.

She wondered what it would have been like if she had accepted the divers' invitation to join them, to become a diver herself. And she wondered what she would have done if she had decided to become a diver, and Victoria's invitation to join the alien contact team had come after that.

I probably would have joined the expedition anyway, she thought. Because having a diver on the alien contact team is not a bad idea. I wonder if I can persuade Victoria to let Zev join us officially?

She dove again. Underwater, she called Zev's name in true speech.

Lying quiet in the water as she rose toward the surface, J.D. listened carefully for an answer. She wished she had her weight belt, her artificial lung.

Perhaps she could get a lung grown for her. Except the equipment would have been concentrated in the genetics department...

We must have backups, she thought.

The distorted echoes of her voice traced out the size of the lake, the topography of its bottom. A sparkle of sound revealed a school of fish; a shimmering surface gave her the location of a stand of water weed.

The water parted across her back, cold water giving way to cool night air and the chill of evaporation across her skin. She turned over to breathe; she floated in the quiet darkness, grateful for a few moments to rest, to stop thinking, to stop worrying about Zev, even to stop rejoicing about the expedition.

She heard a splash near shore. A moment later, a gentle touch stroked her from heel to her shoulder. Startled, she splashed over and trod water. Ripples from her motion spread out across the lake. J.D. pulled herself under with powerful strokes.

She called Zev again, and this time the notes of the cry of his name-sound traced out his body. She felt the low-frequency tones of his voice against her skin. She gestured upward and surfaced again.

Zev rose beside her. The water was not deep enough for him to accelerate from the bottom, leap into the air, and land with an explosive splash like an orca. He hovered before her, water dripping from his short pale hair. He reached out and touched her again. J.D. took his hands and held them against her. His warmth radiated against her body, arousing her.

"I was worried about you," she said.

He wrapped his arms around her and rested his head against her breasts. Her body was buoyant but Zev's was not; together, they sank. J.D. had to kick to keep her head above the surface, and kicking was difficult with Zev's legs twining about hers. His claws slid carefully over her calf.

"Zev, I don't have my lung here, I can't breathe underwater now."

He let her free and floated nearby.

"Come on."

She swam to shore. She and Zev sat in the sand, waist deep in warmer water. He drew his legs up, let his elbows rest on his knees, and slumped forward. He combed his hair back, unnecessarily, with his long fingers.

"Where were you?" J.D. asked. "I couldn't hear you in the lake."

"I was up the beach a little. I was coming to find you. How did you know I was here?"

"It's the nearest place to swim. If you weren't here I was going to look for you in the wetlands."

"The water's all very shallow here, J.D.," he said sadly.

"I know, Zev. I told you it would be."

He gazed across the lake. The surface was very still.

"Tell me what's the matter."

He put his hand flat in the water, spread his fingers to extend the webs, and moved it up and down like waves. Ripples radiated from his fingertips. The water rose and fell against J.D.'s breasts.

"I know what's wrong with Stephen Thomas." Zev spoke in a rush. "It shouldn't have been possible. I never did it on purpose. I only just figured out what happened when he said his fingers itched. I'm sorry, J.D."

"Stop apologizing," J.D. said gently, "and tell me."

"It was for you!" Zev cried, and threw himself into J.D.'s arms.

His tears fell on her shoulder, hot, then cold, as they trickled down her skin. She stroked his wet hair and his velvety back.

"Shh, shh," she said. "Stop crying."

She was afraid that she knew what had happened.

Zev drew back. He ducked his head for a moment, putting his face underwater and scrubbing his eyes and his runny nose.

He sat up straight again.

"When my mother asked you to become a diver, we thought you would accept. I thought you would. Lykos had the sensitizer to give you. You can just take it like a pill, it's hard to kill that stuff."

"Yes."

"But you didn't want to be a diver—"

"It wasn't that simple. Never mind. Go on."

"—so we destroyed the sensitizer. I was sorry, J.D. I was the person who was allowed to help you become a diver. I was chosen to bring the changer to you."

"I see," J.D. said.

"When I came to *Starfarer* I didn't worry. I didn't even think about it. I couldn't give it to you or to anybody else because you didn't have the sensitizer. Without the sensitizer, it dies out. My body rejected it. It's probably all gone now."

J.D. took a deep breath and let it out very slowly.

"Professor Thanthavong said she thought we were all right," Zev said, "when we came out of the genetics building. But Stephen Thomas . . . he was injured, and he must have been exposed to sensitizer that way. But I didn't know. And I stopped the bleeding where he got cut . . ."

"Oh, dear," J.D. said.

"Satoshi was so worried," Zev said. "He thought Stephen Thomas would bleed to death. He wouldn't, but it did look scary." Zev touched his own forehead in the place where Stephen Thomas had been gashed in the collapse. "Lots of blood vessels. Lots of blood. So I just put my tongue on the place."

Bleeding could be fatal in the sea. It could attract sharks. So divers intensified the clotting ability of their blood with a component of their saliva.

Zev glanced sidelong at J.D., a little amused despite everything. "Victoria thinks I'm a vampire, I think."

"Of course she doesn't," J.D. said.

Zev sobered again. "And that's how it happened. All by mistake. Stephen Thomas will be mad, won't he?"

"He'll probably be a bit put out, yes," J.D. said.

"Are you mad?"

J.D. tried to sort out her feelings. "Not mad," she said. "I'm . . . jealous."

"I don't understand."

"He got a gift that was meant for me. A gift I wish I'd had the courage to take. He won't even want it. They'll mix up a viral depolymerase and he'll take it and it will make him just the way he was before. You'll be the only diver left on board."

"I'm sorry," Zev said again.

"I know it. Oh, Zev . . ." She remembered not to shake her head, just in time. The inner ear and the rotation of the starship interacted to produce strange sensory illusions if one shook one's head or nodded. "We'd better go back to the partnership's house and tell them what happened."

"I don't want to. I'm..." He shrugged.

"Embarrassed?"

"Uh-huh."

"Have you ever heard of Murphy's Law?"

"I don't think so."

"'Whatever can go wrong, will go wrong.'"

Zev thought about Murphy's Law.

"That would be funny," he said. "Some other time."

"Let's go."

Zev stood up. Lake water streamed from his body. They waded ashore. Sand stuck to J.D.'s feet. She had no towel. Still damp, she put on her pants and her shirt. Her cotton clothes turned clammy in the cold night air. She shivered and brushed futilely at her feet, trying to get rid of the worst of the sand.

"Do I have to get dressed?" Zev asked.

"I think it would be a good idea for you to tell Stephen Thomas what happened. I know it's scary, Zev, but it would be bad manners not to talk to him."

"That isn't what I asked," Zev said. "I just want to know if I have to put on my pants." He stood there naked, holding the baggy pants.

"I'm afraid so. People are pretty informal up here, but I don't think the informality extends to complete nudity. I thought you liked your suit."

"I did. At first. But it itches. And it rubs my fur."

J.D. stroked the place on Zev's hip where the waistband of the trousers had chafed away at his fine golden pelt, leaving a raw place on his skin. All divers bore the scars and marks of their outdoor life, and Zev was no different. Even J.D. carried healed cuts from rocks and oysters and barnacles. This was the first mark Zev had gained in his new life. Somehow, it was not the same.

"Wear the trousers for now," J.D. said. "We'll find something else later."

"I thought clothes would be fun. But I don't like them after all. Why do you wear them?"

"Modesty. Custom."

"But I have nothing to be modest about," Zev said. "Unless I choose."

"You have quite a lot to be modest about."

Reluctantly, Zev slipped into the trousers and fastened them. J.D. led the way along the trail, carrying her shoes.

"The clothes Stephen Thomas wears looks like they wouldn't hurt," Zev said. "But after I talk to him he probably won't want to lend me any."

Infinity woke the moment the sun tubes radiated the first rays of light into *Starfarer*. He had only had a couple of hours of sleep, but he had been waiting, anxious about both the mechanism and the control programs. He was glad they were back on track, but he would be uncomfortable until he found out what had gone wrong.

Beside him, Esther slept with a delicate, buzzing snore. He was usually sensitive to sounds at night; strange that her snoring never kept him awake.

He slid out of bed and tucked the blankets in around her shoulders. She never stirred.

The day brightened as the sun tubes reflected more light from Tau Ceti into *Starfarer*.

He looked around for his clothes. The AS had not taken anything to the laundry. He kicked yesterday's jeans with his bare foot, caught them, and put them on. Maybe the web crash had scrambled the programming of his housekeeper as well as the sun tubes. He went outside.

The direction of the sunlight, always from straight overhead, no longer bothered him. It used to, when he was working on the space construction team that built the starship. When the sun tubes first became operational, he would wake up, every daybreak, convinced he had slept till noon.

No one else ever noticed the straight-down sunlight. Infinity mentioned it to a couple of coworkers, including Esther, and got no reaction but blank incomprehension. They were all city folks, accustomed to sunlight coming only from above. The bulk of huge buildings cut off the morning light, the evening light, the sunrises and sunsets.

The dewy grass washed his bare feet. He shivered in the coolness of the morning.

The other side of the cylinder was covered with clouds, a heavy concentration for morning. The common weather pattern within *Starfarer* consisted of night showers and clear days, with a few daytime clouds thrown in for visual interest.

Today, clouds covered even the desert. This worried him, because if the desert received too much shade, too little heat and energy, its temperature would not increase, the air above it would not heat and rise toward the center of the cylinder, and the weather patterns would stagnate.

Ordinarily he would assume that the ecology department had the weather well under control, and keep his opinions to himself. He was, after all, a gardener. His responsibility was to what grew from the ground, not what fell from the sky. But after talking to Alzena, he knew that someone else would have to assume responsibility for the weather. The ecology department would not do it anymore. There *was* no ecology department.

The cactus in his garden looked unhappier today than it did yesterday. Grass sprouted around it. Not weeds: *Starfarer* had, by definition, no weeds. The plants on board had been considered, chosen, imported, and carefully placed. Nevertheless, every species did not always grow exactly according to plan.

Infinity sat on his heels and pulled up the sprouts of grass. This was the job he had asked the household AS to concentrate on. Most of its internal memory was dedicated to knowing when something was growing where it should not. Infinity reached out into the web to call the household robot.

He could not find it.

J.D. and Zev returned to the partnership's house as morning brightened *Starfarer*. The grass was very wet, the day colder than usual. J.D. supposed Arachne must vary the temperature. The climate was supposed to be mild and constant, but not static.

Satoshi was sitting on the front porch, leaning back against one of the porch supports, his eyes closed.

J.D. stopped. She did not want to wake Satoshi, who had apparently come outside for some quiet. Beyond him, in the main room, several graduate students, Avvaiyar, and Iphigenie were eating breakfast, buffet style, with Victoria and Feral. The fragrance of French toast made J.D's stomach growl.

Zev fidgeted in clothes made more uncomfortable by being damp. His claws scraped on the rock-foam path.

Satoshi jerked awake. "I'm not asleep!" he said, then saw J.D., and remembered where he was.

"I can see that," J.D. said. "Why aren't you?"

Satoshi gave a wry grin. "I hate to nap," he said. "If I take a nap I feel like a zombie for hours. And I don't have time to sleep all day. So I thought I'd stay up. I was only resting."

"I must talk to Stephen Thomas," Zev said.

"He's in his room eating breakfast. Do you want some?"

"Yes," Zev said. "Do you want some fish?" He reached into his pocket and pulled out a good-sized trout, so fresh its eyes were still shiny.

Satoshi accepted the fish with considerable equanimity.

"Thanks. I don't know how to cook a fish . . ."

"You don't have to cook it, you can just eat it. I already ate one. I could get some more."

". . . but Feral might." Satoshi stood up. "You're supposed to use saltwater fish for sashimi."

"It tasted good. You should try it."

"Maybe I will, if you try it cooked. Deal?"

"Sure."

Bits of fog drifted through the garden, giving the sunlight a silver cast, as if it were shining on a scene in a romantic novel.

Stephen Thomas was sitting up in his bed, surrounded by the tangle of his bright quilt, wearing a purple *hapi* coat, balancing on his lap a tray that held the remains of his breakfast, both French toast and fresh trout. The bruises around his eyes had nearly faded, and the cut on his forehead healed. He did not look at all ill; rather, a few degrees more ascetic than usual, the acute grace of his features honed by fever.

J.D. watched him as he listened to Zev. Her first reaction to him, that of speechless astonishment at his beauty, had never moderated. She hoped she was getting better at concealing it.

Stephen Thomas acted as if he were more interested in breakfast than in what Zev was telling him. He separated the last bite of fish from the skeleton and ate it delicately; he picked up his coffee cup and sipped from it.

"I am very sorry, Stephen Thomas," Zev said. "I didn't mean it."

Stephen Thomas put down his coffee cup. The silence of

the touch of the cup to the saucer was the only indication of how carefully he was controlling himself, his reactions.

"Christ on a crustacean," he said. "You're telling me I'm turning into a *diver*."

"Um," Zev said. "Yes."

Stephen Thomas took another sip of coffee and ate the last corner of a piece of toast.

"Professor Thanthavong can change you back," Zev said. "J.D. told me so. Before anybody even notices."

Stephen Thomas poked at the fish bones, found one final morsel, and nibbled it from the tip of one tine of his fork.

"Maybe I should have tried this raw, like Satoshi did," he said.

"*Can't* she change you back?" Zev said. "Satoshi didn't like it raw."

"Professor Thanthavong just developed viral depolymerase, she doesn't keep a lock hold on it," Stephen Thomas said. "*I* can change me back."

"Then everything is all right." Zev sounded relieved.

"If I decide to."

J.D. was shocked. "You aren't considering—"

"Why not?" Stephen Thomas said.

"Because . . ."

"Think about it for a minute. It might be interesting to change that way."

"I *have* thought about it." J.D. tried to keep the bitterness from her voice. "I've thought about it for a lot more than a minute." The reasons she had turned down the divers' invitation had nothing to do with her apprehension—though she had been apprehensive—about the physical changes involved in becoming a diver.

"What do you think, Zev?" Stephen Thomas asked. "How would you like it if you weren't the only diver on board?"

Zev fidgeted, looked through the open window into the garden, glanced at J.D., and pressed his hands against his knees, spreading the swimming webs.

"I'm already not," he said. "J.D. is one of us even though she doesn't look like us. You'd look like us, Stephen Thomas, but you wouldn't *be* one of us. You've never lived with the orcas and you don't know true speech."

"I speak a little French," Stephen Thomas said, trying to make a joke.

"That's a start," Zev said.

"On true speech?" Stephen Thomas asked, surprised.

"Most of the divers speak French," J.D. said. "The ones in Puget Sound, anyway. I used to think they learned it because they traveled between the United States and Canada. But now I wonder if they haven't been planning to apply for political asylum in Canada for a long time. Zev, do you know?"

Zev shrugged. "I don't get to help make decisions till I'm older. Lykos always talked to me in French and English. For a long time I thought there were only two languages—true speech and lander."

Stephen Thomas put his breakfast tray on the floor. The dishes and utensils rattled.

"So you think I should cure myself from being a diver."

"I think you should do as you please," Zev said. "It would be nice for J.D. and me to have somebody else to swim with. Do you like to swim?"

"I know how," Stephen Thomas said. He got most of his exercise through the intramural team sports that set up competitions between the departments on campus. "I played water polo one semester."

"Divers aren't allowed to compete in water polo," Zev said. "Not with ordinary people. We have an unfair advantage."

"Don't you think," J.D. said, impatient, "that you ought to tell Victoria and Satoshi what's happened?" She stood up.

"I guess so," Stephen Thomas said.

J.D. went to call them.

"Get Feral to come, too," Stephen Thomas said without any more explanation.

Victoria and Satoshi and Feral returned with J.D.

Victoria still looked worried, Satoshi distracted. Feral, as always, remained prepared to participate in any story that came his way.

"Have you seen the housekeeper?" Satoshi said.

"What? No. Why? I couldn't even get it to bring me a glass of juice."

"I thought it might be buried in here someplace."

"Very funny. Sit down, you guys. I have something to tell you."

Infinity tried a couple of different pathways, searching for his AS garden weeder. It was smart enough to get itself repaired, if it started to break down, but Repairs had no record of it. It did not need a new battery and it was not in the house recharging.

Gerald Hemminge had made a foolish threat, back in the meeting, but he could not have been serious.

Infinity called emergency services to find out if the artificials had been recalled. All he got was a busy signal. And he still could not find his garden weeder.

He went back in the house. Esther slept, buried under the blankets with just her curly hair and the tips of her fingers showing. Infinity sat on the edge of the bed.

Esther erupted out of the blankets and pounced on him, pulling him sideways. Infinity yelped with surprise. Esther started laughing and kissing him, and he found himself laughing too, with Esther on top of him, straddling his hips.

"You get up so early!" she said. "My Native American samurai, do all Native American samurai get up so early?"

"Don't know," he said. "I thought I was the only one."

"Can I take your clothes back off?" She unbuttoned the top button of his pants.

"I can't find the AS," he said.

"Kinky," she said.

He stroked her sides and her waist and her hips with the palms of his hands, with his fingertips. She opened the rest of the buttons.

Infinity bent his knees and pushed himself up so he could slide his pants off. Esther tried to help without changing her position. The pants legs bunched and crumpled around his ankles. He sat up, with Esther, giggling, in his lap, holding him hard between her knees, tangling her hands in his long black hair. Infinity tried to kiss her, cradle her breast in one hand, and free himself of his pants all at the same time. He finally kicked his jeans aside as she pushed him back onto the bed, taking him, not laughing now, hungry and intense.

Stephen Thomas told Zev's story, with additions and corrections and apologies from the diver.

"God, what a great story!" Feral said. "You are so lucky— We've got to document how it feels."

Victoria buried her face in her hands.

"I don't believe it," she said. "I can't stand it. What did we do to deserve *everything* going wrong?"

"Hey, Victoria, it isn't that bad."

"No matter what, you're going to be sick for another couple of weeks. Damn! How soon can you start reverting?"

"I'm not sick now," Stephen Thomas said. "I feel terrific. Satoshi, what do you think?"

"Are you seriously asking whether I think you ought to turn into a diver?"

"Yeah."

"Stephen Thomas!" Victoria sounded bewildered.

"I like you the way you are," Satoshi said.

Stephen Thomas pushed himself back against his pillows, slumping down and folding his arms across his chest.

"You guys have got no spirit of adventure."

"We have a job to do!" Victoria exclaimed. "If you keep on with this, you're going to be involved in your own changes, you won't be part of the team—"

"Of course I'm part of the team!" Stephen Thomas exclaimed. "I don't see what difference this would make. We don't even know that we'll find anything on the other side of transition. In the meantime, I've got no specimens from Sea, no samples, no nothing! I don't have a fucking thing to do! So why the hell should anybody care *what* I do, even if I decide to turn into a fish?"

"You aren't turning into a fish, Stephen Thomas," Zev said, his tone solemn. "Divers are still mammals."

"I *know* that, Zev!"

"Then why did you say—"

J.D. put her hand on Zev's arm. He started, glanced over at her, and fell silent, frowning and confused.

Satoshi leaned forward and took Stephen Thomas's hand. Stephen Thomas flinched and jerked away.

"My hands still itch," he said.

"Look, Stephen Thomas, if we find the alien ship—"

"The alien ship—if there is an alien ship—is running away from **us**! We could end up in interstellar space a hundred million light-years from anyplace. Shit, I shouldn't change into a diver, I should design a change that'll let me breathe hard vacuum!"

He pulled the quilt up over his head and flung himself over onto his face. The bedding twisted around him.

"Stephen Thomas," Victoria said.

"Go away, will you all? I'm going back to sleep."

"You're doing no such thing, Stephen Thomas." Professor Thanthavong stood just outside his open windows, gazing in at him with her hands on her hips. "Sit up, I want to talk to you."

Stephen Thomas obeyed, abashed. He shot a glance at Victoria, but it was clear she had not called Thanthavong as reinforcements, nor had she expected the head of the genetics department to turn up for breakfast.

"Thanks for coming," Satoshi said.

"Traitor," Stephen Thomas muttered.

Professor Thanthavong ignored his comment. "What's this nonsense about your turning into a diver?"

"If I am, it's my business."

"Not if it's happening because of an accident in my lab. And not if it's happening because of a mistake."

"I'm not blaming Zev. I don't see why anybody else ought to."

"That's very considerate of you. Nevertheless, it's an illegal act in our country to become a Changeling."

Stephen Thomas shrugged. "So I'll get one life sentence for helping steal *Starfarer*, and another for being able to breathe underwater."

"It's also an illegal act to help someone become a Changeling. Zev is innocent of helping take the starship, but he may be imprisoned for helping you."

Stephen Thomas had no reply.

"It *is* a factor to contemplate," Professor Thanthavong said.

"But I'm already in trouble with your country, Stephen Thomas," Zev said. "I ran away from the soldiers. I sneaked on board *Starfarer*. Sort of. But they can't do anything to me. I'm a Canadian now."

Victoria groaned softly, but Satoshi and Feral both laughed, and even J.D. smiled.

"Come along," Thanthavong said to Stephen Thomas. "Get dressed. We can get to work within the hour. Bring your medical records so we can restore Arachne's files."

With the original record of his DNA, his genetic structure, Stephen Thomas could select out and dispose of the new DNA that the changing virus had inserted into his chromosomes.

"Yes, well," Stephen Thomas said, without meeting Thanthavong's eye. "That's kind of a problem."

"You can't mean to tell me," Thanthavong said, horrified, "you *can't* mean to tell me that you didn't make a backup."

"I did!" he said.

"It's true," Victoria said. "We all went together for new scans a couple of months ago. We all have backups. Stephen Thomas, I saw yours."

"I had it," he said. "But it was in my office."

His office was in the heap of rubble that used to be the genetics building.

"I thought it would be safer there," he said.

9

So far today, the sun tubes functioned properly and Arachne remained up and alert, its web strong and responsive.

J.D. crossed campus to her office in the physics building. Her mood was a curious mixture of elation and apprehension: elation that the expedition would continue; apprehension that whoever had tried to stop *Starfarer* before would try, this time, to prevent it from going anywhere but to Earth.

On either side of the path, spring flowers lay wilted by last night's unseasonable and untimely light and heat. J.D. doubted the ecosystem of the starship could survive many insults like that one. The environment possessed some resilience, but its size made it vulnerable.

Victoria had put Arachne to work on a self-examination, searching for anomalous programming, for anything that might turn out to be the virus or worm or mole or Trojan horse. J.D. was on her way to help look at whatever bits of code Arachne turned up. Victoria hoped that someone, somehow, would find the flaw. It was a long shot.

J.D. entered Physics Hill. Victoria and Stephen Thomas and Satoshi stood in the hallway, a message display hanging between them.

"I don't believe this," Victoria said.

J.D. joined them. "What is it?"

"Official communication from the chancellor." Victoria sounded curious.

"I didn't know he *could* communicate," Satoshi said.

"Shit, I wouldn't talk to people, either, if I knew that all anybody was going to do was yell at me about the administration. Besides, he's got a lot to do."

"Yeah?" Satoshi said. "Important stuff like this?"

J.D. read the communication. To her surprise, it supported

183

the meeting's decision to follow the alien ship. She had assumed, since Gerald Hemminge was so opposed to continuing, that he must be following the administration line.

J.D. did not understand why Victoria and Satoshi were so annoyed. The other two paragraphs were equally reasonable. One set out a work schedule for planting crops. The other described a plan for the fair allocation of scarce resources, ordering all the members of the expedition to pool what they had brought to *Starfarer* in their personal allowances.

"Oh, dear," J.D. said, embarrassed by the second plan.

"What?" Victoria asked.

"I'll do my share of planting, of course. And turn in my allowance, since it's for the good of the expedition..."

"Nonsense!" Victoria said.

J.D. glanced at her, confused. "But, it's true we came away without the reserves we planned."

"Yes. But there are two problems with this communication. First, the whole idea of having personal allowances was so everybody could bring something they particularly liked. Luxuries. It's ridiculous to pool them. Suppose Stephen Thomas gave up his champagne."

"Don't hold your breath," Stephen Thomas said.

"I thought you were supporting the chancellor," Satoshi said. He may have meant his comment to sound like a joke, but it had a definite edge to it.

"I didn't say that," Stephen Thomas said. "I said he wasn't a bad guy. I'm sure this sounded better when he was writing it than it does when we're reading it. And I'm not going to pool my champagne. The next time I open a bottle of it, I want more than half a sip."

"See what I mean?" Victoria said to J.D. "And if Stephen Thomas did pool it, it wouldn't do you any good, because you don't drink. What would anybody do with my gold shirt, or your—whatever you brought?"

J.D. felt herself blushing.

"You don't have to tell me what it is," Victoria said quickly.

"I don't mind, really," J.D. said. "I'm not embarrassed to tell you, and I shouldn't even mind sharing it. It just sounds so frivolous to admit I brought a couple of pounds of chocolate into space with me."

"Chocolate, you might have to put a guard around," Satoshi

aid. "Victoria's right, though. Your allowance is *supposed* to e frivolous."

"It's selfish, though, to refuse to pool it. What are you oing to do?"

"I'm going to do nothing," Victoria said.

"What about the order?"

"He doesn't have the authority to give orders!" Victoria xclaimed. "I can't imagine what he's thinking of, to put out a ommunication like this."

"But we do have to grow food," J.D. said.

"Of course we do. And we will. But this isn't how we work. We'll have a committee, like the housing committee, and verybody will do their share."

"Growing food is part of what the ASes are for, anyway," Stephen Thomas said.

"Can you get Blades to withdraw the order?" Victoria asked Stephen Thomas. "If he *is* reasonable, then he'll want to know it if he's put his foot wrong. This message isn't doing his eputation any good, and it's lousy for morale."

"I get to tell the chancellor he screwed up, huh?" Stephen Thomas said.

"That's about it."

"Okay, I'll call him." His eyelids flickered and Stephen Thomas went away for a moment. When he opened his eyes again, he was frowning.

"No luck?" Victoria said.

"Got my message bounced, with a copy of the order. Weird. He said to call whenever."

A second message display formed before them: the image of Infinity Mendez.

"Hi," Stephen Thomas said. "What's up?"

"Kolya and Esther and I are out here checking the sun tubes," Infinity said. "We can't find any malfunction."

"At this point, I wish I knew if that was good or bad," Victoria said.

"Something is bad. The silver slugs have shut down. I can't even get a response from them. As far as I can tell they haven't worked on the crater since last night. Does anybody have any idea what's going on?"

"Damned if I know," Stephen Thomas said.

"*Something's* wrong with the artificials," Victoria said. "Damn! Maybe Arachne hasn't healed the controllers yet."

"The slugs started working after the web crash," Infinity said. "It's just since last night that they stopped. This hole needs fixing. The course changes put the cylinder under a lot of strain."

"We'll do our best to find out what happened," Stephen Thomas said.

"Thanks."

Infinity's image faded.

"I didn't believe Gerald would do anything with the artificials," Victoria said. "But if he did.... Doesn't he realize how dangerous—dammit! Where *is* he?" Her eyelids flickered.

"Victoria," Satoshi said.

She opened her eyes again.

"What?"

"Suppose I go talk to Gerald. In person."

"That's ... probably a good idea," she said, abashed. "You get along with him a lot better than I do."

"Okay." He headed out of the physics building.

"Satoshi," Victoria called after him.

"Yeah?"

"See what he says about this order, too."

Satoshi waved without turning and broke into a jog down the path.

"No more procrastination," Victoria said.

"I love debugging computer code," Stephen Thomas said, joking. "I look on it as exploring an earlier stage of evolution."

"It's awful, I know, but I can't think of anything else to do," Victoria said. "If anybody comes up with any other idea, I'll be the first to try it."

They went to their offices and set to work, looking at interpretations of Arachne's neural patterns.

Satoshi climbed the steps to the administration building. It was one of the few places on campus built above ground. If he had planned the cylinder, if he had been told that one building must be visible, he would have chosen a library, a museum. And he would have chosen something beautiful, a building with some architectural design to recommend it, not this ugly gray block of rock-foam brick.

The bureaucratic mentality at work, he thought. If something has to be impressive, it has to be concerned with the hierarchy.

But the hierarchy on *Starfarer* was far more complicated; it rested more on esteem than on position. Professor Thanthavong or Kolya Cherenkov would receive more cooperation with a request than the new chancellor could demand. Satoshi hoped he could get Gerald to persuade the chancellor to withdraw his orders before they did real damage.

Satoshi ran up the stairs to the top floor—the second floor; at least the planners had not insisted on making the administration building an edifice. A hallway led past closed offices, and finally ended at the entrance of a reception room. Satoshi went inside.

It was deserted, though there was an AI pattern hovering over the desk.

The room was better furnished than any place else on board *Starfarer*. The rug was of woven wool, the desk of rock foam polished and heat stained to look like wood. The wooden chairs had been imported from one of the O'Neill colonies, which had been in existence long enough to harvest a first crop of trees. On the starship, most people made do with bamboo and rattan.

Two other doors, both closed, opened off the reception area. One led to the chancellor's office, the other to Gerald's. Satoshi knocked on Gerald's door. He had no wish at all to talk to the chancellor. Satoshi had met him once, and found him aloof, overbearing, and uninformed on the aims of the deep space expedition. He was a political appointee. Satoshi believed he had come here to engineer the starship's dismantling. Events had offered considerable evidence for his beliefs.

Satoshi could not figure out why his partner liked the chancellor. Stephen Thomas and Chancellor Blades had spent most of the chancellor's welcoming party talking together. Blades had spoken to almost no one else. Gerald had taken umbrage at being ignored by the guest of honor of the party Gerald had arranged.

No one answered Satoshi's knock.

Blades *had* surprised Satoshi by remaining with the starship, rather than boarding the last transport and trying to go home. But as far as Satoshi was concerned, all it meant was that Blades had more nerve than sense.

He knocked again.

He had expected to find Gerald in. Unlike almost everyone

else on the starship, whose schedules were highly variable, the assistant chancellor kept regular working hours. He could almost always be found here between ten and four, unless he had some other official task.

Satoshi addressed the AI.

"Where's Gerald?"

The intelligence had been waiting in silence; that was its job, unless someone requested its help.

"Assistant Chancellor Hemminge is unavailable."

"Where is he?"

"The assistant chancellor has not publicized his schedule."

"I want to talk to him."

"The assistant chancellor is unavailable."

An AI that had been damped down as far as this one would never make any sense; it would simply go around in circles. He had encountered forbiddingly intelligent AIs, but he had never met one that revealed any hint of frustration. They could not be worn down, circumvented, or tricked.

Satoshi paced the reception room a few times, knocked again, loudly, sat on the upholstered couch, got up again. He tried sending a message to Gerald through Arachne, but received no reply.

On impulse, Satoshi spoke to the AI again. "What's happened to the mobile ASes and AIs?"

"The artificials are under impound."

That answers that, Satoshi thought. At least it's useful information—!

"Release them, please," he said.

"Impound is under the control of Chancellor Blades."

Damn, Satoshi thought. It was worth a try. I guess I'll have to talk to the chancellor after all.

He knocked on the chancellor's door. He had not expected a reply. He received none.

"Where's the chancellor?"

"The chancellor has not publicized his schedule."

After going through the same routine about the chancellor that he had gone through about Gerald, Satoshi sat on the couch, and waited.

Paragraphs and paragraphs and paragraphs of esoteric instructions washed past J.D.'s eyes. Translated from molecular code, they vaguely resembled English, but they fought interpretation. J.D. watched them fly by, hoping a phrase would leap out at her, obviously corrupted, and give her some clue how the web had crashed, or even how the sun tubes had realigned and frozen. Occasionally she stopped the inundation of information and changed the parameters of the search. Arachne had been asked to search for unusual states within its own mental processes. Any complex system contained unusual states, and Arachne was monumentally complex. J.D. experimented with limits on what was unusual. The trouble was, any limit she specified might exclude exactly what she was looking for.

Part of the problem was that Arachne was self-programming. It was difficult enough to understand a program written by another human being, much less one developed by an artificial intelligence that learned and changed and grew. The programming evolved all the time, so even if J.D. found something worrisome, she had no guarantee that it would be in the same place, or even exist, when someone went in to try to fix it.

And if Arachne is making mistakes in its reprogramming, J.D. thought, we are in more trouble than we ever dreamed.

She stretched. She felt as if she had been staring at the same fixed point for an hour. When she looked at the time, she found that several hours had passed.

"I'm not a programmer!" Griffith's voice startled her. She stopped the scrolling and went to see what was wrong. She had to push herself out of her chair.

"You're the one who mentioned Trojan horses!" Victoria said.

In the hallway outside J.D.'s office, Victoria folded her arms and glared at Marion Griffith.

"No, I'm not," Griffith said. "I said if there *was* something like that, it would probably work more than once. I'm not a programmer. I don't know how to write a horse, or what it would say. I don't know what to suggest you look for. If you gave me a program, and said, 'get this into a computer,' then—look, I'm sorry, I shouldn't talk about this sort of stuff."

Victoria blew her breath out in frustration, turned her back on Griffith, and disappeared into her office. Griffith, watching her go, noticed J.D. watching him. She expected him to snarl at her and stamp away, or ignore her completely, as he had on the transport coming up to the starship.

He shrugged, dispirited.

"I'm always saying the wrong thing up here," he said. "I think..."

J.D. hesitated, ready to back off, but Griffith waited for her to continue. Till now she had estimated his age to be at least thirty-five, and perhaps over forty. Now she revised her estimates downward five years. When he came out of his "I'm just an accountant" pose, he acted with an absolute assurance that matured him. The uncertainties of the past few days had stripped away both the assurance and the air of maturity.

"Mr. Griffith, it seems to me that if you expect us to believe you're on our side, you're going to have to be more open than... than perhaps you're used to."

"I'm not—" He stopped. "I see what you mean." His forehead creased in concentration. "The trouble is, I honestly am not a programmer."

"What *are* you?" J.D. asked.

"I'm an accountant."

J.D. thought of a couple of Stephen Thomas's choicer epithets, but instead of cursing made a brief, sharp whistle that meant, superficially, "very rotten fish," with the connotations of wasted time, disgust, and ridicule.

"I didn't think you'd believe me," he said. "I don't know what you just said, but I'll lay odds it means you don't believe me."

"You'd win," J.D. said, and went back into her office.

In the sailhouse, Feral let himself drift toward Iphigenie. He watched her huddle over the hard link; he wished he could be of some use to her.

She glanced toward him. Their gazes met.

"Why are you staring at me?" she cried, startling him with her anger. "Stop criticizing me, stop—"

"I'm not doing anything!" he said.

"—Stop... thinking about what a failure I am." Her voice fell, and she turned away.

"Iphigenie, please, I have nothing but respect and admiration for you. You've been through more than I can imagine. I only wish I could help."

"I'm frightened," she whispered. "I'm so frightened."

He moved closer and put his arm around her shoulders. Her hair's thin braids drifted against his sleeve.

"I've tried to connect with Arachne," she said. "But I just can't do it."

He remembered her cold hands, the beaten look in her eyes, after the web crashed with her deeply involved in it.

"Keep using the hard link," he said. "Everything will be all right."

"I don't know," Iphigenie said. "I hope so. We had so much more data on the first cosmic string, and it was moving much more slowly. I'm afraid we'll get near transition point, and we'll need a change that I can't do fast enough through the hard link. I'm afraid I'll hook in . . . and the web will crash again."

"Don't worry. We'll find the flaw. It won't crash."

Iphigenie shook her head. She spent so little time in the false gravity of the cylinder that she never got out of the habit of shaking her head or nodding.

"They couldn't check all Arachne's systems in a hundred years, my friend. In a hundred years they'd still have more to look at than they started out with."

She slipped from within his arms, and returned to her work.

Feral stayed near her. But he trusted Arachne's reconstruction. He wandered through the web, exploring, testing, searching. So far, he had found nothing definite, nothing to use as evidence for the cause of the crash. He put most of his attention into searching through the information files that Stephen Thomas had gotten him access to.

Occasionally he checked on the progress of several of his stories. Being old-fashioned on the subject, he planned to do the writing himself, but he let Arachne gather information for him. He took a moment to query his interview list: several positive responses from people he had asked to talk to, though most of them wanted to wait for calmer circumstances.

Have to see if I can talk them out of waiting, he said to himself. Derjaguin—of course he said yes. Orazio. I wonder if she still has any sympathy for us at all. The interview with Infinity Mendez turned out well. Follow up on that one. No reply at all from Chancellor Blades. Damn.

He composed a second request to the chancellor, aiming for a perfect balance of urgency and courtesy.

After he had sent it, he thought, I wonder if I can get

Stephen Thomas to introduce me? That might be the key I need.

A pattern shift caught his attention. He moved closer within the web, pushed by excitement. He had nothing definite yet, just the sensation of information waiting to be discovered, to be attached to the proper connections, to resonate.

Without warning, his access shut down.

Feral yelped with shock and pain.

Dazed, he struggled to maintain consciousness. He opened his eyes to a flash of scarlet, then blurred, light-spattered blackness.

After a moment of panic he remembered that he was floating free in the sailhouse. His body turned, pushed by a random air current. The speckles of colored light resolved themselves into the mass of the Milky Way. He pressed his hand against his face, his eyes. He could move; he could see.

His heart pounded so hard it scared him; he relaxed, making his pulse slow. The draft pressed him toward Iphigenie. Feral drew a deep, shuddering breath.

Iphigenie heard him. Huddled over the hard link, she glanced toward him. She frowned.

"What's the matter?"

"I . . . I don't . . ." he said, stumbling over the words.

"Feral, what's wrong?"

He did not want to frighten her any more, but he did not want to keep information from her, either. That was too dangerous. He reached out, hesitantly, to Arachne, ready to pull back.

The computer responded, smooth and strong, with no hint of any problem. Except that his access level had gone back to guest status, and he could only make superficial contact.

"I don't know," he said. "Jennie, what happens when you ask Arachne for information it doesn't want to give you?"

"I don't know," she said, puzzled. "Its purpose is to give information. There's nothing secret about what it holds. I suppose it would escort you back to a public area, if you asked it for something private or personal."

"Escort" was not the word Feral would have used for the heave-ho he had just been given.

"What were you doing?" Iphigenie asked. "Nosing about where you oughtn't?"

"I didn't think so," Feral said. "But I just had my access level lowered."

"That is odd."

"I'm going down to campus for a little while," he said. "I won't be gone long."

I need to talk to Stephen Thomas, he thought.

"Satoshi!"

"Huh? What?"

He flung his arm across his face to shut out the light. It was too early to get up, and he was still sleepy.

"What are you doing here? Wake up!"

He sat up, remembering where he was, but still groggy with sleep. Gerald Hemminge shook him again.

"Wake up!"

"All right, I'm awake." Satoshi rubbed his face and combed his hair back with his fingers.

"What are you doing here?"

"I'm waiting to talk to you. Or the chancellor."

"He isn't here."

"Where is he?"

"I think I'd best not say. You don't sound particularly rational to me just at this moment."

"It's you I want to talk to. Gerald, what do you know about the impound of the artificials?"

"They're being reserved for emergencies."

"Emergencies! If this doesn't qualify as an emergency, what will?"

"You are all such hardy conspirators. Deprived of your mechanical servants for an entire day—"

"Now, look, Gerald—"

"Satoshi, do your own laundry. It would gratify me to see Stephen Thomas Gregory beating his fancy shirts on a rock."

"Wait," Satoshi said. "You don't know the whole story, do you?"

"I believe I have a fair grasp—"

"It isn't just the interior artificials that are impounded. The silver slugs are down, too. Did *you* pull them off the repair site? Gerald—we're flying with a hole halfway through our skin!"

"I—" He stopped.

Satoshi had surprised him, but whether it was because the

assistant chancellor had miscalculated or because he was covering for the chancellor, Satoshi could not tell.

"Even if we did what you want, and returned home, *Starfarer* needs its structural integrity! The stresses on the cylinder are going to keep up no matter what we do. That crater's got to be fixed. Anything else is suicidal."

Gerald Hemminge could be pompous, and he could be disagreeable. He was not, however, stupid; his intelligence made him tolerable in Satoshi's view.

"I'm sure this is an oversight," Gerald said.

"Okay. Let's go talk to the chancellor and get it straightened out. Or," he said, hopefully, "can you do it on your own authority?"

"I'll talk to the chancellor," Gerald said. "That's all I can promise."

Satoshi folded his arms, unwilling to leave without more assurance.

"I could just wait here," he said stubbornly. "He'd have to pass me sooner or later."

"Do you think so?" Gerald asked. "Didn't you ever teach at university, back home? Surely you don't think administrators give up their favorite amenities just because they're on board a starship."

"What favorite amenities? Gerald, don't you want some help? I can back you up, if you'd like."

"I shall deal with it. I'm in a most unpleasant position."

"I understand that. But if the starship comes apart around us and we never get home at all, it's going to be hard for you to prove the rest of us are wrong."

"I shall deal with it. Don't make it worse."

He passed Satoshi, opened the door to his office, and went inside.

Satoshi was halfway across the reception room before he remembered that he had promised to question Chancellor Blades's orders as well as the artificials' impound. He went back.

Gerald's door stood ajar. Satoshi knocked once and opened it.

"By the way, Gerald—"

Gerald's office was empty.

Satoshi looked around, confused.

Then he realized what Gerald had been talking about when

he referred to administrators and their favorite amenities: Satoshi *had* taught at a regular university, and he had heard the rumors.

He had been a junior member of the faculty at the time, not someone regularly invited to fancy administration dinners, fund-raisers, awards ceremonies, or confidential meetings. He had always assumed the rumors to be the usual exaggerations of faculty and students who considered administrators their natural enemies.

But maybe not. The rumors were that the administration buildings all contained hidden hallways, inaccessible to anyone without the right keys, or identification, or status. Hidden hallways that university vice-presidents, say, use to get from one room to another, even one building to another, without exposing themselves to the hoi polloi.

Apparently the rumors were true.

Kolya Petrovich returned to his house, amused. Infinity Mendez had ordered him home to get some rest.

For someone who claimed not to take well to leadership, Infinity was doing quite a good job.

Halfway up the stairs, Kolya saw Griffith sitting on his porch, waiting. Kolya hesitated, then continued.

"Are you speaking to me?" Griffith said.

"I suppose I am. All deals are off, these days, including the one I made with you. Come inside."

Griffith followed him. Kolya got out some bread and cheese. He did not ask Griffith if he was hungry; he made sandwiches and handed one to Griffith.

"Beer?"

"Sure," Griffith said, surprised. "I didn't know you had beer here."

"Several people brew it. Quite well. They take their hobbies seriously. Cheerful competition."

He carried his sandwiches and beer onto the porch. Infinity had made a good decision. There was still work to do out on the surface, but it was not quite so pressing now that the silver slugs promised to return.

The human beings would function better for rest and real food. It was possible to eat in a space suit, but the sustenance came in tubes, semisolid, barely edible, much less palatable.

"Did you find the malfunction?"

Kolya bit into his sandwich, savoring the sharp cheese, chewing it slowly, swallowing.

"We found nothing." He wondered how long the cheese would last, whether *Starfarer* carried stores of it. There were no cows on board the starship. He wondered if anyone had started making goat cheese.

Not that it matters much to me, Kolya thought. He was not partial to goat cheese.

Griffith wolfed a bite of his sandwich. Kolya started to regret wasting the good cheese on him.

"I'd like to help with the inspection when you go back out," Griffith said. "I had Arachne put me through the spacewalk orientation."

"There's no mechanical malfunction of the sun tubes."

"You know that for sure? What did you find?"

"We found *nothing*. And I doubt Victoria and her colleagues will find anything in Arachne's programming. They'll be overwhelmed with information."

Griffith put his sandwich down.

"Something is wrong?" Kolya asked.

"Not with the sandwich." Griffith stared into the mug of beer. It was dark and thick, nearly opaque. "Arachne could crash again. We don't know what the signal was, or who sent it, so there's no way to stop it if somebody wants it to happen again."

"There's no way to stop it by looking for mechanical malfunctions or corrupt programming."

"They're going to blame me. Again."

"Yes, probably. I'm sorry that it's true. But you made yourself the most likely suspect."

"Will you help me prove I'm innocent?"

"I've done what I can, Marion," Kolya said, and this time Griffith did not object to the use of his given name.

"If somebody's watching me when the system crashes again—"

"'When'? You're that sure it will?"

"It would if I'd had anything to do with planning its reactions, and I'm not nearly the sneakiest person I ever worked with."

"You aren't, hmm?"

"No."

"What do you think I could do? You don't react like most

people, when you connect with Arachne. Your communication is invisible. Your attention doesn't wander, you don't close your eyes. You can carry on a conversation."

"I worked hard on that."

"To your disadvantage. If I can't even tell when you're connecting under ordinary conditions, how do you expect me to tell if you were, or weren't, telling the system to shut down?"

"I've thought about that. Maybe I should have my link removed."

Kolya flinched. The idea of removing one's link with the web felt like a threat of blindness, deafness, lack of sensation.

"Or paralyze the node I'm connected to."

"Is that possible?"

"I don't know. I thought you would." He paused, looking at Kolya hopefully, expectantly.

"You expect too much of me," Kolya said. "As usual. I'm not a scientist. I'm not an engineer."

"Won't you even try to help me?"

"I will, if you wish, if I'm not needed elsewhere, and if you can think of a way. How can I defend you against the charge that you could place a delayed trigger within Arachne's web?"

Griffith shrugged unhappily. "I don't know."

"Do you mind if I make a suggestion?"

"Please," Griffith said gratefully. "Please do."

"I think you'd be better off to spend your energy helping Victoria and the others find the real trigger. If it is one of us—"

"You don't want it to be, do you?"

"It doesn't matter what I want! What matters is the truth. I think it unlikely that Arachne is programmed to crash itself. I think someone has to pull the trigger. I think we have to find that person. If it's one of us, all the more important."

"If I helped track the person down, would everyone trust me?"

"People might stop distrusting you so emphatically."

"Victoria Fraser MacKenzie thinks I'm a jerk."

"That is possible."

"Thanks."

"She's devoted to the deep space expedition. You worked against it. What do you expect of her?"

Griffith shrugged. He picked up his sandwich again, took another bite, and swallowed, barely chewing.

"Didn't your mother ever tell you to chew your food?"

"No," Griffith said, suddenly angry, dangerous again.

Kolya did not press him. Griffith changed the subject.

"I did try to help, but I can't tell them what they need to know because I don't know what it is. Jesus, I barely opened my mouth to J.D. Sauvage and now she thinks I'm a jerk, too."

"That doesn't sound like J.D. Whatever did you say to her to make her react like that?"

"I told her," Griffith said, "that I'm an accountant."

Kolya started to laugh.

"Dammit, it's true! Why does everybody laugh or swear or both when I tell them the truth?" He drained his mug and set the glass down hard. "GAO would be a lousy cover to use if I weren't an accountant."

Still chuckling, Kolya said, "For someone expert in manipulating people, you are terribly naive."

Griffith looked away. "I'm not used to trying to manipulate people . . . with the truth."

"Stop trying to manipulate them at all."

Griffith frowned curiously. "Then how do you get them to do what you want?"

In frustration, Kolya ran his hand through his streaky gray hair.

"Marion, sometimes they won't do what you want. That's all there is to it."

"Is it?" His voice was cold, determined. "I know . . . a lot of ways to manipulate people that don't have anything to do with words."

Kolya's sharp anger was far hotter than Griffith's had been. For a moment he managed to hide it.

"And just who would you choose to torture?"

"That weaselly vice-chancellor might be a good place to start. I'd have to look at the transport passenger list, too . . ."

Kolya flung his beer mug down the stairs and across the garden. It crashed against a rock and exploded into tiny, sharp shards. Griffith was on his feet, poised for defense, before the end of the shocking sound. Kolya had made no move toward him. Griffith straightened up, confused.

"If you lay hands on anyone on board," Kolya said, "anyone . . . I will kill you. Do you understand me? I'm the only person on the starship who would make that threat. And I'm the only person on the starship who can carry it out."

Humiliated and bewildered, Griffith backed up, staring at him. When he was five meters distant, he turned, in silence, and walked away.

Stephen Thomas's vision blurred. Translated code fled past him, unseen, incomprehensible. He had been looking at it so long that it no longer meant anything—if it ever had meant anything. He froze the display and put the heels of his hands against his closed eyelids, trying to force away the burning.

His vision was changing, like his body. The changes both intrigued and frightened him. Victoria and Satoshi had tried to talk to him about what was happening, and he had put them off. How could he talk to anyone when he did not know what he thought himself?

Professor Thanthavong had offered, hesitantly, reluctantly, to do a subtraction comparison between Zev, Stephen Thomas, and a standard human genome. Lacking Stephen Thomas's medical record, she could use the comparison to try to single out the DNA sequences that had inserted themselves into his chromosomes.

A subtraction comparison was a risky procedure. It offered no assurance of a correct solution. Stephen Thomas did not trust it to take out only the diver genes and leave his own uniqueness alone. Trusting himself, his originality, perhaps even his personality, to a subtraction comparison scared him much more than it scared him to change into a diver. At least as he was, he would be himself with something added. The other procedure could leave him as himself with something missing.

Someone's hands touched his shoulders, the taut, sore trapezius muscles, and kneaded deftly.

Stephen Thomas relaxed.

"God, Feral, that's wonderful."

"Looked like you could use it." He pushed Stephen Thomas forward in his chair so he could rub his back. His thumbs dug deep, seeking out the aches, intensifying them, pressing them away. Feral slid his hands under the azure silk shirt. His hands were warm and powerful. Stephen Thomas pulled his shirt off and leaned forward to pillow his head on his arms and the tangled silk.

"Stephen Thomas, I think I found something—"

"What! Where? When?" He raised his head. Feral moved his hands lower on his back, digging his thumbs into the tight muscles beneath his shoulder blades.

"I can't pinpoint it. I was right on the edge of something. Then the access you got for me cut out. It was... kind of a shock. Was there a limit on it?"

"Hell, no." Stephen Thomas's eyelids fluttered. His display changed abruptly; he opened his eyes and leaned forward, peering intently into it. "You're right, your access got frapped. Damn! The system's *still* not finished healing." One word changed, and the new display riffled through successive layers of interconnected updates.

"Great, I've got it. Thanks." He rubbed the small of Stephen Thomas's back. His touch lightened as he made connection with Arachne.

"Can I see what you were looking at when you got thrown off?"

"Sure..." But after a moment, Feral scowled and came out of his communications fugue. "No. It's gone. I can't even describe it. It was just a feeling, a way I can look at patterns..."

"Where were you when this happened? Physically, I mean."

"Out in the sailhouse. Jennie—I think she's more comfortable with somebody around."

"Yeah," Stephen Thomas said, "I can understand that. I don't know how you got frapped, Feral. A stray cosmic ray? The sailhouse should have stopped it. Maybe *Arachne* got whacked with one. I just don't know. At this point nothing would surprise me. We're thinking of changing the name of the ship to *Murphy's Law*."

Feral chuckled in bleak appreciation.

"I'll keep looking," he said.

Stephen Thomas straightened up. Feral hugged him, hiding his face in Stephen Thomas's hair.

Stephen Thomas felt a thrill of yearning. Reluctantly, he held it in check.

"I missed you guys," Feral said. "Your house was so quiet while you were gone. Back on Earth, I live alone. It never bothered me that there wasn't anybody around to talk to. But it bothered me here."

"We missed you, too."

"Did you? That's good to know."

Stephen Thomas suddenly thought of something.

"Did you put my still away?" When he boarded the *Chi*, the distilling equipment was sitting in the middle of the partnership's main room, waiting for him to get around to dismantling it. Now it was gone.

"Yes. It's in the storeroom. Is that okay?"

"It's just fine. Thanks."

"I've been trying to make myself useful," Feral said. "But I wondered..."

Feral sat on the edge of his desk, facing him. Feral's elbow edged into the frozen display. With a touch to Arachne, Stephen Thomas moved the image sideways. He put his shirt back on.

"I wondered..." Feral said, "if I ought to move. Get out of you guys' way."

"I guess the housing committee can reassign the vacant houses..."

"Oh," Feral said, crestfallen.

"I mean I could understand it if you wanted a place of your own," Stephen Thomas said quickly. "I don't mean you *should* move."

"You're sure?"

"It gets pretty crazy around our household sometimes. But it's great having you there. It's great having somebody in that room."

No one had ever lived in the fourth bedroom before Feral arrived; Stephen Thomas had begun to wonder if the family partnership was going to keep it empty forever, a shrine to their late eldest partner. Stephen Thomas still missed Merry... but Merry had never slept in the fourth bedroom. Merry had never even been into space.

"I'd like to stay."

"I want you to. Feral, you're the world's best house guest. Among other things."

Feral grinned. He had a terrific smile. "Okay."

Stephen Thomas stretched. "I guess I better get back to work." He gestured toward the frozen display. "For all the good it's going to do."

"Maybe I shouldn't bring this up right now..." Feral said.

Stephen Thomas barely managed not to sigh.

Why is it always me? Stephen Thomas wondered. Every

time he turned around, someone wanted to tell him deep personal troubles. He was the first to hear about it when J.D. thought she might have to leave the expedition to help Zev's people. His graduate students told him the messy details of their personal lives. Even Fox, who was Satoshi's graduate student, had come to Stephen Thomas for advice on staying with the expedition even though she was underage.

Stephen Thomas usually said what he thought, but when someone came to him for sympathy or advice, he found it impossible to send them away. He could not even cultivate the cool distant listening that looked like sympathy, but discouraged continued confidences.

Of course he said nothing to stop Feral. Even if he could stop people from telling him their troubles, he wanted to listen to Feral.

"What's the matter?"

"It's just . . ." Feral clenched his fingers around the edge of the desk. His gentle brown eyes looked hurt.

"Tell me," Stephen Thomas said.

"If you were going to take people along who weren't with the expedition, why only Zev? He can't do what I can for the team and for *Starfarer*! I could document everything. I'm a *good* writer, Stephen Thomas—!"

"Christ, Feral, I know that! Practically everybody on board reads your stuff."

Feral glanced away, pleased by the compliment, but still unhappy.

"Taking Zev wasn't deliberate," Stephen Thomas said. "Shit, I should have realized how you'd feel. Everything was so confused when we got to the *Chi*. Zev had only just got here, he didn't have his bearings . . ." He stopped. "Forget all that. I sound like there was some plan to it. You know. 'Zev doesn't know his way around, so we better take him with us.' But that isn't how it was. He was just . . . there." He grinned. "And attached to J.D. at the hips."

"Oh. Is that how it is?"

"I think it is now. I don't know for sure about before, when they were back on Earth."

"Will he go with you next time?"

"I doubt it. Victoria was uncomfortable about his being with us. He doesn't have any training, and he's awfully young."

"I asked the wrong question," Feral said. "What I want to know is, how do I get to go, too?"

"The official answer is probably, you don't," Stephen Thomas said. Feral's expression made him wish he had dissembled for once. "You could apply to the team. Ask for auxiliary status."

"What are my chances?"

"Hey, if it were only up to me, a hundred percent. But it's not."

"Okay. I understand. Thanks." He brushed his fingertips across the back of Stephen Thomas's hand, pausing where the skin was hot and red and itchy.

"Does it hurt?"

"Not much. Itches like hell."

"You are so damned lucky," Feral said.

"Tell me so again, when the skeletal changes start. That's supposed to feel like growing pains, *cum laude*."

He changed the display back to the search pattern. His shoulders slumped. His eyes burned, and he could not even rub them because of the bruises.

"I better get back to this. For all the good it will do."

"Too bad you can't backtrack what happened," Feral said, in sympathy.

"We could have, at the time, if we'd been ready. Too late now..." He stopped. An idea blossomed in his mind, and he reacted to it with his whole body: a glow inside him, a burst of laughter, a groan of ecstasy. All his best projects had started with exactly this feeling. "Damn, Feral," he said. "That might work."

The scrolling display froze of its own accord. J.D. straightened up, too tired to be surprised. Her eyes hurt. Her head hurt. Her tailbone hurt.

An image overrode the display. It was Stephen Thomas.

"This is a waste of time," he said. "I have an idea. Everybody meet me in the sailhouse."

His image faded.

"The sailhouse—!" The last thing she would have expected was to have Stephen Thomas call a meeting in zero gravity.

J.D. let the frozen display fade, not at all sorry to send it away. She stood, stiffly and slowly.

Zev rose from where he had been napping, in one of the

too-soft fabric-sculpture chairs that J.D. had inherited from her predecessor in the alien contact department.

"Did you fix it?" he said.

"I wish," she said.

He stood very close to her, his body radiating heat. He could have been touching her, caressing her, for the way he made her feel. When J.D. headed for the sailhouse, Zev came along with her. He maintained his land manners. Difficult as it was, so did she.

Stephen Thomas and Feral were waiting with Iphigenie in the sailhouse when J.D. and Zev arrived.

"Why are we meeting out here?" J.D. asked.

"That's a complicated question—no, it isn't, but it needs a complicated answer. Let's wait till the others get here."

Victoria and Satoshi and Professor Thanthavong arrived a few minutes later, and Avvaiyar floated in soon thereafter.

"How'd you get the slugs going?" Stephen Thomas asked Satoshi.

"Sweet reason," Satoshi said.

The harmonies of the sailhouse sang around them. The volume increased.

"Is that necessary?" J.D. shouted. Her ears hurt, and the noise intensified her headache. Zev looked like he was in intense pain.

Stephen Thomas let a couple of white noise generators loose to float around them. The generators went to work creating a bubble of fuzzy sound aimed outward. Stephen Thomas allowed the sensor harmonies to fade.

"I don't know," Stephen Thomas said, his voice barely audible above the buzz. "Maybe I'm just getting paranoid. But I don't trust Arachne anymore, and I don't trust the buildings not to be bugged. This was the best I could think of."

Avvaiyar groaned. "If you extend your fears, we can't even trust ourselves. We might be spied upon through our links."

"I wish you hadn't said that," Stephen Thomas said.

"I wish I hadn't thought of it."

The group formed into a sphere, heads in, feet out. Stephen Thomas had none of his usual trouble joining in; he moved comfortably in zero g. J.D. searched him for signs of the changes. It was tempting to ascribe his ease to becoming a diver, but it was simpler to assume it was due to forced experience during the trip around Tau Ceti II.

"We're wasting our time," Stephen Thomas said. "We're looking for stuff that Arachne is protected against. The damned computer is vaccinated and backed up and crammed full of mole traps and supplied with every redundancy technology can offer. And it still crashed. The backups crashed. Stored data got garbaged. I think it's going to happen again."

"I think you're probably right," Victoria said. "If I wanted *Starfarer* to return to Earth, I'd crash the web... and keep crashing it until everybody gave up and did what I wanted them to."

"Which means Griffith wasn't making up paranoid fantasies," Stephen Thomas said. "Or maybe he was... but they were *accurate* paranoid fantasies."

"You think a crash routine *is* built in?" Victoria said. "Programmed in, deliberately? Why can't we *find* it?"

"Because it would be a routine Arachne needs, but one you could invoke at the wrong time or the wrong place or in the wrong amounts. The biological metaphor is an oncogene—"

"An oncogene!" Thanthavong exclaimed, horrified.

"It's possible," Stephen Thomas said, defending his speculation. "The bioelectronics are so complicated—"

"I don't doubt it's possible," Thanthavong said. "But who in their right mind..."

J.D. knew something about oncogenes. She made it her business to know something about as many subjects as she could. Oncogenes were ordinary genes that mutated slightly, or mutated in their control regions, and transformed the cells they affected into tumor cells.

They caused cancer.

And as Professor Thanthavong had asked, Who in their right mind would build self-destruction into a computer?

"Stephen Thomas," Thanthavong said, "this is an appalling idea. Imaginative, but appalling. Very difficult to accept. Someone quite responsible in the hierarchy of EarthSpace would have had to plan the expedition's failure."

"Not planning our failure," J.D. said. "Just... planning. Planning for all the possibilities."

"Griffith," Iphigenie said, her tone strained and angry.

"No," Victoria said. She continued quickly, interrupting Iphigenie's objection. "He probably would have done it if he could. And maybe he triggered it. But he isn't the one who designed the code. If he could, he'd be too valuable, eh? To send out as a regular spy?"

"No doubt that's true," Thanthavong said. "It takes talent to design a system that's useful under most circumstances, but pathological in others."

"Or one that can be easily mutated into the computer equivalent of a neuroma," Stephen Thomas said. "It wiped out all Arachne's higher functions almost instantaneously. That's one hell of a rate of metastasis."

"Oncogene," Iphigenie said. "Mutation. Metastasis. These are the terms one uses for cancer. Arachne has . . . a brain tumor?"

"That was the effect, yeah. The tumor's got nothing to grow on but neural tissue. So the result is confusion, memory loss—psychosis."

"And Arachne is still running the starship? We're still linking with its web? Why haven't you warned us before this?"

"Because Arachne's already healed itself," Stephen Thomas said. "Besides, I only just figured out what must have happened."

"It might give *us* cancer," Iphigenie said.

"Of course it won't," Victoria said. "That's impossible, Iphigenie. You're not physically connected with Arachne. Besides, you could hardly catch an organic disease from a bioelectronic entity."

"A psychosis, maybe." Stephen Thomas started to laugh, then stopped, realizing he had, for once, gone over the line in saying what he thought. "Bad joke," he said. "Very bad joke." Even his charm could not erase this misstep.

Iphigenie looked ill. "It nearly killed me once!"

And it could try to kill her, or anyone, again, J.D. thought. Overload the autonomous nervous system, blast your blood pressure into the stratosphere, crush your brain. . . . She shivered.

"We're assuming," she said, "that the crash was deliberate. There's no possibility of a random mutation?"

"Anything's *possible*," Stephen Thomas said. "But that's an awful lot of coincidences to believe in before breakfast."

"Lacking such convenient coincidence," Professor Thanthavong said, "the mutation would require a mutagen. You're the bioelectronics expert, Stephen Thomas. What could trigger the change?"

"Most of the mutagens that can damage carbon-based biological systems—" Stephen Thomas said.

"Oh, lord," said Victoria.

"—as well as any of the processes that can trigger a virus or a Trojan horse in an ordinary computer."

"You must keep it from happening again," Iphigenie said.

"We can't," Thanthavong said. "Not unless we can trace the source of the mutagen."

Stephen Thomas grimaced. "That's what I love about you, Dr. Thanthavong. You never bother with the easy problems."

She paused, considering. "The mutagen will have broken down by now."

"It would have broken down a few seconds after it appeared. The physical part of the computer acts like a living system. Its enzymes detect mistakes and correct them. Its immune system reacts to foreign toxins. But the oncogene propagates so fast, the repair mechanisms can't quite keep up. If the web crashes again, the mutagen will exist. For a few seconds. Until Arachne creates antibodies against it and neutralizes it and breaks it down."

"But we'd have a few minutes to follow the immune response. If Arachne built marked antibodies. We could backtrack."

"Right."

Thanthavong considered. "We ought to be able to mark the precursors in time . . . even without the genetics lab."

Stephen Thomas shrugged. "Sure. It isn't certain that it'll work. But if it does, we could follow the trail straight to the neural node of whoever released the mutagen."

"In that case, you'd better get to work, hadn't you?" Professor Thanthavong said.

"You're going to *let* the web crash again?" Iphigenie cried. The undertone of her complexion was gray with fatigue and distress.

Victoria floated closer to her and put her arm around her. Iphigenie pushed her away.

"It isn't comfort I want! I'll have no comfort till I know the web is secure!"

Stephen Thomas frowned, insulted and hurt that his theories and solutions had not met with approval and agreement.

"We're no closer to knowing who crashed the web than we were when we went into transition!" he said. "If you have any great ideas about how to track the person down, I'd sure like to hear them."

"It was Griffith," Iphigenie said. "Who else could it be?"

"It could be anyone," Thanthavong said. "I'm sorry, my dear, but it could be anyone. This is a deliberate flaw, designed to be accessible through the lowest levels of use. Anyone who can touch the web could trigger the mutagen. Even one of us."

"It wasn't. You know it wasn't. We all know who it must have been. We've got to stop him!"

Stephen Thomas had let himself drift out of the sphere. Now he did a backward roll, touched one foot to the wall of the sailhouse, and cut through the air toward the access tunnel.

"Fuck it," he said angrily, "I'm doing the best I can."

The noise generators turned off and the increasing beat of the sensors washed over J.D. She flinched and reached out to Arachne to turn down the volume. The web touched her. Frightened, she winced away. At the request of someone else, the sensor volume fell. Embarrassed at her reaction, J.D. grasped the web firmly, stroked it, tested its gleaming strands.

Arachne looked and felt to her as strong and willing and flexible as it had before the crash. Waiting patiently for her requests, her demands, it stretched out in all directions, in directions she could not name, clean and beautiful and elegantly complex.

10

J.D.'s imagination created a scene that bore no relation to the inside of a computer or to the inside of an organic system. She had wondered what she would see when her attention left the main room of the partnership's house, whether she would enter a phantom world of hugely magnified digital gates or pulsing translucent neural tissue.

Instead, she closed her eyes and found herself on the exterior of *Starfarer*'s campus cylinder.

The first time, the only time, she had walked on the outside of *Starfarer*, she had nearly been killed. Her mind had recreated a setting of imminent danger. She shivered.

The metaphor was, unfortunately, perfectly appropriate.

She sat on the inspection net, her feet dangling. The starship loomed overhead, a curving low stone ceiling. *Starfarer*'s spin pressed her outward, downward, toward the stars that sped past her feet. If she slid between the strands of the net, unfastened her safety line, and let go, she would be flung off into space.

But she was not wearing a safety line; she was not even wearing a spacesuit. In her imagination, she could live and breathe in the vacuum of space.

She walked around and looked around, without any constraints, wondering what, exactly, she was supposed to be looking for. Stephen Thomas had not been able to tell her what form her perception would take, how her mind would interpret the information or the search. He had said, Look for something unusual. Follow it. Follow it *fast*. And then get out.

Stephen Thomas and Avvaiyar and Satoshi and Professor Thanthavong were somewhere nearby, perhaps—probably— all seeing entirely different surroundings, all waiting for the same undefinable event. Victoria had gone out to the sailhouse to help Iphigenie, if she could. Feral had gone with her, still trying to persuade her to let him join the antibody chase. He was not an official member of the expedition; she refused to allow him to expose himself to danger.

J.D. wished Victoria had relented about Feral. The hunt could use more help. Stephen Thomas said he could finish only the five antibody interfaces before *Starfarer* reached the cosmic string. Maybe that was true. Maybe he had only finished as many interfaces as he had trustworthy people to use them. He would have trusted Feral.

Standing, J.D. balanced on the cable. *Starfarer* loomed above her. If she stretched, she could reach the surface with her fingertips.

The cable vibrated against the soles of J.D.'s feet. She followed the wave form, moving along the length of the starship, parallel to its axis of rotation.

The last time she was out here, *Starfarer* had plunged into transition. She wished she could have stopped everything and simply watched it, experienced it. That had not been possible, and it would not be possible this time, either.

The rotation brought her into the valley between the campus cylinder and its twin, the wild cylinder; the motion plunged her toward the endless quivering silver sky that lay beyond the valley. Between the starship and its sail, the crystal bead of the sailhouse hung as if suspended by invisible tethers. The framework that secured it to the starship, that held the cylinders in their parallel orientation, blended in and disappeared against the moving background of the sail.

Reflected light from the sail's surface dazzled her. She closed her eyes and turned away.

J.D. felt a shiver through her body, through her mind, through the rocks above her and the cables beneath her feet. She waited, wishing she knew exactly what she was waiting for. Should she try to follow the tremor, chasing invisible vibrations?

She opened her eyes again. The rotation of the cylinder had brought her back out among the stars. Soon it would spin her into the light of Tau Ceti.

The blaze of the sail's reflection had died away. Sparks gathered at J.D.'s feet. At first she thought they were illusory, an artifact of moving from brightness to darkness. But they

were real, as real as anything in this mind-created world. The
sparks flowed in thread-thin streams past her feet, running
like water along the cables of the inspection net, spiraling like
vines up the net's supporting rods, skipping from point to
point on the rough stone overhead.

J.D. followed the flow of the sparks, running like a tight-
rope walker along the springy cables. The glittery line was so
tenuous that she feared she would lose sight of it, but every
time it dissipated, like a stream spreading into a wide flat
meadow, it recreated itself farther on.

When Stephen Thomas spoke of seeing auras, this was the
sight he described. J.D. wondered if his perceptions had
influenced her, helping her create a reality like the one he
saw. Perhaps she had created it this way in an attempt to
understand him.

It did not matter how she saw what she was seeing. She did
see it.

Griffith was right. The web was going to crash again. And
Stephen Thomas was right about the method. Somewhere
within *Starfarer*, someone had released a foreign chemical
signal. Arachne, detecting it, formed antibodies to it from the
store of precursors Stephen Thomas had marked.

The marked antibodies, which she perceived as sparks,
could be tracked to the source of the chemical signal.

If she could reach it before Arachne crashed and threw her
into the real world.

The sparks scattered around the curve of *Starfarer*'s skin.
J.D. chased them, breathing as hard as if she were surrounded
by air instead of nothingness. They congregated in a rising
whirlpool, a flickering whirlwind, and vanished through the
portal of an inspection hatch. J.D. climbed up into it and
cycled through the air lock, wondering, as she did, why she
had to use the air lock if her imagined reality thought the
starship was flying in air, why she could not dissolve through
the starship's skin like the sparks.

The air lock opened. She hurried out. In the distance, the
end of the spark trail vanished around a curve. She ran after
it, chasing the sparks through the tunnel.

The sides of the corridor roughened. They no longer
looked manufactured, but natural. J.D. felt as if she were
running through a cave. The passage bore the sour tang of
limestone, though there was not a natural piece of sedimenta-

ry rock to be found anywhere within the starship. She reminded herself that she was making it all up; her surroundings were metaphor.

She had survived in space, unprotected by a suit; now she ran through dark underground tunnels, able to see without any illumination. She caught up to the spark trail. It glowed, an actinic yellow streak only a few molecules wide. It skittered along, now on the floor, now the wall, now the ceiling, occasionally fading out, only to reemerge as a trace of light a few meters away. J.D. followed the sparks through the darkness that was not truly dark.

The tremors around her strengthened. When she touched the wall, she could feel the starship quake and quiver.

She could not stop to figure it all out. She ran as fast as she could through the dreamworld. When the sparks fluttered from the stony wall to the rippled surface of an underground lake, she dived in after them without hesitation.

The frigid water embraced her, sliding around her like a caress. She swam, naked, pushed along by her powerful legs, her feet with their webbed, clawed toes. She had made herself a diver.

She swept through the water, feeling no resistance to her sleek-furred body. The metabolic enhancer kicked in and she followed the sparking signal of concentrated antibodies at an exhilarating speed.

The lake narrowed to a river, a great mass of water compressed into a steep cleft. The water rose and billowed into rapids. Waves crashed with a rushing roar, tumbling her through the channel. In real life, without her artificial lung, without a life vest, she would be dead: drowned or crushed against boulders that tumbled and rumbled beneath her, drumming the rhythm of their own inexorable stone dance.

The rapids crashed over a shelf in the riverbed and dragged and pushed her underwater. The pressure forced her to the bottom; her hands brushed naked bedrock scoured into long smooth ripples by the current. The water was icy green. She struggled against its weight, against its crashing chaos. She leapt upward across the current. The translucent green gave way to roiling white. She broke the surface and gasped for half a breath before another wave slapped her in the face and sent her downstream again, tumbling and choking. But she had escaped the hole. The antibody sparks skipped along the edges of columnar basalt.

The river washed her, exhausted, into an eddy. The flow, opposing the main current, carried her in a half-circle toward shore. Staggering, she waded onto the beach. In real life, even a diver might not have survived that transition.

The sparks flickered from sand grain to pebble. J.D. boosted her metabolic enhancer to its limit, to her body's limit. Suddenly she was dry.

Her feet dug into the wet cold gravelly sand, sank into the dry coarse sand just above the high-water mark, scuffed through the warm powdery sand at the highest edge of the beach. She clambered onto the trail and plunged after the antibodies again.

She moved across a landscape of black basalt, an ancient lava flow, tubes and caves of hollow stone that pounded like drums in response to her steps. Long tendrils of basalt stretched out from a distant rise, like tree roots, like the sprawling tentacles of a beached octopus.

The antibodies congregated, glowing, on one of the tendrils. The tendrils began to move.

J.D. became aware of the passage of time. The danger increased with each second. She pushed herself into a run, wishing she had remained waterborne. She was an excellent long-distance swimmer, a poor runner, and her imagination had not extended to changing that.

The rock tubes writhed beside and around and over her, lifting from their substrate of black rock, twining together in labyrinthine patterns. This stone octopus had far more than its share of tentacles.

The tentacles looped and knitted together overhead. J.D. found herself running through another tunnel, like the access veins in the skin of *Starfarer*. The antibodies had collected in puffy, shining streaks along the walls and ceiling. They traced the outlines of some of the lava tentacles, though all the tentacles had melded to form a glossy, textured surface. The antibodies flowed like the tributaries of tiny streams, running together all in one direction.

J.D. knew she should get out, but she was so close, the antibodies were so thick here, such perfect markers, that she kept going. The flowing sparks continued to cluster and clot, till they formed glittering arteries, pulsing rivulets of flowing organic gold.

She rounded a turn in the maze of tunnels, and entered a central chamber.

Stephen Thomas plunged out of a tunnel on the other side of the cavern and ran toward her.

Between them, all the lines of antibodies flowed together, forming an organic mass of translucent spark-shot gold, pulsing and throbbing and drawing the heat out of its surroundings. J.D. shivered.

"Got you, you fucker!" Stephen Thomas shouted.

"Oh, my god," J.D. said.

She recognized the node.

It belonged to Chancellor Blades.

Stephen Thomas recognized it, too.

"Son of a bitch!" Stephen Thomas's voice was full of anger and betrayal. "You treacherous bastard!"

He was blushing, embarrassed and humiliated in a way J.D. had never seen him. He kicked the neural node as hard as he could, a practiced martial-arts side kick with all the impact projected through his heel. The blow hit full force with a crushing thud. The force shuddered through the node's golden body. The footprint turned silver, then darkened to bloodred.

Stephen Thomas drew back his foot to kick the node again. J.D. grabbed his arm and jerked him away. He staggered.

"We don't have time for this!" J.D. had to raise her voice to be heard. The sounds around her were increasing: the pulse of pumps, mechanical and organic, the flood and flow of nutrients, the dissolution of outworn connections, the highstrung harp note of new connections made. And underneath it all, the sinister baritone hum.

Stephen Thomas stared at her, as astonished by her actions as she had been by his embarrassment.

"We've found what we needed! We've got to get out of here!" Even as she shouted at him, she was sending a message to the others, to Satoshi and Thanthavong and Avvaiyar, to anyone still connected with the web: Get out fast, the web's going to crash! We found it. We found it, get out fast.

Stephen Thomas pulled himself away from anger, from revenge. He turned sharply and jerked open a door with a

fan-shaped top. The door had appeared from nowhere—or
had it always been there, and J.D. had not noticed it?
Stephen Thomas stood aside for her to pass through before
him.

They stepped out into the main room of the partnership's
house.

In the sailhouse, Victoria doggedly brought the sensors
into tune.

Feral hovered nearby, making her nervous.

It's okay, she told herself. Let him stay here where you can
keep an eye on him.

Her attention left the control strands for an instant, and
when she caught them up again, she had a sail shimmer to
damp.

He drifted to her side. "Let me help."

Victoria eased the sail into equilibrium. When it lay quiet
in her mind, she gave Feral another moment. The sensors
balanced on the edge of harmony.

"No. You're a *guest*." She spoke with odd pauses between
her words, turning her mind's eye from Feral to Iphigenie to
the sail. "I want you out of the web and out of danger until
we get things resolved."

"But—"

"I can't talk to you now!" As soon as she spoke, she
regretted her tone.

The sensors moaned a minor fugue.

She put her attention entirely on the sail, the approach,
the limited transition point. Iphigenie crouched over the
hard link, working furiously but slowly. Lacking a direct connection, she could not hope to keep up with the changes.

"Jennie—" Victoria said.

"No," Iphigenie said, her voice high and tight. "I won't. I
can do it this way."

I'll have to do this myself, Victoria thought. She immersed
herself in the songs, wrestling them toward perfection.

The last discord remained, stubbornly resistant, growing
louder with every effort Victoria made to fix it. *Starfarer*
plunged toward transition, a fraction of a fraction of a degree
off its true course.

"We're going to miss!" Victoria said. "Jennie, please, I
need you in the web."

"No!"

This isn't going to work, Victoria thought. We're going to have to come around and try again. Then maybe we'll catch up to the alien ship, or maybe we won't, maybe it will have moved on, maybe it will always remain beyond our reach.

Maybe it doesn't even exist.

She snarled with despair and dived back into the symphony, trying to find the source of the error. She felt as if she were swimming against the current of a multicolored, multidimensional stream of musical notes. If she had not been so angry and baffled and aggravated, she might have found it funny, but the sound, growing painfully loud, overwhelmed her senses.

"Let me buffer you," Feral said to Iphigenie. "You can port your orders through me. Whatever happens, you'll be cushioned."

It took Victoria a moment to disentangle Feral's words from the screaming music; it took her another moment to realize that Iphigenie's hesitation meant acceptance rather than refusal.

"All right," Iphigenie said.

Her eyelids flickered.

"Feral," Victoria cried, "stay out of the web!"

The sensor chords sank to a whisper of perfect harmony.

Starfarer's magnetic claws stretched out to the cosmic string, touched it, grasped it. They began feeding on its limitless stores of energy, using the remnants of the creation of the universe to bring the starship toward transition potential.

"Get out fast, the web's going to crash!"

An emergency message, with J.D.'s voice and personality, flashed through the web to everyone involved in it.

"We found it. We found it, get out fast. We found it!"

Victoria responded by reflex to the urgency in J.D.'s voice. She pulled back from the web, from the warning of danger.

But Feral and Iphigenie remained hooked in. Iphigenie's shields blocked the warning, or Feral took a terrible risk to prove himself to Victoria, or they both pushed past the limits to finish the approach.

"Feral! Iphigenie! Get out of the web!"

She stroked toward them, grabbing at the air. Weightlessness, for once, defeated her. She floundered, out of reach of any solid object.

Light reflecting from the silver sail silhouetted the figures of her two friends, holding hands. As Victoria struggled toward them, calling their names, the sail began to furl, majestically folding and twisting into its storage configuration. Feral and Iphigenie had been dark shapes against brightness; now they were pale shapes against space and stars.

The symphony ended.

The web crashed.

J.D. felt a moment of disorientation. In her imagination she had been standing, but her physical body was sitting. Her perceptions from within Arachne and the real world flowed together.

She opened her eyes. Zev sat cross-legged in front of her, peering closely at her, worried. When he realized she had returned, he smiled. He touched her face, brushing the back of his fingers against her skin. She covered his hand with hers, pressing his warmth to her cheek.

Satoshi sat on her left, Thanthavong on her right, Avvaiyar and Stephen Thomas across from her.

The neural node map by which they had all been orienting themselves hung in the center, a complex, nearly transparent tracing of interconnections. It reminded J.D. of the labyrinthine alien message. But the path to its center had disappeared; Arachne had already attacked the oncogene, destroyed it, dispersed its components.

Stephen Thomas leapt to his feet and lunged for the hard link in the corner of the room. He snatched his recording module out of the machine.

"Got you, you bastard," he snarled. *"Proof."*

The node map trembled and dissolved.

J.D. flinched, physically, as her connection with Arachne dissolved in a small hot point of pain. She was not in direct communication with the link, but its constant, reassuring potential vanished from her perception.

Inside the partnership's house, the lights went out.

Outside, the light from the sun tubes faded. *Starfarer* plunged into darkness.

Starfarer entered transition.

The web stretched and frayed and exploded.

Iphigenie cried out.

Feral convulsed, his back arching, spasming, his arms and

legs shuddering. He made a single sound, a desperate, groaning gasp.

The holographic map dissolved and vanished. In response to Arachne's crash, to the absence of instructions, the sailhouse walls went to safety default. They darkened to opacity, shutting out the intense, hypnotic sight beyond and cutting off the light.

Victoria finally made it to Feral's side. She grabbed him, as if she could physically drag him away from the web crash.

His body went limp.

"Feral!" She pleaded for a response. "Feral—?"

Without thinking, forgetting that the only free artificials were the silver slugs outside, she tried to call a health center AI. She reached out for Arachne and tripped into the mental hole of the computer's absence. She jerked back, frightened and disoriented in the darkness.

"Is he all right?"

The sailhouse walls luminesced, filling the chamber with a cool green illumination. Iphigenie took Feral's slack hand.

Victoria felt for his pulse. She found nothing. His skin was clammy and cold, his eyes white crescents beneath half-open lids. Blood smeared his face: his nose and ears bled. Opaque scarlet droplets quivered in the air.

"He'll be all right," Iphigenie said. "It's just shock—"

"He isn't breathing! Use the hard link and get us some help." Victoria searched her memory for the zero-g update to CPR training. Breathe for the patient. Compress the chest: one hand on the patient's back, one on the sternum, push hands together hard. She had to alternate between breathing and compression. Awkward. But Iphigenie was making one attempt after another to find someone, something, who could respond.

J.D. felt her way outside into the garden. The spicy, sweet fragrance of carnations surrounded her. Zev joined her, snuggling in the crook of her arm.

"I wish I were out there to see transition again," she said.

"I know," he said. "But, J.D., there is time. There will be another time. Now we can travel wherever we like."

"I hope so. I hope you're right."

Power from the auxiliary systems began to flow. Light

shone, soft, from the floor-to-ceiling windows behind them, laying shadows to the carnation-covered bank that surrounded the yard.

The door crashed open. J.D. jumped in fright. Stephen Thomas sprinted past her.

"Stephen Thomas, what's the matter?"

He disappeared into the night.

"It's pitch-dark out there," J.D. said. "He's going to trip and kill himself."

"No, he isn't," Zev said. "He can see. Like I can."

Without replying, J.D. returned to the house.

"What happened? Where did Stephen Thomas go?"

Satoshi dug through a drawer, pulling out crumpled papers, a pocketknife, a couple of pencil stubs, the sort of things one always intends to throw away, but keeps for just one more use. The litter bounced to the floor.

"I *know* there's a flashlight in here someplace—"

J.D. looked from Thanthavong to Avvaiyar. Avvaiyar turned away; Thanthavong had drawn in on herself. J.D. hardly ever thought about or noticed how elderly she was; but right now the senior geneticist looked old, and frail.

"It's Feral," Thanthavong said. "He was caught in the web crash. Out in the sailhouse. It's bad."

"Oh, no!"

"Here's the damned thing." Satoshi turned on the flashlight. It threw an intense beam across the room, cutting through the somber emergency light. "Let's go."

"I can go faster," Zev said. "Should I follow Stephen Thomas?"

"Yes," J.D. said. "Go on. Go. Hurry."

Stephen Thomas slumped beside the stretcher where Feral lay.

If I'd just been with him, he thought, I might have been able to . . .

If I'd just had more time, I might have figured out how to boost the antibodies so the web didn't crash . . .

If I'd just been able to think of a way to prove who did it, without letting it crash again . . .

If I hadn't given him more access to the web, he wouldn't have been there at all . . .

He searched for the strength to rise. His forearms rested

on his thighs; his hands hung, limp, between his knees. He stared at his hands, hardly seeing the red, irritated skin between his fingers, hardly feeling the itching, barely aware of the ache in all his joints. The pain of the changes blended with and disappeared into the pain of loss, the pain of his grief.

Though Stephen Thomas was aware of the other people in the room, his partners nearby, J.D. and Zev, Professor Thanthavong and Avvaiyar, he felt completely alone.

Feral noticed things no one else noticed, and asked questions other people were afraid to ask. It was unfair, it was ridiculous, it was impossible, that he should be dead.

Victoria came over to Stephen Thomas and laid her hand on his head, stroking his long fair hair.

"I'm so sorry, love. I tried..." Her voice shook. She fell silent.

"How could this happen?" Stephen Thomas cried. "Last time nobody even got hurt! Not like this, not permanently."

"It crashed harder. Faster. The designer knew the antibodies would give Arachne some protection."

Stephen Thomas gripped Feral's cold hand. A harder, faster crash, but a shallower one, one intended to disrupt the starship's course without causing any more damage to its systems. One intended to force it to return home. Oh, and incidentally, only incidentally, to destroy any human being caught in the web.

"He was still alive when you got him here."

"His body was. Just barely." Victoria hesitated. "He was gone, Stephen Thomas. Everything that made him who he was, everything that made him unique..."

"Please, stop," he whispered.

She started to cry. Stephen Thomas put his arms around her. Satoshi knelt beside him and hugged them both.

Stephen Thomas held his partners in his arms, dry-eyed, overwhelmed with rage and despair.

Every academic skill I have is a *joke*, he thought bitterly. I can create life from chemicals. I can turn myself into something that's not really a human being anymore ... but the best thing I can do for someone I love is to concur in his death. Even now, I could make him live. I could repair the arteries that burst, regrow his heart, regenerate his brain.

And then I'd have an infant in an adult body, a child with a quarter of his life already used up. I'd have a new person, but I'd want to turn him into a replica of someone I once knew.

He pushed away the whole perverse idea, disgusted with himself for resenting Victoria because she was strong enough, ethical enough, to let Feral die.

"Oh, god," he said. "I'm going to kill Blades."

"*No,*" Satoshi said.

Stephen Thomas glared at his partner. "I expected you to say, 'I told you so'! When did you get to be his defender? What should we do? Let him stay chancellor? Declare him king?"

"We should make certain he can't do this again. Then we should decide what justice is, and carry it out. Justice. Not revenge."

"You can have the justice. I'll settle for revenge."

Satoshi grabbed him by the shoulders. "Listen to yourself! We can't let ourselves turn into barbarians!"

"I don't care" Stephen Thomas shouted. "I don't—"

"I'm sorry," Satoshi said. "I'm sorry. I know how you felt about him, how he felt about you."

"He was our friend, too," Victoria said.

Across the room, Avvaiyar made a sound of surprise. Everyone felt the quick light touch as Arachne began to revive. The crash had been quick and hard, but shallow.

The change made Stephen Thomas almost too angry to speak. "That was quick," he said. "The fucking computer twitches for a couple of minutes and comes right back to life. The inferior human being *dies.*"

"Take advantage of it," Victoria said. "Put the transcript in the web. As soon as Arachne comes back to strength, everybody will see it. And then we'll decide what to do."

"The chancellor must lose his access to the web," Thanthavong said.

Stephen Thomas rose, moving out of Satoshi's arms, cold to his comfort.

"I can take care of that," he said.

"No," she said. "This is a task that should be done impersonally. Not in blind fury. Show Arachne the evidence. Arachne will do it."

Stephen Thomas stopped, knowing she was right, unwilling to admit it.

"You have another job to do, Stephen Thomas, you and

your teammates," Thanthavong said. "*Starfarer* will complete its transition soon. We don't know what's on the other side. The alien contact team should be ready. For anything."

Victoria glanced gratefully at Thanthavong. She had been afraid to make the same demand of him.

In his mind, Stephen Thomas retreated to the same place he had gone when Merry died, when the partnership trembled on the verge of dissolution, stripped of its center and its stability. He made himself solid. He walled part of himself off behind windows, placing himself above and to one side of his physical body. Sound came through the windows. A little light came through. Nothing else. No warmth, no fragrances, no breezes. And no pain. He watched Victoria from his new, distant vantage point, wondering what she had feared he might do.

"We'd better go out to the *Chi*, then," he said. He did feel something, he still could feel something: a mild surprise that his voice sounded so calm.

He surprised Victoria, too. She took his hands and looked into his eyes.

"You're sure?"

"Yes," he said.

If he had not fallen apart when Merry died, he would not fall apart now.

"Yes," Stephen Thomas said again. "There's nothing I can do to help Feral." And though he knew it was true, he knew he would always question his own actions in the events leading to Feral's death.

"All right," Victoria said. "If we're going to do it, we'd better do it."

She took a deep breath, straightened her shoulders, and left the health center to go up to the *Chi*'s dock. Satoshi followed, but Stephen Thomas hesitated before Professor Thanthavong.

"You won't let Blades back into the web," he said.

"No. You can be sure of that."

"Thank you."

"My friend—"

He tensed, and she stopped.

"What?" Stephen Thomas said.

"Never mind. It will wait. Good luck."

* * *

Infinity Mendez felt no sense of movement or direction, except the ordinary, inescapable spinning of the cylinder.

Transition looked nothing like space. He had not known what to expect out here, and because of Arachne's crash there were no visual records of their first encounter with it. Infinity had—he thought—brought no expectations. So he surprised himself by wanting, by searching for, evidence of their tremendous relative speed through space.

"Where *are* we?" he asked Esther, who sat nearby on the inspection net. Kolya sat apart from them, gazing outward, transfixed.

"Beats me," Esther said.

"Don't you understand"—he waved his hand out, down—"this?"

"No."

"I thought you would."

"Why?"

"Because you're a pilot."

"Don't have my rating for this stuff," Esther said, a laugh in her voice. "Maybe Victoria MacKenzie understands it. She's probably the only one on board who does."

Above lay the rumpled rock of the missile crater, nearly repaired, if not quite restored to its original state.

"The silver slugs are waking up," Infinity said.

The silver slugs huddled in crevices, their skins reflecting an occasional glimmer of transition's unusual light. When the web crashed, they all shut down, fastening themselves securely to *Starfarer*'s skin, waiting for instructions. Now that the computer was returning to life, the slugs flexed and stretched and prepared themselves for work. They were oblivious to transition, concerned only with their obligation to maintain the starship.

The drive to keep *Starfarer* repaired was programmed into the slugs like an instinct. Except for the hours during which the administration had shut them down—Infinity still did not understand the reasoning behind that—they had worked constantly since Arachne returned from its first crash.

They would continue to work, because the ship had not yet regained its full structural strength. Infinity believed, and hoped, that it had achieved enough stability to survive transition, and the inevitable stresses of the sail's deployment at the other end of their voyage.

There was no point in dwelling on the other possibilities. He had done his best; the silver slugs had worked to their limits. People sometimes thought he was fatalistic. Whatever happened now, happened. Infinity thought that the best one could do was approach it with composure.

"Do you see the same things as I do?" Esther asked.

"Sure," Infinity said, his voice low. "Why wouldn't I?" Then, "How would I know if I didn't?"

"That's what I mean." She replied in the same soft tone, as if their conversation might disturb Kolya. They both knew better. Either he had his transceiver turned on, and could hear them no matter whether they whispered or shouted, or he had it turned off and could not hear them at all. Infinity suspected that the cosmonaut had it turned off, that he was experiencing transition in his own private way; and perhaps he was listening for the music of the spheres.

Back in the Tau Ceti system, before they made the change, Kolya had flatly refused to go back inside. He had been out here during their first transition. He wanted to see it again. Infinity was curious about it, too; he had been underground, looking at the damage, seeking the source of the water leaks, and finding Griffith zipped up, helpless, in a survival pouch. Neither one of them had seen anything of that journey.

It was foolish, even dangerous, to remain perched outside the starship's skin during an experimental flight. But if something catastrophic happened to *Starfarer*, it probably would be no safer inside. So Infinity and Esther remained outside with Kolya, and watched transition unprotected.

"So," Esther said, "what do you see?"

They tried to describe to each other what they saw. They could not make their perceptions match; they could not even make them touch at occasional points. Either they were seeing two entirely different things, or they were using two entirely different ways to try to describe them. It was as if they were communicating in different, mutually incomprehensible, languages, languages evolved from different roots.

In frustration, Infinity raised his head and stared into the missile crater. The slugs had come out of their nooks; they nearly covered the irregularly concave surface of the damaged area, seeking out the spaces that should be solid, filling them in around the open places that should carry water, nutrients, information. One slug crawled across the skin, leaving behind an opalescent trail of optical fibers.

Infinity squeezed his eyes closed, looked down, and opened them again.

Transition was gone.

Normal space spread out around him, and the new star system lay clearly in view, Sirius A bright, intense, gilded and damped by the gold shielding of Infinity's faceplate; Sirius B dim and distant.

A few more degrees of spin took Sirius A out of sight.

Infinity started at Esther's yelp of astonishment.

A graceful blue crescent blinked into existence, accompanied by a wash of light.

"Did you see that?" Esther exclaimed. "It just appeared!"

"A trick of the starlight..." Kolya said.

"It must be an optical illusion," Infinity said. "It was there and we just didn't see it."

Infinity admired the planet for a moment, but abruptly, as he adjusted to the return to normal space, as his eyes acclimated to the light, he made out what he was looking at. He drew in his breath, shocked and stunned.

What lay in orbit behind *Starfarer* was a small blue planet, illuminated on one limb, three quarters full and one quarter dark.

It moved fast. Faster than the starship.

It was heading straight for *Starfarer*.

Starfarer plunged through space.

The planet rushed toward the starship from behind.

J.D. flinched back in her couch. Satoshi caught his breath. Victoria muttered a short, sharp oath. Stephen Thomas, uncharacteristically, said nothing. He lay easy and relaxed within his safety straps, watching.

"Where did it come from?" Satoshi exclaimed.

Distances and sizes are impossible to estimate in space, J.D. thought desperately. That thing must be large, and far away. It *must* be.

All *Chi*'s warning reactions began to scream.

"We know!" Victoria said.

The sounds stopped.

Zev let himself free of his couch and drifted to the window

to cup his hands around his face and look out at the strange little world.

A holographic chart showed the sphere to be only a few tens of kilometers in diameter. But it was bigger than *Starfarer,* and its entire bulk would crash into the starship.

The stellar sail untwisted, grand, majestic, and slow. J.D. knew—without doing the math, she *knew*—that the sail could not deploy fast enough, could not change the starship's course radically enough, to avoid the crash.

A blue haze rimmed the illuminated arc of the worldlet, and clouds glowed white in starlight. But clouds were impossible: the planetoid was surely too small to have a permanent atmosphere.

Perhaps it had volcanoes; perhaps one had erupted so recently that the gas and particles had not yet escaped its gravity to fly off into space.

"Not enough time," Victoria said. "Not enough delta *v.*"

"What *is* that thing?" Satoshi asked, fascinated despite the fact that it was going to kill them. "What the hell is it?"

Iphigenie appeared, in image, among them.

"There's nothing I can do," she said. "Even if I were in the web. I can't move the ship fast enough. I'm sorry. If the sail were powerful enough to move us that fast, *Starfarer* would disintegrate under the force."

"I know," Victoria said. "I'm sorry, too, Jennie."

"That's no natural object," Satoshi said.

A chaotic mass of information roiled in front of him; he picked bits out, brought them forward, inspected them, let them fade back into the confusion.

"It's no bigger than a medium-sized asteroid, but it's got an atmosphere. Oxygen, water, land—"

"We should have gone home," Gerald said from his liaison post. "As I told you. I hope you're satisfied!"

"I'm just delighted," Victoria snarled. "And your last words can be 'I told you so'!"

"Victoria, is the *Chi* ready to take off?" Professor Thanthavong asked.

"We can't—"

"If you crash, too—"

"—we go clean," Stephen Thomas said.

"We have time. A few minutes to get everyone into the *Chi*

or the transport or at least into suits or survival pouches. Afterward, there may be enough of the starship to salvage..."

"I..."

J.D. felt a visceral reaction against taking off with the *Chi*, leaving *Starfarer* behind. When the starship crashed, there would be nothing left of it, only the people in the *Chi* and in the transport—could everyone on board fit inside the two small ships? She doubted it. The transport had been overfull when *Starfarer* dragged it into transition, with several hundred people remaining on the starship.

"It isn't going to work," Victoria said.

"We've got to try!" Thanthavong said. "Are you a survivor, or not? I thought you were!"

"Not like this," Stephen Thomas said, very softly.

"We are all trying not to panic, Victoria," Thanthavong said. "Don't make it harder."

"All right," Victoria said. There was no life or hope in her voice. "We'll get as many people on board as we possibly can."

It doesn't matter what we do now, J.D. thought. It doesn't matter a bit.

She opened her safety straps and floated over to Zev's side.

"It's pretty," Zev said. "It looks like it has seas."

"It does have seas," Satoshi said. "It has air. It has a very strong magnetic field, and the gravity of a small planet."

"What!" Victoria exclaimed.

"We're broadcasting our greeting, aren't we?" J.D. said, turning back toward her colleagues with a sudden twinge of hope. "If the alien ship is still in this system, maybe it will hear us. Maybe the alien people will understand that we're in trouble. Maybe they'll come help us."

"We're broadcasting what we agreed on. Our introduction, and a copy of their maze."

"But we've had no reply," J.D. said sadly.

"No reply. And there's no sign of the alien ship."

"It's moving," Zev said.

J.D. joined Zev. She put her arm around him. His fur felt soft and sleek and warm. He snuggled close.

"Of course it is, Zev," she said.

"It's moving *away*."

"It just—"

She stopped. The planetoid appeared to be curving in its course, moving aside from collision.

"What's going on?" J.D. said. She touched Arachne and got back a reply that confirmed what Zev had perceived. As the alien contact team and everyone aboard the starship watched, amazed, the planetoid accelerated. A gradual motion drew it aside from *Starfarer*. In complete astonishment, J.D. watched it as it moved away, slowed, and paced the starship. Messages flashed back and forth between *Starfarer*, Arachne, and the *Chi*, letting people know that they were not going to die today. At least not in the next few minutes.

Before the spin on the cylinder had pulled Infinity and Esther and Kolya out of sight of the planet, Infinity was clambering across the inspection net to the air lock, his colleagues close behind. They hurried toward the air lock, not because they had any illusions about being safer inside. Outside, they were helpless. Inside, they might be able to do some good.

Infinity hooked in with Arachne, hoping for information that would negate his fears. Instead, he received confirmation of them. The planetoid plunged toward the starship.

The air lock cycled. Infinity faced the others. Kolya and Esther looked as shocked as he felt.

They did not speak. There was nothing to say. This was the one possibility that might, in the normal progress of their voyage, destroy the ship. During the blind moment between transition and normal space-time, *Starfarer* could crash into an asteroid.

But it wasn't supposed to happen, Infinity thought. We knew there's a vanishingly small chance that it could. But nobody thought it ever *would*...

And that's the weirdest-looking asteroid...

They heard Thanthavong's plans for the *Chi* and the transport; they heard Victoria's reluctant acquiescence.

"But where am I supposed to fly it?" Esther said. "Earth-type planets orbiting Sirius? No way."

And by the time the air lock opened, the emergency had ended.

Infinity's hands shook with the rush and sudden ebb of adrenaline. He took off his helmet, shook his hair free, opened his suit, and let it collapse on the floor.

Esther flung herself between Infinity and Kolya, catching one man in each arm, hugging them close. Infinity, in his turn, held her gratefully and put his free arm around Kolya. He thought the cosmonaut was going to pull away; instead, he put his arms around his younger colleagues and embraced them, looming over them.

"I have never been so scared in my whole life," Esther said. "I thought the missile carrier was scary! That was nothing."

"Yeah," Infinity said. That was about all he could get out.

"I would not like to repeat the experience," Kolya said.

They broke apart self-consciously. Kolya and Esther did not meet each other's eyes. They were from completely different backgrounds and cultures, but each was a pilot. Pilots were supposed to take every emergency calmly, and coolly, and never reveal their fear. Not even afterwards.

"Strange..." Kolya said. "When I tested fighter planes, when I was the first to use a new spacecraft, I came much closer to death. Seconds from it, instead of minutes. The experiences frightened me. But they were exhilarating. The first thing I wanted to do was fly the plane again. Put the spacecraft through the same routine. Make it work. Get it right. This time it's different. I don't feel exhilarated. Only relieved. Grateful." He shrugged. "Perhaps it's age."

"You've got control, when you test fly," Esther said.

"Yes—?" Kolya said, not understanding her point.

"It's the control that gives you the rush. Knowing you were the one who pulled things together. Here, we couldn't *do* anything."

Kolya considered what she had said. "I believe that may be part of it."

"Everybody was going to die," Infinity said. "That's what I was thinking. It wouldn't have been so bad, if it was only me or a few people. Somehow it felt worse that it was going to be everybody."

They made their way up through the skin of *Starfarer*. Infinity switched his attention back and forth between his own surroundings and the incredible miniature planet pacing *Starfarer*. The ecosystem amazed him and intrigued him. He wondered if he would get a chance to visit it, to talk to the person who designed or directed it. And he wondered if an artificial ecosphere might draw Alzena from her apathy.

* * *

J.D. touched Arachne.

"Professor Thanthavong, is everyone all right?"

"Yes," Thanthavong said. "And we're still . . . trying not to panic."

"Yes." She managed a shaky laugh. "I know how that feels."

Gerald Hemminge interrupted. "You're supposed to talk through me," he said. "I am your liaison, after all."

After a long silence, and at a loss for anything else to say, J.D. answered him.

"I'm sorry, Gerald," she said. "We'll try to follow the protocol from now on."

The blue planetoid hovered nearby.

"You know what it's doing?" Victoria gestured toward it. "It's moving to draw *Starfarer* into orbit."

"How is it possible, Victoria?" J.D. asked.

"I don't know." Victoria sounded stunned. "Maybe it isn't. Maybe we're all undergoing mass hallucination. We're *seeing* it. But I can't explain it. What's that thing using for propulsion? What *is* it?"

"It's the alien ship," J.D. said.

All her teammates stared at her.

"That's the most reasonable explanation, isn't it? We came here looking for a ship: for whatever the craft was that left the spectral signature. We expected . . . I don't know, some kind of mechanical spaceship, a pointy rocketship—"

"A flying saucer," Satoshi said.

"Or a big cigar-shaped blimp thing." She spread her hands, making sketches in the air. "But it won't be anything like that. Why would alien people want to fly around in a tin can? We sure don't. *Starfarer* doesn't look like any classic spaceship."

"So they've replicated a natural environment," Satoshi said. "And they've done it even more accurately than we have."

"But they were way ahead of us," Victoria said.

"And now they're beside us, and when we got here they were behind us."

"Maybe they stopped off to sightsee," Satoshi said dryly. "But J.D.'s idea makes a lot of sense."

"Strange as it is, it's the simplest explanation I can think of," J.D. said.

"Then why don't they answer us!" Victoria exclaimed.

"Let's go see," J.D. said.

Victoria gazed thoughtfully at the natural-looking, wholly unnatural object.

"Very well," she said.

Politely, but more so all their other colleagues could listen in and know what they were doing, they informed Gerald Hemminge of their plans.

The *Chi* pushed free of *Starfarer*, and accelerated toward the planetoid.

"The conditions down there are Earth-like," Satoshi said. "The air's about twenty-two percent oxygen, the rest nitrogen with traces of the usual stuff. Lots of water. Shirtsleeves environment at the middle latitudes, thirty degrees Celsius."

"Shirtsleeves for you, my dear," Victoria said. "Sounds like air-conditioner weather to me."

Satoshi smiled, then sobered.

"Where's the heat coming from?" J.D. said. They were too far from either of the stars in the systems to receive much warmth from starlight.

"Underground."

"Neutronium?" Victoria said.

That made sense to J.D. A chunk of a neutron star, to provide the necessary mass, to create enough gravity to hold the air and the water, to tap for energy. A thick shell of rock and dirt, perhaps even of metal, to absorb extra energy, store it, reradiate it as heat, and protect the inhabitants from the interior radiation. Plants evolved to photosynthesize in the infrared as well as the visual spectrum, when the planetoid left the vicinity of a star.

Results: a miniplanet, no native sun required.

"If you agree, Victoria, I'd like to transmit our regular broadcast toward the..." She waved one hand in the direction of the planetoid, unsure what to call it. "The same transmission we're sending back to *Starfarer*."

Victoria shrugged. "No objection. I don't see how they'd be able to decipher it, without compatible equipment."

"You're right," J.D. said. "Of course. But. Still."

"Go ahead and try it."

J.D. made the necessary request. The *Chi* was still so close to *Starfarer* that she could work through Arachne. The web behaved normally: as if it could read its users' minds. Until it finished healing, Arachne was dedicating most of its attention

to communications between the starship and its scout, but as
far as J.D. could tell, the second crash had left the web with
no tangible damage. That did not seem fair.

Feral would have gotten a kick out of this, J.D. thought.
He might even had persuaded Victoria to let him come along.
She glanced over at Stephen Thomas, wondering what he was
thinking. The cut on his forehead had healed, his black eyes
had faded. He looked as beautiful, and as calm, and as cold,
as a marble statue, not permitting himself to react to Feral's
death; not permitting himself to react to anything.

She turned away and squeezed her eyes shut, willing
herself not to cry.

"Professor Thanthavong," Stephen Thomas said, his words
abrupt. He had remained calm through the threat of imminent destruction and the shock of their deliverance, but he
had not spoken since the emergency ended. He ignored
J.D.'s promise about liaison protocol.

"I am here, Stephen Thomas."

"Did Arachne look at the evidence?" His voice was cold.
"Is Blades out of the web yet?"

"He no longer has access to Arachne," Thanthavong said.
"You may ease your mind on that concern."

"What are you going to do about him?"

"I? Nothing. I did propose that he remain sequestered
until we convene a meeting. Then he may, of course, speak in
his own defense. He has agreed to my suggestion."

"When's the meeting?"

"You and J.D. are the witnesses against him. The meeting
can't take place until you return."

"Good lord, look," Satoshi said. "They're transmitting."

J.D. leaned forward so quickly that she bounced against
her safety straps. She grabbed the arms of her couch.

"It's the maze again," Victoria said.

The complicated twining of light and shadow formed before
them, three-dimensional, transparent on its outside surface,
paths marked with fragile brush strokes that became more
and more solid as they neared the center. J.D. could see the
relationship between this maze and the original, two-dimensional
one, as if the two-dimensional shadow had traced a true
course through the three dimensions.

"Maybe they *can* look at your broadcast," Victoria said to
J.D. "What they're sending us is coming straight through. It

didn't need any more processing than a transmission from *Starfarer*."

J.D. looked directly at the camera that observed the alien contact team.

"We'd like to talk to you, face-to-face," J.D. said.

Stephen Thomas gestured with his chin toward the three-dimensional maze.

"Maybe that *is* their face," he said, bitter and mocking. "Maybe they're already trying to talk to us."

"I'm aware of that possibility, Stephen Thomas," J.D. said. It distressed her to hear him speak in such a tone. "That's why I think we should meet in person."

Her calm dismay silenced him. J.D. felt anything but calm.

"They may have figured out our broadcast system in a couple of days," Victoria said, "but it seems unlikely they could have picked up enough English to understand what you just—"

The image projector produced a rich, full voice.

"We would like to meet you face-to-face, too."

11

J.D. waited in the air lock of the *Chi*. In a few minutes, she would be the first human being to set foot on a living alien world.

Her heart pounded.

She wore neither protective suit nor breathing apparatus, only an LTM, for broadcasting to the *Chi* and to *Starfarer*, on her collar. The alien beings assured her that it was safe to go outside, and she chose to believe them.

Satoshi's voice reached her through the exterior speaker.

"They're right about the air, J.D.," he said. "It's breathable. Chemically it's almost identical to Earth's. That is, Earth's before the Industrial Revolution."

"Yes," J.D. said. She had not doubted it.

"That doesn't say anything about bugs."

"I don't like your exposing yourself to alien pathogens," Victoria said. "I think it would be better to let Stephen Thomas finish testing—"

J.D. felt anxious, but excited, too. She restrained her impatience. She understood Victoria's uneasiness, her uncertainty. She would feel the same if she were in her teammate's place, just having watched a friend die. Having to watch another friend walk into the unknown, alone, would be intolerable. Walking into the unknown herself was easier.

"They have experience with this," J.D. said. "We have to trust them."

"Let her do her job," Stephen Thomas said.

"I'm going outside now." J.D. was unwilling to wait through more delays, to be forced to stand fast through any more discussion. She opened the air lock door.

Warm, fresh air enveloped her, dissipating the inevitable

234

stale odors of shipboard life. The air smelled like roses, like growing grass.

She stepped down.

The *Chi* had landed on a wide patch of white stone, irregular in outline but uniform in smoothness. J.D. had not been able to tell from above it if was natural or manufactured. Standing on it, she still could not tell. It radiated warmth. She took a few steps across the even stone. She left no mark behind her.

The air was so clear it sparkled. The curved horizon lay close; she could walk all the way around this worldlet in a couple of days. Sirius A was high, small and bright and intense in the purple sky. The atmosphere was shallower than that of Earth, so the light from Sirius A was less filtered, less scattered. The result was a strange, cold daylight, and a sky like evening. The brighter stars shone, intense against indigo. Sirius B, small and dim, was barely larger than a distant star.

The worldlet spun, not fast enough to perturb its gravity, but fast enough to give it days and nights, fast enough to keep one side from cooking, fast enough to avert atmospheric turbulence and violent storms.

Satoshi had measured the period of rotation. It was twenty-four hours. Not twenty-three and a half, or twenty-four hours, six minutes, forty-nine seconds: not some number close to Earth's day, some number J.D. could consider an interesting coincidence. The period of rotation was, precisely, twenty-four hours.

She walked away from the *Chi* and onto the land, walking gingerly on the ground cover. She was on an alien world and she expected alienness. The last thing she wanted to do was blunder around and step on the inhabitants.

In itself, the worldlet was strange, but its environment made her feel nearly at home. J.D. found it difficult to believe in such a coincidence; she considered the cost of such extraordinary hospitality.

A soft breeze ruffled her short hair and passed through the velvety leaves beneath her feet. She stooped down and brushed her fingertips across the tops of the plants, but did not pick any. She took the cautious course of waiting till she had some idea of what she was doing, whom and what waited to meet her. She did not want to do anything to abuse her welcome.

The landing stone lay in the midst of a wide meadow. The vegetation was short and bushy, a springy herbaceous species with small round leaves. Her footsteps made no more mark on it than they had on the landing stone.

The meadow spread across a shallow valley that vanished quickly over the horizon. A forest filled the upper end of the valley, but stopped abruptly, leaving a sharp edge of meadow. A narrow stream cut precise loops from the forest, past J.D., and around the curve of the world. Low hillocks rolled away on one side, never rising to foothills or mountains. To the other side, a field of scree rose steeply to a plateau.

Behind her, the *Chi* creaked and pinged, cooling and settling. A musical low hum was the only other sound. J.D. wondered if the sound came from this world's equivalent of birds or insects.

She waited, ready for anything. She waited for the hum to turn to a voice, for the plants beneath her feet to take on sentience, for the entire worldlet to be a living, intelligent creature, the ultimate Gaia.

A puffy cloud passed overhead, barely higher than the weather systems on board *Starfarer*.

J.D. pushed aside the assumptions that her mind kept making about the beings she would meet: they had spoken in English, so they must be flesh and blood, they must have mouths, and ears, and language. But the medium of their communication was electronic signals sent through space, giving no clue to origin. The beings no more had to have mouths, verbal language, ears, faces, than Arachne did.

She sent a brief, direct message to her teammates.

"Any reaction? Instructions?"

"Nothing," Victoria said softly in her mind.

"Thank you for welcoming us," J.D. said aloud.

At the same time, she instructed the *Chi*'s computer to transmit her statement electronically. It occurred to her that the alien beings might not recognize her any more than she could be sure of recognizing them. Who could know how the beings would interpret the alien contact team's message, or J.D.'s greeting, or their regular transmissions, or even her appearance?

I'm prepared for misunderstandings, J.D. thought. I think. I hope they are, too.

She turned slowly, looking around, gazing up the slope of

tumbled rock, wondering if she should climb to higher ground for a better vantage point, or follow the stream...

Something moved.

At the edge of the plateau, a group of small beings stood on their hind legs, their paws crossed delicately over their stomachs, and stared down at her.

She waited.

The meerkats, J.D. thought. They look like meerkats. Like the stone creature I found in the museum. Are these the alien beings? Is that why their statue was the only thing left after the destruction?

If the meerkats *were* the alien beings, a lot of theories about intelligence and body size, brain size, would go out the window. The beings stood no higher than her knee.

Meerkats are communal, she told herself. Maybe meerkat aliens have a communal intelligence.

Oh, *stop*, she thought, aggravated with herself. Stop making assumptions. It isn't even safe to assume their brains— whatever functions as a brain in an alien creature—are in their heads!

She walked toward the scree, her gaze on the meerkats. They stood perfectly still, staring at her.

"J.D., look out!"

As Victoria shouted a warning, as the ground rumbled beneath J.D.'s feet, movement caught the corner of her eye. She spun around.

Roaring with outrage and anger, a huge piebald bull galloped out of the forest and across the meadow, snorting, tossing its head and its long, curved horns.

The *Chi* was too far away.

J.D. sprinted onto the scree, scrambling up the sharp, precarious rocks. Tiny avalanches spilled and clattered behind her. The bull slid to a stop at the edge of the slope. Its hooves dug deep grooves in the soft, damp earth. It pawed and snorted and advanced a few wary paces onto the scree.

It stopped. Twenty meters above it, J.D. clambered onto the edge of the plateau and lay there panting.

Are you all right? Electronic transmission did nothing to temper the shock in Victoria's voice.

"I'm fine," J.D. said aloud. The LTM on her collar would pick up and transmit her voice to the *Chi* and to *Starfarer*.

Her visual transmission must have given everyone quite a jolt. "I'm a bit . . . startled."

She climbed to her feet. The meerkats had vanished.

She was clutching a small dusty plant. She recalled a phrase from a favorite old fairy tale: I have given you my hospitality, and you have stolen my rose.

Don't be silly, J.D. said to herself. You read too much fiction.

She would have replanted the wilting flower, but she had ripped its roots from a narrow crevice. She shoved it, leaves and ruffled white flowers and dirt and roots and all, into her pocket.

She looked over the edge of the cliff. Seeing her, the bull snorted again. Its amazing horns curved up and forward, crowning it.

Like a longhorn, J.D. thought, then, No, like an aurochs.

It looked like a great wild European ox, a creature hunted to extinction, then experimentally backcrossed into existence again. It stood taller than J.D. at the shoulder, and its curved horns added another half meter to its height.

The aurochs's red-and-white spotted coat gleamed as if it had been groomed. The enormous creature snorted a third time, but it had backed off the scree and into the meadow. Looking up at her, it bounced on its forelegs. The playful motion startled her.

J.D. considered climbing down the scree to face the pie-bald bull, but lacking any communication from the alien beings, she decided to choose discretion over valor for the moment.

A shrill cry shocked the quiet.

J.D. looked across the plateau. Up here it was dryer. The trees twisted together, windswept and dark.

Shadows beneath the gnarled trees moved like ghosts. The shadows could be what she was seeking. So could the trees; they might be Ents, as in Tolkien. She stopped searching, and walked, completely open, into the high forest.

She stepped into the shade, expecting coolness. But it was warmer beneath the tangled branches. The trees insulated the heated ground. The air smelled of hot pine pitch. J.D. blinked, waiting for her eyes to become accustomed to the dimmer light.

The meerkats appeared again, their skinny feet and legs

pacing quickly, their bodies staying at the same level when they moved. In life they were not nearly so cute as in sculpture, but strange, alien prowlers. They skittered off together, then stopped and leapt up to watch her.

Beyond them, two figures walked toward J.D.

They paused; the woman came forward.

"Welcome," she said.

J.D.'s knees buckled. She staggered, falling, catching herself on her hands. Her fingers clenched the hot, dry ground. She pushed herself upright, though she felt too shocked to stand.

After a moment's surprised hesitation, the man spoke to the woman.

"I told you she wasn't ready."

"She's just frightened. We should have sent the aurochs to the other hemisphere."

The woman hurried to J.D.'s side.

"I didn't think—I'm so sorry. The bull wouldn't have hurt you; he only wanted to play. Should we call your colleagues?"

At the same time, Victoria was sending a concerned message. The image J.D. was sending to the *Chi* must have swooped and tumbled.

"Nothing's wrong," J.D. said to the woman, and to Victoria. "It wasn't the bull." She was ashamed to have reacted with such shock. But she had been expecting something—anything—so strange, and she had received something so apparently ordinary.

The woman sat beside J.D. The man remained standing.

"I must have..." J.D. decided not to lie to them, even about so trivial, and embarrassing, a matter. "I was surprised to see you," she said. "Because you look so much like us. I was prepared for anything, except human beings. I mean," she said quickly, "other people who look like human beings."

They were small, no taller than Victoria, slender, narrow waisted but muscular, particularly through the legs, dark eyed, their skin dark in the red tones, like Zev's, but more cinnamon than mahogany. The man was young, the woman old. Both wore their hair in ringlets, the man's black, the woman's silver gray, its tighter curls streaked with metallic silver decorations.

The woman wore a skirt and shirt and vest of a simple cut

and simple weave. It looked like homespun, natural-dyed cotton in shades of tan and sand and umber, light and cool.

The youth wore a kilt that flowed around his legs, brilliant white against his skin, glowing in the shadows of the forest. His clothing gave the impression of free-moving liquid, not because of some alien fiber or unique weave, but because of the hundreds of narrow, sharp, vertical pleats in the silky cloth.

Like a Fortuny gown. J.D. started to laugh, restrained herself, and thought, High fashion.

The two people were exquisitely beautiful. They were the only people J.D. had ever met who were as beautiful as Stephen Thomas.

"But we *are* human beings," the man said.

J.D. had been about to stand up again. Instead, she stayed where she was, the woman kneeling beside her, the youth gazing down with his arms crossed on his smooth bare chest.

"We've been waiting for you for a long time," the woman said.

"Then why—" J.D. stopped, before a thousand questions tumbled out of her mouth without any pause for answers. "Maybe we could start again. With proper introductions. My name is J.D. Sauvage. I'm from Earth, more recently from *Starfarer*, the starship that . . ." She hesitated, not sure what to call the worldlet. "That this place avoided hitting. . . . How did you do that?"

"My name is Europa," the old woman said. "I'm from Earth, too, more recently from this place, which is our starship." She did not answer J.D.'s question.

"My name is Androgeos," the youth said. "How did you come here?"

"We followed you. We saw your transition spectrum. I have to explain what happened when we arrived at Tau Ceti—at the star system we just left."

"We know its name," Androgeos said.

"We came as fast as we could." J.D. frowned. "Were you waiting for us? Looking for us? It seemed to us that we arrived here first. Why did you leave Tau Ceti?"

"Androgeos meant, why did it take so long for the people of Earth to build a starship?" Europa said.

J.D. had no idea how to answer that. "How long have you been waiting?"

"Thirty-seven hundred years," Europa said. "Wouldn't you like to stand up now?"

J.D. was not entirely sure she could trust her legs, but she gathered herself and rose. She was steady enough. The meerkats peered out from behind tree trunks. Their curiosity overcoming their wariness, they *pit-patted* toward her, stood up in a group just out of her reach, folded their hands, and watched.

"Come," Europa said, taking J.D.'s hand. "Let's go sit in the sunlight, where it's cooler. I do like the light of Sirius, don't you?"

"I . . . haven't had much chance to sit in the light of Sirius," J.D. said, nonplused.

The light of Sirius was bright and white, but the star was much smaller than the sun as viewed from Earth. Europa led J.D. to a group of boulders near the edge of the plateau. She perched on one. She drew her legs up and rested her elbows on her knees, her chin on her fists. J.D. sat on the warm rock.

"Tell us everything," Europa said.

"Everything? About Earth? Don't you already know it?"

"There's only so much we can learn from remotes," Europa said. "Things change . . . in three and a half millennia."

Androgeos stood apart from them, his arms still folded. His demeanor made J.D. uncomfortable; she wondered if her surprise, or her comment about aliens, somehow had offended him.

"Tell us about your starship," Androgeos said. "How you came to be here."

"We came looking for you," J.D. said simply. "For centuries—I don't know, probably as long as humans were humans—people back on Earth wondered if people lived among the stars."

"So we did," Europa said. "And here we are."

"Why did you run away before?" J.D. asked.

"Because you arrived in a threatening manner," Europa said dryly.

"I want to explain about that. It was an accident."

"How did you come here?" Androgeos asked again.

J.D. explained the method by which *Starfarer* had detected the worldlet's departure.

"Yes, yes, *we* know how to do that," Androgeos said,

impatient. "Interesting that *you* do. But you were a distance from the—what were you calling it?—the transition point, that will suffice. Your ship is ungainly. Yet you traveled very fast."

"I don't know," J.D. said honestly. "Your starship can accelerate much faster than *Starfarer*. As you saw. I'm sure Victoria could explain it. Would you like to go meet her, and my other teammates?"

"Yes, soon," Europa said. "But let's speak a bit more first."

"Where do you come from?" J.D. asked. "What I mean is, if human beings have been out here for more than three millennia, how did your ancestors get into space? Where did they live all this time? How many human beings are out here? How did you build your starship?"

"So many questions!" Europa said.

"Yes," J.D. replied. "Of course. That's why I came here. To ask questions. To find answers."

"We have questions, too," Androgeos said. "In fairness, we should trade. Each ask one in turn."

"That's all right with me," J.D. said. "I'm not going anywhere—I've been waiting all my life to get here."

"We've been waiting all our lives for you to come," Europa said. "I just wish—"

Androgeos interrupted. "Which question do you want us to answer?"

"How did your ancestors get into space?"

"The other people rescued us," Androgeos said.

J.D. waited a moment. The meerkats peered at her across a flat-topped boulder. Androgeos had finished his reply.

"What other people?" J.D. asked. "And what did they rescue your people from?"

Androgeos frowned, as if he might object to her wanting some elaboration, but he could not deny that the answer contained very little information.

"There are many other people out here," Europa said. "Some of them are awfully strange. Frightening to look at, even. But you learn that it doesn't make much difference."

J.D. repressed a twinge of irritation at getting a lecture on prejudice.

"I think I already know that," J.D. said carefully. "You and Androgeos surprised me only because you were so familiar."

I suppose I can't blame Europa for what she assumes about

me, J.D. thought. She's a hundred generations removed from Earth. She probably thinks I'm a barbarian.

J.D. smiled to herself. With their physical features, their Hellenic names and no doubt ancestry, Europa and Androgeos probably did think she was a barbarian. A barbarian by definition: someone who did not speak Greek. Except that thirty-seven hundred years ago would have been well before classical Greek times. Probably even before the classical Greek language.

J.D. sent her bits of information to Arachne, asking for speculation, and returned her attention to Europa and Androgeos.

One of the meerkats bounded onto the flat-topped boulder and stood atop it, staring at J.D.

"The other beings took humans off Earth?" J.D. said.

"They rescued us," Europa said again. "They only take people who are going to die." She leaned back, exposing her face to the light of Sirius, bathing in it. Her eyes closed, she spoke dreamily. "It was terrifying, the air trembled and the sea rose up and roared. We saw the darkness striding toward us across the water. And then there was nothing to breathe, only hot ash all around us, falling, and no light . . ." She shivered. "So no one saw, when the people came down to save us." She opened her eyes again and gazed at J.D. intently. "They're always very careful about that."

Santoríni, Arachne said to J.D. The eruption on Thera. The destruction of the civilization on ancient Crete. Knossos, the Minoans.

The labyrinth.

"At other disasters? Do you mean that they. . ." She hesitated, searching for a word less heavily charged than "kidnap." Besides, if she were about to die, she would welcome someone who swooped down and took her away, kidnapper or not.

"They want a representative of every new sentient species," Europa said. "To do what we will do. To welcome their own kind into civilization. Gently, gradually, without too much distress and fear."

J.D. resisted the idea that she could not be trusted to meet alien beings, real alien beings. She had spent her life preparing to accept being frightened. She struggled to accept Europa and Androgeos as a kindness, a gift; nevertheless, their explanations, their condescension, distressed her. She felt dismay. No: more than that. She felt cheated.

"If there are so many other people out here, how can you be sure none of them have let themselves be seen visiting Earth?" J.D. asked, thinking of the rashes of UFO sightings over the past decades.

"They *didn't*," Androgeos insisted. "It's agreed."

"Agreed by who? How do you know so much about us? You speak English. . . . Surely you didn't learn it in the last couple of days."

"We never visited you," Androgeos said. "I didn't say we didn't watch you."

"Sometimes we sent a ship through your solar system," Europa said. "A contained one, not an open one like ours. For the last few years you would have noticed that it was not an ordinary Apollonian asteroid. So we've stayed away. But we've been waiting."

"Still, maybe one of those other people felt curious and came to Earth to take a look."

"Never."

"How can you be so sure?"

"Because they *wouldn't*," Androgeos said, as if that wrapped the subject up.

"Why do you think they have?" Europa asked.

"Some humans—back on Earth—think they've seen alien spaceships."

"Ships like this?" Europa exclaimed.

"No." J.D. laughed, remembering the team's conversation about alien spaceships. She thought she could detect a resonance of amusement from Victoria, back in the *Chi*, listening to everything.

"No," J.D. said again. "Nothing like this. But they see what they think are spaceships. And alien beings."

"Have you," Europa said hesitantly, "seen such apparitions yourself?"

"Me?" J.D. said. "No, of course not."

"If we had shown ourselves to Earth," Androgeos said, "then we would never know that humans see these fantasies."

"Is it important to you? To know some of us see fantasies?"

"Not particularly," Androgeos said offhand. "I use it only as an example. In simpler words, we leave you alone so you night discover something we don't know. Which you would never do, under our influence."

Against her will, J.D. had taken a sincere dislike to this arrogant young man. Though she felt insulted by his tone and his dismissive attitude, she had to respect his aims.

"I suppose not," she said. "No doubt you're right, and we needed the protection. Culture shock has destroyed—"

Androgeos interrupted. "Do *we* look culture shocked? It has nothing to with culture shock. Nor with protecting you. If we wished to protect you, we *would* have come to Earth, solved your problems, and led you out of barbarity."

"In the past, civilization helped new worlds reach space," Europa said. "But we found it wasn't good for us."

"'Us'—humans?"

"No, *us*—civilization."

"Young cultures sometimes stumble upon new knowledge. Valuable knowledge." Androgeos shrugged. "Unlikely. But it does happen."

"Unlikely," J.D. said dryly.

"But you don't see, J.D.!" Europa said. "You have one chance to offer civilization unique work. Then you're unique, too. You earn respect. If all you do is jump out into space and say, 'Here we are, give things to us,' then you are ordinary."

"We thought we were doing pretty well to jump out into space," J.D. said.

"I didn't mean to offend you."

"I know. Never mind."

"Why did you come," Androgeos asked, "if not to gain honor and recognition and acceptance among other people?"

"We came for a lot of reasons," J.D. said. "Not only because we hoped to meet other people. In fact, there's always been a controversy about that, back on Earth. Some people think other intelligent beings can't possibly exist."

Androgeos snorted. "And do they still believe the Sun circles the Earth?"

"Those of us who thought there must be other people out here had to answer the question, Why haven't any of them visited? We thought it might be a benevolent gesture— because the other beings didn't want to overwhelm and destroy our culture."

"The other beings do not much care about your culture,"

Androgeos said. "And they will have no reason to care, unless you prove yourselves worthy of attention."

"Your culture *will* change now," Europa said. "Nothing can stop that from happening. Even if you never meet any other people, just knowing we exist out here will change things. You did understand that, when you set out, didn't you?"

"Yes."

"It will be up to human beings whether you change it the way you want it, or let it be changed around you."

"What do you mean," J.D. said to Europa, "'Even if you never meet any other people'?"

Europa glanced away, glanced back, shoved her hands between her knees, and hunched her shoulders.

"You ran away from us," J.D. said. "When we arrived at Tau Ceti, and the missile exploded, we frightened you—"

"You frightened us not at all!" Androgeos exclaimed.

"Then why didn't you stay?"

"Didn't you understand what you were supposed to do?" Androgeos cried. "Why did you have to come after us and make things so much more complicated? Why didn't you go back to Earth?"

"Go back to Earth!"

"The message was clear."

"What message?"

"You can't come to civilization with weapons. You can't hunt people down. Your aggression is revolting! You aren't ready to join us. You were supposed to go home and grow up some more!"

"But that's *why* we followed you. Not to be aggressive, not to attack—! To explain about the explosion. It was a mistake."

As she spoke, she wondered, if what he's telling me is true, *why* is he talking to me at all?

"How could a nuclear explosion be a mistake?" Europa scowled at her. "That's just as bad as being armed. No, it's worse, it's careless." She shook her head. "Besides, the explosion didn't matter. What matters is that you were armed in the first place."

"*Starfarer* isn't armed!"

The dispute around that question had gone on for years, in public and private, in legislatures and parliaments, in the press and in living rooms. J.D. had followed the discussion even when she believed she had no chance to belong to the expedition.

"I understand that," Europa said. "But—"

"I don't think you do! For *Starfarer* to leave the solar system unarmed is a leap of faith and trust for human beings. It's a qualitative change in our behavior."

"And yet," Androgeos said, "you brought the warhead."

"It was a *mistake*."

"I'm sorry!" Europa exclaimed, genuinely distressed. "We've been waiting for this day for a long time. I'd make an exception for you if I could, J.D. I don't make the rules."

"Who does? What are the rules?"

"We can't tell you that," Androgeos said.

"Oh—!" J.D. exclaimed, exasperated, outraged.

"We don't *know*," Europa said.

"You—*what?*"

"There's no galactic overlord, making decrees, like in one of your movies. There's no list, one, two, three. What we have is a body of experience and observation."

"Such as—?"

"The cosmic string, of course."

"Then it *is* deliberate," J.D. said, amazed. "The strand that came within Earth's reach . . . someone sent it."

"And placed the intersections around Tau Ceti," Europa said. "Yes."

"And withdrew them when you exploded your bomb," Androgeos said, deliberately, cruelly. "As a protection for all of us. Protection against barbarism." His voice held an undertone of pain and anger: it hurt him as much to point out the reasons as it hurt J.D. to hear them.

"You must go back to Earth because we know, from the experiences of other people, what will happen if you don't go back to Earth. Almost any behavior is permitted—"

"Ignored," Androgeos said.

"As you will. Perhaps 'ignored' is a more accurate description. Weapons of mass destruction, though, attract . . . notice."

"So if we go home and persuade our governments to give up their arms, their armies—"

"That will help not at all," Androgeos said. "They are welcome to keep their toys. Use them on each other."

"No one will stop you, you see," Europa said, "from destroying your own world." She smiled sadly. "Though I very much hope you will not do so. I'd like to see it again. To return to Crete—"

The stories she and Androgeos inherited from their ancestors are as powerful for them as the same stories are for us, J.D. thought.

"They don't care what you do to other human beings," Androgeos said. "But you can't behave that way in civilization."

"Civilization" was sounding less and less civilized to J.D. Less civilized, and even more intriguing.

"We didn't intend to." She tried to explain. As she told Europa and Androgeos what had happened before *Starfarer* reached transition, about the tensions and the attempt of the military to take over the starship, she began to fear that she was only making things more difficult. But she could not think how to make them better, even by lying. She did not want to lie, and she knew that if she did lie, she would find herself in a manufactured story impossible to keep straight.

She finished her story. Neither of the alien humans spoke.

"Can't we ask for a hearing?" J.D. said.

Androgeos laughed.

"I get into arguments with friends," he said, "who claim human beings are so uninteresting that our whole species will never amount to anything. When I tell them what you just said—"

"I wasn't intending to be outrageous," J.D. said.

His dismissive comment about his own people disturbed her. If human beings disparaged each other, still, after so many years' exposure to civilization...

And then she realized Androgeos had not been talking about friends who were human beings. He had been talking about friends who were not human beings.

"It will be difficult to find anyone to ask," Europa said. "Because we have no idea what people, what beings, control the cosmic string. We've looked for them. Everyone has."

"I don't believe they exist," Androgeos said. "Not anymore. They set up controls. Then they vanished."

"It makes no difference whether they exist or not," Europa said. "No more than arguing whether the gods directed the bull during the games."

"How many angels can dance on the head of a pin," J.D. said softly.

Androgeos frowned, confused. "I thought I knew what an

angel looked like," he said. "From one of our information captures. I would have thought they were too big to stand on the head of a pin, much less dance."

So they don't know everything about us, J.D. thought; they aren't so omniscient that they even know all our idioms.

"It's just a saying," J.D. said. "A statement about futile arguments. Now we have a new one, I suppose. 'Where do the ancient astronauts live?'"

"But no one knows," Androgeos said. "Why argue about it?"

"Even if we do go home of our own volition," J.D. said, "I don't see a way to preventing Earth's governments from returning. First they tried to insist that we stay. Now they'll insist that we go."

"It will not be possible," Europa said. "The cosmic string will withdraw."

J.D. jerked up her head, astonished despite herself, despite her thought: Of course. That's exactly how they'll do it.

"And if you stay here," Androgeos said, "they'll withdraw it from the Sirius system, too."

Victoria was listening to everything J.D. said, everything the alien humans said. She would, without question, already be testing her algorithm for transition points that led back to Earth. J.D. feared she already knew what Victoria would find: the solar system emptied of cosmic string.

Starfarer would be able to return to Earth, but it would never be able to leave again. Not until "civilization" threw another lifeline.

"I think you have no choice," Europa said. "I think you are going to have to go home."

"And grow up?" J.D. said. "Just exactly how long do you expect us to stay in our rooms?"

"What?"

"Never mind. Another saying. If we do go home, how long are we supposed to stay?" She wondered if she could stand waiting for another year, another decade.

"They might let you try again in five hundred years."

"*What?*" J.D. cried, bolting to her feet.

J.D. saw the goal of her life's work held just beyond her reach, and about to be snatched away forever.

Europa rose, too, her hands open and spread, imploring her to understand.

"It's all right. Please. We'll be at Tau Ceti, waiting for you, when you return."

"What a comfort! Your twenty-times grandchildren can greet my twenty-times grandchildren, and they'll reminisce about us! *Five hundred years!*"

"It isn't so much," Europa said. "Not when you've waited as long as we have."

J.D. almost sat down again, but she steadied her knees by force of will.

"I thought you meant your ancestors," she said. "I thought it was quaint speech habit, to talk of them as 'us.'"

"We never said ancestors," Androgeos said.

"You meant yourselves, Europa and Androgeos. You lived on Crete when Santoríni erupted. When the tidal wave and the ash from Thera destroyed Knossos. You were the ones the alien people took away with them."

"Yes," Androgeos said, sounding for all the world like Zev when J.D. finally understood something about the orcas or the divers that was, to him, self-evident. "Yes. Of course. We have said so."

A second of the meerkats climbed onto the rock and stood beside the first. It dropped onto all fours and tiptoed toward J.D. It was just the color of the stone. Its pointy, damp nose twitched and glittered as it sniffed at her. Its small dark eyes held wariness, cunning. She held out her hand to it, very slowly, giving it a chance to smell her fingertips.

"They sometimes bite," Androgeos said.

J.D. left her hand outstretched. After a moment, satisfied, the meerkat ran to its companion. They prowled away down the side of the rock, then scampered to join the rest of the group. When they all stood looking at her, black eyes shiny in dark masks, she could not tell which were the two that had come to investigate her.

"I found their statue," she said.

"What statue?" Androgeos asked.

"The statue!" Europa exclaimed in dismay.

"The one of the meerkat. In the museum."

Europa sat up straighter. The lookout meerkat shrieked. All the meerkats dropped down and ran away, disappearing against the dry ground.

"But how could you?" Europa said, stricken. "You didn't land—you couldn't!"

"I'm afraid we did," J.D. said.

"My beautiful museum," Europa said, her voice a sigh. "I worked so hard on it for you."

"I'm sorry," J.D. said.

Distressed, Europa sat on the warm boulder with her hands clasped between her knees, kneading wrinkles into the fabric of her skirt.

"What is it about you Earth humans?" Androgeos said angrily. "You could have joined us a thousand years ago. Instead, no sooner do you gain access to knowledge, than you destroy it. You raze the library at Alexandria. You burn books, you suppress research, and now—!"

J.D. could not stand it; she could not bear to apologize again.

"That isn't fair!" J.D. said. "We didn't know the museum would destroy itself if we tried to look at it! We had no way to know! Why didn't you tell us what would happen? Why didn't you leave a message?"

"We fell silent," Europa said. "We withdrew our welcome."

"The warlike ones never take the hint," Androgeos said ominously. "They have to be shocked into sense."

"If you'd just left it alone!" Europa said. "It would have been waiting for you when you came back."

"Not for me!" J.D. cried. "It doesn't make any difference to *me* if it destroyed itself, or if it's still there in five hundred years!"

She turned away, distressed by the accusation, distressed by her own reaction. The destruction of the library at Alexandria had always seemed to J.D. to be one of the great tragedies of human history. To be accused of being the cause of an equivalent disaster was too much to bear, and too close to the truth.

Europa touched J.D.'s shoulder. Her hand was delicate, long fingered, strong, the nails opalescent.

"Back on Earth," she said. "How long do you live, back on Earth?"

J.D. collected herself, pretended she was all right, and answered.

"Not much more than a hundred years."

"Hardly any different from our birthplace," Androgeos said. "Why so little improvement?"

"You could keep the body going indefinitely. But if you

keep renewing neural tissue, eventually the connections in
your memory get fuzzy. After a while . . . you aren't you
anymore." She could not keep her thoughts away from Feral,
from the destroyed museum, from Stephen Thomas changing
as she watched. She caught her breath, trying so hard not to
cry that her throat hurt. Seeking calm, she stared at the
ground. A minuscule plant grew from a crack in the rock,
dusty green with deep purple flowers, like pinpoint violets.

"You didn't visit the worlds, did you?" Europa asked, "Tau
Ceti II, Tau Ceti III? The living ones? You would have
mentioned it if you did. Wouldn't you?"

J.D. started to answer, then jerked back to stare at Europa
in horror.

"You don't mean—you can't be saying the *worlds* would
have destroyed themselves, too!" Even though she had first
suggested it, she could not believe it might actually be true.

"It's our defense," Europa said. "Not to let them fall into
warlike hands."

"We didn't land," J.D. said.

"I'm so glad," Europa said. "That make things better. The
planets will still be there when Earth humans come back. I
can build you another museum, but five hundred years isn't
nearly enough to reconstruct the ecosystem. And they never
come out the same. Tau Ceti II is so pretty, and Tau Ceti III
is severe, and exciting . . ." She stopped. "But you won't get
to see them."

"No."

"I'm sorry you have to return to Earth."

"I am, too," J.D. said, at a loss. "Please, come and talk to
my colleagues before we go. Don't make them leave without
even meeting you."

Androgeos glanced at her, sidelong, suspicious. "It would
not be to your advantage to kidnap us."

"I've got no intention of kidnapping you!" J.D. exclaimed,
shocked and embarrassed and insulted. "I'm trying to show
you some hospitality."

Androgeos and Europa gazed at her, and she had no idea
what they might be thinking.

"If you don't want to come inside the explorer," she said,
"at least invite my friends out. If you're afraid—"

"We're not afraid of you, J.D.," Europa said.

"All right. But you asked questions my colleagues will have to answer."

The two alien humans hesitated, and then Europa rose.

"We'll meet your colleagues," she said.

They climbed down the scree and walked back toward the *Chi*, Europa and Androgeos flanking J.D. The alien humans were of a height, and J.D. was a head taller.

"You're so fair!" Europa said. "I can see your blood right through your skin!" She reached up and laid her fingertips against J.D.'s skin. J.D. was still flushed with the embarrassment of Androgeos's accusation. Europa felt the heat. She pulled back, startled.

"I *knew* there were colorless people, of course," she said. "But you're the first I've ever met."

It's no easier for the alien humans, meeting us for the first time, J.D. thought, than it is for me, meeting them.

"We come in lots of colors," she said. "Even colorless."

The *Chi* cycled open with a faint sigh of the locking mechanism. The meerkat troop, which had been slinking around and sniffing at the spacecraft's legs, stood up as one. A high, shrill cry: they all scampered off.

"Why meerkats?" J.D. said. "They aren't from Greece."

"Neither are we," Androgeos said. "We were civilized when the Greeks were still barbarians, when there were no Greeks. Our ancestors were the pharaohs. We like to have reminders of our mother continent around us."

Europa laughed. "Andro, you're so pompous. We have meerkats because the people who rescued us rescued them, too, and other creatures. And because they're fun to watch and soft to pet."

"Because they're cute," J.D. said.

"Yes."

"Tell me about the people who rescued you."

Europa glanced away. "I can't do that."

The door opened. Victoria stepped down. Satoshi and Stephen Thomas and Zev followed her.

J.D. made the introductions. The alien humans greeted her teammates civilly, coolly. Androgeos turned all his attention and arrogance on Victoria.

"You can answer questions your colleague did not understand," he said.

"I can answer questions in my area of expertise," Victoria said, "and J.D. can answer questions in the areas of hers. I have questions for you, too." She paused. "Want to trade?"

J.D. caught a quick flash of anger before Androgeos repressed it. Stephen Thomas looked at Androgeos, narrowing his eyes. J.D. wondered what he perceived, what he thought of the alien humans.

Whatever Stephen Thomas thought, J.D. knew she did not trust Androgeos. She had not decided for certain about Europa, though she liked Europa better. She assumed they would back each other up. Europa might tease Androgeos, her—colleague? Lover? Son? All three? Or none? But they must, after all these centuries of waiting, have the same goals.

"I can't explain our transition algorithm in words of one syllable," Victoria was saying to Androgeos. "Or in words at all. We need a graphics display."

J.D. had worried about how to tell Victoria of her suspicions without communicating through Arachne or the *Chi*. The alien humans could, no doubt, pick up transmitted information if they cared to. Now J.D. saw she did not need to voice her warning. Victoria was holding back her explanation, for the *Chi* could create displays out here as easily as inside.

"How many of you are there?" Satoshi asked Europa.

"Just one," she said. "Just me. I never thought it would be much fun to have a younger twin."

"Sorry," Satoshi said. "I meant how many humans did the other people rescue? Were they all from Crete, from the same time and place? Are they here, on your ship? Even if it was only a few, there must be a sizable human population away from Earth."

"Not that many," she said. "We don't have a world of our own, you see."

"What about Tau Ceti's worlds?"

"But," she said, as if explaining to a very young child, "those were made for you."

"'Made'?"

"They were lifeless, waterless."

"And you made them habitable? In three thousand years?" Satoshi sounded incredulous.

"Not I," Europa said. "And not in four thousand years. Your

neighbors placed them and seeded them for you, as a gift. Eons ago. Before there *were* human beings."

"That's remarkably magnanimous," Satoshi said.

Europa smiled. "Earth had life. Sentience always evolves. It just needs time. Someday human beings will terraform some other lifeless world for some other people. For beings who have not yet come into existence."

Satoshi fell silent.

Stephen Thomas crossed the landing stone, headed for the meadow.

"Where are you going?" Androgeos spoke sharply.

"To take a look at your plants," Stephen Thomas said. "To take a few samples."

"You wouldn't find them interesting. The species originated on Earth."

"They're interesting, believe me." Stephen Thomas started away again.

"No," Europa said, with a firmness J.D. had not previously heard in her voice, but did not find surprising.

Stephen Thomas stopped short.

"I'm sorry," Europa said. "That isn't possible."

J.D. winced for Stephen Thomas, feeling the blow as if it had been directed at her. Stephen Thomas stood on the sterile landing stone, looking around him at a world full of, if not precisely alien life forms, species that had been cut off from Earth for three and a half millennia, plants, and microbes, and animals, that must have been engineered for the environment.

"Europa—" Stephen Thomas said.

She circled him and approached Zev.

"You are wonderful," she said, awed. "What are you?"

"I'm Zev," he said. "Can we go swimming?"

"I thought you'd been watching us," J.D. said. "Don't you know about the divers?"

"We're not omniscient, J.D.," Europa said. "We're not omnipotent. What's a diver?"

Zev told her about the divers, the orcas.

"An ichthyocentaur, that's what you are!" Europa said. "I never expected to see one. But you have no scales on your legs."

"I'm not a fish!" Zev said, offended. "I have no scales anywhere." This was obvious. Zev was wearing nothing but a pair of Stephen Thomas's shorts. The fabric was a shade of green that did not compliment his skin tones. J.D. could not imagine the color complimenting anyone, including Stephen Thomas.

J.D. tried to keep track of several conversations at once. To her astonishment, Victoria had persuaded Androgeos that the transition algorithm could only be displayed by Arachne, back on board *Starfarer*.

J.D. regretted the dissembling, but approved. She had arrived to meet the alien humans in a state of deliberate, willful naïveté, and it had been a mistake.

I won't do that again, she promised Victoria silently, though she still refrained from sending her teammate a message. I promise I won't do that again.

12

The landing stone became a white expanse, then an irregular patch in a green meadow, then a decorative gleam against the natural landscape. It disappeared within the flowing pattern of forests and streams, lakes and marshes and island-studded seas.

The *Chi* rose. A herd of aurochs galloped across the meadow, tossing their horns.

The *Chi* rose, and the landscape vanished beneath sweeping white scarves of cloud.

The horizon curved quickly, steeply. The blue of the shallow seas overwhelmed the green of the land. The *Chi* sped away from the small blue planet, the miniature replica of Earth.

Despite the promise Androgeos and Europa had made, to visit *Starfarer,* J.D. expected their world, their ship, to accelerate and vanish, taking the alien humans along with it.

"They're following us," Victoria said. She sounded as surprised as J.D. felt.

The streamlined white blob of the alien humans' short-range spacecraft followed them out of the atmosphere.

J.D. let out her breath. "I didn't dare to believe them," she said.

"What have they got to gain by lying?" Satoshi said.

"What did they have to gain by talking to us at all?" J.D. asked. "If it's true that we've cause them nothing but trouble with our missile, why didn't they just whiz around us and disappear again?"

"I wish you wouldn't refer to that bomb as if it were our fault," Victoria said.

"I have to, Victoria," J.D. said. She met Victoria's sharp glance. "I'm sorry. We *are* responsible for it, we, us, human

257

beings. All of us. People who will, or won't, prove we're worth asking to join civilization. The people who fired the missile, the people who were the target. Maybe Europa is right. Maybe we ought to go back to Earth for five hundred years."

"You're speaking like a guilty child," Victoria said, "and I disagree, I deny, that we deserve to be punished!"

In the amphitheater, Infinity and Esther and Kolya and the rest of the faculty and staff of *Starfarer* watched the transmission from the *Chi*. Infinity found it comforting that so many of his colleagues had, independently, decided to come to *Starfarer*'s heart. Together, as a community, they watched the landing, the first meeting of humans and alien people.

By the time the *Chi* lifted off from the alien humans' spaceship, Infinity was numb with shock. The landing amazed and delighted him; the existence of the alien humans astonished him; Androgeos and Europa first exasperated and then affronted him. They had tremendous power, and they used it the way people always used power. Or misused it.

He leaned forward and rested his forehead on his arms, drained.

"Quite a story for Feral to cover," he muttered.

"Where is Feral?" Kolya asked. "I thought he would be here, but—Oh, *bojemoi . . .*"

The disbelief, the pain, in Kolya's voice, jolted Infinity upright.

"What—?" He automatically reached out to Arachne for information . . .

. . . and discovered the news of Feral's death.

"I was wrong," Infinity said, out loud, but more to himself than to Esther or Kolya. "I was wrong. Losing one person *is* just as bad."

"Look at strand three," Esther said.

As Arachne reached its full strength, regaining all its communications capabilities, a parallel message strand began to carry the recording Stephen Thomas had made of the antibody trace. It spun through the web, requiring no explanation. Infinity watched the evidence J.D. and Stephen Thomas had uncovered, disgusted, appalled, but not surprised. If he had learned one thing in his life, it was that people in authority would behave badly whenever they had the chance.

All around Infinity, other people were discovering the same information. Like whispers, messages vibrated through Arachne's shiny new web, messages echoed by voices in the amphitheater.

"It was Chancellor Blades..."

"Blades crashed the web..."

"Blades caused Feral's death..."

"Blades..."

"Blades..."

"Blades..."

All around Infinity, people cried or cursed, or held each other, or simply stood, stunned, or milled around in confusion and anger and disbelief.

A crowd began to form, cohesive, wrathful.

"This is going to turn into a mob," Kolya said. "We've got to—"

Iphigenie DuPre strode into the amphitheater. At the top of the stairs, she looked down over the crowd.

"Listen to me!" she cried. "Listen to me!"

Her angry voice sliced through the buzz of incredulity and outrage.

"Any of us could have died," Iphigenie said.

She had torn herself free of indecision. She was magnetic, arousing, driven by her fury and her grief.

"It was deliberate murder! It was aimed at *me*—and instead it killed Feral. An innocent, a guest, a friend! He died trying to help us! He died *because* he tried to help us."

She paused, gazing at her colleagues, letting what had happened sink in.

"We can't let Blades do this again! Will you come with me, will you help me stop him?"

She led her colleagues in a stream, out of the amphitheater.

Infinity found himself being pulled along, following Esther. Outside the amphitheater, when the crush eased a little, Kolya caught up to him and grabbed him by the shoulder.

"What are you doing? Infinity! Esther! Where are you going?"

"I'm going with Iphigenie," Esther said. "We've been jerked around enough."

"And then what?"

Infinity stopped. Esther did not hesitate.

"I . . . I don't know," Infinity said. "Maybe there's an explanation. Maybe it was an accident—"

"Feral's death? Perhaps it was an accident. But the crash of the web caused it. And the crash *was* deliberate."

Infinity hurried after Esther. He did not know what else to do. He caught up to her. Kolya strode along beside them.

"What do you do here," Kolya asked, "when someone commits a criminal act?"

"I don't know," Infinity said again.

Esther had never lived on *Starfarer* till now. Though Kolya had lived on the starship since its beginning, he had avoided *Starfarer*'s endless organizational meetings. But Infinity had attended most of them.

"We never even talked about it," he said.

Esther looked at him askance.

"Not even, 'What do we do if a couple of people punch each other out?'"

"Not even that," Infinity admitted.

"What were you thinking of?" Kolya said.

"I guess we were thinking this is a utopia," Infinity said.

They reached the crest of the hill. From it, they could see the ugly, blocky administration building. Other people had already begun to gather outside it.

Infinity took a deep breath. "I guess we were wrong."

The *Chi* was halfway home.

J.D. hesitated, floating in the doorway of the small lab. Within, Stephen Thomas stared at an analysis display, his expression blank.

"Stephen Thomas—?"

He glanced up. "Nothing here," he said. "Europa's ship has very clean air." Shadows of exhaustion and grief darkened the skin beneath his eyes.

J.D. reached into her pocket and pulled out the damp, dirty lump of the wilted plant. The ruffled flowers had closed up into knots of discoloring white petals. J.D. wished she had let Stephen Thomas alone. This effort to ease his disappointment felt not only futile but pathetic.

"I just remembered this," she said. "I know it isn't much. I pulled it up by mistake. It's probably contaminated with pocket lint . . ." She stopped. She had not meant to sound flippant, to make jokes. She wished she had forgotten the

plant completely, wished she had never pulled it up or kept
it. Too late now. Holding out her hand, she offered him the
abused clump of leaves.

The bent, crushed plant floated from her palm. A few
fragments of dirt detached themselves and drifted in slow,
irregular trajectories around it.

"It's from Europa's ship," J.D. said, unnecessarily.

"Christ in a cow pasture," Stephen Thomas said. "J.D.,
you're amazing." He grabbed a sterile petrie dish and floated
toward her. In a moment he had the alien plant, including
even the dirt particles, safely enclosed.

"I'm sorry that's all—"

"Don't apologize!" he said sharply. "You apologize too
much. Don't ever apologize." He left the petrie dish floating,
took J.D. by the shoulders, bent toward her, and kissed her
chastely on the forehead. His lips felt hot and dry. His kiss
made her tremble.

"Thank you," he said.

Professor Thanthavong stood outside the edge of the crowd,
watching Iphigenie, distressed and dismayed. Infinity and
Esther and Kolya joined her.

"The doors are barricaded," Thanthavong said. "If they
rush the building... more people are going to get hurt."

"Be easy," Kolya said. "Blades has to come out eventually,
and what can he do in the meantime? All Iphigenie need do
is wait."

"And when he comes out, then what? Will we become
murderers, too? Why is Iphigenie *doing* this?"

On the other side of the crowd, Iphigenie continued
speaking.

"I'm living on borrowed time," she said. "My life cannot be
mine again unless I find *justice*."

"Send the ASes after him," Infinity said. "They can stop
him."

"I can't do that," Thanthavong said.

"But—"

"It's impossible! He never released them. They're all in the
basement of the administration building, the ASes and the
mobile AIs. If he has enough time he can program them by
hand. If he's good enough, he could program them to protect

him." Without giving Infinity a chance to reply, she hurried toward the crowd. Kolya strode after her.

"Miensaem—" He touched her shoulder.

Turning back, she flung off his hand. "Do you have a better idea?"

He hesitated. "No. I'm sorry, no."

"Then don't stop me!"

Infinity followed her.

"Infinity!" Kolya said.

Infinity glanced back.

"She's right," Kolya said. "Let her try—if this continues— I've seen—"

Kolya looked far more shaken now than he had in the face of his own death.

"I think I can help!" Infinity could not take time to explain. He ran after Thanthavong.

She mounted the stairs.

"We must prevent"—Iphigenie saw Thanthavong; her voice faltered, then strengthened—"prevent more sabotage, more deaths!" Thanthavong walked up to her. At the same time, the senators pushed their way through the crowd.

"Nothing's to be gained by creating a mob," Thanthavong said.

Iphigenie drew herself up, fighting the gravity, her eyes narrow.

"These are our friends and colleagues, not a mob, and I'm a victim of assault, not a demagogue!" Iphigenie said. "The chancellor must surrender himself."

"He's given me his parole, to stay in his office and his house," Thanthavong said.

"You *believe* him?" Iphigenie said, incredulous.

"Does it matter, Iphigenie?" Thanthavong asked. "Arachne is rejecting his neural node. We've suspended his hard link. He's cut off. Harmless."

"And what if he has another way into the system?"

"That's impossible," Thanthavong said.

"So was crashing the web!"

Thanthavong started to answer, then fell silent. She had no reply.

Iphigenie turned to the crowd again. "Blades has the whole administration building at his disposal, all the ASes and the mobile AIs! Who knows what he can do to us from here?"

Senator Derjaguin took the steps two at a time. He was panting. Senator Orazio, smaller, less efficient at pushing through the crush, followed a moment later.

"Chancellor Blades is a U.S. citizen," Derjaguin said. "I warn you, if anything happens to him, my country will prosecute."

"Jag, calm down," Orazio said. "Ms. DuPre—" She walked toward Iphigenie, her hands outstretched.

Iphigenie brushed her aside with indifference borne of desperation. "Your country's kidnap squads can't reach us here."

"I'm offering him sanctuary in the consulate," Derjaguin said.

"Sanctuary?" Iphigenie laughed bitterly. "Or a staging area to make war on us?"

"Let us take charge of him," Orazio said, pleading. "What's happened is tragic. But vigilante—"

"You're making things worse, Senators," Thanthavong said. "You have no authority here."

Iphigenie turned her back on Derjaguin and Orazio.

"Blades *can't* remain here," she said to Thanthavong. "You must see that. If we have to storm the building—"

"Storm the building! Batter it down with your bare hands?"

"This is anarchy!" Derjaguin exclaimed. "Good god—"

"There's another way," Infinity said.

They all stopped talking and stared at him. He looked down. He had just interrupted a multimillionaire, a U.S. senator, and a Nobel laureate.

"What is it, Infinity?" Thanthavong said.

"Who the hell are you?" Derjaguin snarled.

"He's a member of this expedition!" Iphigenie turned on Derjaguin. "He has a right to speak. You do not."

"The chancellor doesn't have all the ASes," Infinity said.

"But he does. He called them in."

"Not the outside workers—the silver slugs."

"What use are they in here?" Thanthavong asked.

Everyone thought the silver slugs could only work outside. Infinity supposed the chancellor had made the same assumption, or he might never have freed them.

Infinity gestured to the plaza.

"Here they come."

Responding to his call, the big silver slugs pressed themselves through the access tunnels to the interior of *Starfarer*, through the ground-level hatches and up into the field around the administration building. The plaza glittered with the smooth shiny glow of the lithoclasts' skin. They were slow, for each one gripped the ground tightly, flowing into its front end and securing itself before it eased its back end forward. On the starship's outer surface, losing hold meant being flung off into space.

They were slow, but they were steady. Inexorable, the slugs oozed toward the administration building.

Is this right? Infinity wondered. If I'd kept quiet, would everybody have gotten tired of waiting, and gone away?

He glanced at Iphigenie, then at Thanthavong. Iphigenie could have kept everyone at a pitch of anger. Professor Thanthavong watched the slugs, speechless.

Derjaguin glared at him. "What will those things do to him?"

"Nothing," Infinity said.

The immense slugs hoisted themselves up the stairs. One crawled up the door, obscuring it. Infinity stood back, motioning to the other people not to crowd the slugs. A haze of acid and vaporized stone spurted from the entryway. As the door collapsed, the slug slumped with it, then crawled into the building.

Iphigenie, impatient, was first to slide through the slug-sized hole. In a moment the halls were full of people. They surged past the slugs and upstairs to the chancellor's office, only to be faced by another set of mechanically locked doors.

Infinity and Esther paced the silver slugs. Thanthavong remained with them, still anxious, and Kolya followed, bemused.

"We may avoid our own Bastille yet," Thanthavong said softly.

The mood, inevitably, had eased. Iphigenie no longer controlled a mob that might pull down a building bare-handed, not to free the person within but to make him a prisoner. Perhaps that was the result of the leisurely pace of the slugs. Perhaps it was because the expedition members were peaceable people, pushed to extremes. Or perhaps everyone had realized the absurdity of having to stand aside while artificial stupids, each the size of a boneless rhinoceros, humped their way up the stairs.

The door to the waiting room dissolved as easily as the

front door. As Infinity threw open a window to help disperse the corrosive haze, Iphigenie slipped through the hole. Again the crowd surged through; again everyone had to stop and wait for the slugs to come and eat through the door of the chancellor's office proper.

The first silver slug crawled into the waiting room. The leading edge of the slug encountered the trailing edge of the good carpet. The carpet bunched up under the slug's flat belly, the surface that served as its foot, and the slug crawled in place for several minutes, rumpling the rug and forcing it backward.

Fox tried to stifle her giggles, but could to keep from laughing. Others began laughing, too: the crowd changed into a group of individuals. It was as if, before, their anger made them faceless.

The slug passed the leading edge of the rug and resumed its forward progress. Esther grabbed the carpet and pulled it aside before the next slug ran afoul of it.

The slug dissolved a hole in the third door.

This time, Iphigenie held back.

"Come out!" she shouted.

No one answered. The slug continued to nibble away at the door. The bolt dissolved; the door collapsed to dust.

The office was empty.

"He was here!" Iphigenie cried. "He *was* here! Where did he go?"

"Into the passages," Infinity said.

"What passages? Why didn't you tell us?"

"You didn't ask. I thought everybody knew about them."

She grabbed him by the shoulders, but before she could shake him he put his hands on top of hers. He moved quickly, freeing himself, keeping hold of her wrists.

"You let him get away? Why? He'll do it to us *again*!"

"You wanted him out of here—"

She tried to fight him, tried to pull away. He pressed her hands toward her and downward, bending her wrists in their natural range of motion but also in such a way that she could neither free herself nor struggle. Her knees bent and she leaned forward to escape the pressure.

"Stop it," Infinity said softly. "Please. Stop it. Listen to me."

"What are these passages?" she asked. "How do you know about them?"

"I helped build them," Infinity said. "I thought they were common knowledge. But I never understood what they were *for*. This, maybe."

Her shoulders slumped. Infinity let her go. She straightened and flung herself away from him.

The slug began to munch at a door that opened into a cabinet that in turn concealed a passageway.

Their work finished, the slugs that had come up the stairs had congregated in a rest mass in the middle of the office.

"Look."

Beyond the dissolved cabinet door, where the hidden passage began, another silver slug appeared.

The moiré pattern of its skin identified it as a lithoblast. It created new rock foam rather than clearing away damaged material. It backed (or perhaps crawled forward; Infinity had never been sure, and was not entirely certain it made a difference to the slugs) out of the passageway, extruding a great frothy mass of light, strong rock foam that filled and blocked the passage.

"Holy christ, have you buried the chancellor in that stuff? You're worse than he is!" Derjaguin looked sick. "He didn't *plan* anyone's death!"

The rock foam sagged from the mouth of the passageway, then solidified, pale gray, like moldy whipped cream.

The slug left off emitting rock foam, crept over to its fellows, and snuggled in with them. Except for the diffraction-grating pattern of its skin, rainbowing the light, the lithoblast was indistinguishable from the lithoclasts. The lithoclasts began to feed it, transferring dissolved rock mouth to mouth.

Burying the chancellor would simplify the future, for everyone except Infinity. The point was moot: He had no idea how to program the silver slugs to bury a living creature.

"He isn't buried," he said. "He's just blocked off from all the passageways. Except the one that leads to his house."

Iphigenie stared at him.

"We *did* decide we wanted him out of here," Infinity said. "Didn't we?"

Chancellor Blades had escaped to his house. He would be

safe there, but he would be cut off from the rest of the starship, and he would be without resources.

Like almost everyone on the starship, the chancellor lived in a house built beneath a sculpted hill. His residence, including as it did rooms for putting up visiting academic dignitaries, plus a large kitchen and dining room for entertaining them, was three stories high, with balconies and bay windows, terraces and small gardens at several levels.

Silver slugs, mostly lithoblasts, clustered around it. Half the windows had already disappeared beneath thick, irregular, overlapping layers of rock foam. Beneath the house, out of sight, lithoclasts severed the house's connections with the rest of the campus, and lithoblasts filled in the resulting spaces.

"Send in one of the eating kind," Iphigenie said. "Bring him out."

"And then what?" Derjaguin said. "Hanging? Or maybe you'll burn him at the stake?"

"You shut up!" Iphigenie shouted.

"Why do you want him out?" Infinity asked.

After a long shocked silence, Esther began to laugh.

"What kind of a stupid question is that?" Iphigenie was offended and angry.

Esther recovered her composure. "Leave him in there! All alone, and cut off . . ."

"Infinity," Thanthavong said, with sorrow and appreciation, "you have got it exactly right."

Infinity was grateful to Esther for speaking up for him, glad that Professor Thanthavong understood and agreed with what he intended. He disliked controversy; he disliked acting in important matters without the agreement and support of the community he had joined. But everyone had been so angry, so ready to rush off with assumptions rather than information, that this was the first time anyone had been willing to listen to his solution to the problem.

"Leave Blades in there, Iphigenie," Professor Thanthavong said. "Send him food, send him water. The lithoblasts will block him from the passageways—the secret ones and the public ones." She glanced at Infinity for confirmation.

"They already have," he said.

"Look." Thanthavong gestured toward the house. "They're

closing the windows. After that, a few ASes will be able to
guard him. He won't be a danger anymore."

"What about his access to Arachne?" Iphigenie asked,
doubtful, suspicious.

"Arachne has rejected him. He can't form another node."

Iphigenie started to object again.

"The slugs dissolved the hard link connections," Infinity
said quickly. "He can't touch Arachne at all."

Silence fell. Every person there used Arachne a thousand
times each day, automatically, as if it were an extra sense and
an extra limb. And everyone had felt what it was like to lose
contact with the powerful entity.

It was like dying a little. For Blades, the perception of
dying would not end.

"Very well," Iphigenie said abruptly. "For the time being,
that is satisfactory."

She passed Infinity without looking back, intent on returning
to the sailhouse, zero gravity, and stars.

The faculty and staff of *Starfarer*, no longer an enraged
crowd, hurried toward the end of the campus cylinder where
the *Chi* and the alien humans were about to dock. People
scattered over the path, alone, in pairs, in small groups.

Kolya watched them go.

They are, I hope, he thought, wondering what possessed
them for the little while. They are, I hope, making the
decision never to let it possess them again.

He would follow in a moment. He was equally anxious to
meet the alien humans, but he had a task to perform first.

Kolya turned to Infinity and offered him his hand. Infinity
took it. Infinity's hand was hard, calloused.

"Thank you," Kolya said.

Infinity had no reply. Esther tapped his arm.

"Let's go up to the dock. I don't want to miss this."

"No," Infinity said, "I don't either."

"Go ahead," Kolya told them. "I'll be along soon."

When they had left, Kolya crossed the lawn. A solitary
figure leaned against the rock outcrop that bordered the yard.

Griffith gazed at the foam-enshrouded cocoon that had
been the chancellor's house. Three silver slugs sprawled like
huge shapeless lions in front of the single opening that
remained.

Kolya approached. Griffith turned toward him, his expression wary. He was too well trained to reveal that he was ready either to run or to defend himself. But Kolya knew.

Kolya leaned on the rock next to him. He kept his silence for some minutes.

"I was wrong," he said finally.

"About what?" Griffith said.

"About a great number of things," Kolya said. "But at this particular time, I was wrong to threaten you."

"Maybe it was lousy etiquette," Griffith said. "But you got through to me."

"Unfortunately."

Griffith glanced at him, sidelong, quizzical.

"'Unfortunately'?"

"If you had forced someone to tell us how Arachne could be crashed, Feral would be alive. If I hadn't stopped you."

"Maybe." Griffith shrugged. "I would have had to pick the person who knew. I might have hurt someone who just got in the way. That's what happened to Feral. He just got in the way."

"I wouldn't have chosen correctly, either." Kolya gestured toward the cocoon house. "And you would have had the difficulty of reaching the chancellor."

"Difficulty?" Griffith shrugged again. "No. No difficulty."

13

The *Chi* reached *Starfarer* and settled into its dock. The alien humans' tiny short-distance craft, following in the *Chi*'s wake, moved up next to it.

"I want to watch this," Victoria said.

Androgeos had the irritating habit of replying to questions with variations of "Don't worry about that," shrugging off detailed explanation. The team was not to worry about interchange of disease, the problem had been solved millennia before. They were not to be curious about other alien beings. The alien humans' ship moved; Victoria must not be concerned with its mechanics. The questions of how and where their craft would dock must not trouble the alien contact team.

J.D. wondered if Europa might be more forthcoming if she were alone. It seemed to J.D. that she had to work awfully hard to present a united front with Androgeos. On the other hand, she might simply prefer to let her younger colleague supply the negatives.

The short-range craft hovered over a nearby access hatch.

The ship changed.

Its skin quivered and reformed, extending, projecting, then everting to form a tunnel. It reminded J.D. of the ASes that crawled around the surface of *Starfarer,* but it was much more changeable, more mobile, more versatile. The craft regenerated itself into a new form and a new function.

"We are ready," Androgeos said, speaking through the *Chi*'s audio system. "Whenever you are prepared to invite us in."

* * *

J.D. propelled herself out of the *Chi*, following Victoria into the waiting room. Zev and Satoshi and Stephen Thomas were right behind her.

The faculty and staff of *Starfarer* filled the waiting room. It looked to J.D. as if everyone on board had come to see and meet the alien humans, and perhaps everyone had. Gerald Hemminge drifted at the front of the crowd, but he looked terrible, with bags under his eyes and his face still irritated from shaving.

No one spoke.

I never thought I'd see my colleagues awed to silence, J.D. thought.

She was glad to be back among them. She glanced around, finding strength in the somber faces.

Maybe, she thought, somehow, together, we can persuade the alien humans to help us fight exile.

J.D. noticed the presence of most of her colleagues, and the absence of a few. Alzena had not come; that distressed J.D. without surprising her. Iphigenie was nowhere to be seen; perhaps the sail needed her attention. To her astonishment, J.D. could not find Kolya anywhere.

She glanced around again, then closed her eyes for a second. She had been looking for Feral, missing him in particular, seeking him out, expecting him to be in the midst of everything.

Victoria floated to the auxiliary air lock.

"Victoria—" Gerald said.

The door hissed, equalizing the last few millimeters of pressure.

"Yes, Gerald?"

Kolya Cherenkov floated into the waiting room. J.D. smiled at him, glad to see him, not so glad to see Griffith, who as usual tagged along.

"Victoria, wait," Gerald said. "I *must* tell you—"

The air-lock door opened.

Europa and Androgeos entered the starship. Their commune of meerkats paddled through the air between them.

The alien humans moved confidently, though their clothing was not quite appropriate in zero g. The knife-pleated skirt Androgeos wore hiked high above his knees. J.D. could not help but notice—though she pretended not to—that his body was the same rich cinnamon brown all over.

Absently, he pushed his kilt to cover himself.

"Europa, Androgeos," Victoria said, "I'd like to introduce Gerald Hemminge, our—"

"Acting chancellor," Gerald said. "It is a great honor."

Acting chancellor? J.D. thought. Did Blades resign? Did they have the meeting about him already? What happened, while we were gone?

She glanced toward Professor Thanthavong, hoping for a word of explanation. Thanthavong pressed her lips together. J.D. got the hint to wait.

Victoria looked rather startled, Satoshi bemused, and Stephen Thomas...

Stephen Thomas was nowhere to be seen.

Gerald introduced the alien humans to the people in the waiting room. Everyone wanted to meet, if not exactly alien beings, people who had themselves met alien beings.

Europa accepted the courtesies with grace, Androgeos impatiently, now and then pushing down his skirt. The fabric of Europa's skirt remained in place despite the effects of zero g. The metallic silver strands in her hair moved in weightlessness, writhing lifelike of their own accord.

Two young meerkats, curious but shy, hid behind Europa's vest, peering out occasionally, then disappearing. A third clung to Androgeos's bare ankle and occasionally emitted a sharp squeal. The others paddled around. Zev was right. They looked not at all like otters. They maintained their pacing gait in zero g, kicking first with the feet on one side, then with the feet on the other. One meerkat hovered alone in a corner, watching, supine, trying to keep its weightless paws crossed over its belly.

Androgeos turned to Victoria. "Now show us—"

"—Your ship, if that is allowed." Europa interrupted her younger colleague, in a tone meant to take the sting out of his peremptory demand.

"Certainly," Gerald Hemminge replied.

Gerald gracefully extricated Europa from the charge of the alien contact team. Androgeos hung back, but Europa gestured to him. He followed her; Gerald led them toward the exit.

Victoria hovered next to J.D.

"Do you have any idea what's going on?" she said.

"None."

"'Acting' chancellor?" Satoshi said.

Avvaiyar and Thanthavong joined them.

"You look confused, my friends," Thanthavong said.

She told them what had happened while they were gone.

"Good lord," Victoria said. "I'm glad you isolated Blades, but couldn't you have given us a word of warning?"

"I'm sorry. Gerald objected to broadcasting our troubles to the whole system. To the alien humans. For once, I agreed with him."

"Androgeos has an opinion of us that's about as low as it can go. As for Europa..." She shrugged. "Who knows? But a little matter of a lynch mob probably wouldn't make any difference."

"It wasn't a lynch mob!" Avvaiyar said. "Anyway, no one got hurt."

"And Blades is locked out of the web by any route," Thanthavong said. "Stephen Thomas will be glad to hear that.... Where is he?"

Victoria looked around. "I have no idea," she said. "He must have followed Gerald."

"An excellent idea," Thanthavong said. "I believe I will do the same."

For the next hour, J.D. and Zev and Victoria and Satoshi and most of the other members of the expedition trailed Gerald Hemminge as he showed the starship to the alien humans. He took very well to being acting chancellor.

Zev trudged beside J.D. He was barefoot, and he was not used to walking long distances. He started to limp.

This is silly, J.D. thought. We can't see Europa and Androgeos. We can't even hear what they're saying except through Arachne.

J.D. felt herself fading into the crowd.

Is this what happens to explorers? she wondered. After we've done our exploring, are we supposed to stay out of the way and not mind what happens next?

Infinity and Esther were walking together a little way ahead. J.D. caught up to them.

"Infinity—?"

He acknowledged her. "Hi."

"Feral Korzybski was a friend of mine," J.D. said. "Thank you. For stopping Blades. For..."

Infinity looked into her eyes, then away.

"Yeah," he said. "I liked Feral, too."

J.D. could think of nothing else to say.

The meerkats scurried past them, going the opposite direction, sniffing and climbing, now and then stopping to dig furiously and send small fountains of dirt spraying out behind them.

Infinity grimaced. "Alzena wouldn't like to see those critters on board. She'd think weasels were worse than dogs and cats combined."

"Maybe we should tell her," J.D. said. Telling Alzena that someone had smuggled predators on board might even draw her from her depression.

"It couldn't make things any worse for her," Infinity said.

J.D. fell back to rejoin Zev. Footsore, he slowed down.

Gerald wore an LTM, recording and broadcasting everything. Most people, J.D. included, found it awkward to receive a direct audiovisual transmission from Arachne and simultaneously function in the real world. It would make more sense to sit down on a pleasant hillside, in the weird, intense light from Sirius A, and let Arachne create an image of what was happening up ahead.

J.D. was about to do exactly that when Victoria joined her.

"Is this how it was supposed to work?" J.D. asked.

"We had in mind that first meetings would be...a bit more formal," Victoria said. "And stranger."

J.D. chuckled wryly.

"J.D., I've just had an odd report from Arachne. Would you take a look at something for me?"

They stepped off the side of the path with Satoshi and Zev. Arachne reproduced Victoria's findings. At first they looked unexceptional: a lifeless, cratered asteroid. Unusually spherical for a rock its size.... J.D. let her eyelids flutter, went into a communications fugue, and took in the asteroid's physical measurements. Astonished, she opened her eyes again. Victoria was smiling.

"What is it? Who are they?"

"Another alien ship," Satoshi said. "An artificial construction. The same anomalously high gravity."

"But no ecosphere. No atmosphere."

"Not on the surface," Satoshi said. "But a lot of outgassing. Something's there. Underground."

The planetoid Victoria had discovered, circling Sirius A not far distant, looked to the eye like an ordinary bit of leftover planet, nothing astounding. No free-flowing water. No obvious life.

To other methods than the eye, though, it had enough unusual states to attract Arachne's attention. Its gravity, its interior structure, its odd orbit, its solitude.

"The question now," Victoria said, "is whether we should ask our guests about it. They must know it's there—did they think we wouldn't find it?"

"They might have thought we were preoccupied with them." J.D. hesitated before she replied to Victoria's question. "A couple of days ago, I'd have said, Yes, ask them. Don't keep secrets, assume they aren't keeping any secrets. But today . . ."

"You don't think we should ask them?"

"I do think we should ask them. Because we haven't got anything to lose."

Stephen Thomas left the explorer, left the gathering, left the axis of *Starfarer* behind. He had no interest at all in spending more time with Europa and Androgeos. Someone else could show them around *Starfarer;* someone else could smile and be polite. They wanted to stop the deep space expedition as short and as dead as if the nuclear missile had detonated when it hit. They were out for whatever they could get. He wanted no more part of them.

Returning to gravity, he trudged down the hill. Always before, he had welcomed the return of the pull of the Earth, the sensation of his body moving with the force, against it, conquering it.

Now it did not matter. Gravity, zero g, it was all the same to Stephen Thomas.

He strode across *Starfarer,* stopping at the edge of the garden of Chancellor Blades's house.

Three silver slugs lay on the grass, crushing the hyacinths scattered through it. The house looked like a giant wasps' nest, thrown to the ground and broken. Irregular layers of rock foam, ragged and unplanned and overlapping, covered all but one of its openings, and much of the hillside as well. Underground, the slugs were surrounding the house with a layer of foam. When they finished, Blades would be completely and finally cut off. The secret passages out of the administration building were being filled in; the tough rock foam would prevent Blades's digging out into the open access tunnels.

A rain cloud passed near overhead, thick and dark. The downpour caught Stephen Thomas, drenching him. The air turned cold and electric. Chill rain dripped down his face, trickled through his hair, and soaked his shirt. He shivered.

He expected to be furious, thoughtless, driven by rage. But he found himself watching himself as if from a distance, doing what he was doing because he had decided, a long time ago, that it should be done.

But Professor Thanthavong was right. This was a task that should be done coldly. Stephen Thomas felt cold physically, intellectually, emotionally. Even revenge was chilled out of him. He could perform this task, or not. It made no difference. He kept going.

He reached out to Arachne, testing the strands. They quivered, sending vibrations to a point that no longer existed. The vibrations of his message passed completely through the location of Blades's disintegrating neural node, and returned to him unchanged and unacknowledged. Arachne had observed the proof Stephen Thomas recorded, and made its decision, and created immunities against the chancellor. Without a long course of desensitization, the system would always recognize him, and never again let him pass.

That relieved Stephen Thomas, but did not satisfy him. He crossed the sodden lawn. The soft cool grass, the bright flowers, sprinkled droplets of water over his feet.

As he moved closer, the silver slugs stirred. Their blind, sensitive bodies clenched and rippled, flexing, reorienting. Stephen Thomas spoke to Arachne. Though the system ignored his orders to the slugs, he paid them no more attention. They were slow, and not very bright.

One of the slugs blocked his path. He tried to get around it, but it moved to stop him. He was faster than they were, but they were so big, and so close to the open doorway, that they could blockade it with their bulk. Frustrated, Stephen Thomas retreated.

"I want to talk to you!" he shouted.

Blades did not reply.

The slugs clustered before the door, relaxing from their defense, sprawling over the grass. They obscured the bottom half of the open doorway, but the room beyond was as dark and silent as if it were deserted.

Stephen Thomas prowled across the lawn, back and forth, wondering if it were all a sham, if Blades had escaped, and the slugs guarded the empty shell of a house; or if they had quietly and efficiently killed him already, and walled his body up in rock foam or dissolved it into slime. Everyone claimed the artificials could not contravene their programming and deliberately injure a person, but what proof did anyone have of that?

He strained to see beyond the silver slugs and into the cavern of the ruined house.

A shadow moved: a shadow against shadows. Wraithlike, Blades paused in the half-light.

Stephen Thomas sprinted toward the doorway.

He ran across the lawn and leapt up the side of the leading slug. He moved so fast it could not rise up to stop him.

Its body clenched.

His feet slid on its slick silver moiré sides. He scrabbled and clutched and scrambled to a precarious balance.

As he jumped toward the empty doorway, the silver slug twitched its skin, stealing his balance and adding momentum to his leap.

The slug threw Stephen Thomas to the ground. He hit hard. The fall knocked the breath from his body.

Shit, the damn thing's malfunctioning, Stephen Thomas thought.

Stephen Thomas struggled for air, trying to rise. One of the slugs loomed over him, and a more sinister possibility occurred to him.

Blades planned a secret route into Arachne, he thought. Just like he planned a secret trap that caught Feral, and a secret route out of the administration building. He's sent the slug to kill me!

The silver slug arched its great body and curled down on top of him. He shouted for help with his voice and through Arachne, but too late. Calmly, but inexorably, the slug enveloped him. It pinned him to the ground. It cut off his web link, the daylight, and the air.

Androgeos and Europa submitted to the tour of *Starfarer* with magnanimity, or condescension.

"A very pretty arrangement," Europa said, standing on a hilltop from which both ends of the cylinder could be seen. The wetlands lay beneath a soft light fog, and the sea was silver gray.

The meerkats suddenly rose and stared, poised, ready to disappear. Halfway down the hillside, the herd of miniature horses grazed in a luxuriant patch of grass. The appaloosa stallion flung up his head, snorted, squealed, and bullied the mares and foals into a gallop down the slope. The meerkats dropped to all fours and vanished behind a rock.

"How charming," Europa said.

"There's quite a range of animal life in the wild cylinder," Gerald said. "Would you like to visit it? We could be there in an hour or so."

J.D. had not yet had time to visit it herself, since she had been on board such a short time and so much had happened.

I'd much rather have that hour with Europa, she thought, alone, sitting and talking over coffee.

"Would you like to see it?" Gerald said again.

"No," Europa said. "Thank you, but no. I think we had better finish here."

"Very well," Gerald said stiffly. "The path follows the river."

Europa and Androgeos were preparing to depart. They were bored, or they were so dismayed by their own kind that they could not bear to spend a few hours, out of their infinite life spans, with ordinary human beings. Or... since *Starfarer*'s presence would cause the cosmic string to withdraw, they were afraid of being stranded here in the Sirius system, where no one had, so thoughtfully, seeded and tended a sterile world until it bloomed.

J.D. had no more ideas on how to persuade them to remain, and perhaps she should not even try. She followed the tour.

When she passed her own house, she had an inspiration. Whether it was a good inspiration or a foolish one she could not decide. She ran inside and rummaged through a net bag of belongings that she had not yet had time to put away.

When she rejoined Zev on the path, she carried two small packages.

Zev trudged on, his head down, sweat plastering his fine gold hair to his body.

"I'm tired, J.D.," he said.

"I know," J.D. said. "We'll stop soon, I think."

The path plunged down into the canyon cut for the river. Zev left the trail, waded into the water, and splashed forward, floating.

One of the meerkats clambered up the striped bank and began digging. Bits of dirt skittered out behind it.

Europa stopped.

"What is this?" She left the path. At the canyon wall, she urged the meerkat aside, then brushed her fingertips across a band of artificial sedimentary rock and exposed the tip of a bone.

Gerald chuckled. "It's an art project. One of our artists has . . . a bizarre sense of the unique."

Crimson Ng slid through the crowd. "It's a fossil bed," she said, serious and straight-faced. "We found it in the moon rock we made *Starfarer* out of. I'm a paleontologist. I'm excavating it."

"For heaven's sake—!" Gerald turned toward Europa and spread his hands in dismay. "She has a bizarre sense of humor, too."

The fossils Crimson had made were of strange, nightmarish alien beings. She had created a perfect illusion, exactly as if a paleontologist had begun to excavate the site. Europa knelt before the exposed fossils, gazing at them, fascinated.

Stupid of Gerald to laugh at Crimson, to make fun of her work. She was small; she appeared fragile, delicate, and very young. She was none of those, and she had a powerful temper, close to the surface. Instead of releasing her irritation, she was using it to drive the deception, to exasperate Gerald.

The assistant—acting—chancellor should have laughed at himself; he should have apologized.

"This isn't worth any more of our time." He spoke abruptly; his smile was artificial. He offered his hand to Europa, and ushered her and Androgeos along the path. Crimson glared after them.

J.D. thought she saw Androgeos slip a fossil into his pocket. But she was not sure, so she said nothing. For one thing, Crimson would be delighted if the alien humans took one of her fossils and puzzled over it. She claimed the bones to be indistinguishable from real fossils, except that they came from no creature ever to evolve on Earth.

Besides, J.D. could not figure out where Androgeos would fit a pocket in the knife-pleated elegance of his garment.

J.D. caught up to Crimson and gave her arm a comforting squeeze.

"Gerald is such a *jerk*," Crimson said.

Up ahead, Europa stopped.

"You are correct," she said to Gerald.

"I beg your pardon?"

"You are correct about time. Ours is spent."

"Come with me a little farther," Gerald said urgently. "The river leads into the wetlands. It's spring . . . the Canada geese will be hatching their goslings—"

Europa listened in silence. Androgeos shrugged, sullen, disinterested.

"We might even see the eagle . . ." Gerald hesitated when Europa showed no reaction. "We have so much to tell each other . . ."

Despite herself, J.D. felt touched by his desperation. For all his contrariness, he wanted success. If the expedition could not succeed magnificently, he wanted it to succeed in some small way. He thought he had taken control of it, and now he held it in his hands as it collapsed, withering in the cold gaze of Androgeos. No one controlled it any longer.

His voice trailed off.

Nothing he could say would make a difference. J.D. knew it was too late. It had been too late since the missile exploded.

"I haven't seen an eagle in many years." Europa smiled, not unkindly. "I'd like to see one again. Someday. But Andro and I have indulged ourselves long enough. It's been good, spending time with our own people."

Our own people, J.D. thought. Could she mean, could she possibly mean she and Andro are the only human beings in civilization? How isolated they must feel!

Stephen Thomas thought he would suffocate. He thought his body was being crushed. The weight above him pressed him against the flattened grass. The cool green smell, sweetened with the fragrance of hyacinths and tinged with a metallic sheen, permeated the darkness. After a few minutes the sickly sweetness nauseated him. He started to gag. He fought to control the reaction. If he threw up, he would suffocate.

A trickle of warm air caressed his face. He gasped at it. He tried to breathe without moving: impossible. The weight of the slug took advantage of each exhalation, never pushing air from him, but forcing each inhalation to be shallower and more difficult.

Stephen Thomas panicked. Clamped flat against the dank grass, he fought against the slug. His struggle was motionless, and futile.

He fought again, this time to win detachment. He lay very still, trying only to survive as long as he could.

A rippled passed through the body of the slug. It squeezed him tighter to the ground, moving over his feet, up his legs and body, across his face. He would have cried out, but even that was impossible.

This is it, he thought. Blades figured out how to break the programming. I've had it.

Daylight and cool air burst over him. The silver slug reared up, exposing Stephen Thomas's face, his shoulders, his chest. Stephen Thomas gasped at the air, sure it would be his last breath.

Instead of crushing him, the slug lurched off him and crawled away. Its body slid across his legs, leaving him free. The silver slug returned to its guard post, joining the others as they lay across the doorway like faithful dogs, like a three-bodied, headless Cerberus guarding the gates of hell.

As soon as the slug released him, the interference on his web link vanished. He clutched for the web, hung on tight, then, gradually, released his grasp. Now that he was free, he had nothing to say to anyone.

He tried to get up.

"Stephen Thomas, what in the world are you doing here?"

His legs were asleep, his arms full of pins and needles. His joints ached fiercely and his hands itched.

Professor Thanthavong helped him to sit.

The air smelled clean and cool, after the metallic scent of the slug, the crushed grass, the bruised flowers. His fingernails were packed with dirt.

"The damned thing tried to kill me!" he said. "If you hadn't come along—"

"The damned thing *called* me," Thanthavong said. "They're keeping the chancellor in. And everybody else out. What were you *doing*?"

With her support, he was able to stand. He was still damp

from the rainstorm, chilled from lying on the wet ground. He shivered. His legs trembled.

"God, it hurts," he said. His feet felt like sacks of rocks.

"You should have let me give you the depolymerase."

"Great. I'd be throwing up instead of aching." He shuddered: he would be dead instead of in pain. "No thanks."

He stumbled when he tried to walk. The blood rushed, fiery, to his toes. Leaning on Professor Thanthavong's shoulder, he limped to the stone outcrop and sank onto the warm rock.

"You wanted revenge," Thanthavong said sadly.

Stephen Thomas looked at the ugly wreckage of the chancellor's residence. He thought he saw the shadow again, the human-shaped shadow in the dark doorway. Thanthavong laid her hand on his shoulder, restraining him, but Stephen Thomas did not move.

"I thought I did," he said, more to himself than to her. "I should have."

"Stephen Thomas, get hold of yourself!"

"I'm not allowed to love anyone," he said. "First Merry, then Feral . . ."

"What nonsense."

He leaned forward, breathing deep and hard. He could not explain.

"Come along," she said. "Don't make Feral's death more of a tragedy by behaving like a fool."

Her tone allowed no argument. Stephen Thomas made himself watch what was happening from a distance, from inside the glass box where nothing could touch him.

The path led toward the steep hill that formed the end of *Starfarer's* campus cylinder. Europa and Androgeos walked with Gerald at the front of the straggling group of expedition members.

J.D. lengthened her stride till she was walking beside Europa.

"Let us show you *some* hospitality," J.D. said. "At least stay long enough to eat with us."

Europa took so long to reply that J.D. thought she would not answer at all.

"It would be improper," she said.

The words gave J.D. a deep, quick shiver. The symbolism

of eating together, breaking bread, remained powerful. In civilization—in Europa's part of humanity's civilization—one did not eat the food of someone not a friend.

"I'm sorry," J.D. said softly.

"I, too," Europa said. "Please believe me. I am sorry, too."

"Will you accept a gift from us, at least?"

Europa hesitated. "I suppose I could do that."

J.D. handed Europa the packages.

"I didn't have time to wrap them, I'm afraid." Or anything to wrap them in. Purely frivolous items like wrapping paper were in short supply on the starship, passed around and reused till they dissolved in tatters.

"What is this?" Europa asked.

"Chocolate, and coffee."

"Indeed!"

"Psychoactive substances," Androgeos said, disapproving.

"I suppose so, technically," J.D. said. "But fairly mild, as recreational drugs go."

"Thank you very much, J.D.," Europa said. "I've heard of these, but of course we've never tasted them."

"I thought you wouldn't have seen chocolate. I wasn't sure about coffee. Do you know how to prepare it?"

"You will have to tell me."

"Grind the beans up fine, boil water, let the water cool for a minute or two—" J.D. suddenly choked up. It was Feral who had told her about never letting coffee boil. She managed to finish giving Europa the instructions, but her voice shook and her vision blurred, from holding back the tears.

"All that's happened is a great disappointment to you," Europa said. "I know it. I'm sorry to be the cause of it. Thank you for the gifts."

J.D. turned away, embarrassed, and scrubbed her eyes on her sleeve.

At the foot of the hill, Europa stopped and extended her free hand to Gerald, who clasped it gingerly.

"Thank you for showing us your home," Europa said. "We'll take our leave of you now. I think it would be best if the same people who first met us bid us farewell."

For once in his life, Gerald Hemminge had no heart to argue.

* * *

Europa and Androgeos hovered by the air lock. Victoria and J.D., Satoshi and Zev floated nearby. J.D. felt in shock with disbelief, that the first meeting with alien beings could begin and end so quickly.

"Finish your business with Victoria, Andro," Europa said. "Then we must leave."

"What business?" Victoria said.

"You promised to show me your algorithm," Androgeos said. "That's why we came over here, after all."

"Who *cares* about the algorithm!" Victoria exclaimed. "There's got to be a way for us to talk to the people in charge. The people who control—"

"I've explained all that to you." Europa's tone was cold and final. "You broke the rules of civilization. The reasons don't matter. In a few decades—"

"Why should we believe you?" Victoria was angry. "You tell us nothing, you won't answer our questions, you conceal things from us—"

"What things?" Androgeos challenged Victoria. "We never concealed anything you could comprehend!"

Satoshi's sharp laugh cut itself short. "You wouldn't let Stephen Thomas cut one damned grass blade to look at!"

"Oh, that. I told you, it's only ordinary grass. That doesn't count."

"It counted to Stephen Thomas!"

"Victoria, your algorithm sounded very pretty. Won't you show it to me before I go?" Androgeos tried to charm her, but managed only to sound ingratiating. Victoria ignored his request.

The image of a barren, cratered sphere, slowly turning, formed nearby.

"What's this," Victoria asked, "if not something you concealed?"

Androgeos glanced at the image of the bleak alien ship. At first he looked startled, then amused.

"Did you know they were here?" he asked Europa.

"Yes. Of course. But they always are."

"Who are they?" J.D. asked.

"Just the squidmoths." Europa dismissed the second alien ship with a graceful flick of her long fingers. "There were probably some back at Tau Ceti. I didn't look."

"The . . . squidmoths?" The strangest thing about Europa's

behavior was that she did not consider it strange at all, that she expected J.D. to accept her disinterest and to share it.

"They're everywhere," Europa said. "Whatever system you visit, there's likely to be one of their ships. They're like... like rats."

J.D. laughed in disbelief. "Europa... if you leave us behind, we'll talk to them. You may think we're hopelessly prejudiced, but we're not. Civilization may think we're only capable of dealing with people of our own species. But we're not."

"You may not be," Androgeos said, self-satisfied, still amused. "But they are."

"I'm sure this seems an opportunity to you, J.D.," Europa said. "I assure you, it isn't. They won't talk to you. They seldom talk to anyone. They... I don't know what they do. They listen to the starlight. They exist."

"I see," J.D. said. *Squidmoths?*

"I see you don't believe me." Europa sighed. "When I was an Earthling, we believed what our betters told us."

"Your betters?" Satoshi asked. "Who was better than the descendants of the pharaohs?"

"No one," Androgeos said, smooth as silk. "Europa speaks metaphorically. As children believe parents, you should believe us."

"Who *were* your parents?" Satoshi asked. "Kings and gods? Pharaohs?"

Androgeos glared at him.

"Or more ordinary folks?" Satoshi asked.

"What does it matter?" Androgeos exclaimed angrily.

"It doesn't, to me," Satoshi said. "But you keep bringing it up."

"You can remain here and waste your time trying to talk to the squidmoths," Europa said, ignoring the exchange between Androgeos and Satoshi. "But I warn you, don't waste too much time. If you do, you'll find yourself severed not only from civilization, but from Earth." She touched the wall, propelling herself slowly toward the hatch. "Victoria, show Androgeos your algorithm. We must go."

Victoria took a long, deep breath, a sigh of sadness and loss. Her eyelids flickered, and the edges of a second image began to form beside the desolate planetoid.

"Victoria," J.D. said, abruptly understanding what Androgeos planned. "Victoria, don't."

Victoria opened her eyes. The algorithm graphic flickered. "What?"

"I want to see it!" Androgeos shouted, ugly and desperate.

"They want to *take* it, Victoria!" J.D. said. "They want it badly."

The algorithm faded to invisibility as Victoria realized what J.D. meant.

"Your ship appeared *behind* us," Victoria said to Europa. "That's why Androgeos asked how we followed you so quickly. We entered transition a long time after you did . . . but we got here sooner."

Outrage disturbed even Satoshi's equanimity.

"This is what you're always looking for, isn't it?" he said. "Something new, something unique. Victoria's work, but you'd take it, for yourselves, without a second thought."

"It isn't like that," Europa said.

"Let us take it with us," Androgeos said. "It might make a difference. It might help you be banned for a short time instead of a long one."

"How short?" Satoshi said.

"You *can* talk to the—to the 'ancient astronauts'!" J.D. said. "Or are they just a tall tale?"

"They aren't. We can't talk to them. We don't know how. But they know . . . somehow they know it, when civilization changes."

"Why didn't you tell us all this in the first place?" Victoria said.

"I didn't think you'd believe us, I didn't think you'd trust us."

"I walked out onto your planet unprotected." J.D. whispered her words; she could not speak louder, or she would sob. "I trusted you with my life, but you didn't trust me at all."

"I'm sorry," Androgeos said. "I'm sorry! You're right, I didn't trust you. You exploded a bomb! If you trust me now—"

"*How short a time?*" Satoshi said again.

"I can't promise," Androgeos said. "But maybe only a hundred more years."

"Good lord," Satoshi said. "Androgeos, you've been living with your labyrinth too long. Your brain is tangled."

"A hundred years?" Victoria exclaimed. "Forget it."

"Keeping the algorithm won't do *you* any good," Androgeos cried.

"No?" Victoria said. "If civilization wants it, they'll have it. But they'll have it from me."

Victoria had made her decision. Even Androgeos recognized it.

"Fine," he said sullenly. "You can wander around until you find someone to give it to."

"I intend to!"

"In five hundred years."

Androgeos opened the air lock and entered without another word. A little troop of meerkats followed him.

Europa hesitated in the entrance, balancing herself on its edge, half in the ship, half out.

"I'm sorry things happened this way," she said. "I—"

Alzena Dadkhah plunged into the waiting room. Her head cloth had come loose, and her beautiful long hair flew wild. This was much more the way J.D. expected to see her, not trapped in the conventions of her heritage.

But then J.D. saw her gaunt face, her staring eyes, her desperate expression.

"Take me with you." Alzena's voice cracked. She tried to wet her lips with her tongue. "Please."

"We can't," Europa said. "You must . . ."

Alzena stopped, awkwardly hitting the wall, too distracted for grace. Her fingernails scratched on the rock foam as she pulled herself toward Europa.

She wrapped one arm around Europa's knees and reached up and touched her cheek, suppliant, pleading.

Europa shivered back, then steadied herself.

"I don't have power over your life," she said.

"You do," Alzena said.

"Will you die if you stay here?"

"Yes."

"Then, come," Europa said abruptly, and drew her into the air lock. The door sealed shut.

"Alzena!"

J.D. touched Satoshi's arm, not holding him back, but stopping him anyway.

"Let her go," J.D. said. "She meant what she said."

As the alien humans' strange little craft rearranged itself for flight, Miensaem Thanthavong propelled herself into the waiting room. Stephen Thomas, damp, grass stained, and bedraggled, followed close behind.

"Alzena!"

"She's gone," J.D. said.

"How could you let her?" Thanthavong said. "How could you?"

"How could we stop her?"

Thanthavong started to retort. Instead, she hesitated.

"I was too late," she said. "Perhaps it's.... No. I was too late. We'll leave it at that."

Stephen Thomas let himself drift to Victoria's side.

"Where were you?" Victoria exclaimed. She noticed his muddy clothes and unkempt hair. "Stephen Thomas, what happened?"

"That ... would take a while to explain," he said.

"You should have been here," Satoshi said.

"I know." He looked disconsolate. His breathing was ragged. "I know. No excuses."

Zev moved close to J.D. "I don't understand anything, I think," he said. "What are we going to do now?"

J.D. had no answer. She hugged him instead.

As the alien humans' craft accelerated away from *Starfarer*, the rest of the members of the deep-space expedition joined the alien contact team in the zero-g waiting room. Gerald, Senator Orazio, even Senator Derjaguin; Kolya Petrovich, Chandra, Crimson Ng, Griffith. Florrie Brown and Fox and Avvaiyar and Iphigenie; Infinity Mendez and Esther Klein, the faculty and staff and students. Everyone but Blades. And Feral.

"That's a good question, Zev," Victoria said. She faced their colleagues. "What *are* we going to do now?"

Starfarer's great sail turned, catching the bright strong light of Sirius A. The starship began a slow, steady acceleration.

The alien humans' ship fled toward a nearby coil of cosmic string. *Starfarer* could not catch the worldlet, not in the normal dimensions of space-time. But the starship could track the alien humans; it could follow them into transition. Once there ... who could tell? Perhaps they would reach the destination before their quarry, perhaps after. Perhaps the alien humans were traveling to civilization, to report on the actions of the expedition; perhaps they were traveling to the galaxy's version of a desert. It did not matter. *Starfarer* would keep moving, keep searching. It would—everyone hoped—remain one step ahead, one transition ahead, of the powers trying to isolate it.

J.D. strapped herself into her couch in the observers' circle. As the *Chi* departed from *Starfarer*, heading starward, Zev took J.D.'s hand. His swimming webs surrounded her fingers like warm satin.

Starfarer would not reach its new transition point for several weeks. In the meantime, the alien contact team planned to explore in the system of Sirius A.

The ship of the squidmoths was a tiny point of reflected light ahead; it was an image, detailed yet mysterious, in the center of the observers' circle.

The *Chi* accelerated toward it, carrying the alien contact team. Five members, instead of four, Zev's tacit acceptance confirmed. J.D. wished for a sixth member of the department.

Feral was right, she thought. We should have included a journalist.

Stephen Thomas, in his usual place, remained withdrawn. He rubbed the skin between the thumb and forefinger of one hand with the fingertips of the other, massaging the itchy new swimming webs. His skin had begun to take on the darker hue of a diver; he glowed with a pale gold tan. All his injuries had healed. His physical injuries, at least.

Victoria and Satoshi bent over the image of the squidmoth's ship, extracting esoteric information from its shape, from the imperceptible veil of molecules escaping from its interior, from the light reflecting off its surface. Victoria's concentration had intensified; Satoshi's cheerful self-possession had sobered.

J.D. found her own anticipation tempered with prudence, not with joy.

"A waste of time!" J.D. repeated Europa's words, still amazed by them. "A waste of time!"

Victoria grinned at her. "A challenge, J.D., eh? To talk to beings who don't talk to anybody?"

"Maybe nobody ever talks to them," J.D. said. "I wonder if Europa considered that?"

"At least if they don't talk to us," Satoshi said, "we won't have done worse than anyone else."

J.D. chuckled wryly. She looked through the edge of the observers' circle, seeking out the luminous silver gray pinpoint of the second alien ship.

Here I am again, winging it, she thought. I wish I didn't have to; I wish I knew more about where we were going.

In spite of everything that had happened, J.D. felt more intrigued than apprehensive.

She thought: *Squidmoths?*

About the Author

VONDA N. MCINTYRE has been writing and publishing science fiction since she was 20. Her novels include **Dreamsnake** (winner of the Hugo Award, presented at the World Science Fiction Convention, and the Nebula Award, presented by the Science Fiction Writers of America), **The Exile Waiting,** and **Superluminal.** She has written one children's book, **Barbary.** Her books and short stories have been translated into more than a dozen languages. The *Starfarers* series includes the national bestsellers **Starfarers, Transition, Metaphase** and **Nautilus,** a series that has the distinction of having had a fan club before the first novel was even written. She is also the author of Bantam's next *Star Wars* novel, **The Crystal Star.**